The
Empire Girls

Also by this author

When My Ship Comes In

The
Empire Girls

SUE WILSHER

sphere

SPHERE

First published in Great Britain in 2017 by Sphere

1 3 5 7 9 10 8 6 4 2

A CIP catalogue record for this book
is available from the British Library.

ISBN 978-0-7515-6461-7

Typeset in Bembo by M Rules
Printed and bound in Great Britain by
Clays Ltd, St Ives plc

Papers used by Sphere are from well-managed forests
and other responsible sources.

Sphere
An imprint of
Little, Brown Book Group
Carmelite House
50 Victoria Embankment
London EC4Y 0DZ

An Hachette UK Company
www.hachette.co.uk

www.littlebrown.co.uk

For Kev

The
Empire Girls

PART 1

Tilbury Docks, February 1952

1

Vi

Vi breathed the pub in. The Empire pub. The ale, ashtrays and tang of working men's sweat and snuff mingled with the sweetness of her lipstick and perfume. It was the precious aroma of the life she had built and would protect no matter what. She leant her forearms down on the bar and smiled. It was busy tonight. The punters were well-oiled and bellowing their two-penn'orth, banging the tables with the side of their fists for emphasis. The dockers and stevedores, the farmers, labourers, crane drivers and tugboatmen, in collarless shirts and cloth caps. Men with hard work creased into the lines of their faces and the cold brand of war stamped onto their bodies and minds.

'Where's Kenny?' Archie pulled a pint of mild and frowned. 'The empties are building up.' Her brother-in-law lifted his chin at the foam-smudged pint glasses strewn on the pub tables and winked at Sally the Whelk, doing the rounds with her tray of shellfish.

It was well and good owning a pub but you needed a man at the helm. And Archie suited the job, *built like a brick shithouse*, as the punters would say. He liked a joke, a wager and the occasional backhander but he stood no nonsense and everyone knew it.

Vi stood straight and reached for a rag to do the tables herself. She paused as the door of the pub opened and her attention was caught by a coloured man stepping inside. She nudged Archie with her elbow. He grinned – they liked a bit of a game, and the punters enjoyed their banter. They made a good pair, the two of them front of house.

The man wore a light suit, too thin for winter, the trousers wide, the jacket long, and a trilby at an angle, dapper and cocksure. He carried a cardboard suitcase and held some papers in his fist. Vi tutted. One of them off the boats. They usually got off the ship and straight onto the boat train to London, and that's how she liked it. If they hung around in Tilbury they soon got the message they weren't wanted. Not in The Empire anyway. She'd been meaning to put up a sign in the window to save the bother of sending them away.

He walked with a swagger into the fog of cigarette smoke and hugged his arms. It was warm in the pub. The pub fire got most of the coal – what with the shortage there wasn't much left for upstairs. The punters nearest him went quiet and then the next group caught it. Soon the whole place had fallen silent as they watched him walk towards the bar.

'Oi, oi, look what the cat dragged in!' Archie called out.

The punters sniggered and the man swivelled around to

see what was behind him. He saw nothing there and a look of realisation dawned on his face, his eyes wide with shock as though someone had pinched his backside. He came to the bar, said something in his funny voice.

'What was that, Vi?' Archie said it loud, comical-like, leaning his ear down to Vi.

'Dunno, Arch, I think he's asking about the next boat home!' Vi played her part well, put her hand on her hip and laughed around at her audience.

The punters chuckled and the coloured man didn't know what to do with himself. He backed away, turned and strode out, but without his swagger now. Vi and Archie exchanged glances, pleased that it was such a good night.

There were enough Johnny foreigners around the docks already – a smattering of Indians and Orientals, cliques of Czechs and Maltese. Everyone was used to seeing the native workers on the ships, thousands of seamen in and out of the port, Portuguese, Arabs, men in turbans. It didn't mean Vi's punters wanted to share a watering hole with them. There was always the Seaman's Mission they could go to, and it took the biscuit now the coloureds were coming over in droves since the war and thinking it was all right to stay here.

'Where's that bloody Kenny?' said Archie.

Instinctively, Vi checked the hallway that led off from the back of the bar. She saw an empty stool there and her stomach turned over.

'And where's Doris?' she hissed, striding out through to the tap room at the back of the pub where Kenny the potboy cleaned the glasses. Her heels rapped the wooden floor as she walked. Bloody Doris, slipping away when Vi's back was turned. When you had a teenage daughter, sweet bloody sixteen, you had to be careful. A momentary lapse and all could be lost.

'Doris!' she called up the stairs as she passed the stair-foot door. She heard a sound coming from the tap room and sped up, nearly leaping to get there to catch whatever was going on.

There – she saw it – a flicker of the hem of Doris's dress falling to her knees. A second later and she would have seen them as they were now, standing there as though butter wouldn't melt.

Kenny, a seventeen-year-old bag of hormones and hair cream, turned to grab his crate of glasses as if nothing had happened. Doris stood straight, her eyes wide, her face flushed red against the whitewashed walls. Vi noticed that one of her hairpins had come loose, and that made Vi even crosser – Doris knew how important it was for young ladies to remain well-groomed and decent at all times. She was lazy about keeping herself slim and Vi had berated her only the previous week for having to let out the side seam of her dresses.

'Archie!' Vi screamed over her shoulder into the pub, her fists balled at her side. Kenny stopped dead and Doris glanced at the door as if she was thinking of making a run for it.

2

Doris

The Empire pub. Doris had been born in the front bedroom and had grown up emptying ashtrays before school. The pub stood close enough to Tilbury Docks for the outside noises to creep in through the windows and cracks – clanking cranes, shouting men, ships' horns and a sense of things shifting from one place to another. The smell of rubber and tea and engine grease would waft in through an open window to mingle with the stale beer and fag ends inside. It was busy tonight. The dockers had been paid and Sally the Whelk was walking round with her tray. It was good for business – the seafood made the punters thirsty. Sally nudged round to the end of the bar, held out a little paper bowl of cockles to Doris and motioned when Vi wasn't looking. Doris stepped forward out of the hallway, grabbed them with a silent thanks and rushed back into the dim passage.

Once she'd finished her cleaning jobs she was allowed to sit on a stool by the stair-foot door and watch the pub, staying out of sight. *Pubs are no place for young ladies*, Vi would say. There was Vi, pulling a pint, her corset making her stand rod-straight, hair set and styled and face painted, chin up, giving the punters a piece of her mind, but with a wink. She eyed Doris slouching on the stool, eating the cockles. Doris sat up straight and put out a foot to rotate her ankle, to keep them slim – Vi had been on at her lately about putting on weight. *There are two types of girl*, Vi would say, *good girls and good-time girls*. You had to be a good girl to find a nice husband.

Doris's Uncle Archie was behind the bar, a big bloke with a big neck, in a waistcoat and shirt sleeves with a silly bowler hat on his head to be funny. He sniffed a pinch of snuff, cocky and assured, always seeming to take up more room than he ought, with his loud voice and air of authority. He and Vi ran the pub together.

There was Old Bill sitting at his same spot at the bar. When the pub was quiet Doris would listen to him talking – he was shell-shocked in the first war. Doris would draw him sometimes, try to catch that look in his eye. She learned a lot from drawing people, it made her really look at a person. Like Old Bill. Something can happen to you in life and change you forever.

Doris was sixteen and went to secretarial college, so she could get a job in an office and meet the right sort of husband. Vi walked her to college and back, just like she used to walk her to school and back, once Doris had begun her monthlies. That's when she started keeping her in, too. *You're a woman now*, she said. *You have to start taking care of the four Fs: feet, face, fanny and fellas.* By fellas she meant take care to stay away from them. She watched Doris in the same way the punters watched each other's card hands. Doris stayed in and did the cleaning. Knowing how to keep house and make yourself look nice were vital.

Kenny, the potboy, came through with four dimpled pint mugs in each hand. He stopped in front of Doris.

'Let's have one.' He nodded at the cockles and opened his mouth. Doris giggled and popped one in. He winked and headed out the back to wash the glasses. If it weren't for Kenny, Doris would be really lonely. Vi kept her eye on him though. If she knew he was Doris's secret boy he'd be out on his ear.

The pub door opened and one of the dark fellas off the boat walked in. Doris took her chance and slipped off her stool to go and see Kenny out the back. Vi and Archie would be distracted for a minute – no one liked those dark fellas coming in the pub and they would make a show of it to entertain the punters.

'Hello sweetheart, feeling brave?'

Kenny always messed with her about being trapped in the pub. Doris stuck out her tongue at him and hitched herself up onto the draining board next to the butler sink.

'So when am I taking you out to the pictures, then?'

Doris laughed. 'How about tomorrow night?'

Kenny paused as he turned on the cold tap, looked at her with raised eyebrows and his face creased into a smile.

'Yeah, lovely, let's go to the milk bar in town first, play the jukebox and that.'

Doris's heart sank. She'd dearly love to go to the Palace

on Dock Road and the milk bar in Grays with Kenny, but Vi would never let her. Doris was trapped there, under Vi's watchful eye. She was like a sparrow hawk, always hovering and ready to strike should Doris put a foot wrong or do anything that involved having fun or being a modern girl. Vi had drummed the same thing into Doris her whole life. *You need to be a good girl, keep decent and you'll make a good wife.* Doris didn't have the strength to go against her.

'All right, then,' she said, carrying on the charade. 'What time will you pick me up? I'll let Mum know and she'll help me do my hair.'

'Oh, I dunno, let's say seven, I'll tell Archie I want tomorrow off and that he needs to sub me next week's pay.'

They chuckled at the thought of Vi and Archie doing anything to help her and Kenny to go out courting.

'And you'd better get that hair sorted out,' he said, reaching behind her head and plucking one of the bobby pins out of her brown hair.

'Stop it,' Doris giggled, and grabbed the pin back from him. He was always doing that – he knew how particular she had been brought up to be about her appearance.

'You can ask your pal Maisie to come along with her fella too,' said Kenny.

It was a stretch for Doris to laugh about that one but she did. She'd lost touch with her one friend from school, Maisie, who had given up on her a long time ago, since she'd been kept in by Vi. Now she had no one but Kenny.

'I dunno,' she said. 'Maisie's getting sick of me always going out, I think she wants to stay in tomorrow night.'

'Give us a kiss,' said Kenny, leaning across with his hands

still in the sink to push his lips against hers. A jolt of pleasure ran through her body. 'You're so pretty, you know that?' he said.

'Doris?'

They froze at the sound of Vi's voice and the tap of her heels on the hallway floor. Doris slid off the draining board and stood up straight just as Vi walked into the tap room. Her face was a picture, like her head might explode.

'Archie!' she screamed.

Cold streaks of fear ran down Doris's arms. She glanced at Kenny, who looked like she felt. Archie came clomping down the hallway.

'What is it?'

'These two,' said Vi, jerking her arm towards them, 'up to no good.'

'What you up to?' said Archie, frowning at them both.

'Nothing,' said Kenny, 'just talking a bit while I'm doing the glasses.'

'Pah, believe that and you believe anything,' said Vi. 'You get upstairs now, you'll not be sitting in the hallway again.'

'I didn't even do anything,' cried Doris. She winced at a pain in her stomach, tried to rub it away.

'You want him out, Vi?' said Archie, nodding his head towards Kenny.

Vi considered him. 'You're on thin ice, Kenny. If I catch you around Doris again, you're out, understand?'

Kenny nodded with a face like he wanted to kill someone and turned his back on them to wash the glasses at the sink.

Doris breathed with relief. At least Kenny hadn't been sacked. If she lost him she didn't know what she'd do. They'd still be able to see each other when Vi and Archie weren't looking, they'd managed it so far without being caught. When Vi was serving someone at the bar and Archie was in the cellar, she and Kenny would slip out to the back yard for ten minutes, or when Vi went upstairs for something and Archie did a bit of business across the bar while she was out of the way, Doris would take her chance and meet Kenny in the cellar. They'd become quite good at finding ways of being alone. It'd be harder now, but she'd wait for her chance. She'd be really good for a while and Vi might let her sit in the hallway again of an evening.

The pub noise quietened as Doris made her way upstairs, hearing Auntie Win's radio on in the front room. She paused midway, her stomach twisting with pain again like she was getting some sort of tummy bug. In her bedroom she sat on the bed and reached down to pull her wad of drawings out from underneath. As she bent over, she winced and sucked in a breath, wondering if those cockles were off or if she'd caught something. She waited for a second, let out a big fart and it passed.

Looking through her drawings always gave her a happy feeling. She drew things looking out the pub windows. Two women standing talking, one with her hand on the back of her neck. A labourer pushing his barrow, bent back and flat cap. Women on their knees washing their front steps in Wharf Road behind the pub. She considered how it was strange that art was like a part of her body, she needed it to stay alive. At school her art teacher used to say she could see the beauty in ordinary things. Her smile dropped when she thought about her row with Vi, when Vi said art college wasn't a good way of finding a husband. But you didn't fight with Vi without knowing when to stop.

A sudden terrible pain in her stomach made her drop the drawings to the floor. She nudged them back under the bed with her foot. Hunched over, she pulled the chamber pot out, held up her dress and squatted over it, the cramps in her stomach bad as though she had the runs. A big pain came around her back and made it hard to stay squatting but she felt she really needed to go and wondered whether to chance it and run out to the lav. It died down and she waited there like that. Then out of nowhere she felt herself being sick and just about managed to move the pot in time to catch it. She started to cry and slid the pot back under herself again because she could feel herself going. But it didn't feel right and then a massive pain made her groan and she thought she might call out to Auntie Win. She put out one hand to the floor to steady herself and, god help her, her guts dropped out.

There was a god-awful pain like she was being torn limb from limb and a terrible feeling of something that couldn't wait. Looking down she saw a great big lump sliding out of her. It missed the pot and fell onto the floor with a wet thud. It was like something from the butchers, a red bloody lump, that's all it looked like, and it was big and of course she thought she was going to die. You can't survive something like that – there must be something terribly wrong with you if a big bit of your body just falls out like that. She crouched there staring at it and tried to edge away but felt, with horror, that it was still attached to her. Looking down, she saw a long thick silvery-grey squidgy rope thing coming from inside her. All of a sudden the lump on the floor moved and she thought she'd pass out from the shock. It moved and then a hole opened up at one end and it started to cry.

Doris screamed and Auntie Win came running in, her hair in turbaned rollers, her tatty yellow quilted pre-war housecoat flapping open, no longer able to stretch across her uncorseted girth. She looked at Doris and looked at the thing on the floor, her hand flying to her chest, her face ghoulish white with shock and cold cream. She turned to the door and opened her mouth, straining to shout but no sound came out. She tried again and this time shrieked for all she was worth.

'VI!'

3

Vi

Old Bill pushed his pewter mug across the bar to Vi for another. She pulled his usual pint of mild and waited for his usual comment. His hand shook as he took a long gulp, drawing in his cheeks that were grey with stubble. 'The rain's got into that, Vi. Give us a bottle of brown to liven it up,' he said, smacking his lips.

Vi smiled, prised the top off a bottle of brown ale, slid it over to him. It was the same every time.

She could swear she could hear Win shouting upstairs. She called over to Archie, leaning on the bar with his elbows, talking low with one of the punters. Vi pointed to the ceiling to say she was going up. He nodded and went back to his conversation. The stair banister needed a polish, and the skirting on the landing needed a wash. Vi made a mental note to get Doris on to that in the morning. Win had her cold cream on but when Vi saw her eyes she stopped dead. Win shook her head as if what had happened was too awful to say out loud. Straight away Vi thought something must be wrong with Doris, she'd had an accident. Win nodded her through into Doris's room and what Vi saw there would stay with her for the rest of her days.

Doris was half-standing, half-crouching over the pot, shaking like a whippet. Her dress was above her knees at the front but hanging down at the back and it was soaked with blood. Vi started to say her name, took a step towards her, but she was staring at something on the floor by the pot and Vi looked in the same direction. At first glance it looked like a large trussed-up joint of beef, covered in blood and slime. It moved suddenly – Vi screamed and jumped back. A baby. The face was turned away and the body didn't look right but it was a baby. And the cord led from the baby up inside Doris's dress.

Vi stared at her daughter like she'd never seen her before. She didn't understand. When she looked closer at the baby she realised it was still in the sac, apart from its head, so its arms and legs were curled up around it like it had been pushed into a nylon stocking. Vi stood there open-mouthed, looked at Doris, who wouldn't meet her eye, at Win, who shook her head at her again, her hand over her mouth.

'Doris!' blurted Vi. Her daughter didn't register, just stared down at the baby. 'Doris, what have you done?'

'I'll run for the doctor,' said Win.

'No, don't.'

'But the baby, the cord?' Win threw her hand towards the

mess on the floor and Vi knew she was right, they needed a doctor there right now, but her brain was switching back on. She started to think fast and she didn't want the doctor there. She'd sort it out herself.

'I'll do it. Stay here.'

Win looked at her sister like she was mad. Vi ran through to the kitchen, stoked up the fire in the range, got the kettle on. She ran to the blanket box in the bedroom and got some old towels. Somehow her instincts took over and she knew what to do.

'Wrap it up in this.' She thrust the towels into Win's arms and ran back to the kitchen. While she waited for the kettle to boil she got the dressmaking shears and a kitchen knife. Eventually the pot boiled, she poured hot water on the knife and the shears and brought a bowl through to Doris's bedroom. She stopped to think, tried to remember when Doris was born and realised she hadn't the foggiest how to do it properly. Win was kneeling down near Doris with the baby wrapped up in her lap. Doris was still half-crouching, in some sort of stupor.

'Snap out of it, Doris, we've got to sort this out.' She didn't answer. Win looked scared stiff. Opening up the towel, Vi could see that the sac was stuck to the baby's shoulders. With the shears she snipped some of it near the feet and some reddish water dripped out onto the floor. She pulled the sac away from the baby's body and it came away well enough, freeing the baby's grey-coloured limbs, but still stuck to its shoulders so she left it hanging there.

'Is it breathing?' Win asked.

'I don't know.'

Vi lifted the wet baby off the towel and it opened its eyes and mouth for a second, then closed them. Vi nodded at Win. They looked at each other as if to say that could have been a problem solved, but it wasn't. The baby started to cry. It was that pitiful heart-wrenching new-born cry.

'Shut the doors, quick!'

Win went out to shut all the doors. Vi heard her turning the wireless up. She held the baby under its arms with its legs dangling down. It seemed very small and one of its feet was twisted. She grabbed the towel and wrapped it around the baby's shoulders. Win came back in and sat on the floor. Vi set the baby on her lap, glanced at her and got the knife.

'A girl,' said Win.

'You ever done this before?' Vi asked her.

Win shook her head. 'You?'

Vi shook hers and took hold of the cord. It was grey and slippery and thick. Her hand trembled. She lined the blade up underneath it and brought it up quickly through the cord. Blood seeped out from both cut ends. It made her gag. She panicked. Instinctively she pinched the ends to stop the bleeding. She looked at Win, tried to think.

'Pinch it,' Vi said to her. Win's eyes widened with fright but she squeezed the cord and Vi darted away to the kitchen to find some string. They managed to tie it around the baby's end of the cord and it stopped dripping. Blood still dripped out of the other end of it and Doris looked down at it with horror. Vi got some more string and tied that bit off too and pulled Doris's dress down at the front.

Giving a small laugh of relief, Vi sat back on her heels and rinsed her hands in the bowl. Just the fact that she'd cut it away from Doris made her feel a bit better. Win was wrapping the baby up and looking at Vi like she shouldn't have done it herself.

'Rock it to stop it crying,' Vi said to her. Turning to Doris, she felt rage explode inside her. Doris was still staring at the floor. Grabbing her shoulders, Vi shook her, shouted into her face, 'What the hell is going on, you ungrateful little sod?' She didn't answer. Vi jerked her chin up to force Doris to look at her. 'And whose is that bastard?' Vi pointed to the baby in Win's arms. 'Do you know what you've done? Well?' Nothing. 'Wicked girl.'

'Win?'

Archie stood in the doorway looking like he'd seen a ghost. Win nodded towards Doris.

'What the hell is going on?' he said.

'What do you think?' Vi shouted. 'The wicked bitch has had a bloody baby.'

'What?' he roared. 'Whose is it?'

'Yes, Doris,' Vi shook her again, 'who's the father? Tell me!'

She just stood there, hunched over, and Vi couldn't take it. She slapped Doris's face. The force pushed her backwards and she landed on the bed, just flopped there like a sack of flour.

'Tell me, Doris, you have to tell me. If you don't I'll have to send you away, I swear I will.'

The ungrateful sod wouldn't say a thing. Vi stood up, put her hands on her head, tried to think. Archie growled and stamped away downstairs. In a few seconds he was dragging Kenny to the bedroom doorway.

'What the hell's he doing here? Get him away!' shouted Vi.

Archie ignored her. 'You been touching our Doris, you little git?' he said, his huge hands gripping Kenny's shoulders.

'What?' said Kenny, trying to look into the room. He saw Win holding the baby and Doris on the bed, pale and staring, grimaced at the sight of blood on the rag rug on the floor. 'What?'

'You heard. Have you been touching her?'

'What?' Kenny looked like he was going to be sick.

'You little bastard.' Vi came at him, punching and slapping, grabbing his hair. It was Archie who put out a hand to stop her. She sobbed and let out a yell of agony.

'What have you done?' she screamed at him. She looked from him to Doris to the baby, tried to think, tried to find some way of saving them all from the mess. 'Win,' she said, 'Win, stay here, watch them both . . .' She didn't know what to say. Leaving Win to look after Doris and the baby was cruel but she had to try to sort things out.

'Come on, bring him, where do you live, you little bleeder?'

Archie pushed Kenny out of the door and Vi followed. They bundled down the stairs, Vi grabbing her coat.

'No, damn it, out the back,' she said when Archie started walking down the hallway towards the bar.

'Where do you live, I said? Sydney Road, isn't it? What number?'

Kenny was as pale as his shirt. He shook his head, said something Vi couldn't hear.

'What?' she said, glaring at him.

'Please don't, my dad will . . . I didn't do it.'

'Course you bloody well did,' said Archie, pushing him through the back door. 'Be a man, take it on the chin.'

They made their way to Sydney Road. Kenny tried to pull away several times, but Archie had him in a stronghold.

'Where does this bleeder live?' said Archie to an elderly woman passing by. She opened her eyes wide and told them number twelve.

Archie thumped the door of number twelve and Kenny whimpered, looking like he might cry. Vi regarded him with disgust.

The door was opened by a woman in her late forties wearing a spotless apron and holding a baby. She started in surprise.

'Kenny? What is it?'

'Hello, Mrs Holdsworth?' said Vi through gritted teeth.

The woman nodded.

'Your son here has got something to tell you.'

The woman stared at her son. Kenny looked at her pleadingly and shook his head.

'What is all this?' the woman demanded, taking on an aggressive tone.

'Your boy has knocked up my daughter. And he'd better do the right thing or Archie here will make him.'

The woman covered her mouth with her hand. 'Kenny? Is this true?'

'No,' Kenny cried, trying to pull away from Archie's grip.

The woman considered her son for a moment and looked at Vi and Archie.

'He said it's not true so why don't you both just fuck off.'

With that, she pulled Kenny inside and slammed the door in their faces.

Archie hammered on the door until it bounced on its

hinges. They could hear Kenny's mother shouting at him indoors but no one answered. Vi was beside herself. If the little bugger wouldn't take responsibility that really left them all in the lurch. She hurried home with Archie, back upstairs to the awful bloody scene in the bedroom. Doris still lay on the bed whimpering and clutching her stomach. Win sat on the floor holding the baby, which had fortunately gone to sleep.

'Right,' said Vi. 'Get up, get up.' She pulled Doris's arm roughly until she was standing. 'Get her coat, Win,' she said, taking the baby. 'Archie, you're taking her out.'

Win scuttled off and came back with the coats. They had to get Doris into hers, she was limp with shock. Win put Doris's shoes on for her and Vi gave the baby to Archie. He held it like it was an unexploded bomb.

'Take her to the Sally Army home in Grays. The big house by the park, you know it?' Archie nodded. 'She'll have to go in the sidecar with the baby. Just get her out of here. Go out the back door. Hurry, don't let anyone see. Put the baby under your coat. Oh my god, someone'll see.'

They bundled out onto the landing and down the stairs, the sheer momentum driving Doris along. In the scullery at the back door, Vi grabbed her arm.

'You go to the home and you get rid of that thing, that bastard, you hear me? Get it adopted or anything. Just don't come back here with it, I'm telling you Doris, don't you come back here with it.' Vi's voice broke. 'After all I've done for you. You'll be punished, Doris, no one'll come near you now. Do you know what you've done?'

Archie led her out of the back door, one arm holding the

baby beneath his coat. And they were gone. Win looked at Vi, wiped the cream off her face with a rag.

'The pub,' she said.

'I'll go,' said Vi. 'You sort out the mess upstairs.' Vi took a deep breath, slapped her cheeks with both hands and strode through to the pub. First thing, she grabbed a glass and jabbed it twice at the brandy optic, downed it in one while she faced the wall. The pub was strangely quiet. She shuddered and realised that they must all have heard the shouting, they must all know what had happened. She could hardly bring herself to turn around but when she did she frowned. It was something else.

'The King's dead,' said Old Bill at the bar.

'What's that, Bill?'

'The King died, Vi, we just heard.' He put his head down and Vi looked around. Everyone was sitting in silence staring into space, clutching their cloth caps to their chests.

'King George is dead?' Vi bit her lip but she was crying. She put her hand over her mouth and looked at the sad faces and she cried. No one said a thing and no one knew. The shock of what had just happened hit her. Her Doris. Ruined. All her life she'd been so careful. So worried. Her little girl.

She reached across to ring the bell to call time early. Two rings clanged into the silence, vibrated through her heart and soul. They all looked over at her and they stood up. She put the towels on the pump handles and watched them walk out.

4

Doris

Doris was in a dreadful nightmare. In the motorcycle sidecar she swayed this way and that, Uncle Archie driving, staring ahead, steering round the bends in the dark road. The February wind whipped her scarf-less hair across her face. She was sliding on a wet seat. There was a baby in her arms. She was dizzy and shaking, her teeth were chattering but her head and body were hot. The baby was so wrapped up she could only see its eyes, nose and mouth. It kept looking at her. It started to cry, the sound mixed up with the roar of the motorcycle engine, its face screwed up, its toothless mouth open and angry. There was a pain deep in Doris's gut but it was as if it wasn't her. She saw a girl lurching in a wind-whipped sidecar holding a screaming swaddled new-born and clutching herself down there to hold her insides in.

A large looming house. *Salvation Army Home for Unwed Mothers.*

'This is it,' said Archie, pushing the motorcycle stand down with his foot. He came round to Doris's side, reached down to lift up the baby, held it in the crook of his arm and held his other hand down to Doris. He wanted her to get out. Her legs wouldn't move. Her brain stopped working. Her arms were frozen in the shape of the baby's swaddling. Without a word, he reached down to put his arm around her shoulders and under her arm, pulled her up to standing and lifted her gently over the side. Something warm dripped on to the backs of her cold legs and her dress was stuck to her. He pressed her to his side and pulled her along. Her feet climbed some grey steps, her shoes slapped on the cold concrete. The door opened. There was a woman's voice and Archie's voice and Doris's feet shuffled forward over the threshold onto some black and white tiles. In the light she saw that her feet had turned red and the tiles had red spots on them. Urgent voices called out and there were people either side of her, black leather lace-up shoes next to hers. She could smell furniture polish and Dettol.

She was lifted up and placed on a bed. The ceiling was white. The light was bright. There were lots of new voices and she couldn't hear Archie. Someone lifted up her dress. Her hands flapped down to bat them away. Her arms were held down. Someone was near her face, shining a light, speaking. She smelled coffee breath and Lysol and heard metal clanking on metal. Someone touched her down there, pushed something inside. She kicked her legs. Someone held her legs down. There was pain, a bad, bad pain. She screamed out. Her arm was grabbed. There was a sharp sting in the crook of her elbow and the light and voices faded.

*

When she opened her eyes she was in a little white room. Her mouth was dry and she was sore down there. There was a glass-fronted cabinet with metal things on steel trays inside. A nurse on a chair looked up from her book, a Bible, and stood up. She held Doris's wrist and looked at her upside-down watch and she smiled.

'Good morning, Doris. How are you feeling?'

Tears ran down the sides of Doris's face.

'Now, now, you are all right, there's no need to worry. Shall we try to sit you up?'

She slid her arm between Doris's back and the pillow and drew her up the bed a few inches. Doris winced at the pain. The nurse held up a bedpan to show her and raised her eyebrows, slipped the thing under her and Doris let herself go, gritting her teeth at the sting.

'Good,' the nurse said. 'Hungry?'

'A bit,' said Doris, and her voice sounded all thick.

The nurse brought a bowl of rice pudding and a cup of tea and sat by Doris while she ate.

'What happened?' said Doris.

The nurse shook her head and frowned.

'I mean, something happened, what happened?'

'Do you mean your condition when you came in?'

'No,' said Doris. 'Before that. There was a baby. Where did it come from?'

The nurse looked sad and let out a sigh from her nose. She put her hand on Doris's. 'You had a baby, Doris. It came from you.'

Doris started crying. 'But how?'

*

Doris woke up and her mouth was dry again. It didn't hurt as much down there but her chest was sore. She was in a different room, still small and white but no cupboard with metal things on a tray. No one was in the room but there was a little bell on the bedside table. Doris rang it and the same nurse came in. She did the same bedpan and food routine.

'I think you're ready to sit up, Doris.'

Doris's head spun when she sat up but then she felt better.

'Doris, I'm going to take you to the sluice room for a bath.'

She smiled and Doris groaned when she helped her off the bed. She held Doris's arm as she shuffled out of the little white room and a short way down a deserted corridor and into a bathroom with a large bath with claw feet. The tap squeaked when the nurse turned it on. She reached over to a big bin full of white stuff, scooped out a cupful and tipped it into the water.

'Salt,' she said. 'To help you heal.'

The sound of water hitting water echoed around the room. Doris didn't want to get undressed in front of the nurse so she stood there watching it get deeper. The nurse stepped away and pulled a curtain closed around the bath.

'Take your time, Doris, I'll pop back in soon.'

The water was warm and silky. Doris let herself down gingerly and lay back, breathing in the steam. It stung down there but her body didn't look any different except her chest was swollen. She started to cry. She didn't understand.

The nurse took her back to the plain white room.

'Now, Doris. I'm going to bring Matron to see you.'

She opened the blind at the window and left. It was a grey day out there, bare trees and brown straggly flower beds in what would otherwise have been a nice big garden. A patchy lawn sloped up from the window. A large magpie flapped down to the grass and hopped across to a grey lump on the ground. *One for sorrow.* It pecked at the lump with its large black beak and downy feathers flew up. It was a dead wood pigeon – the magpie was plucking it. When there were several feathers strewn about the grass the magpie began pecking at the pigeon's flesh. It turned Doris's stomach to see it but she couldn't stop watching. The pigeon had a red bloody hole in its side. The magpie pecked and pecked, holding the carcass still with its foot, looking this way and that to see if it was being watched.

Doris jumped when the door opened and a vicar walked in. He was tall in a long black frock thing and stood there staring at her and smiling for a few seconds before speaking.

'Hello Doris. I'm Reverend Allen. May I come in and speak with you?'

She nodded at him and wished he'd go away. He was so happy with himself it seemed to strain him to force a look of sympathy. He was young and blond and wore little round wire glasses. He pulled up a chair next to the bed.

'I hope you're feeling well?'

Doris nodded. He nodded.

'Doris, this is just a quick visit. I'll come back when you're feeling stronger. I just want you to know that I'm here for you, and God is here for you.'

Doris nodded again and didn't know what to say.

'Doris, I want you to know that you can make things right

with God and start afresh. I can help you with that in church. For now, Doris, I urge you to pray. If you repent for what you have done, ask God to forgive you your sins for the sake of his son, Jesus Christ, who died for you. Can you do that for me, Doris?'

Doris nodded at him and the door opened. He leant down to her and said, 'Bye-bye for now, Doris, God bless you.'

A different nurse came in. She was small but seemed to fill the room. Her dark grey-speckled hair was dead straight, and was two inches longer than her nurse's hat all around, in much the same way mothers cut around pudding bowls. Doris imagined her hair had led her to this exact calling in life. From behind her, another woman stepped into the room. She was dressed in smart clothes, not a nurse's uniform, and she was looking at a clipboard.

The nurse gave Doris a nice smile.

'I'm glad to see you sitting up, Doris.' She sat on the chair the vicar had been in. 'I'm Matron Docherty.' Her accent was Scottish, her voice soft. 'Now Doris, I think you've had quite a shock?' Doris nodded and looked at her hands. 'Your uncle told us they didn't know you were expecting a baby.'

Doris shook her head and tried not to cry. 'I didn't know, either.'

The Matron looked at the other woman. 'Well, Doris, it is known to happen sometimes, but it is very unusual. Still, all is well now. When you came in you had a fever because you hadn't delivered the afterbirth and you were losing blood. Luckily Dr Stewart came quickly and saw to you in time. Would you like to see your baby?'

Doris's insides clutched up. She was hoping it wasn't real,

that there wasn't really a baby at all; she was hoping they weren't going to say this. She shrugged her shoulders.

'I think it will help, Doris. If you don't mind, I will go and fetch her.'

Her.

The Matron opened the door and beckoned to another nurse waiting there with a bundle.

'Doris, this is our deputy matron, Nurse Pim.' The other nurse came in, glanced at Doris and looked away. She was tall with broad shoulders but had no bust or hips and looked the shape of a shilling kite. A churning fear kneaded Doris's stomach with pushing knuckles and made her feel sick. Still not looking at her, Nurse Pim gave her the bundle.

'Make sure to hold up her head,' she said, like Doris had done something wrong. She hovered there in case Doris dropped it.

The baby was asleep. Its mouth was tiny. It had a bonnet on but Doris could see it had blonde hair. She didn't want to hold it and gave it back to the nurse, who looked like she knew as much, and went to stand at the foot of the bed.

'She's bonny,' said Matron. 'She's small though, she has come early. And some of the sac had fused onto her shoulders – that may cause a scar. And there's something else but for now, Doris, the priority is to get you well and back on your feet and taking care of Baby. But we do need to ask you a couple of questions if that is all right. This is Mrs Brown,' she said, indicating the smart woman with the clipboard, 'who would like to have a quick word.'

Mrs Brown stepped forward to the bedside. She smelled of the perfume Vi wore in the pub, Evening in Paris. The cobalt blue bottle on Vi's dressing table. Vi's disgust the other night, the terrible look on her face.

'Hello Doris, I'm your moral welfare officer. I can help with arrangements for the baby.'

Doris nodded at her.

'The baby needs to be baptised and registered. Do you . . . your uncle mentioned that you might be considering putting the baby up for adoption?'

Vi's words came fast.

You go to the home and you get rid of that thing, that bastard, you hear me?

What was Vi thinking about it all? She must have been livid.

Get it adopted or anything.

Doris nodded at Mrs Brown. 'Yes, I'm not to go home with it.'

'Well, that's as may be, Doris. But I think we need to talk to your parents, sorry, your mother, at some point. You see, Doris, adoption is not a straightforward thing. There are many difficulties. For example, a baby must be perfect to be considered. Any physical impairment makes it impossible for a baby to be placed.'

After all I've done for you. You'll be punished, Doris. Do you know what you've done?

'I'm afraid, Doris, that Baby has been born with talipes, a club foot.' She nodded at Matron to show her. Matron gave her a look like she didn't want to yet, but opened the blanket, put her hand under the baby's tiny left leg and held it up to show Doris. The foot was bent inwards at a right angle, with the sole facing backwards. It looked more like a hand than a foot.

'I'm sorry to say that makes her ineligible for adoption, Doris,' said Mrs Brown.

Matron said something about how the Salvation Army discouraged adoption whenever possible, that a child's best chance in life was with its own mother. But Doris couldn't concentrate, couldn't hear her properly. Vi's words were louder and Doris felt like she was in a nightmare again.

Just don't come back here with it, I'm telling you Doris, don't you come back here with it.

5

Vi

Doris should have been doing this washing.

'She should be doing this,' said Vi.

Win grated more soap into the hot copper boiler. Vi popped some coals into the fire underneath and wiped her hands on her hip. When she saw the black streaks she tutted — Archie liked their aprons to be spotless.

Dropping the bar towels into the boiling water, she stirred them round with the copper stick.

'Who's going to turn out the bedrooms and do the shopping if we have to do this?'

Win shrugged. 'We'll manage,' she said.

'Manage? It's a bloody disgrace, Win.'

Vi took a breath, tried to calm down. When she thought about Doris she felt enraged. After all the effort she'd made to make sure this exact thing didn't happen. The shame of it.

The waste. A decent upbringing wasted, secretarial college wasted.

Win was at the mangle, feeding one of Vi's dresses through. That dress was worse for wear. All her clothes were but she made the best of them. Material was still in short supply and she didn't like to squander money in the shops. She bought her magazines and saw the new fashions that way, it was good enough for her. The new spring collections and make-up to colour match. Pearl White and Anthracite Black, Canberra Claret, Kookaburra Pink. A Shortie coat would have been lovely, but she made do. An electric cooker or washing machine would have made all the difference, but Vi taught Doris to do things the right way, she wanted her to have a decent start in life. Win turned the mangle handle and the drips fell down.

Vi stirred the towels round, prodded them with the stick, stood back from the soapy steam that would make her set curls droop and her face shine with sweat.

'We can carry on like before, can't we, when she comes back?' Things she wouldn't normally say out loud she could say to Win, her sister.

Win rinsed a sheet in the sink and glanced at her, as if to say nothing was a safe bet at that point in time.

'I don't know what the boys would think about it all, Vi.'

Archie and Win had two sons, Jim and George. They had both gone away to sea to work on the liners. They came back every couple of years in their smart suits showing off their photographs of the rich and famous passengers they had met.

'Well it's not like we see them much, is it?' said Vi, helping her sister to pull the sheet through the mangle. Win looked away. She missed her boys.

Vi took the sheet out to the back yard and looked at the sky. It was grey and there was a cold wind. The clouds looked heavy with snow, but the washing would still go out. It'd be stiff with ice and would take longer to dry, but it would still go out. She knew before she looked at the row of terraced houses leading off from the pub that they'd all have washing strung up in the back gardens. It was Monday morning. If you hadn't got your washing out by midday Monday, you weren't fit to keep house.

She let down the line and pegged on the sheet, pulled it up as it cracked in the wind. Bright white, the whitest of whites. She called good morning to Betty next door and eyed her washing. Betty eyed Vi's. If Betty knew about Doris, good god.

The magnolia tree was starting to bud. They were coming to the end of winter. The tree reached up to the top floor of the pub, it was so big. It struck Vi that magnolia trees must be coming into bud everywhere. Set by nature's clock. She thought about Doris and her clock. Would this have happened no matter how careful Vi had been? She did more than most mothers and kept her in, but Doris had still managed to go behind her back. Vi had had plans for her: train her up in keeping house and teach her how to make the best of herself, go to secretarial college – none of that silly talk about art school. Get a good job and meet a good husband – the type of husband who would give her security – be a good mother and a good wife. She swallowed back the shame for the umpteenth time. Betrayed by her own daughter. It sickened her to the core.

'We'll put her on the spring cleaning when she gets back.'

Cleanliness was next to godliness, not that you'd find Vi in a church that much. 'She can wash away her sins.'

Win nodded and handed Vi a damp sheet. That morning Vi had read in the problem page about an unmarried girl expecting a baby. It was disgusting. The columnist told her to confide in her mother because she'd be hurt when she found out. Hurt? That'd be the least of it. She was advised to write to the National Council for Unmarried Mothers or something. What would they have done for Doris, turned back time? Made the wicked girl see sense before it was too late? No, there was only one thing she could do now, get rid of it. Bastard daughters had bad blood. Vi wouldn't have her cheapening the street or jeopardising Vi's position. War widows were respectable.

Bloody war. If Cyril had still been around this wouldn't have happened. They'd still be running the pub together. Doris wouldn't have dared to stray. There'd be no housing crisis, Archie and Win wouldn't have moved in. Vi would have given anything to go back to those days, before rationing and bomb sites. A husband gives security, takes charge, makes a woman decent. It was important to have a man around the house. Archie had to serve that purpose now.

Late in the evening, at ten thirty, Archie called time in the pub and Vi put the towels on. Doris normally did the ashtrays in the mornings but Vi would have to do them tomorrow. Vi wondered how long she'd be gone – she needed her back there to help with the cleaning. A small voice in her head asked how Doris was doing, if she was all right, but Vi slapped it away. Of course she was all right, she'd taken care of herself all right, hadn't she? Sneaking around with Kenny, up to all sorts.

Upstairs, she nearly bumped into Win, who was ready for bed. In that terrible too-small housecoat she was bursting out of, her hair in steel curlers, her face shiny with cream. Vi shook her head at her. She'd told her a hundred times that she owed it to her husband to look attractive. And that's what the magazines said. *It's up to you to look nice for Archie,* Vi would tell her, *he has to look at you all day.*

The magazines said it was possible to look glamorous day *and* night. Vi would save up to get her hair permed or she'd put setting lotion on in the morning before work so she didn't go to bed with a head full of ironmongery. She put her face cream on *before* bed for twenty minutes so her face wasn't shiny and stuck to the pillow case. She brushed her eyelashes with castor oil so they would look pretty before she went to sleep. It wasn't hard to do those little things to make sure you looked your loveliest at all times.

At her dressing table she brushed her hair until it shone and buffed her nails. She took her bottle of Evening in Paris, dabbed a touch in the crook of each elbow, behind her ears and at her hairline.

There was a tap at the door and she looked over her shoulder. Archie walked in, looking back to close the door quietly. Vi tutted when she saw a hole in his sock – Win wasn't looking after him properly. She stood up to greet him. He put his arms around her and his hands gripped her backside. His head dropped, his face met hers, their lips almost touched but he bent further to kiss her neck. She undid the buttons on his waistcoat and his shirt and before she'd finished he lifted her up on to the bed, took off his trousers and climbed on top of her.

6

Doris

Doris looked down at the wood pigeon. Feathers littered the grass around it and all that was left were the wings. The bones of the body had been stripped clean and the head was gone. She hugged her coat and closed her eyes, felt the chill breeze against her cheek and tried to find herself, remember who she was. She started to cry when she thought that everything was different now. She wondered if she was being watched and opened her eyes, wiping her nose on the back of her wrist. Once more around the garden to clear her head, slowly though as she was still sore.

The house was massive. Bricks the colour of yellow ochre. Tall windows painted white with their own little roofs above them. So many windows, sixteen just at the front, not counting the little triangle ones in the roof. Big chimney stacks and a bare wisteria plant that clung all over the front and around one side like it was holding the whole thing together.

The girls used a door in the side porch. Inside the house was all dark wood walls and curved panels over the doorways, high fancy ceilings and a wide staircase in the entrance hall. The floors were scrubbed clean by the girls, the wood polished to a glossy shine, but still the whole place was rough around the edges, the plaster crumbling in the corners and a smell of damp, like there was no money to keep it up.

It was time for prayers so she made her way to the front parlour. They had to sing hymns before they were allowed breakfast. Most of the girls were already in there and Nurse Pim gave Doris a stern look. She started up Jesus Thy Blood and Righteousness and they all mumbled along. Doris had only been there a few days but she'd already noticed that when Matron took prayers she did the jolly songs like Morning Has Broken. Nurse Pim's prayers and hymns were always about repentance and sin and that kind of thing. Doris just prayed that none of it was real. Sometimes she prayed that the baby would die.

They said Amen and went through to the dining room for breakfast.

'I hate kidneys.'

It was Sherie, one of the girls.

Doris nodded and wrinkled her nose. 'Me too.' She spooned some porridge into a bowl and tasted it. Salted today.

'How you feeling?' Sherie asked. She was older than Doris, her hair was bleached and she had plucked her eyebrows into thin arches.

Doris shrugged and nodded.

'Seen the baby much?'

Doris shook her head. She didn't want to see it, she wanted to forget all about it.

'Doris? Matron wants to see you after breakfast,' said one of the nurses.

'She'll be putting you to work soon,' said Sherie. 'They think it's good for the morals, a bit of hard work.'

Doris ate her porridge and didn't know what to say.

'So do you mind me asking? Who's the father?'

Doris's spoon stopped midway, a glob of porridge dropped down into the bowl.

'Who's the father of yours?' She said it too quickly.

Sherie laughed and gave a look of mock shock. 'A boy I've got, he used his wily ways with me and I was stupid enough to get caught. Thought we'd be all right taking the kettle off before it boiled,' she said, tapping her nose.

Doris forced a small smile to pretend she understood.

'My dad locked me in the cellar when he found out.' Sherie said.

Doris put her spoon to her lips, pulled off the porridge that felt too thick to swallow.

'I've got a boy, too,' she said. 'Kenny he's called.'

Sherie looked interested, leant forward with shining eyes. 'How old?' she said.

'I'd better go and see Matron,' said Doris.

Matron smiled and waved her into a chair when Doris tapped on her open door.

'How are you feeling, Doris?'

'All right, thanks.'

'Good. I think it's time to get you started on some little jobs around the place, it'll be good for you.'

'All right.'

'I understand you have refused to feed Baby yourself?'

Doris went rigid.

'It's all right, it's just that it might have been better if you'd tried first before making that decision.'

Doris looked at the parquet floor and wondered which girl had been on her hands and knees polishing it.

'I'll arrange for some tablets to stop the milk, it must be painful. Have you thought of a name for Baby?'

Doris shook her head.

'She'll be going into hospital for an operation soon, Doris. It's called a tenotomy, where they cut the Achilles tendon at the back of the foot. Baby will need a leg brace and manual manipulation once she's recovered from the operation. It's a long treatment process, Doris, and Baby will need a lot of help, and love.'

She waited for Doris to look up.

'Doris, have you given any more thought to keeping Baby? The Salvation Army are keen for mother and baby to stay together whenever possible. Perhaps I could speak with your mother – with the support of your family, or if you were to marry the father, perhaps . . . '

The look on Doris's face stopped her. Vi and Archie would have banged down Kenny's door by now and dragged him to church – if it was going to happen it already would have. Vi hadn't even been to see Doris, not even a letter or anything.

'It wouldn't be easy if you chose to do it independently. Council housing wouldn't be an option I'm afraid, and it would be difficult for you to find other accommodation. In cases such as these, adoption is usually the correct course of action, but with Baby's health problems . . . '

Doris stared at her lap, feeling like strong hands were pushing down on her shoulders. She had never asked for any of this.

'The Salvation Army may be able to assist you. There may be a hostel place, but they are few and far between. The National Council for the Unmarried Mother and her Child may also be able to offer some help from their Lettice Fisher Fund. Otherwise, the only other option would be to put her into care. We would help you find a foster mother in the first instance, until we can find a children's home for cripples that will take her. In all likelihood she'll be in a home until she's sixteen.'

Doris stared at her but could see only a blurred face, a stranger saying impossible things. Matron paused, tapped her fingers on the desk top, seemed to make up her mind about something.

'Doris, with your mother's consent, we would like you to stay here with Baby for the time being to help her through her treatment.'

Doris blinked and Matron came back into focus. 'How long for?'

'Well, it would be months, maybe ten months, until she's undergone most of her treatment.'

The parquet floor was so shiny. Doris spread her fingers and held her hands away from her lap. In the reflection, she saw ten fingers. Ten months not at the pub. Ten months away from Vi and secretarial school. Ten months of freedom. She swallowed away a lump in her throat at the thought of not seeing Kenny for so long. He hadn't been to see her though, hadn't even bothered writing. Maybe he didn't love her after all. She'd been kidding herself. He probably had other girls as well as her.

'All right,' she said.

'Well, that's wonderful, Doris.' Matron slapped the desk with both hands and beamed a broad smile. 'I'll draft a letter to your mother. Off you go then, ask Nurse Pim for a job to do, something light to begin with.'

As Doris left the office, she turned back to say, 'Laura. That's what I'll call it.'

Doris went upstairs to the dorm, looked down from the window at the nurses pushing the babies out in their prams to cry themselves to sleep under the oak tree. Laura. After Laura Knight, the artist. She realised she hadn't thought about drawing since all of this had happened. She might have fancied drawing the prams under the tree but she didn't, she just didn't feel like it.

Sherie came in and lay down on her bed.

'What did Matron say?' she asked.

'Just like you said, to put me to work.'

'Thought so. What's wrong with your little one's foot then?'

Doris turned around from the window. Sherie was lying back, her left foot crossed over her bent right knee, her leg kicking up and down. She was just bored, she wasn't being nosey for the sake of it.

'Club foot.'

She nodded her head. 'Is it from, you know ...'

43

She gave Doris a look like she'd know what she meant.
'What?'

'You know, did you try and get rid of it yourself?'

'What? No. Why, did you?'

Sherie's face clouded over. 'My little one's got a funny eye, they say she'll be blind on that side . . . it must have been the knitting needle I used . . . '

'Oh.'

'What on earth is going on? You two have work to do.'

It was Nurse Pim, and her arms were crossed. 'Doris, we need some coal brought in. Sherie will show you what to do.'

Sherie's face dropped. They went downstairs and Sherie showed Doris the coal cellar. It was dark and spidery and Doris saw something dart across the floor. Sherie screamed and ran back up the cellar steps. Doris grabbed the shovel and started loading up the tin bucket with coal. Matron was right, a bit of hard work would do her good.

7

Doris

In the kitchen, Doris was scraping carrots when a nurse popped her head in.

'Doris, your mother is here to see you.'

The knife slipped and cut her finger and she gasped a breath. She'd been in the home for three months with no visitors at all. Taking off her apron, she sucked her finger and went through to the entrance hall. When she saw Auntie Win standing there in her hat and coat, clutching her bag in front of her, Doris breathed out a sigh of relief.

'Auntie Win!' She ran over to her and choked back a sob at the sight of a familiar face. Win patted her shoulder and shushed her.

'I'm supposed to be your mother, Doris,' she whispered.

'Why?'

She bunched herself up and pursed her lips. 'Is there somewhere we can talk in private?'

Doris looked around. There was no privacy in the home – there would be girls in the kitchen chopping veg, girls in the rec room knitting booties, postnatal girls lounging in the dorm and others polishing and mopping and sweeping all over the place. 'The garden, maybe,' said Doris.

They sat on a little bench away from the house and spoke in hushed voices.

'Why didn't Mum come?'

Win looked like she was sugar-coating her words before saying them.

'Your mum's busy with the pub, Doris. I said I'd come to see you instead.'

'So she knows you're here?'

Win hesitated. 'Yes, course she does. Now then, how are you holding up? You look well enough. I brought you some Lucozade.' She pulled a pimply glass bottle covered with a yellow plastic wrap out of her bag and handed it to Doris.

'I'm all right. I'm making myself useful, Mum's coaching has come in handy, I help with the cooking and cleaning. The Matron's nice but the deputy's a witch.' Doris held the bottle, squeezed and let go to make the plastic crackle.

'And the baby?' Win's brow creased into a frown.

Doris shrugged, 'All right.'

'Where is the baby?'

'It's over there,' she said, pointing to the group of prams under the large oak tree about a hundred feet away from where they were sitting.

Win looked like she was shocked to realise it was so close by. 'Can I see?' she asked.

'I suppose. They don't like us around the babies unless we're feeding them.'

Clutching her Lucozade to her chest she stood up and Win followed her over there. There were no nurses around. They peered into the prams. All of the babies were asleep, there must have been at least a dozen there.

'Which one?' Win asked, her face softening when she saw them.

'I think this is it.'

'It?' Win tutted and went to look, gave a soppy smile when she gazed in.

'No, wait a minute, it's this one.'

'Don't you know which one?'

Doris frowned and looked at the baby. They all looked the same to her. This one turned its head in its sleep and Doris saw a purple mark on its cheek. She looked into another pram.

'It's the one with the funny foot.' But the babies were bundled up, and Doris couldn't see their feet. She started lifting up the blankets and one of the babies woke up and started to cry. She lifted up some more blankets until she saw the foot brace, a steel bar with a little baby shoe fixed on to each end to keep the baby's feet in place.

The one crying baby woke the rest of them up in turn until they were all screaming with purple faces and kicking their blankets off.

'This one,' Doris called out, pleased, and Win rushed over to see. She looked down and put her hand over her mouth, went all sad and started to cry. The baby cried too, and it tried to kick its legs and couldn't because its feet were fixed into the brace. It sort of rocked side to side instead and lifted its arms up, its fists tight and angry.

'Can I help you?' Nurse Pim was striding across the lawn to them.

'I was just showing my . . . mum the baby.'

'Well you've woken them all up now, haven't you?' She gave them both a dirty look and marched back indoors, leaving the babies crying. Doris couldn't stand the noise and Win looked worried and started rocking one of the prams. Doris beckoned to her to go back over to the bench.

'How come you don't know which one is yours?' she said, looking back at the prams.

'I do. I do if I see the foot. It's all twisted round. That's why I'm still here, did Mum get the letter from Matron? About the baby needing to get its foot sorted out? It's been in hospital, had an operation and now I have to help *manipulate* it, so it goes back to normal. It wears that brace as well.'

The babies were still crying under the tree but no one came to see. They had to learn that no one would come.

'Doris.'

One of the babies was crying louder than the others, really wailing.

'Doris, what's going to happen?'

'About what?'

'The Matron's letter, it said that the baby can't get adopted because of its foot. So, what's going to happen to it?'

'I don't know. I'm staying here to help it get better and then I don't know. They said it'll get fostered and then go into a home.'

'Doris, what about bringing her home? Have you thought about that?'

'Is that what Mum said?'

Win shifted in her seat, opened her bag for her hankie, dabbed her nose and put it back again.

'No, your mum is still very cross about it all, Doris. She's shocked, that's all, and she's glad you're staying here for now, until things settle down.'

'I don't want to bring it home. It's shameful. Mum wouldn't like it.'

'Doris, has your mum ever told you about where me and your mum were brought up?'

Doris stopped to think. That one baby was so loud it grated on her nerves. 'No, she never talks about when she was little, she gives me jobs to do if I ask her.'

'I never talk about it either, Doris. It's nothing to shout about.' She paused. 'We grew up in Grays Cottage Children's Home, an orphanage.'

Doris's heart quickened.

'Mum never said. Where were your mum and dad then?'

'We don't know, we never did know. We were doorstepped in Whitechapel, in London.'

'Doorstepped?'

Win shrugged. 'Left on an orphanage doorstep in East London. They sent us down to the home in Essex, me a baby and your mum a nipper.'

Doris stared back at her. How was she supposed to take it in, something like that?

'There was a note saying . . . saying there wasn't a father and she couldn't cope.' Win smirked. 'They didn't tell us that bit until we left the home at sixteen years old. Vi first, then me a couple of years later.'

They listened to that baby cry. The others were quietening down.

'What was it like?'

'The home?' Win's eyes looked at something far away. 'Unnatural. That's the best word I can think of, Doris. But you don't know that when you're little, you just feel sad. A child needs love. In the home there was no love, only survival. We got through it the best we could. When people came looking to adopt one of us, we'd run to smile at them, cling to their legs, hope they'd take us. We knew it would be good to be chosen and get out of the home. We just knew that.'

'But no one chose you?'

'No, no one chose us. And it wasn't for the want of dreaming about it and wishing for it. And sending us to the local school so we could pretend we were normal just made it worse. All it did was show us how proper families lived, what they had that we didn't have. And it made us targets. We were bullied without mercy, called things, and if we cried about it at the home, we were punished and taunted.' Win's face twisted with spite. '"Your mummy's not coming for you," things like that.'

'That's horrible.'

'Oh yes, it is. If I could get my hands round the neck of that house mother now, I'd . . . well, it hardens you up, doesn't it? You have to toughen up quick when you're young, grow up before your time.'

The thought of Vi and Auntie Win in that place. Doris stared at the oak tree and tried to take it all in. She knew it was awful but it was like Win was telling her a story, not something that really happened. Then it dawned on Doris why Win was telling her.

'Don't do it to your little one, Doris.' Win was crying now. Quiet little tears rolling slowly down. 'Don't do it to her, Doris. I can't tell you what it does to a person. It makes you feel ... not human, unwanted, like you don't belong anywhere. It makes you wish you were dead. It gives you a fierce hatred of the people who didn't want you. It stays with you forever, Doris, you can never, never get rid of it. You're never good enough. Please. Don't do it to the baby. She's got enough on her plate as it is, no father and crippled. That's a hard enough start in life.'

Doris was numb. Vi had drummed it into her all her life. She must be decent, be able to hold her head up in public, not shame the family. Anyone who had a baby without being married was a tart and their children were bastards. They brought the street down, you crossed the road to avoid them. They were rubbish, shameful rubbish.

'But Mum—'

'I know, but when she sees the baby she'll remember, we can talk her round. It's worth a try, Doris. I'm here for you, all right?'

Doris looked at Win's hand. She was scratching her wrist, over and over on the same spot, she didn't even realise she was doing it.

'Look at what it's done to your mum, look what it's done to me. We were branded bastards, Doris, and we still don't tell people that. Haven't you ever wondered why we haven't got any friends? We're afraid the truth will come out. You know what a bastard is, don't you? Course, everyone knows that. They're bad blood, they infect people around them.'

She gave Doris a long look and she scratched and scratched and the skin was red and raw like it would start bleeding any minute.

'We had to work hard for a decent life when we grew up, but we had each other. But your baby, we can help you.'

'What about Kenny? Have you seen him?' said Doris.

Win paused. 'Your mum and Archie went to see his mother, but they didn't want to know, Doris, I'm sorry.'

Doris felt the prickle of tears in her eyes. She'd been hoping Kenny might be trying to sort things out. So that was it then, was it? She couldn't believe Kenny would let her down so badly. It just went to show, you couldn't trust anyone.

'Maybe you'll meet another boy who'll take the baby on?' said Win, hopefully.

God, that one baby was still crying, it wouldn't shut up. Doris stood up and walked over there, looked into each pram to see which one it was. The quiet ones were staring up at the oak tree, the dappled sunlight was moving over them like Mother Nature had made a toy for them to look at. Doris went to the crying one, it was that cry that sounded so desperate, so needy, like it was trying to say *Please just help me*. She lifted up the blanket at its feet and saw that it was hers, its face red and wet. Doris put her hands on the pram handle, pressed down on it gently and let go, pressed and let go, pressed and let go, and the rocking started to soothe her. She calmed down, sobbed a few gulps of air and went quiet, staring at Doris. There was a sudden breeze and the leaves on the tree flapped, they flapped and clapped, like they were giving Doris a round of applause.

8

Doris

'Nurse Pim has told me to leave,' said Doris, carrying Laura into the nursery and sitting on the floor with Kathy, one of the married ones. Kathy's hand paused mid-air as she patted her baby's back.

'When have you got to go?'

'Next week. She's only saying it because Matron's away. I hate her.'

Kathy shook her head and resumed her patting, the baby rewarding her efforts with a loud burp.

'I'm supposed to have a couple more weeks left here,' said Doris. Matron had said she could stay for ten months to look after Laura. She'd made friends with Kathy, who had got married while she was at the home, which meant she was allowed to take her baby when she left. Matron treated her more like the married ones than those who would leave without their babies. So she washed Laura and fed her and changed her and did her foot exercises. She was nine and a half months old now.

Doris bent Laura's foot sideways really gently the way they had shown her at the hospital but she was trying to wriggle away.

'I've just got used to being here, that's all.'

Kathy nodded and offered her baby the bottle again. Laura tried to crawl away but Doris held her in her lap and put her feet into the brace. She hated it and cried but that's what Doris was supposed to do.

'What's gonna happen with Laura then?'

Doris glanced at Kathy and her stomach turned over. She hadn't been able to sleep for thinking about it, what Win had said about growing up in an orphanage. But the thought of going home to Vi with a baby . . . There was no question that she, Doris, would have to go home. She liked being at the Salvation Army home but she could feel the tug of Vi's apron strings. She wasn't ready to go it alone yet, she was scared. And she didn't think she could leave Laura now. It wasn't that she felt like Doris's, or that Doris cooed over her like the other girls did with their babies. Doris still couldn't believe any of it had happened and she wished none of it had, but Laura didn't ask to be born and Doris didn't want this strange little cripple baby to hate her for her whole horrible life.

'I'm gonna get churched and take her home.'

'What?' said Kathy, frowning. 'Carol said when you've had a baby you're dirty so you have to be blessed in church then you're clean and it's all right to go home. Carol's mum told

54

her if you go home before you're churched you infect the neighbourhood with bad luck.'

'Oh yeah, I'm doing that too, but we're Catholic so it's different – you can only get blessed if you're married.' Kathy gave Doris a smile of pity. It was all right for her, her baby had a dad. But that vicar said she could get churched and make things right and Doris could tell Vi she had been cleansed.

'So your mum's given permission to take Laura home?'

Doris nodded. Auntie Win gave permission, Matron thought she was Vi.

The next day, in her best dress and a borrowed coat, Doris pushed Laura in the pram to the St Peter and St Paul Church. She shivered as much from nerves as from the bitterly cold air. It was quiet, not the song of a bird, not the bump of a bicycle. Only the loud clonk of her shoes on the path and she realised how fast she was walking, her footsteps matching her heartbeat. The short path to the church went through the graveyard, the headstones standing strong through the years, nothing able to knock them out of place. The blue and brass clock over the door showed twelve o'clock. It was judgement day for Doris. She hoisted the pram up the little step, went through the stone arched porch and struggled to push open the iron-studded wooden door to get the pram through.

She found herself on her knees at the vicar's feet in the empty church with Laura in her pram at the back of the pews. And she thought about Vi and that she'd think it was all right for her to go home with the baby because she'd done this.

'Forasmuch as it hath pleased Almighty God, of his good-ness, to give you safe deliverance, and to preserve you in the great danger of childbirth; you shall therefore give hearty thanks unto God, and say . . . '

Doris looked at her prayer book and said that bit with the vicar.

'I found trouble and heaviness; then called I upon the Name of the Lord; O Lord, I beseech thee, deliver my soul.'

Her voice was a low mumble but it echoed in the big cold church. God was going to help her and she was going to be all right.

'I will receive the cup of salvation, and call upon the Name of the Lord.'

Salvation meant saved.

'O Lord, save this woman thy servant.'

Yes, she was going to be saved.

'O Almighty God, we give thee humble thanks for that thou hast been graciously pleased to preserve, through the great pain and peril of childbirth, this woman, thy servant, who desireth now to offer her praises and thanksgivings unto thee. Grant, we beseech thee, most merciful Father, that she, through thy help, may faithfully live according to thy will in this life, and also may be partaker of everlasting glory in the life to come; through Jesus Christ our Lord . . . '

The vicar nodded at her with wide eyes and they said together, 'Amen.'

Doris got up from her knees and the vicar took back the prayer book.

'Am I clean now?' she said.

9

Vi

'Bring back the birch, I say.'

That was Jack's answer to everything. He was talking about the two Teddy boys in the corner of the public bar, wearing narrow trouser legs and long suit jackets.

'They haven't done anything to me, so live and let live.'

That was Archie's two-penn'orth.

'Arch, a couple of months ago, four of them robbed an old woman after burning her face with a fag-end, didn't you hear?'

And that was Harry's. Jack and Harry, two of The Empire's regulars. Always at the bar having a banter with Archie. Both from old Tilbury families, Harry was a lighterman on the river and Jack worked a plot of land – he used work horses and his house wasn't on the electric; he'd be on about mechanisation given half a chance.

'Never mind the birch, stick them in the loony bin and throw away the key,' said Jack. Archie nodded sagely and pointed his cig at Jack to say he liked that idea.

'Or send them out to Korea first,' said Harry, chuckling.

The regulars all sat in the same place. Vi knew them as much by where they sat and what they drank as by anything else. They were reliable like that. There was a good camaraderie in The Empire. They knew each other well, their punters were loyal to them and they in turn looked after the punters. Good men, working men. Dockers and farmers who took pride in their work and knew they made a difference, knew that the country couldn't cope without them. Men disabled from the war defending their country. They were together in the pub when the King died and they'd be together when the new Queen was crowned – Archie had even talked about renting a television set for the coronation. Freddy over there had his wedding reception in the pub and sent them a postcard from his honeymoon in Skegness. John there captained The Empire's darts team and kept a thriving pigeon loft. This was real life, decent life, people grafting to feed their families and coming to their local for a pint of mild to forget their troubles.

'Where's Old Bill tonight?' Jack nodded towards Bill's stool, empty for a change.

Vi shrugged. 'Didn't want to come out in the fog I expect.'

They were saying it was the worst London smog ever recorded. And it came down to Tilbury too, first a drifting fog and then a cloud of smog that made it hard to see indoors without lights. It was yellow with the coal fumes from all the factories and works; there were enough smokestacks to pump grime into the cold air around there. People were dropping like flies, especially the old ones. It got into the lungs, made you choke, made your eyes water. You could only see six feet in front of you.

'What I don't get,' said Harry, 'is how come there's smog when our coal's still on the ration?'

They all raised their eyebrows and shook their heads.

'What I don't get,' said Jack, 'is how can coal still be on the ration when we bloody well mine it in this country.'

'Bloody politicians, that's what,' said Archie. 'Spending people's pensions on atomic bombs.'

'And sugar still on ration,' said Vi.

'That really takes the biscuit – if you pardon the pun – bloody sugar on the ration, that says it all, that does.'

'British Empire's fading fast,' said Harry, picking up a pinch of ash from the ashtray to show his point and crumbling it like an Oxo cube. It floated down in specks and they all watched and nodded like they hadn't had this same conversation a hundred times.

'Yep,' said Jack. 'The Yanks and the Soviets are in charge now and we've been left holding the debtors' bill.' He stared into his pint of mild like he was looking in there for the old Britain, the Great Britain the world admired and feared, the one with the upper hand, the one that hadn't been crippled by austerity. He swilled his glass round and drank down the dregs.

'Here Jack, we're still in charge, don't you worry,' said Archie, reaching under the counter with a wink. Jack and Harry sat up and sniffed as though this whole talk hadn't been leading up to Archie reaching under the counter. He put a little parcel of sugar in front of each of them and they slid them off and into their coat pockets. Archie tapped the side of his nose with his finger and the men cleared their throats and their consciences at the same time. It wasn't like Vi and Archie had to worry about sugar shortages, with all the dock-ers who came in the pub with damaged goods that had been *accidentally* dropped at work, and with Archie's little sideline in black market goods. If Vi had her way she'd rather he didn't, she didn't want to put her pub at risk, but he was the man and he knew best so she let it be. They were all fed up with the shortages anyway, the bloody war was over, wasn't it?

The sound of the foghorns downstream grew louder when the pub doors were opened.

'Archie! Vi!'

John the butcher was standing at the open door beckoning to them with a dreadful face on him. Vi went to call through to the scullery.

'Win!'

'Old Bill, he's taken bad,' said John the butcher, gesturing for them to go outside.

Win came through to the bar, patting her hair into place.

'Watch the bar, Win, something's up,' said Vi, and followed John and Archie outside.

About ten feet away Vi could just make out in the fog some people crowding around a person on the floor. Pinching her nose against the fog, she dashed towards them and they became clearer by degrees until she was almost on top of them and they gave way to let her through. Poor old Bill. She dropped to her knees next to him, put her hand under his head.

'What's happened, love?'

His chest was rattling.

'It's the bloody smog, he can't breathe,' someone said. 'The doctor's coming.'

Vi smoothed back Bill's grey fringe and looked around for his hat but couldn't see it. He must have been coming for a pint after all. Daft old sod out in that weather. It just showed you that the punters saw the pub like their own home, like coming home. The doctor nudged her aside gently and started to examine Bill. Everyone went quiet to give them some breathing space, some of them stifling their coughs into their coat lapels.

The tring of a bicycle bell caught Vi's attention. She looked through the fog and saw Sharp Sid coming on his three-wheeler, with the grinding stone on the handlebars and a sign in the frame that said *Knives Scissors Garden Shears Lawn Mowers Saws Sharpened*. What on earth was he doing out in the fog? He rang his bell and nodded at Vi as he went by. She turned around to the pub and saw that Win had come out, holding a tea towel against her nose and mouth. Vi tutted, she should be watching the bar. But she was looking at something and Vi followed her gaze.

Someone was walking through the fog towards them. Vi squinted and her heart lurched when she saw that it was her Doris, becoming clearer as she got closer. Vi stood straight, took a few steps towards her to get away from the group around Old Bill. And then someone may as well have kicked her in the stomach. Doris was carrying a baby. In panic, Vi looked at the small crowd, saw that they had turned to stare. Her hands flapped up to her face. What the hell was she doing? Everyone would see.

Vi ran the few yards to meet her, pulled her roughly away towards the dock wall, far enough so they couldn't be seen through the fog.

'What the hell are you doing?' said Vi.

Doris's face dropped. Did she think Vi would be pleased to see her with her bastard in her arms? She wasn't right in the head.

'Mum, it's all right, I've been churched, the vicar said I'm clean now.'

Vi shook her head, tried to make sense of what Doris was telling her.

'What are you talking about? I told you not to bring that thing back here, didn't I?'

'Yes, but Auntie Win thought . . .'

'What?'

'Sorry Vi,' said Win behind her.

Vi swung around, saw Win and Archie standing there, saw other faces surrounding them in the gloom. She gasped for breath, her throat closing up.

'Vi, we can manage, we can help her, I think it will be all right, Vi.'

Vi screwed up her face, tried to find the words that she needed to shout into the stupid woman's face, her own sister who should have known better, who should have known well enough the reason it was not all right, it would never be all right.

'You should know better than anyone, Win,' Vi growled at her, low so no one could hear.

A thought occurred to her. The one thing that would make this horrible mess all right.

'Are you getting married then? Are you marrying Kenny?'

Doris frowned, looked at Win, and shook her head.

'No, I . . .'

'Archie!' Vi shouted. He was at her side in a second. 'Tell her, Arch, get rid of her, I can't bear it.'

Archie stepped towards Doris. 'Go on now, we'll put you in the loony bin if you don't get gone, you can't stay here, you're not bringing that thing home.'

'Yes,' Vi said. 'I can have you put away, I'll do it. You're a disgrace, how dare you come back here with that thing when I told you not to. It's immoral, it's not proper, you'll be sleeping all over the place looking for a husband to take that thing on.'

'Yeah, she's made her bed now, she'll be fair game,' said Archie.

'No, Archie,' said Win, clutching his arm. He shrugged her off, he knew what made sense.

'You get gone, my girl, or I'll have you put away, do you hear me?' said Archie.

Doris fell back against the sea wall, her face as white as the blanket around the thing she was holding. The cover slipped away from the baby's legs and Vi saw some sort of metal brace with the feet strapped on.

'You keep it, you keep that thing, it's your punishment for your wickedness,' said Vi.

Vi wouldn't have Doris spoiling the decency she'd worked so hard for. She would not be dragged down.

Doris looked at Vi, looked at Archie and Win and sobbed, stumbling away into the fog. One step, two steps, three, four, five. Six feet into the fog and she started to disappear and she was gone into nothing.

Vi took a deep breath of the vile air that stung her nose like pepper and she closed her eyes. When she turned around she realised there were no gloomy figures standing around in the yellow mist and she heard hushed voices in the direction that Old Bill had gone down. She walked over there slowly, and as he came clear, she saw the men had taken off their hats and were holding them close to their chests. The doctor was closing Bill's eyes and Vi pushed her fist against her mouth. Bloody smog. The people were dropping like flies.

PART 2

Tilbury Docks, April 1955

10

Doris

The kid leant over the sea wall, looking for the green slime you can see when the tide's out. The grey water slopped up and down from the wake of the passing boats, up to where the algae clinging to the wall was lime green and down to where it was brown and always underwater with the barnacles, never seeing the light of day. If Doris was that way inclined she'd run up quick behind the kid and pitch her over into the river. But the thought made her shiver. Doris could look at the water for an hour – the shades and shadows, the reflections of the sky, the innocent ripples and angry wakes, the river opaque like it was a solid swelling mass.

The kid saw something, ran over to the pub and grabbed a wooden beer crate, took it and pushed it against the wall to stand on, leant right over to grab at something, one of her feet lifting off the crate. Just a snail. Doris knew she'd poke it out of the shell with a stick and tread on its body. She looked at Doris for a sign of recognition and Doris looked away towards the pub. The Empire pub. Big. Big like a bully in a playground.

The public bar door opened and a woman came out. It was what Doris had been waiting for – Vi coming out of the pub door to scrub the step. Every morning, as reliable as the tide itself. Doris waited for her moment. Vi didn't turn her head but gave a quick sidelong glance over to where Doris sat. There was a small crunching sound. The kid had trodden on the snail. Doris shot up her arm to wave a greeting and, as usual, Vi looked away and continued with her work. But she had seen and that's what Doris lived for these days. To make sure Vi knew she still wanted to come home.

Vi and Doris had an unspoken understanding. As long as Doris kept her distance, Vi would let her be. Like there, on the sea wall, a hundred feet away from the pub. If she got any closer Vi would tell her to get away or she'd have her taken away. It was nothing to Vi that Doris and the kid were living like stray dogs. Nothing that she could take them in with a nod of her head or a wave of her hand.

Doris had struggled on her own now for more than two years. It felt longer. She often thought about that girl in the pub, practising homemaking and going to secretarial school, and it wasn't her. She was the one who gave birth on her bedroom floor and left a Salvation Army home holding a baby, the one who brought the baby home and was thrown out on to the street. The kid was ten months old then. Doris tried to block that night out of her memory but she still remembered a vague kind of coldness like the blood draining out of her body. It was fear. Cold fear that she could have caught in a bucket and poured over her head time and time again. Vi used to tell her that there were good girls and good-time girls. Doris wasn't good any more – she was the kind who had brought shame on her family.

Doris had disappeared that night into the fog. She was crying so hard, she needed air but there wasn't any, the fog was choking her. Turning blindly this way and that, she got lost, stumbled up a kerb and dropped the baby. It cried for half an hour. Doris stopped, stood still, heard footsteps further off, someone walking carefully, feeling their way. She came up against the butcher's shop, recoiled from the headless carcasses of cows that hung in the window, the pink-grey pigs' heads with oranges stuck in the mouths arranged below, staring out at her. She imagined the heady tang of the meat inside, the smell of the sawdust on the floor to absorb the blood. She knew where she was at least and followed the road round to Kenny's street.

His horrified face when he opened the door – the sight of Doris there with the baby and her bag of possessions. When his dad called out in the background to see who it was, Kenny shut the door quick. So quick that Doris had to step back. She stood there staring at the door – she wanted to kick it and shout *Help me Kenny* but Kenny's dad would come out and the neighbours would come out. In the back of her mind she'd known he would shun her. Why else hadn't he come to visit her in the home? She had hoped it was because Archie had threatened him or his mum and dad had said they wouldn't hear of it, but that look on his face. She looked down at the baby, asleep now and heavy in her arms. A dead weight. Doris turned away and the baby woke up and started to cry again because she was holding it too tightly, crushing the air out of it. It was getting hungry too.

Her old friend Maisie lived on the next street over. The last door in Tilbury she could knock at. Maisie's mum, Sylvie, opened the door, her eyes flicked down to the baby and she took a step back with the shock of seeing her there. Doris gathered her courage and stood up straight. *Good posture is a sign of class*, Vi used to tell her that.

'Hello, Mrs Hurrell. I'm sorry but can I come in? I've got nowhere to go.'

'Doris, what on earth?'

She couldn't shut her out quick enough. The bolt was drawn across with a clap. Hard bitch, no better than Vi. If Doris hadn't been standing on her doorstep she'd have crossed the road to avoid her. That was it then, she had no choice but to go back to the home. As she passed the side passage of Maisie's house, Doris saw the mother's pushbike resting there. There was a large wicker basket fixed to the front wheel arch. With a thumping heart, Doris put the baby in the basket, strapped her bag to the carrier on the back and wheeled the bike away. After a couple of minutes they were hidden by the fog. Never in her life had she stolen something. But needs must when the devil drives. Doris pulled the baby's blanket loosely over its mouth and nose against the fog, mounted the bike and cycled for all she was worth the four miles to Grays, back to the home, through the choking yellow cloud.

When she arrived, she was coughing hard and exhausted from cycling uphill. The deputy matron, Nurse Pim, opened the door to her and Doris started to sob. Nurse Pim gave an impatient sigh like she knew she'd be seeing Doris again.

'You'd better come in,' she said. 'But only for the night, we haven't room.'

She led Doris through to the delivery room where there was a little bed and a cot by its side.

'I suppose the baby shall want some milk?'

'Yes please, and me as well please.'

Nurse Pim indicated that Doris should get it herself. Doris heard her lock the front door and go up to bed and she carried the snivelling baby through to the kitchen to make up a bottle to shut it up. The baby held the bottle itself while Doris cut some bread off a loaf, one-handed. She poured some milk and sank into a chair in the dining room. Her dry throat made it hard to swallow.

After breakfast the next morning Nurse Pim called Doris into the office.

'You're out of luck. There shan't be a place in the Salvation Army refuge for you and the baby for some time.'

Refuge. It was a strange word.

'But what will I do? Can't we stay here?'

'I'm sorry, we haven't the room, and this home isn't supposed to be for long-term stays.'

Nurse Pim ran her finger over the fine dark hairs on her upper lip as she stared at her desk and thought.

'And you'll not get housed if you're not married. Have you any money?'

Doris shook her head.

'Well, even if you had you'd find it hard finding a room to rent. People don't want unmarried mothers, it brings the place down they say.' She paused. 'There is a place you could try. But it's not Salvation Army and we would have no responsibility for you there. Matron wouldn't normally send our girls, but given the circumstances . . . it's up to you . . . '

'Where is it?'

'Southend, you'd get the train.'

'Is Matron back yet?'

'No, she is not.'

Doris searched the woman's face for a sign that there were other options but she saw none there. It was an open door after all, when all others were closed. Last night in the fog, was it really only yesterday? Vi and Archie and their hate-filled faces, then Kenny's horror and Maisie's mum's disgust. No one wanted to help her, she had become some sort of abandoned thing, cast out. A far cry from the girl she had been before, so keenly aware of how to behave properly, how to keep house and make herself look her best. And now this offer of a refuge. That strange word. Refuge from danger and a roof over their heads was top priority.

Win had told her to keep the baby. Win should be help-ing her. But she had just stood there when Archie gave his two-penn'orth and now Doris was stuck. She looked at the baby sitting in her lap. It was trying to pull itself up, grabbing handfuls of Doris's dress and concentrating hard. It found its feet and stood up unsteadily, one foot in a special boot, smil-ing into Doris's face triumphantly, bent its knees and bounced with excitement, fell back down on its backside with a bump, its blonde curls puffing up, and started its ascent again.

'Thank you, yes, we'll go.'

'Good. You both need a wash. Go and use the facilities and I'll look for the train timetable.'

*

Nurse Pim lent her the money for the train fare, said she could pay it back when she was working. Doris wondered what she meant. How was she supposed to work when she had the baby to take care of? The baby liked the train; she held on to Doris and looked out of the window at the passing fields, covered in a low mist. A woman sitting opposite with her hair up in a scarf smiled at them, then gave a look of pity when she saw the baby's special boot.

'She's bonny, how old?'

'Ten months.'

The woman held out her finger and the baby grabbed it and laughed.

'What's your name, bonny baby? What's your name then?'

The woman looked at Doris.

'Her name's Laura.'

'Are you on the choo choo train, Laura?' said the woman with raised eyebrows and open mouth. 'Cow,' she said, pointing out the window. 'Moo. Say moo. Moo.'

The baby laughed at her and pointed too. 'Mah mah,' she said.

'Ah, she said mamma,' said the woman.

Doris gave a small smile. She didn't think it was mamma, the baby didn't say that.

'You are lovely, yes you are.' The woman pinched the baby's cheek lightly. 'Her hair is a beautiful colour.'

Doris looked at Laura's short blonde curls. It was a lovely colour. And it was strange having a stranger's perspective on Laura. Without everything else that went along with being an unmarried mother.

'She's nothing but trouble,' said Doris, and pulled Laura away from the woman to sit back on her lap.

The woman frowned and tutted quietly, took out her knitting from her bag. Laura strained forward, holding out her hand to the woman, but Doris tapped it and pressed it down.

The train pulled into Southend Central train station. Doris put the baby on her hip and stepped onto the platform with her bag, then walked past the hissing engine to the exit. She had been there before, on a school outing, had eaten a toffee apple on the pier. A million years ago. Vi nearly hadn't let her go on that trip. She'd been into the school to get the teacher's assurance that Doris would be under supervision at all times. Look at her now. Doris felt that familiar dip of shame.

'Do you know where this is, please?' Doris showed the guard the address that Nurse Pim had given her.

'Yes, miss, turn left out the station on to the Broadway, second left on to Queens Road and Gordon Road crosses Queens after the school.'

'Thank you.'

The guard stared after her and Doris wished she had a pram to put the baby in. Coming out on to the pavement, she felt the sea salt in the air wash over her. The baby looked towards a seagull that sat atop a road sign, its mouth open in a long screech. Looking right was the high street, busy with local shoppers. Cars, motorcycles, people standing under bus shelters, women pushing prams. In the summer it would be packed with holidaymakers and day trippers. She turned left and checked the Broadway Road sign, hitched the baby up on her hip and walked along, turned left into Queens Road and gave silent thanks that the station guard had given her the right directions.

The school buildings came into view on the right and then a crossroads. Doris checked the address and looked at the door numbers of the semi-detached brown brick houses. She turned right and found number seventeen. It looked just like a normal house except for the line of prams in the side alley. Over the door was a discreet sign. *Southend Christian Women's Mission*. Doris's arms were aching. For a second she wanted to burst into tears. This was another strange door to knock at.

It was opened by a dumpy woman with a round red face wearing a blue and white striped apron. She looked like a mini butcher, all she needed was a straw boater on her head. At the sight of Doris she smiled and Doris didn't know what to say.

'Hello, dear, can I help you?'

'Yes please, the Salvation Army home said I can stay here with my baby.'

'Oh, did they now?' She frowned and then chuckled. 'Come in, come in, all in need welcome here.'

Doris tried to smile but couldn't. She just wanted to put the baby and her bag down.

'Come through, dear.'

Doris followed her into a parlour type room with a desk in the corner.

'Please, sit down. And who is this?'

The woman sat next to her on a settee and put her face close to the baby's.

'This is Laura, she's ten months old.'

'Is she now? Are you now? Are you indeed?' Laura caught onto the baby talk and smiled. 'You are sweet, yes you are, very sweet, sweet indeed.'

The blanket fell away from the baby's feet and the woman flinched when she saw the special brown boot.

'Club foot,' said Doris.

'Ah, yes, it happens,' she said to the baby, 'yes it does, it happens, yes it does.'

Doris waited, sneaked a glance around the room. It was tidy and looked like it was kept for best. The wooden floor shone, but the smell of polish was overlaid with a damp, musty odour. There was a large crucifix on one wall over the mantel.

'Well my name is Mrs Bottomley. I'm the housekeeper here. Housekeeper and Jack of all trades more like.' She nudged Doris with her elbow. 'And what do we call you then, dear?'

'Doris.'

'Doris. Yes.' Mrs Bottomley nodded and regarded her for a moment. 'And if I may ask, Doris, what is your situation?'

'I'm . . . I've got nowhere to go.'

'Family?'

Doris shook her head.

'The father?'

'No,' Doris looked at the crucifix and down at her lap.

'I see. Yes I do.'

The baby wriggled on Doris's lap, wanted to get down. Doris put her on the wooden floor and she got herself to sitting and shuffled across to the fireplace, started batting at the grate brush dangling from a hook.

'Don't. Naughty,' said Doris, giving Mrs Bottomley an apologetic look.

'It's all right, leave her be. Doris, you're in luck. I do have a spare bed here, if you're interested. Our arrangement here at the refuge is that most of the girls go out to work for a living, while a couple stay here to watch the children. The workers give a share of their earnings to the carers. That way everyone can pay for their keep. It's an arrangement that works well, as long as everyone pulls their weight and does their best to keep the peace.'

'Really? You'd let me stay?' Doris couldn't help a smile spreading across her face.

Mrs Bottomley stood up to pick up the baby before she pulled the poker onto the floor. She bounced her on her hip.

'Yes, really. Really, really,' she said to the baby. Laura laughed and tried to catch hold of Mrs Bottomley's necklace, a double string of pearls. 'La, laah, la, la.' Mrs Bottomley la'd the Blue Danube and started to waltz around the room with Laura, slow at first then faster and faster, laughing at Laura and Laura delighted with it all. They spun around, Mrs Bottomley making the correct steps and holding out the side of her skirt with one hand, the other clutching Laura on her hip. Doris stared, not sure where to look. Mrs Bottomley suddenly flopped down on to the sofa, out of breath, laughing, her cheeks redder than before.

'Right, come on, I'll show you around.'

Mrs Bottomley smiled at Doris, nodded with her head for her to follow her out of the room. And Doris stayed there for more than a year.

On that first day at the refuge, Mrs Bottomley, despite her size, tripped gracefully around the house, introducing Doris and Laura with great excitement to some of the other women and showing Doris where she'd sleep. There were three large bedrooms for the women, each with two bunk beds and two or three little cribs, some of the children too old for a cot and sleeping with their mothers in the bunk beds. The fourth bedroom belonged to Mr and Mrs Bottomley. Mr Bottomley hadn't surfaced from his room yet – he always had a late breakfast, Mrs Bottomley advised her. The nursery was downstairs. In it were two women, two babies and three toddlers.

'Min, Glor, meet Doris, our new girl, and her lovely little one Laura.'

Min and Glor looked up from where they sat on a settee pushed up against one wall. They both held cigarettes, both looked sullen and somehow drained of life. Doris didn't know which was which. She nodded her head and smiled at them uncertainly. The one on the left had curlers in her hair beneath a floral turban, her face was pasty white and her teeth stuck out on to her top lip. She wore a brown dress, had her bare legs curled up beside her and was picking at one of her toenails. The other one had brown hair that hung limply around her face. Doris couldn't tell if it was greasy or wet. Her floral dress was stained and dirty, her legs bare, her feet in worn house slippers. They looked Doris up and down and went back to their cigarettes.

One of the toddlers got up from where it sat and waddled over to one of the babies who sat up holding a rattle. The toddler snatched the rattle away and the baby started to cry.

'Give it back,' Min and Glor snapped at the toddler in unison. The toddler jerked with shock and stood still. Min and Glor shuffled forward in their seat and held up the flat of their hands. The toddler dropped the rattle and ran over to the window, hid behind the long curtain tied back there.

'Oh you naughty, where's the naughty?' sang Mrs Bottomley, and pranced over to the curtain on tiptoe. 'I'll find you, naughty.' At this the toddler shot out from behind the curtain and made a run for it. Mrs Bottomley caught it round the waist and whisked it into the air. The toddler fought to get free and cried out. Mrs Bottomley put her face into the child's stomach and blew a big raspberry on it. The child stopped wriggling and cried out with glee.

'Gen, gen,' it said.

'No, not again. You play nicely, you naughty little thing, or I'll tell Mr Bottomley.'

The child sat down on the floor, picked up a block of wood, its red paint faded and chipped, and placed it on another block. Min and Glor sat back on the settee and took drags of their cigarettes, ignoring Doris.

'Min and Glor are the house mothers, as we call them. They take care of the children while the other girls go out to work and they pick the older ones up from school. They'll take care of Laura when you get a job. I'll get one of the girls to take you over to Cardinal tomorrow to ask for work. Most of them work there. Plastics factory. The company aren't bad really, they don't mind our girls, you know.'

Doris hadn't had a proper job before, Vi hadn't let her. But Vi worked her hard enough at home and Doris wasn't afraid of getting her hands dirty. She'd be all right.

'Why don't you stay here and get to know everyone while I go and put the old man's breakfast on.'

Mrs Bottomley sashayed out of the room. Doris stepped forward and put Laura down on the floor to play. She took one of the wooden blocks to give to her.

'Mine,' said the toddler and took it back. Doris glanced up at Min and Glor but they sat back watching her. Doris looked in her bag, took out a little doll that one of the girls at the home had knitted for Laura, and gave it to her. The toddler saw it and got up, went over and snatched it away. Laura watched him, her mouth turning down, but she didn't cry. She held out her arms. But the boy turned his back and sat down. Laura shuffled on her backside to him, put her hand on his shoulder and looked into his face.

'Urgh, what that?' said the boy, pointing at Laura's foot.

Min and Glor leant forward to see.

'Cripple, is it?' said one, the other making a face.

'Cripple,' said the boy and bashed Laura's foot with her doll. 'Cripple, cripple.'

Doris snatched the doll away from him and picked up Laura. 'Stop it,' she said to the boy. 'Don't call her that.'

Min and Glor smiled cruel smiles and leant back to take another puff.

Doris sat in the opposite corner on an armchair next to the fire with Laura playing in her lap. No one spoke. Presently the door opened and a man walked in. He was tall and walked with a slouch, which seemed to Doris to be more broken than slovenly. It was his eyes that Doris noticed, as he glanced at her and away again quickly. It was like he was haunted by something he didn't want to look at. He wore slacks and a shirt and tie beneath a cardigan. His hair was cut into a short back and sides, the receding fringe combed back with hair cream. His cheeks were slightly sunken in, his nose slightly bent and his mouth was a thin straight line. He walked over to where Doris sat, without looking at her.

'That's Mr Bottomley's chair,' said Min or Glor.

'Oh,' said Doris, getting up with Laura. She went to sit in a wooden chair in the other corner, away from the benefit of the fire's heat. Mr Bottomley sat down, saying nothing. Doris sneaked a look at him. He was watching the children play and with his forefinger he made tiny circles on the middle of his closed lips, round and round. Doris couldn't help watching him. She didn't know whether to introduce herself and he didn't enquire as to who she was so she stayed quiet.

The following morning, after a sleepless night in a draughty bedroom shared with three other women and their two toddlers and one six-year-old boy, all of whom were awake at different times in the night, Doris had breakfast and left Laura with Min and Glor. Laura looked up at her from the floor as she left.

Doris went along with a group of seven women who worked at Cardinal Plastics. It was close by on London Road, a large red-brick factory building within a fenced-off compound. She was shown into the office of the manager, a Mr Dawson, who spoke to her kindly enough and said she could have a job making plastic buckets for the seafront shops. She came back to the refuge after her shift dizzy from the fumes and with her fingers burnt from pulling hot plastic off the moulds. When she came into the nursery she heard raised voices.

'What am I supposed to do with *that?*'

It was Mrs Bottomley. Doris was taken aback at the difference in her. She was pointing at Laura and talking to Mr Bottomley, who sat in his chair. When Laura saw Doris walk in, she jerked with shock as if she thought she'd been abandoned for good. With relief her little face broke into tears. She tried to shuffle towards Doris while holding up her arms. Doris frowned and scooped her up.

Mrs Bottomley made no move to disguise her mood. She stood with her hands on her hips, her red face gurning with rage.

'What is it?' said Doris.

Mrs Bottomley turned on her. 'Never you mind, nosey parker.' She brushed past Doris out of the room and as she went by she pressed the side of Doris's nose so hard with her forefinger she pushed Doris's face to one side. Doris felt the sting of tears and glanced at Min and Glor who were watching her with evident glee. She turned and went up to her room, sat on her bed and let Laura cry into her neck.

Over the following weeks, Doris settled into her job but never settled at the refuge. The women were distant, disconnected, getting from one day to the next, not knowing what kind of mood Mrs Bottomley would be in. Two months after her arrival, she had come home from the factory early with a stomach ache and had seen a smart couple sitting with Mrs Bottomley in the front room. Mrs Bottomley had waved her away. A week later, she'd come home from work with the group of girls, went with them to collect their children from Min and Glor, and found one of the children was missing. It was Ethel's baby, Thomas.

'Where's Thomas?' asked Ethel.

'Ask Mrs B,' said Min or Glor.

Mrs Bottomley came into the room, downcast and holding a white handkerchief. She saw Ethel and held out her arms.

'I'm so sorry, my dear, there was nothing we could do.'

Doris looked at the other women, all staring on with horror. Ethel, in shock, laughed.

'What are you talking about? Where's my Thomas?'

Taking her arm and leading her to an armchair, Mrs Bottomley sat her down and crouched by her, holding her hand.

'Now be strong, my dear. Baby Thomas put a button in his mouth and it choked him. We couldn't get it out, could we?' She looked across at Min and Glor, who both shook their heads.

Ethel shook her head, her eyes wide. 'No, no, no he wouldn't, he wouldn't do it.'

'It happens, my dear, you know as well as I do, babies put things in their mouths. He's gone, I'm so sorry.'

Ethel stood up quick, brushed Mrs Bottomley away. 'Where is he? I want to see him.'

'The doctor took him, my dear, he couldn't stay here. He's with the good Lord now, he's at peace.' Mrs Bottomley crossed herself. 'We'll have a little funeral for him, put him away proper, won't we dear?'

Ethel looked at her like she'd gone mad and burst into tears. The other women rushed to her side, united for once, consoling her. Doris grabbed hold of Laura from the floor and held her tight against her chest. She looked over at Mr Bottomley, silent in his chair as usual, his forefinger making circles on his closed lips.

The Bottomleys bought a new television set the week after baby Thomas died. Ethel had already gone, no one knew where, but Mrs Bottomley alluded to the idea that she had been released from her difficult situation in life. Some months later, when some of the other women had left and new ones had arrived, it happened again. A baby choked, on a piece of apple this time, under the care of Min and Glor while the mother was at work with the other women. Doris went cold when she heard. A week later, the Bottomleys bought a new car.

Mrs Bottomley could not be relied upon to be in the same mood from one week to the next. She was either skipping around the house, playing with the children and making cakes for everyone, or she'd be slumped in a chair or smacking someone for doing something trivial that annoyed her. She slapped Doris's face on one occasion for saying she needed time off work to take Laura to hospital to see about her foot.

'It's not a cripple's home, you know, she'll have to get on with it like everyone else.'

But sure enough, a week later, Mrs Bottomley ordered a taxi to take them to the hospital, paid for it herself and came with them too. Doris noticed her asking the doctor a lot of questions about Laura's foot – whether it was permanent, whether it could look normal with treatment – and the doctor's answers seemed to have the effect on Mrs Bottomley of plunging her into a dark pit. She insisted they get the bus home and that Doris pay her own fare and she stared out of the window gloomily, slapping Laura away when she tried to play with her.

Laura was looking big for her cot when Doris tucked her in one evening. She'd had her second birthday a month before and would climb out of her cot into bed with Doris some nights. Doris would let herself enjoy the warmth and closeness before telling Laura off.

As Doris tucked her in, Laura kicked off the blanket and laughed.

'Stop it,' said Doris. She was tired from work and wanted to go to sleep herself. Mrs Bottomley came into the bedroom, her face drawn tight.

'Get your things and come downstairs,' she said.

Doris looked round to see who she was talking to. Mrs Bottomley was looking at her.

'Sorry?'

'I said, get your things together and come downstairs. Some-one new needs your bed so you've got to go.'

A chill shot through Doris's body. 'What? You can't just throw us out, this is where we live.'

'No, young lady, this is where you've been staying at the liberty of the Christian Mission. And now someone else needs help so you'll have to go, you've been here long enough and I've done my best to . . . '

The woman stood there like they were strangers.

'Oh never mind . . . your time's up and that's that.'

'But where will we go?'

'I don't know, Doris,' shot back Mrs Bottomley, 'that's not my concern. You've had plenty of time to sort something out for yourself, you've been here well over a year.'

'But I've got nowhere to go.' Doris burst into tears, cried openly, everything suddenly bleak again.

'Well go back to your home town, someone will help you. I bet you miss it anyway, don't you?'

Doris did miss it. She yearned to go back to Tilbury, to see her family again. But she knew what kind of reception she would get and she had very little money, most of her wages having gone to the refuge.

'Can't we stay here tonight?'

Mrs Bottomley gave an exaggerated sigh and adjusted her position to lean on her other hip.

'I suppose you can sleep on the settee in the nursery. Just one night, though.'

Doris nodded, looking at the floor. 'Thank you.'

Laura was delighted when Doris lifted her out of the cot. They slept that night in the nursery, huddled together on the settee. Doris held Laura close, needing the comfort. But she couldn't help thinking that her chances of being let back home would be better if she left Laura at the refuge and went back to Tilbury without her. Mr and Mrs Bottomley could sell Laura to a rich American and buy a new fridge or something. But Doris had realised that they couldn't sell her because of her foot. She had heard whispers during her time there, the women's various ideas about the Bottomleys and what sort of racket they were running. Doris should have known her wages from the factory wouldn't be enough to keep her there for much longer.

On the train back to Tilbury the next morning, Doris felt her life running in reverse. Like when the projectionist at the pictures has to rewind the film. She hadn't been back there all this time. What would Vi say about it? Doris wouldn't knock at her door, she had more pride than that. But she would make herself known, she'd give Vi the chance to take her back. She'd stay close but not too close. Vi would see her grandchild from a distance and want to know her. She would regret throwing them out, she'd want to make it up to them.

11

Doris

Stepping off the train at Tilbury felt like coming back home. It was the smell of the place – it had the seagulls and the farm crows, the salty air of the estuary, just like Southend, but there was something else about Tilbury, the hustle and bustle of a busy port, the aroma of rubber and engine oil and the hay-scented waft coming from the grain terminal. Doris could see the black cranes towering over the dock wall, leaning this way and that, lifting their burdens. It gave her courage. She lifted Laura onto the platform and lugged her bag over her shoulder. Laura tottered along holding Doris's skirt, attracting doting looks from passing women.

'Where we, Mumma?'

'Home, we're back home.' Doris wanted to run, run all the way to the pub, she wanted to push open the door and charge upstairs to her bedroom and put the covers over her head and wish it all away. Maybe Auntie Win would help. She felt a shot of anger run through her. Fat lot of good she'd been. They made their way down Dock Road. Two of the old neighbours passed them and made no attempt at hiding their scorn when they saw her. Shivering in the cold wind, they walked over the hairpin bridge and along Ferry Road, past the docks and down Fort Road to the river where Doris saw The Empire pub looming. Her heart folded itself up like a slice of cooked ham. She pushed on past, not daring to look into the windows, and a little way off she sat down to rest on the sea wall.

A man had left his copy of the *Essex and Thurrock Gazette* on the train. Doris, her heart thumping, opened it now, thumbed through looking for the job adverts. There was the one that had always been in there. Thames Board Mills, the 'Mill' in Purfleet a few miles away, calling for girls aged six-teen to twenty-two for the casemaking factory. *Good wages, welfare and sports facilities, two-shift work 6am to 2pm and 2pm to 10pm.* Doris read with interest and then turned the page. What was she supposed to do with the kid while she was at work? She glanced across at the pub and saw no movement, went back to her paper and flicked through to the Situations Vacant. *Lady assistants required for boot and shoe department. Must be single.* Well, she was single, but not the right kind of single. *Wanted: a respectable woman to share home with widow.* Doris wouldn't be classed as respectable so that was no good. *Help req. for housework also plain cooking. 4 in family. Live in or out. Good home.* Live in or out. Doris's stomach turned over. It was worth a try. Laura could live with them, be part of the family with the other children. They'd have a job and somewhere to live. Doris looked down at herself. Her clothes were worse for wear. She knew her hair needed at least a wash and cut, not to mention setting. In the corner of her eye she saw the net curtain upstairs at the pub draw aside then fall back into place. Her heart banged in her chest. She daren't hope. She held her breath, kept her head down, but her eyes searched the pub eagerly. If Vi let her back, she wouldn't have to worry about finding a job and somewhere to live. It would all be so much easier and such a relief.

The bolts of the pub door shot back loudly in quick succession and the door opened suddenly. Archie strode out with a face that would have scared a docker. He came straight for Doris.

'What the hell are you doing here?' he growled, standing over her.

Doris could barely speak. She saw Laura shrink back against the wall, too afraid even to seek Doris's side.

'Where's Mum?' It was all she could manage.

'Your mother's indoors, and god help you if she sees you. Get gone, go on, you're not welcome here.'

He grabbed Doris's arm and pulled her roughly to her feet.

'Get off me, I want to see Mum.'

'Be off with you, and take that with you.' Archie pointed at Laura. 'If you make any trouble round here we'll call the madhouse, we told you that. Now get gone.'

He shoved her. Her legs buckled but she recovered enough to stay standing. She whimpered, grabbed her things and Laura's hand and scuttled away, looking back to see Archie standing there staring after her.

Laura was crying because Doris was crying. They kept

walking until they were out of sight of the pub. It was just as it had been before, turned away like an unwelcome door-to-door salesman. Doris felt sick; why did she think it would be any different this time? They walked along the dock wall until they came to a derelict tenement building, half of it bombed out during the war and still sitting there waiting to be bulldozed. Doris slumped down on to a little wall. Laura tried to get on to her lap but Doris pushed her down.

'Go and play,' she said.

Wiping her nose on her arm, Laura looked down, saw a sandy ants' nest at the base of the wall and found a stick to poke it with. The red ants ran about frantically. Laura stirred up the nest, disturbing their peace. Doris found her hankie and wiped her face, humiliated and despondent. She opened the local paper to the right page and ripped out the advert for the home help. They needed somewhere to sleep tonight.

'Come on, we're going to the phone box.'

Laura was engrossed with the nest, trying to press her finger on the insects as they ran about.

'Come on, I said.'

Laura brought the stick with her, turning it round to keep the two ants on it from falling off or running up her arm.

'Hello?'

'Hello. I'm enquiring about the housekeeper job.' Doris squeezed the Bakelite telephone receiver in her hand to steady her nerves.

'Oh yes. Well, do you have experience and can you provide references?'

'Yes,' said Doris, thinking quickly. Maybe Matron at the home and Mrs Bottomley at the refuge would give references, she'd done plenty of housework there. 'Yes, I have experience and I can get references.'

'Super. Are you married?'

'No, single. I'd be interested in the live-in position.'

'Super. I'd like to interview you. When would you be available to come to the house? We're on Bridge Road, Grays.'

'I can come now.'

'Really? Would you? That's marvellous. Well, my name is Mrs Pierce and we're at number seven Bridge Road. Will you be able to find us?'

'Yes, I'll manage. I'll be there in about half an hour.'

'Splendid. See you then . . . what did you say your name was?'

The bus was cheaper than the train, and the driver said he went to Bridge Road for tuppence.

'There it is, number seven,' said Doris, crouching down to Laura's level. 'Now Mumma needs to go to that house and you need to wait for me there.' Doris pointed to a path at the side of the house. 'You need to wait there with the bag and you mustn't move or make a noise. Mumma needs to make sure first.' Doris looked sternly into Laura's face until the child nodded. They approached the house on the same side of the road, sidled into the side passage so as to be unobserved from the window. Doris smoothed her hair back, picked the dirt out of her fingernails and pinched her face along her cheekbones the way she had seen Vi do.

'Oh, hello,' said the woman brightly when Doris knocked at the door. 'You must be Doris?' Doris nodded and realised from the look of the woman that it was going to be a very smart house. She was led through to the front parlour where they sat on upholstered upright chairs set by a cosy fire.

'Would you like some tea?'

'Yes, please. I mean, no thank you, I am fine.'

Mrs Pierce cocked her head and smiled.

'Now then, tell me what kind of experience you have.'

'Lots. My mother brought me up to know how to keep house and we learnt homemaking at school. I've done lots of cooking at home too. I've also done a lot of cleaning at a Salvation Army establishment in Grays and I'm sure they will provide a reference and I've also done a lot of cleaning at a Christian mission in Southend.'

'Well, that all sounds ideal. And do you like children? We have William, who is six and Jessica, eight.'

'Oh yes, very much, and I learnt about mother care at school too.' Doris sat up very straight and smiled her sweetest smile.

'Well, Doris, I think you are a very polite young lady. When do you think you would be able to start?'

'Really? I've got the job?'

'Yes, you have. You mentioned you'd like to live in? Well we have a lovely single room, and your wages would be adjusted accordingly to take account of your room and board. What do you think?'

'Oh, thank you, Mrs Pierce. I can start right away.'

'I see.' Mrs Pierce clapped her hands. 'I suppose we could seek references during your training period. Well, isn't this all working out beautifully? We'll get you a nice new nylon overall. Would you like to go home to collect some things?'

'My things are just outside, I'll go and get them.'

With a look of surprise, Mrs Pierce stood up to show her to the door.

'Won't be a tick.' Doris slipped outside, down the front steps and round to the side path. She picked up her bag. 'Come on now, and make sure to be good and quiet, you hear?' she whispered into Laura's ear and led her by her cold little hand back up the steps to the front door that Mrs Pierce had left ajar. They walked into the warm front parlour.

Mrs Pierce turned around from winding the carriage clock on the mantel and the clock slipped out of her hands and crashed to the parquet floor. Everyone stared at it for a second.

'What's the meaning of this?' she said, her voice higher and harsher than it had been a minute ago.

'Please, Mrs Pierce, she won't be any trouble. She's really good and she can just play with your children and I'll look after all of them and get all of my work done, I promise.'

'Doris, do you mean to tell me that you are *unmarried* and have *a child*?'

Doris nodded and tried to smile.

'This is outrageous, in all my life.'

'Please, Mrs Pierce, we've got nowhere else to go, nowhere to sleep tonight. I'll work really hard for you, you won't regret it, honestly.'

'You're right about that, young lady. I don't want you near my children. Get off my premises immediately before I call the police. Get out, go on.'

Mrs Pierce ushered them out of her door and closed it quick.

Doris wanted to spit at her door, she wanted to kick it until it splintered. She wanted to leave Laura there on the doorstep and run away as fast as she could.

'Mumma?'

Laura looked up at her, unable to grasp what was happening.

'Oh, just come on.' Doris took her hand, pulled her stumbling down the steps on her little legs and walked towards the bus stop. It took twenty minutes for the bus to come and Laura said she was cold and hungry for every minute they waited. They got back to Tilbury and Doris bought a bag of chips for their tea. They carried them round to the derelict tenement and sat on the wall near the ants' nest Laura had been playing with. Doris turned to look at the tumbledown building behind them.

Half of the tenement block was still standing. She wondered whether it was safe and got up to investigate. Laura followed, stumbling over the fallen bricks and rubbish that had accumulated there. They walked up the stairs to the first floor and along the communal balcony, tried one of the doors. It was locked. She tried a few more, all locked. Then one that was also locked but gave a little when Doris pushed at the handle. She leant her shoulder into it and shoved. The jamb splintered, soft and porous with damp and woodworm.

It opened on to a dark, dank room that had once been someone's living room. Doris stepped in tentatively and jumped back when something rustled and ran across the floor. She waited for it to go and went in further. There was no furniture in the room. The cooking range over the fireplace was hung with cobwebs and the wallpaper had peeled away from the wall at several places, revealing large patches of grey mould. Damp ran down the walls. She went through into the scullery and tried the tap over the sink. It groaned and no water came out. She left it for a bit and, as if dredging the pits of hell, the tap spat out some dark brown sludge and gradually ran clear. Opening the larder door, Doris shrank back from the dozens of black beetles on the shelves. In the one bedroom there was a bedstead with a dirty mattress but rainwater had seeped on to the floor and when Doris touched the mattress it was damp.

'A right little palace,' said Doris, prodding a chipped chamber pot on the floor with the toe of her shoe.

Laura looked up at Doris, trying to guess her thoughts.

'Looks like we found somewhere to stay tonight, eh kid?'

'Mumma?' said Laura, looking around.

'Well, don't blame me, it's not my fault.'

Laura pulled up her dress and squatted over the pot, her little face straining and red. That was one good thing about Min and Glor, they didn't let the toddlers stay in nappies. Doris took out the newspaper job advert from her pocket and used it to wipe Laura with. Then she squatted over the pot herself.

'Might as well christen the place, eh?'

All Doris wanted to do was lie down and sleep but the bed was damp. She told Laura to stay put while she went to look at the other flats. She got into one but the windows had blown out and bird mess streaked the walls. She did find a tarpaulin though, and took it back with her, draping it over the mattress so they could at least sleep there. Doris lay on the tarpaulin in her coat and curled up on it. She thought she could hear music and strained to listen. Laura snuggled into her and they kept each other warm that night.

*

Doris woke up in a sweat. She had dreamed she'd jumped into the river. The water was cold, it had forced the breath out of her lungs. Laura was there, looking over the river bank, her blonde curls blowing across her face, her mouth screaming *Don't blame me, it's not my fault.* And Doris had given up and sunk down into the water, her arms trailing above her head.

She sat up on the bed and her movement made Laura stir. She opened her eyes and moved in close to Doris.

'Hungry, Mumma.'

'Yes, all right.'

Doris counted the coins in her purse. She had two pounds and six shillings to her name. She needed to start earning some money somehow.

'Let's go and get some bread.'

They walked to the bakers, asked for the loaf to be sliced, ate some as they walked along. In the grocers, Doris spent two shillings on a bottle of Scrubb's cloudy ammonia, a penny on a box of matches and tuppence on a jar of strawberry jam. On the way back to the flat, Doris picked up a bottle of milk from someone's doorstep. She didn't break her stride but her heart pounded in her chest. They went back to the flat and started cleaning. Doris scoured the other flats, breaking into windows to get the doors open. She found a can opener and a blunt paring knife in one, and some curtains and old sacks in another. She found a broom without a handle and an old saucepan and even a wooden chair. She used the curtains for a bedspread and for cleaning cloths and got Laura to sweep the floor with the broken broom. She stuffed rags into the cracks around the bedroom window. She got rid of the beetles, for now at least, and with the bits of coal she had found in the other flats she started to build up a fire in the grate.

'Go outside and look for any bits of wood and bring them back here,' she said to Laura.

When an hour had gone by, she wondered where Laura had got to. And presently there was a knock at the door. Doris jumped, afraid it was the police, or Archie. She opened the door slowly and peered out. It was Auntie Win with Laura.

'Hello, love,' she said, her face a picture of relief and guilt. 'How have you been?'

Doris bit her bottom lip. She didn't want to cry. But it was Win's fault she was in this mess, it was Win who had told her to keep Laura, to not send her to a home.

'Mumma,' said Laura, holding up a small twig with a big smile on her face.

'Is that it? That's not going to do much, is it?' said Doris, tutting.

With Win there, Doris realised that Laura's face was smeared with dirt, that her baggy pinafore frock needed washing, that she herself was covered in grime from cleaning the flat. She could see pity in Win's eyes and wanted to use it to her full advantage.

'Have you come to take us home, then?' said Doris, still on the threshold of the flat.

'What? Oh Doris, I just wanted to see you. Archie said you were back and I've thought about you every day since you left.'

'Well, thinking doesn't do much.'

Win looked taken aback at the change in Doris, her loss of innocence, the way she spoke.

'No.' Win looked down at Laura and smiled. 'So I've met your Laura.'

'You've seen her before, remember?'

'Yes, but now she's a little girl and we can talk to each other, can't we? Why was she out on her own?' The look on Doris's face made her reconsider her question. 'You must be two years old by now?'

Laura smiled back at Win and gave her the twig.

'Is this where you're living then?' said Win, peering inside and unable to disguise her shock.

'Looks like it,' said Doris.

'Where have you been all this time? I came looking for you when Vi sent you off.'

'What, when you didn't stop her, like you said you would? When you told me to keep the baby and you'd help me?'

Win had no answer.

'I've been to hell and back. That's where.'

'Look, maybe I'll come back another time. Is there anything you need?'

Doris screwed up her face with disbelief. 'Anything I need? Only my life back.' Doris thought quickly. 'But you can bring us some money and food and blankets . . . and clothes.'

Win nodded. 'Course. I'll do my best, Doris.'

'And you can talk to Mum for me, tell her she needs to take us back in before we die out here.'

Laura looked up at Doris, her bottom lip curled down and tears appeared in her eyes.

'Don't talk like that around the little one, Doris.'

'Don't dare tell me what to do with her, Win,' Doris snapped back.

Doris had always called her Auntie Win, but times had changed. Doris was eighteen, grown up and embittered. She looked at Win, who was struggling for something to say. She said she'd go and come back soon. Doris closed the door and sat down on the floor, put her face into her hands and sobbed.

Laura put her hand on Doris's shoulder, her face close. 'Stick?' she said with concern.

Doris looked at her through her tears.

'Go on then, and get some more this time.' She got up to let Laura out, wiped her nose on the back of her hand and started cleaning the windows.

On the outside of the glass the dirt was rain-splattered, inside it was mildew and dead flies. Doris enjoyed the cleaning. It was good manual work, and it felt like she had achieved something when she'd finished. She went outside to buff away the smears and heard a high-pitched scream from below. It was Laura. The sound was full of urgency and fear and Doris found herself running.

She slipped down the stairs and skidded round the corner into the open waste ground. There she saw a man, a coloured man bending down to Laura.

'Oi!' she shouted, 'Get away.'

The man straightened up and waited for her to approach. Doris picked Laura up and hitched her on to her hip away from the man.

'What you doing?' she said, frowning and stepping away.

'The girl fell down, looked lost,' he said. 'You her mudda?'

'What?'

'You her mudda?' he said.

'Yes, I'm her mother, and she wasn't lost,' said Doris, blotting Laura's bleeding knee with her hand.

'My mistake,' he said. 'Homesick,' he said, holding out his hand.

'What?'

'My name, they call me Homesick. And you?'

Doris looked at his hand, dark brown on the back and light on the palm. She'd never touched a coloured man's hand before and didn't want to now. She shifted Laura on to her other hip as an excuse not to.

'Doris,' she said.

'And who's this?' His accent was funny, almost not English.

'I'm Laura.'

Homesick held out his hand to Laura and she grabbed his finger and laughed, self-assured now that Doris was there. He smiled, his face creased with good humour, and Doris relaxed a little. With a start she noticed that in the man's other hand there dangled a dead rabbit.

'For the pot,' he said when he saw her looking.

The rabbit looked diseased. It had gummy eyes and a lumpy head.

'Myxomatosis,' said Homesick. 'The farmer gave them a disease, but they're good to eat if you cook it well. They're easy to catch like this.' He laughed and held up the rabbit for Laura to see. Her eyes were wide with interest.

'You live here?' he said.

'Mind your own business,' said Doris and turned on her heel. She stood by the wall waiting for him to go before going back up to the flat. He walked around to the other side of the tenement block and disappeared. He must be living there too.

'Naughty.' Doris put Laura down and smacked the back of her leg. 'Don't talk to men like that, do you hear?'

Laura cried but stopped soon enough. She knew Doris would hit her again if she felt sorry for herself for too long. They walked back up to the flat, Doris checking that the man wasn't watching where they were going. 'I'll have you taken away if you're naughty, do you hear? I can have you put in a children's home, you know.'

Doris was hungry. The thought of a rabbit stew made her mouth water. She hoped Win would be back soon with some decent food. They waited but Win didn't come so they had bread and jam for tea again.

Win didn't come the next day either. Doris woke up with Laura snuggled into her. She felt something warm against her leg and put her hand down. A brown rat jerked with fright and jumped off the bed. Doris gave a yelp of disgust and sat up to watch it run through to the scullery. She followed it, clapping loudly and shouting *Get out* and when she saw it disappear through the wall beneath the sink, she stuffed some cardboard into the hole and went to brush the bed off with her hand over and over, got a wet cloth and scrubbed her coat where the rat had been sleeping. When Win came, she'd ask for some candles and a trap. If she left a candle to burn at night it might keep them away.

Laura's lips were purple with cold. Doris wanted to get the fire going to take the chill off the room but needed to save the coal for when they had something to cook.

'Get your coat and shoes on, we're going out.'

Laura struggled with her coat and waited for Doris to pull

it on roughly for her. Outside was colder and barely light. There was a low mist on the river. They walked away from the docks, down Dock Road and up the Broadway to the farm-land north of Tilbury town, where the freshly furrowed fields were planted with spring wheat. Stretching away, the brown earth butted up against a small grassy hill, the edge of a chalk quarry. From this distance Doris could see the movement of perhaps two dozen wild rabbits, bobbing and grey. She skirted the field, telling Laura to be quiet and tread carefully. They approached the hill and kept close to the bank, edging around to spy on the rabbits, who hadn't seen them yet.

'Wait, wait . . .' breathed Doris. Laura watched the rabbits and her mother's face in turn. The rabbits were nibbling the tiny green wheat shoots, stopping to prick up their ears and watch for danger. Suddenly Laura shouted *Stick* and ran to pick up a fallen twig. The rabbits scattered, Doris sprang out from her hiding place and chased them. Most darted back to their burrows in the hill but many were sluggish and dopey. Laura joined in the chase, squealing and shouting, Doris lunged at one, hopping slowly back to its hole. She got a hand on it, but it writhed and pulled away; she lunged again and caught it with both hands. It struggled to get free, wide-eyed and panicked, sick with disease. Doris knelt in the dirt, held the rabbit down with one hand and took out the paring knife she had found at the tenement. She hesitated, glanced at Laura, took a deep breath, pulled the rabbit's head back by the ears and drew the knife across its throat. The knife was blunt – the rabbit squealed to get free, twisted up on to its hind legs. Doris felt a stab of panic, held the animal down and tried again, pressing the knife harder until it went through.

The animal fell limp, blood seeping on to the ground. Laura screamed *No Mumma* and ran around in circles.

'Shush,' said Doris. She grabbed the rabbit's back legs and they walked home with it dangling down, dripping blood. Doris held her head high – she had done it, and Laura trotted after, gazing with awe at the rabbit and at her mother.

It was still early and as they made their way back to the river, they passed the Melbourne Road allotments. Doris stopped there at the gate, looked for movement and saw none.

'Be quiet and wait here,' she told Laura, and crept inside. At the first allotment she saw the green heads of something growing, crouched down, took hold and pulled up a parsnip, and another. On the next plot there was a row of onions, not quite ready but they would do. She pulled two and slipped away.

Back at the flat she put the rabbit carcass down in the sink, stood looking at it. At school they had learned how to butcher a rabbit but not to skin or gut it. She took the knife and gouged at the furry skin on the stomach until it punctured through. Using her bare hands she took the skin and pulled it apart at the hole until it ripped the length of the belly. She cut the belly open, wincing and trying not to gag. The shining grey guts appeared, coiled and steaming. Standing on a wooden box, Laura leaned in to see, fascinated. Doris put her hand inside, pulled out the warm intestines in one piece, retching at the smell where the knife had nicked a hole in them, reached in again for the burgundy liver and further up the pink heart and lungs.

'What, Mumma?'

'Its guts, you can't eat that bit.'

Laura prodded the grey intestines with her finger and pulled away with a squeal, gathered her courage and touched them again, lifted a strand of guts into the air with her stick.

'Get out the way,' said Doris, scraping out the insides. She started to pull off the skin, and it came away from the flesh easily but stuck on the legs. Using the blunt knife, she hacked off the back legs, breaking the bones to get them off, and tugged the skin away from the upper body, chopping off the front legs. With the pelt pulled inside out over the head she cut at the neck, not wanting to look at the gummy eyes and lumpy head. And then it was clean and looked like something Vi might have bought at the butchers. She ran the water, washing her hands and the rabbit. She held it up, pink and glistening, and smiled.

With what she had, a small amount of coal, an old saucepan, onions, parsnips and water, she made a rabbit stew. The chimney was blocked and smoked out the room, but that was one of the best meals Doris had ever eaten. They ate it out of the pan with their fingers.

'Wabbit, Mumma?'

'Yes, rabbit.'

The following day, Win knocked at the door carrying a plump flour sack.

'Hello love, sorry I haven't been.'

Doris let her in, saying nothing.

'I've brought some bits and pieces,' said Win, unpacking the sack and giving Doris furtive glances. 'Here's two blankets and a couple of plates and cups, a couple of spoons and forks.' She checked Doris for a reaction but Doris gave none. 'Loaf of bread, some spuds and lard, apples.' She held an apple out for Laura, who took it with a smile and tried to take a bite but couldn't sink her teeth into it. 'Bit of sugar and tea,' she looked around the flat, 'but I expect you haven't got a strainer, have you?' Doris shook her head and raised her eyebrows. 'As for clothes, I haven't managed much at the moment, but here's a cardie of mine for now and I'll go to the St Mary's rummage sale, get some bits for the little one.'

Win put her hands on her hips and smiled uncertainly. 'That all right, then?'

'You got any money?'

'Oh, not really, love, you know what Archie's like with the purse strings. But I'll try and bring you some more bits of food and that soon.'

'All right.' Doris took the apple from Laura, wiped the saliva onto her skirt, bit into it and handed it back to Laura, who proceeded to take little bites, slapping her lips at the sour taste. 'Did you talk to Mum?'

Doris guessed that the answer would be no, otherwise why would Win have brought all the stuff? She might otherwise have just told them to come home.

Win looked at the wall. 'I tried, Doris, but it's no good.' Win faced her with a look of defeat. 'Just leave it for a bit, eh?'

'What, two years not long enough?'

Win shrugged. 'You know what she's like, love.'

12

Doris

Win came again the week after, and then almost every week after that. Doris relied on the food she brought. But it wasn't enough to live on and Doris devised ways of getting by. She'd get up early every day to lift a bottle of milk from a doorstep, making sure to vary the street and house each time. She went to church on Sundays and hung around for the tea and biscuits after the service, filled her pockets when no one was looking. She pilfered from the allotment now and again but was careful not to take too much. Sometimes Win would bring them fish and chips, sometimes some tapioca pudding, a slab of lard for cooking, some hard-boiled eggs, a jar of fish paste.

She stayed away from the Bobbies on the beat and the police station on Dock Road, kept her head down. When the coast was clear she and Laura would carry any bits of metal or rags they found around the bomb sites to the scrap yard to be weighed and exchanged for cash. Any empty beer and fizz bottles they found they'd return to the shop for tuppence. There was no rent to pay and no bills and gradually with what Win brought and what they could find in the other abandoned flats, they made a little home for themselves.

Doris made a point of going to sit outside the pub every day, unless it was raining too heavily. She wanted Vi to see her, to remind her what she was doing to them. Doris would always wave, give a clear sign of her intentions. And she hoped that one day Vi would back down and let them come home.

Through the summer months, Doris and Laura would generally get there early. They knew the routine of the delivery men, would watch the labourers pushing their wooden barrows down the road to work and the dockers ambling along, smoking. And Vi would always be up early to scrub her step. She was the first there every weekday morning in her cross-over pinny, six o'clock sometimes, on her knees, praying to the altar of the god of cleanliness, decency and good morals, scrubbing the stone doorstep and surrounding flagstones, washing it down, rubbing it with the donkey stone until it was clean and creamy white. A fleeting whiteness – tainted by dirty shoes or a heavy rain, the whiteness would fade away and need to be redone the following morning. When Vi came out of the pub door she would step over the step so as to save the colour. She'd be there ready for when the postman came at seven, then the milkman, bread man and coalman. Doris would watch the comings and goings. And Vi would be there for her public appearances, making a show that she was up and out and doing her duty. Before she'd been thrown out, Doris would do the work behind the scenes. She wondered who was doing that now. She would wash the clothes and Vi would hang them out.

The other women in the adjoining terrace came out one by one to clean their steps, chatting to one another and looking over at Vi, who held up her head and kept herself to herself and kept her standards up. She had no friends. Doris hadn't fully realised that before, but now she understood, since Win had told her their story. Now Vi used the donkey stone to preserve her good reputation.

When winter came, they hibernated, ransacked the flats for anything to insulate and keep warm, stuffed their coats with newspaper and stayed in bed all day. Doris would wish she could draw, wish she could go home. Thinking about the roaring fire in the pub, she would plan to take Laura to an orphanage or leave her at the church or hand her over somewhere else. She went through the motions in her head, visualised every detail, lived the moment when she turned away and walked back into the decent life she'd had before she became an outcast. But the part where Laura looked at her for the last time, not knowing it was the last time, that was the part Doris couldn't quite see, and she skirted around it in her mind, to where she was walking away.

She never did it. She asked herself why she carried on living hand to mouth when there was another way but she had no answer. They had chilblains and chapped legs and life was bleak and boring. She tried knocking on doors asking for any old cardboard or newspapers to be taken to the scrap yard but people looked at her like she was a beggar. Only kids did that kind of thing, so she gave it up.

They became the local oddities. Kids playing football in the street with jumpers for goalposts would kick the ball towards them, laugh and call out things like bastard and tart. They must have heard those things from their parents. Doris tried to keep them looking decent but she didn't have a wash tub or mangle at the flat, so she sometimes snuck into another tenement at night, down to the basement to wash their clothes in the copper boilers. There was usually enough coal to get a fire going to heat up the water. But she was worried someone would catch her and call the police, so they went dirty most of the time. When Doris wore out her shoes she put cardboard in the soles. When Laura outgrew hers, Doris cut the toes off them, too scared to go to the doctors about Laura's foot in case they called the police. Laura cried about it and Doris could see she was humiliated even though she didn't really understand.

Somehow Doris clung on to the hope of going home the way mouldy fruit clings to a leafless tree. But as the months stretched away, winter turned to spring and Doris became more overwhelmed with the bleakness of it all.

For thirteen months they had been surviving at the tenement. On this April morning, as Doris sat on the sea wall and raised her hand in greeting to Vi coming out to clean her step, she was ignored, as usual. The kid Laura stamped on her snail and hitched herself up to the top of the sea wall by jamming her good foot into the cracks in the stones. There was a rusty mooring ring bolted into the top of the wall. With just her arms over the top and her body hanging down, Laura played with the mooring ring, looking through it to the river, making her own little framed picture, and then letting the ring clang back down again.

Doris heard the sound of a ship's horn coming off the river into the dock. The kid jumped up on her crate to get a good look. From the tone, Doris knew it was a big one and when she turned around she saw it was a migrant ship, over from Jamaica probably. All the hats leaning forward and the arms waving like they were expecting some sort of grand welcome. Doris tutted, someone should tell them not to bother. There wasn't anything here for them to get excited about, they'd soon see. She turned back, watched the door of the pub for any movement. This might be the day that Vi walked out of the front door over her clean white step and strode towards Doris with a tentative smile. It might be the day that Vi brought a bag of sweets for Laura and told them that they were welcome to come home.

An hour later she was still there. A dark fella came walking by, one of them off the boat. He had a light in his eye, looking around and up at the sky. He lifted his hat to Doris and she scowled back at him. He frowned and swung his suitcase in a devil-may-care way. When he came to the pub he stopped short and the light went right out of his eye. For a second, Doris wondered what he was gawping at. Then she realised it was the sign in the pub window, popped in between the leaded lights and the half-length lace curtains, showing through a space in the potted nasturtiums on the windowsill. *No Coloureds, No Dogs.*

He looked around like he needed to check he wasn't seeing things and his gaze fell on Doris and the kid. He half gestured to the sign then thought better of it. His mouth drew into a pinch and he jammed his hands deep into his trouser pockets and Doris almost wanted to laugh – that's what The Empire pub does to you. That was Vi and Archie for you, they didn't serve the coloureds, they put the sign up a few years ago when the migrant ships started coming. They didn't much like the Irish either but there were a lot of them around there since the old days when the docks were built and they had their own pub anyway. They should have added *No unmarried mothers, No bastard children* to that sign – that would have been about right.

Doris turned away, looked down into the river, the water the colour of an army uniform, going darker when the sun clouded over. Lonely clumps of brown seaweed drifted by, along the estuary and out to open sea, or got stuck in the exposed mud banks at low tide and joined the other washed-up rubbish there. Laura clanged the rusty mooring ring from one side to another. It sounded like the toll of a bell.

13

Vi

It was one of those really blustery days when if you were indoors everything rattled and it sounded like a big devil was rushing at the pub and rushing away again, and if you were outside it was mad and lawless and the devil pushed you around and you couldn't do a thing about it. In Vi's bedroom the top branches of the magnolia tree in the back yard tapped against the window. She'd been meaning to cut those branches off.

Vi thought about seeing Doris over on the sea wall again that morning. She made sure she was there for when Vi cleaned the step. Everyone else saw her too. Vi's daughter, the fallen woman – the ungrateful swine. Vi refused to let Doris ruin her too. She'd carry on with her head up, she'd clean her step the same as always. That child was three years old. It should have been with a proper family, adopted, given a decent start in life.

After Vi sent Doris away that first time when she'd had the baby on her bedroom floor, she had grieved. She had lost her Doris. She had told her what to do: go to the home and get rid of the baby. She told her that. It would have been so easy, they could have gone back to how they were without anyone knowing any different. What possessed her to keep it Vi didn't know. Bringing shame on them – a bastard child, a whore for a mother. Vi knew how those things can hurt you in life, she'd been that bastard child and so had Win. All she could do was do her best to keep it away, to build up a decent life for herself. They said if the mother's tainted then so is the child. Bad blood and bad morals. Maybe they were right. Maybe Vi was fated to go wrong no matter how hard she tried.

When Doris came back from the Salvation Army home with the baby and Vi sent her away into the fog, Vi had stayed in bed for two weeks, couldn't face going down to the pub. Then she snapped out of it and pulled herself together. Vi had lost her daughter and that was that. She had a pub to run and a respectable life to uphold. When Doris came back around here a year ago it wasn't Doris, it was a ghost of her, come to haunt Vi. Vi didn't know where she'd been but the child was still with her and it was two years old then, tottering around. She had the gall to come and sit on the sea wall practically under Vi's window, looking across at the pub, still with her bags. The shame of it. Vi nearly saw her breakfast again that morning when she happened to look out of the upstairs window. Of course she got Archie quick, told him to go out there, get rid of them. He was only too pleased to oblige – he knew the value of a good reputation. Vi watched as he moved her on, the child trailing behind, and yes, she wondered where they would go. Not least because she didn't want them hanging around again.

The next day Win came back in from shopping with a flush about her face – she wouldn't catch Vi's eye and Vi knew why. She'd been out looking for them. God only knew why she'd do such a thing. Vi gave her till evening to tell her, and sure enough, she knew her sister.

'Vi,' she said in the kitchen after tea when Archie had gone down to open up. Vi pretended not to hear.

'Vi, I saw Doris today and her little one, Laura.'

'What the hell are you doing, Win?' Vi turned on her, snapped close to her face and dug her nails into Win's arm. She winced and pulled away.

'Nothing, Vi, I just bumped into her, that's all, when I was shopping.'

Vi gave her a look – it was a likely story.

'She's in a bad way, Vi, no money, living in a bomb site with beetles running up the walls and the stench of a lav that no one's emptying. She wants you to let her come home.'

Vi turned away, looked out of the window over to the river. Her throat tightened.

'What? With that bastard child I suppose?'

'With her daughter, yes. A sweet little thing she is, Vi. But you should see her, so scruffy, in a dress that's filthy and too big, her teeth are bad.'

'What in god's name are you thinking, Win?' said Vi, her voice cracking. 'After everything we've worked for here, I'm not throwing it all away. I won't do it.'

'Vi, she's our blood, they both are.'

She was Vi's sister, yes, but Vi went up to her and ground the words in her teeth. 'You watch yourself, Win. You want me to tell Archie?'

Win stared at her with her stupid face and said nothing.

'I'll tell Archie and we'll make sure she doesn't hang around any more.'

'Don't, Vi, let her be.'

Vi dried her hands on the tea towel. 'I'm going down to open up for business, Win. My business that me and my Cyril built up. If you dare to jeopardise that you'll have me to answer to. Do you understand me?'

The next day, Vi saw Win putting some blankets into a basket.

'What you doing with those?'

'Nothing, Vi, just sorting some bits for the church jumble, that's all.'

'Oh? Well, why don't you take the clothes off my back as well?'

Vi unbuttoned her blouse and stuffed it into the basket with the blankets. Win looked at her like she was mad. Like *she* was mad.

'Here, take our food, come on.' In her corset, Vi grabbed the basket away from her, went to the larder, put a loaf of bread in there, some cheese, a box of biscuits.

'Stop it,' Win cried. 'Just stop it.'

'Why? Don't you think the church is a good cause? Here, take my coat, my shoes.'

Vi ran around like mad, dropping things into the basket. Win pulled her arm roughly, made her sit down. She took the basket away and started emptying it. She took everything out of there and put the basket away.

Three days later, Vi saw Win with a bulging flour sack slipping out the back door. She must have thought Vi was stupid. A week later, she slipped out with a covered basket and the same a week after that. Vi didn't have the strength to say anything, but she kept an eye on her.

Doris started appearing on the sea wall every morning soon after that. The months passed by and Vi got used to seeing Doris on the wall and sometimes around the town. It was an embarrassment that she tried to distance herself from. Doris looked like a ragtag and so did her child. Vi had brought her up better than that. The hours she'd spent teaching her how to groom herself, how to make clothes and keep house. All gone to waste. It broke Vi's heart to see it and it would have broken Cyril's heart if he'd been around. The punters didn't say anything but Vi could see it in their eyes and a couple of them had started drinking somewhere else. They probably wanted to tell her how disgusted they were, how they thought better of her. She managed to keep things going, keep the pub jolly. But the wives didn't make it easy. They elbowed each other, said snide things in the queues in the shops. Vi held her head up and ignored it. She kept her step clean and her windows washed and she showed the world that there were good morals in her house.

She went downstairs. Archie came in from outside carrying a cardboard box carefully with both hands.

'She's out there again,' he said.

'I know,' said Vi. 'But what's the point, Arch? We've moved her on enough times now and the ghost still comes back. If she causes any trouble I'll be down that doctor's, don't you worry.'

'Well, it's not good for business, Vi, tarts hanging around.'

'No? Maybe she should go and hang around on Ship Street?'

Archie chuckled. 'There's plenty of work round there for her.'

Vi laughed but she didn't think it was funny.

'This bloody paper strike is pissing me off now, bet the bookies hate it,' Archie said, putting his box down on the bar.

Vi stepped back when she heard a scratching sound coming from the box. 'What's in there?' she said.

'Finches, I'm gonna sell them on, they fetch a pretty penny.'

'Where will you keep them?'

'I'm gonna get a cage for upstairs, what's the problem?'

Vi shrugged.

Archie turned on the wireless behind the bar. 'Old Churchill's stepped down,' he said.

Churchill. The name only reminded her of losing Cyril. Warmongering and the casualties of war. We won the war. Yes. But the war had beaten Vi. If Cyril had still been around things would have been different.

'What would Cyril think, Arch?' she said.

'About Churchill?'

'No, about her out there.'

'He'd be ashamed, of course, just like we are.'

Vi nodded and wiped the bar down, noticed that the till was empty. 'Shall I get the float?'

'No, I'll get it.'

Archie didn't let her touch the till these days except to ring

117

up the rounds. He counted the money, he sorted out the float. Vi didn't even know what the takings were most of the time.

'Win needs to go and pay the coalman and get some bits from the shops.'

'What bits?' he said.

'Don't know, some meat and spuds and some soap powder.'

'Soap powder? Again? I don't know what you women do with that stuff, we spend a fortune on it. You'll have to start using less of it.'

He went upstairs to the safe and came in with the float, started emptying bags of change into the till. 'How much?' he said.

'Don't know, give her a couple of quid.'

'No Vi, tell her to find out how much then I'll give her the right money.'

'She doesn't know how much the meat will be.'

'Tell her to go down to Brown's and get the coal ticket and bring it back here, then I'll give her the money.'

It's my pub, Arch, she wanted to say. But she could guess his thoughts too. *It might be your pub, Vi, but it's my licence, so do as you're told.*

He stood up, glanced around for Win.

'Don't worry your pretty head about it, Vi, it's just boring men's stuff.'

He pulled her towards him with his hand at the back of her neck and planted a kiss on her lips.

14

Doris

And that's when Stanley came along. A local fella Doris had seen in the pub often enough. Smart looking and chipper in a green tweed overcoat. One of the few men around there who had a motor car, a black one that he drove rod-straight and smiling above the wheel. Since Doris had been living rough, he'd made a point of stopping to look at her from a distance whenever he saw her around. And one day he approached her.

'You're Cyril's girl, aren't you?'

Doris shrugged. People usually made a point of avoiding her, crossing the road when they saw her coming.

'You boarding somewhere?'

'What's it to you?' Doris surprised herself with her tone and manner. Living rough had taken its toll on her.

Stanley laughed. 'And who's this, then?' He crouched down to Laura, standing by Doris's leg.

'Laura,' said Laura.

Stanley put his hand in his pocket and brought out a little paper bag, opened it out and offered it to her.

'My name's Stanley. Strawberry bonbon?'

Laura looked up at Doris and Doris shrugged, wanting one too.

The little girl sucked her sweet with relish and Stanley popped one into his own mouth, offered the bag to Doris.

'No, thanks.'

'You look hungry. Can I take you both for a bit of tea?'

Doris said nothing.

'In the cafe on Dock Road? Bit of egg and chips maybe?'

Laura tugged on Doris's skirt.

'No strings. I used to know your dad.'

His hair was dark and slicked back with cream. He was clean shaven and had cupid's bow lips that didn't quite meet even when his mouth was closed, so the front of his teeth always showed. He looked harmless enough. Doris accepted his offer and they walked with him to the cafe.

The egg and chips were sublime. Laura put too much salt on her chips and had to swap them with Doris. Stanley bought them spotted dick and custard and steaming mugs of tea. Laura bounced in her seat, barely able to reach the table top.

'Do you want a job?' Stanley took a cigarette out of a pack of Weights but didn't light it.

Doris looked at him. Her heart thumped.

'What sort of job?'

'In my office. Can you type?'

Doris nodded and wanted to cry. 'What sort of office?'

'I'm a private detective – I keep myself to myself, you have

120

to in my business.' He tapped the side of his nose. 'I need someone who can be discreet, type letters for me, confidential letters, someone I can rely on.'

Doris didn't realise private detectives looked like Stanley. He wore smart slacks and a kind of jacket knitted in grey four-ply with a zip and collar, a shirt and tie underneath. 'I haven't got anyone to watch the kid,' she said.

'You can bring her with you. I've got a back room you can put her in if I've got a client in. What do you think?'

'Why me?' she said.

Stanley shrugged. 'I was a pal of your father's and I've noticed you hanging around, I'd like to do you a good turn.'

Doris thought it was right up her alley.

Stanley paid for the meal and they followed him out.

'Where's this office, then?' asked Doris.

'Ship Street,' he said, smiling.

Ship Street. She gave him a sideways glance.

'It's all right, it's at the decent end of the street.' He chuckled. 'It's only a short walk but my motor's parked here if you want a lift?'

The only time Doris had been in a car was when Mrs Bottomley had paid for a taxi to take Laura to the hospital. She looked down at Laura, who was pulling at her skirt and trying to say something without Stanley hearing.

'Beauty, isn't she?' said Stanley, stopping by a black car parked on Dock Road. He patted the bonnet. '1951 Rover 75, goes like a dream. Chromium grille, streamlined body. They don't do that any more,' he said, tapping the single light in the middle of the front grille. 'Six cylinder, two point one litre. I've done seventy miles an hour in her.'

In her lopsided way Laura jumped up and down and pulled at Doris's hand. Stanley opened the passenger door and beckoned Laura inside. She was too excited to speak and climbed in, on to the red leather seat, the colour of that rabbit's liver Doris had gutted. Doris, trying to appear unimpressed, slid in beside Laura, breathed in the smell of leather and polish, reached out to stroke the wooden pan-elled dashboard. Stanley closed the door on them, ran round the front of the car with a skip and climbed in himself, the leather seat sighing as he sat down. He turned the key and the car stuttered to life, chugging like a tugboat. He pulled at the gear stick, turned the thin plastic wheel and steered them out on to the road. Doris looked over her shoulder through the back window, watched as the road behind her stretched away into the distance.

They pulled up on Ship Street. Doris glanced warily down to the other end of the road where she could see some women hanging around on the pavement. The tarts on Ship Street, she'd heard Archie and Vi say that before. But Stanley's office looked all right, it was at the end of a row of terraced houses. Just a plain glass window with some blinds pulled down and there was a plaque on the door that said Stanley Blackshaw, Private Detective.

'That's my humble abode,' said Stanley when Doris looked at the flat above the office.

He unlocked the door and showed them in. It was sparse but professional looking. A desk with typewriter and papers, two chairs in front and one behind.

'This is the back room,' he said, opening a door. 'There's nothing much in there but I might set you up in there with a desk and typewriter. It's time I got some help with that side of things. Please,' he said, motioning her into a chair. He sat down himself on his side and seemed distracted for a moment by the papers on the desk, putting one hand up to twiddle the hair on the crown of his head around his fingers.

'I do mostly divorce work these days. It's big business now, for me anyway, since the war.' He opened a desk drawer, looked inside, closed it again. 'You know, the men came home, their wives were different people, doing all kinds for the war effort, and then they wanted different things in life. That's where I come in. Did you know that divorce is six times higher now than it was before the war?'

Doris shook her head. She hadn't heard of anyone getting a divorce, except Wallis Simpson. And Group Captain Peter Townsend. But no one she knew of in Tilbury.

'I don't know, times are changing. Married women out working, wanting to be paid the same as men.' Stanley shook his head absent-mindedly. 'Last year there were over twenty-seven *thousand* divorces. *Thousand.* Course, that's not to say it's easy to get a divorce. Lucky for me, it's not. By any means.'

Laura climbed up on to the second chair, sat for a moment listening to Stanley then started to look around for something to do. She leant forward to pull one of the papers towards her. Stanley put his finger on it to stop her.

'That's why you get a lot of sham marriages now.' He looked at Doris for a sign she understood but found her face blank. 'You know, sham second marriages where the woman changes her name by deed poll. Course then you get the first wife or husband turning up, exposing the bigamy, bastard

children, all that.' He shrugged and took out his unlit cigarette from behind his ear to look at it. 'Better to do it properly
in the first place, if you can afford it.'

Doris nodded, not knowing what to say.

'That's the irony. There are certain things in life that are
all too easy to get into but nigh on impossible to get out of.
It's like signing a pact with the devil, isn't it?' He chuckled.

'Yeah, well, you might not have much choice sometimes.'

'Very wisely said, Doris.' He nodded at her. 'So, you can
type? What speed?'

'About forty words a minute.'

'Not bad,' he said. 'And can you be discreet? Are you good
at keeping secrets?'

'Oh yes, very good.'

'Well then, would you like the job? Let's say mornings for
now?'

'Yes, please.'

He waited, looking at her with raised eyebrows. 'You
mustn't be so passive, Doris. State your terms, assert yourself.'

'What?'

'Money, Doris. Aren't you going to negotiate terms?'

Doris looked blankly at the wall behind him. 'How much
does it pay?' she said uncertainly.

'That's more like it. Well, that depends. I don't want to pry,
but it seems to me you might be down on your luck at the
moment? Have you got somewhere decent to live? I might
be able to arrange something for you.'

'Like what?'

'Like, a friend of mine runs the boarding house down the
road and there's a spare room for you and the little one if you

want it. A woman there could help look after her sometimes when you're working.'

'You said she could come to work with me.'

'Yes, but Doris, the nature of my work is varied, I might need you to do other things sometimes, besides typing.'

'What things?'

He laughed. 'Well, let's take it one step at a time. There might be some travel and adventure involved if you play your cards right. I'm just saying for now, are you interested in lodgings or not?'

'Yes.'

'Right then, we got there in the end. In that case, if you're working for me part time and paying for lodgings out of your pay, I reckon it'll be a minimal amount in your pocket.' He twiddled his hair as he thought. 'Let's say one pound, five shillings a week for now?'

'All right.'

'All right.' He stood up, patted his pockets, found his keys. 'Come on, I'll show you your new digs.'

They followed him down the street. Towards the women hanging around on the pavement. Doris's insides clutched up. As they got nearer, she saw there were three women and they all adjusted their positions when they saw Stanley. One leant back against the wall and pulled the front of her coat open to show her low-cut top. The other two stood on the edge of the kerb to look up and down the road.

'Working hard, girls?' he said.

'Yes, Stanley,' they chorused.

Doris was surprised. They all knew him, in fact they

seemed to be wary of him. They had on high heels and red lipstick and lots of rouge and eye make-up, but not put on nicely the way Vi did – it looked garish, like they wanted it to be seen from a distance. These must be the tarts Vi and Archie talked about. Doris realised she didn't know what tarts meant – they all looked friendly enough. Stanley led Doris and Laura in through the front door of the boarding house. There in the wide hallway, sitting at a desk, was an older woman with a low-cut top and a long wrinkled cleavage.

'All right, Lil?'

'Stanley,' she said, nodding. 'How's you?'

'I'm well, how's business?'

Lil turned down the corners of her mouth and shrugged, took a puff from her cigarette and eyed Doris. 'Not bad, Stan.'

'This is Doris, and this little one is Laura, and they'd like to take the free room.'

Lil raised her eyebrows and nodded. 'I see. Of course, I'll get it ready. ' She called out to the back room, 'Fred.' A woman dressed in the same style as those outside came along the hallway. She wore a green halter neck dress and big black plastic beads. 'Fred,' said Lil, 'get the empty room ready. This here's Doris.'

'Oh, nice to meet you, Doris,' said Fred. She looked into Doris's eyes, seemed to see something there that she thought she might see, and smiled. 'And who's this then?'

'Laura,' said Doris.

'I'm three,' said Laura.

'Are you now? Well, that's a big girl. I bet you don't like sweets, do you?'

Laura frowned. 'Yes,' she said, nodding her head like she was going to head butt Fred, 'yes I do, I do like sweets.'

'Oh right, you might want one of these, then.'

She took a jar off the front desk and offered Laura a mint imperial. Laura pushed it into the side of her cheek with her tongue.

'Don't you say thank you?' said Fred.

'Thank you,' she said around the sweet, dribbling and wiping her mouth with her hand.

'That's all right, chicken,' said Fred, laughing. 'I'll go and do the room, then. Oh, Stan . . . '

'Fred?'

'There's a fella out the back, wants a job, I told him to hang around to ask you if you've got anything. Nice fella, but one of them coloureds.'

'Thanks, Fred, I'll go and have a look.'

Stanley walked through into a back room. Lil on the front desk was regarding Doris through her cigarette smoke and, feeling unnerved, Doris followed Stanley and gestured to Laura to come on.

They walked down a long hallway and through a door into a smoke-filled back room with several men sitting and standing around, listening to the horse racing blaring out of a radio. One of the men was black. He had on a smart suit, one of them with the long jacket, a colourful necktie and a new-looking hat. He looked like the fella who Doris had seen the other day, the one who saw the sign in the pub window. When Stanley approached him, he took off his hat and held out his hand.

'Mr Stanley?'

'Stanley Blackshaw, how do you do?'

The man looked cross with himself that he'd got Stanley's surname wrong.

'How do you do, Mr Blackshaw. Claude Vernon. I understand you're the man I need to talk to, to ask for a work?'

'That's right. What can you do?'

Claude looked animated at the prospect that he was being given attention, like he expected to be turned away.

'I can turn my hand to most things. I have done farming and labouring, I like people, I can read and write.'

'Jack of all trades, eh?'

Claude smiled as though he wanted to know what the phrase meant.

'I might have something for you, Claude, as a matter of fact.' Stanley smoothed back his hair and smiled, seemed to find something funny. 'Yes, you know what? I might have something for you. Where can I find you?'

Claude looked embarrassed, glanced at Doris, then looked down at Laura with surprise. 'I only just arrived, from Jamaica, and I'm looking for lodgings.'

'Right, I see, well I can't help you there I'm afraid. There's no room here.'

'No, there's no room here.' It was a younger man, came to stand at Stanley's shoulder. He was one of those Teddy boys, dressed up in his funny bootlace tie and thick-soled shoes. He looked like he didn't like the coloured one.

'Room's all ready,' said Fred, coming back down and not hearing what had just been said. 'I've kicked Sally out, she'll be in with me,' she said to Stanley. She turned to Doris, 'You can bring your things along if you like.'

Claude's face altered slightly. Doris didn't know why she spoke – it might have been because Stanley was there and she wanted to show she was grateful for the room and the job. It might have been because she had seen the Teddy boy in the pub with his pals and they sometimes said things to Vi when Archie wasn't around, and once one of them had called out to Doris when they saw her sitting in the hall behind the bar and had said something lurid to make her squirm. It certainly wasn't because she liked this coloured fella or felt sorry for taking a room when there wasn't one for him.

'I might know where you can stay.' The sound of her voice surprised her. Everyone looked at her expectantly. 'If you don't mind roughing it.'

'I don't mind roughing it,' he said in his funny voice. 'Claude Vernon.' He held out his hand and Doris couldn't do anything else but put her hand against his for a split second and take it away again.

'Doris.'

Stanley nodded appreciatively. 'You go and bring your things then, and show Claude where to stay. Claude, you come back tomorrow.'

In an instant, Doris regretted saying anything. Now she was going to have to show this fella where to go. She'd have to talk to him and be seen with him. As if her reputation wasn't bad enough already.

She grabbed Laura's hand and turned to go.

'You're welcome,' called out Fred. Doris spun around to look at the woman's face. She was grinning, one hand on her hip.

'Thanks,' said Doris, 'for doing the room.'

'Like I said.' Fred turned on her heel and headed into the back room.

Doris walked out of the front door and looked over her shoulder to check the coloured fella was there.

Claude joined her and she stole a glance at his face – he was grinning up at the sky. He suddenly clapped his hands together and sprang into the air.

'My luck is changing,' he said, with a laugh at Doris's surprised face. 'Thank you, for this, where is it, what kind of rooms?'

'Don't get too excited. It's only in a bombed-out tenement. I think one of your lot lives there, that's all. Fella called Homesick.'

'I'm three,' piped up Laura.

Claude stopped to crouch down by her. 'You're three?'

Laura nodded proudly.

'That's big!'

Laura nodded again, looking very serious about her achievement.

He stood up and continued walking. 'One of my lot? You mean Jamaican?'

Doris shrugged. 'I suppose.' As they walked over the hair-pin bridge and turned the corner, Doris saw Kenny coming towards them, fifty yards away, and he saw her at the same moment. Doris swallowed and felt sick, slowed her pace, tried to think what to do. She managed a tight-lipped smile and when Kenny was thirty yards from them, he looked with disgust at Laura and at Claude and he changed direction and crossed the road.

'You're brown,' said Laura. 'Like mud.'

Claude stopped, serious for a moment. 'And you pink,' he said, 'like a pig.'

Laura looked down at herself, pulled up the sleeve of her coat, regarded her bare arm and pouted. She walked along in silence for a few minutes, looking up at Claude now and again.

'Where you staying at now?' said Claude, unaware of Kenny going by.

'In that bombed-out tenement,' Doris replied, 'but round the other side. It's a dump but I haven't had anywhere else.'

'You're brown,' said Laura, 'like burn sausage.'

Claude put back his head and laughed so hard that his hat fell off. He picked it up and thought for a moment.

'You pink,' he said, 'like sausage that hasn't been cook yet.'

Laura looked at the colour of her hand, pouted again and narrowed her eyes.

'Here it is,' said Doris, walking across the forecourt covered in scrubby weeds and heading around the back way.

Claude looked up at the building and whistled. 'A palace,' he said.

Doris didn't tell him she had said the same thing when she first saw it.

They clambered over some loose rocks and through the entrance into the central courtyard. Doris found her way round to the flats on the west side.

'You're brown,' said Laura, stumbling along, 'like cocoa.'

Claude smiled at her. 'And you pink, like a marshmallow.'

Laura smiled, pleased. Claude put out his hand to help her walk over the rubble and she took it.

'What happen to your foot?' he said to her.

131

She frowned. 'It bad,' she said.

'I bet you are fast though. I'm gonna call you Blaze-A-Glory.'

Her little face lit up.

'Come on, Blaze,' he said, pulling her along.

'I don't know where, I just saw him come this way,' said Doris, looking for signs of habitation. They worked their way back through into the central courtyard, down the end that wasn't visible from Doris's flat window. And there they saw sure signs that someone lived there. A cooking fire with a spit had been rigged up outside one of the ground floor flats. Four old wooden dining chairs, dark with rain water, surrounded it. Claude went ahead, knocked at the door, called out.

'Anyone home?'

They heard the sound of a man's voice inside, the door opened and there stood a coloured fella with crumpled shirt and trousers, bare feet, rubbing the sleep out of his eyes and looking for all the world like he'd been hibernating for winter and wondered why the sun was up.

He started when he saw them there, looked confused, saw Claude and nodded a greeting, held out his hand.

'Hey, man.'

'Hey,' said Claude, shaking his hand. 'Sorry to disturb, you sleeping?'

'No, no, don't worry your head, I was just taking a little nap.'

'You Jamaican?'

'Yeah, we all, except Smallie, he's Trinidadian.'

Claude looked past the man for the others.

'They all out working,' he said. 'They be back soon. Come in, sit, I will make a cup of char.'

132

'I'll be off then,' said Doris, backing away.

'No, no, come, come in, please,' said the man. 'I am Goodfor,' he said, holding out his hand to Doris, 'I mean, that is what the boys call me anyway.'

'Doris,' she said, taking his hand. He put out his arm to guide her inside.

'It is all right, take it easy, I am not gonna hurt you,' he said, laughing at her expression and holding up his hands.

It smelled funny inside, pungent, not unpleasant though.

Laura hid behind Doris's leg. Goodfor beckoned for them to sit down on the settee. There were also two mismatching armchairs in the room, even a rug on the floor. It looked much nicer than Doris's flat.

'Been here long?' said Claude, taking one of the armchairs.

'Me? Yes, long time, three year.'

'Three year?' said Claude, shocked.

'Oh, not three year here in Tilbury, three year in Old England. I been here about eight months.'

'You got a work?'

Goodfor looked vague. 'Oh yes, yes, not at the moment though.'

'It is not easy, man,' said Claude. 'The doors I have knocked on, no work, nowhere to stay. I been to factories, folk say there is a work, I get there, jobs all gone. I see rooms to rent, I knock, rooms are gone. I got a work now, just now, so it is good.'

'You hustled a work? Where is it?'

'With a fella Stanley, he does have a boarding house here, says I can have a work, don't know what I will be doing yet.'

Goodfor nodded slowly. 'You got somewhere to stay?'

Shaking his head, Claude said, 'No, I ain't have.'

'You can stay here, man, I ease you up,' said Goodfor, slouching into a chair and forgetting about the tea. 'It have a room in the flat next door with RAF.'

'Truly?' said Claude, leaning forward in his seat.

'Yes, man, I ease you up.'

Claude leaned back, let his shoulders drop. 'Thanks, man, I appreciate that.'

Doris stayed for an hour at Goodfor's insistence, even though she tried to get away. Claude entertained Laura and chatted to Goodfor. The door opened and two more men came in, expressed surprise at seeing visitors there.

'Hey man,' they said to Claude.

Claude stood up to greet them and shake hands, hear their names.

'RAF,' said one.

'Smallie,' said another.

'This your piece of skin, man?' they said to Claude.

'Nah, this is Doris, she showed me this place and this is her girl Laura.'

Doris gave them uncertain smiles and Laura squashed closer to her mother on the settee.

'You not made coffee, you lazy dog?' said RAF to Goodfor. He swiped Goodfor's legs off the arm of the chair where he'd been lounging. 'You hit a weed?'

'Nah, man, I been resting.'

'I can smell it. Good for Nothing, that's you. He always makes excuse for not having a work, he signs on the dole,' said RAF to Claude. 'Makes a bad name for the rest of us.'

'Why should I get a work, no one give me a work anyway, they don't want me – they say it to my face. I am sick of it.'

'You ain't gonna save for your passage home if you're on the dole.'

'Hey,' said Claude, leaning forward. 'You see the sign in that pub? No coloureds and no dogs?'

'Yeah, we seen it,' said Smallie, 'so what?'

'So what? So I was expecting a welcome, welcome to the Great Britain, the mother country, that is what.'

The three other men started laughing. It broke the tension in the room between Goodfor and the others. They slapped their thighs, tears in their eyes. Laura started to laugh with them even though she didn't understand.

'You think that is bad?' said Smallie. 'You go to London, you'll really feel the colour bar. It is a struggle, it is.'

Claude leant back in his chair and frowned. 'I don't understand it, man. We are British citizens, we brought up British.'

RAF gave a snort of derision. 'Yeah, why you think we all here, then? Saving up to go home?'

'Saving up to go home? Truly?'

Doris sneaked a look at Claude's face. He looked paler than before. Like he'd been told someone had died.

'I ain't going home, man, it is my dream to come here. I am a writer, I am gonna make something of my writing. It have no opportunity in Jamaica, a quarter of the country out of work.'

'Don't tell me,' said Smallie, holding up his hand, 'you saw the posters the English put at home, the adverts in the *Jamaican Times*, tell you you're needed in England, it have a work in England, good wages, prospects, fresh start?' Smallie tried keeping a straight face but couldn't. RAF and Goodfor chuckled with him. They erupted into belly laughs.

Claude looked horrified and suspicious. Doris wondered what kind of thing he wrote.

'I tell you, man, it cheaper to go to Australia with the ten-pound poms than go back home, but they don't want spades,' said Smallie.

'Why you wanna go there then? It'll be just like here,' said RAF.

'They give you a house and a job and wages are higher, I heard it, and the sun shines more than here.'

'Ha that is not difficult,' said another man walking through the door. He nodded at Claude and looked with interest at Doris. 'If the sun shines here my skin gets a shock,' he said and laughed. 'I seen you before,' he said to Doris.

'Yes, hello,' said Doris to the man who called himself Homesick, the one who helped Laura that time, the one who told her about the sick rabbits.

'And you, Blondie,' he said, smiling at Laura. 'You catch a rabbit like I told you?' he asked Doris.

She nodded. 'Yes, I caught one. Skinned and gutted it too.'

Homesick nodded, impressed. 'So who this then?' he said, extending his hand to Claude. Claude sat up to shake it.

'Claude,' he began to say.

'He is a writer. We'll call he Shakespeare,' said RAF laughing.

Claude smiled and shrugged like he didn't mind being called that. He seemed to accept that they'd call him something and Shakespeare would do.

'You all got a work?' Claude asked.

'Me and him hustled a work in the tannery,' said RAF,

motioning to Smallie. 'It stinks to high heaven but they don't mind giving the bad jobs to the spades.'

'You served in the war?' Claude said to RAF.

'Sure. And a lot of good it did me. They call me British when I willing to give my life for them – now I want to live and get a work here I am not British any more.'

'My father died in the war,' said Claude. 'He was proud to serve the King.'

The men regarded him in silence, a silence that said, you just wait and see what you're saying once you've been here a little while.

'I'm three,' said Laura into the void and immediately dove to bury her face behind Doris's back.

'Hey, what is your name, Blondie?' called out RAF.

Laura stayed where it was safe.

'I'll be going now,' said Doris, getting up, Laura clinging on to the back of Doris's dress, and Doris trying to get her off, conscious that her dress was being pulled tight over her chest.

'Sit, sit, I will make that coffee Goodfor should have made you.'

Goodfor tutted at RAF and rubbed his hand over his face. Doris sat back down wondering when she'd be able to get out of there. She was supposed to be getting her things from the flat.

'I need to get my things from the flat to take to Ship Street.'

'Ship Street?' said Smallie.

'Yes, I've just got a room there and a job with a private detective, typing.'

'Ah, good. That is good,' said Smallie, looking at the others.

'Who, that Stanley with the motor car?' said Goodfor. Doris nodded.

'She in the racket, man?' said Goodfor to no one in particular, and Doris wondered what he meant. No one said anything. Claude hugged himself to warm up.

'You will get used to the cold,' said Smallie. 'There no heat from the sun here. I ain't fooling, man, people burn fires inside the house to keep warm and all the smoke pours out house chimney and makes a smog that you choke on, it gets down your throat and comes out your mouth.'

'Take it easy,' said Homesick. 'That's just your warm breath hitting the cold air, looks like smoke. You bring any food from home, man?' he asked Claude.

'None left now,' said Claude.

'I can't wait to get some salt fish when I get home,' said Homesick.

'Curry goat,' said RAF rubbing his belly. 'Here they eat potato, bread, eggs, does not taste of anything,' he said to Claude. 'Ah, it don't matter,' he said, waving away his comments, he seemed mindful that Claude was just starting his adventure, he'd find out soon enough.

'You want a help, taking your things over there?' said RAF to Doris.

'No it's all right thank you, I'll manage.'

'Manage? You do not need to manage, you got five strong spades to give you a help.'

Goodfor tutted and shuffled in his seat.

'Thank you,' said Doris, wondering what she'd got herself into.

*

After they'd had coffee, Doris managed to extract herself with just Claude to help her with her things and not all five of them.

'I just need to pack up some stuff,' she said, eyeing him warily as he hovered in the doorway of her flat.

'How long you lived here?' he said, looking round.

'About a year.'

She thought he'd ask why but he didn't.

'You been to London?'

Doris shook her head.

'It can't be as bad as they say,' he said, almost to himself. 'Seeing that pub sign was a son of a bitch though.'

Doris didn't feel like telling him she grew up in that pub. She went into the bedroom to get the blankets off the bed. She lifted the tarpaulin to look at the mattress, spotted with grey-green mildew, and was glad to be going somewhere else. The piss pot was half full but she didn't want to carry it past Claude to empty it so she pushed it under the bed with her foot. She rolled their few spare clothes up in the blankets and tied the bundle with string. She wanted to take the wooden chair she had found, and the food from the larder. She didn't know what the food arrangements would be at the boarding house, she'd never lived in one before.

Claude carried the chair and the blanket roll, Laura carried her doll and her favourite stick and Doris managed the box of food and kitchen things. She turned to see the flat before leaving and felt the sting of tears in her eyes that she had been living like a tramp for so long. The damp and the bugs and the foul stink of the lav along the balcony that no one emptied. She hoped that where she was going would be a step up to something better, and hoped in her heart that Vi would give way and let them back home to save them from any of this.

On the walk back to Ship Street, Claude looked around and shivered.

'Man, it is grey and bleak here, no leaves on the trees even.'

Doris was going to say that the trees were starting to bud and would be green again soon. She wanted to say she was sad about that, but stayed silent, not trusting this man she hardly knew. She might have told him that a tree in the winter is a piece of art. The limbs branching off smaller and smaller, each splitting into two or more, and in turn that one splits too. The bare skeleton of a tree is far more beautiful than one covered in leaves. It is the substance, the innards, what holds it together. For a second, Doris felt the need to draw, but just as quickly the feeling faded.

When they got back to the Ship Street boarding house it was late. There were more women out on the pavement. Doris saw a man walk up to the door and slip in furtively. He spoke to Lil on the desk, who called out to one of the girls, one with bleached white hair and purple lipstick, and they disappeared upstairs together. The place just didn't seem right and Doris wanted to turn around and walk out. But Laura was almost asleep against her leg and the thought of going back to the damp tenement gave her the spark she needed to decide that she'd give it a go. She could always go back to the tenement if she didn't want to stay. She'd have a look at the room.

Lil called Fred from the back room.

'Hello again,' said Fred.

'Hello,' said Doris, not wanting to be too friendly, just in case.

'You want to see your room I suppose?' She looked at Claude carrying the things. 'You two together, are you?'

Doris started. 'What? No.'

'You her pimp, then? Stanley won't like that.'

Claude and Doris looked at each other, completely mystified.

Fred laughed. 'Don't worry about it. You stay here then, I'll take that.'

She took the blanket roll from Claude and left the chair in the hallway. She went up the stairs and Doris followed with Laura.

The room was small but Doris thought it was lovely. Hung with scarlet drapes at the windows, the large bed covered in an embroidered satin eiderdown, a lamp with a pink scarf draped over it. A sweet dressing table and mirror. She sighed with relief. Laura tried to be excited but was too tired. She climbed up on to the bed and was asleep within a minute.

'It's lovely,' she said.

Fred smiled. 'It's all right, isn't it? They look after you here. That's why I've stayed so long — the East End is bad news now — too organised, too many patches and territories, the girls haven't got any control, they're like slaves. Give Stanley the odd *handshake* now and then,' she said with a wink, 'to keep him sweet and you'll be fine.'

'What?'

'You working tonight?'

'I don't think so, I'll probably start tomorrow. Stanley said it's mainly typing letters to start with.'

'Typing letters? Oh.' Fred laughed. 'Oh right, he's warming you up, is he? Shouldn't have stuck my nose in, should I?'

'Warming me up?'

'Oh nothing, I didn't realise you were doing office work. That'll be good, won't it?' Fred gave a strange smile. 'I'll get back to it, then. Have a good sleep and don't worry about the noise, you'll get used to it.'

Doris watched her leave and lay down on the bed. She hadn't realised how tired she was. It was like the strain of the past year on her own was draining out of her into that bed; she was stuck to it. She let herself fall into sleep, Fred's words going through her mind. Warming her up, what did it mean? Warming her up to start her new job maybe. That was all. She had somewhere nice to live and she had a job. Things were really looking up.

Doris woke the next morning feeling like she hadn't slept a wink. The noise through the night had been awful. Shouting and laughing coming from downstairs, upstairs, through the walls, stamping up and down the stairs. She could hear everything, even someone using the pot upstairs. There had been a lot of banging and calling out – she couldn't think what all the noise could have been.

Laura had slept through it all and woke up excited to be in a new room. They went downstairs to see about something to eat. No one was around, everyone must have still been in bed. It smelled like the pub the morning after a busy night. Doris found the kitchen and some bread, put the kettle on the stove and made some tea. The clock on the wall said it was half past eight. Doris thought it would be a good idea to go along to Stanley's office to see about starting work.

Outside it was cold but the sun had struggled into the sky and was shining weakly through the grey cloud. The office door was locked. She looked through the glass with cupped hands and saw no movement. Stanley's car was parked in the road so she banged on the door and waited. She banged on the door again and Laura joined in too. The window of the upstairs flat opened and Stanley stuck his ruffled head out.

'What you playing at?'

'I've come to work,' she said, standing back in the dirt road to look up.

Stanley squinted down at her. 'Well just wait for a decent hour, would you?' He closed the window and they sat down on the kerb to wait.

15

Vi

'Says here she chased him round the car to shoot him.'

Archie looked over at Vi's paper and grunted. 'She looks like a tart,' he said.

'Outside a pub it happened. That poor man, only twenty-five, a racing driver.'

Vi looked at the picture of the smiling woman in the paper. Ruth Ellis, bleached blonde hair, dark lipstick, pencilled-in eyebrows and dangly earrings. She looked like a good-time girl.

'She's been charged with murder.'

'She'll swing for it,' said Archie.

'Nah, you think?'

'She shot him in cold blood, didn't she?'

'She's a model and runs a night club.' Vi tutted. What can you expect if you live an immoral life? 'Two men in her life, well, that just goes to show.' She'd always told Doris that there were good girls and good-time girls. 'Puh, on Easter Sunday, too, terrible. Says that after she shot him he was lying face down on the pavement, and she came round and shot him again in the back. It makes you go cold, doesn't it?'

Turning over the page, there was an article about abandoned babies. *On average, four babies are dumped every day in Britain. In telephone boxes, on doorsteps, in other children's prams, underneath train seats . . . the mothers are usually unmarried.* Vi scanned the page, her eyes darting from one sentence to the next in a morbid curiosity, not really wanting to read it. *The mother often wants to keep her baby but can't face the shame of what her relatives and neighbours would think.* Vi turned the page over quickly. Those babies were better off adopted, with a proper family, she didn't know what all the fuss was about. Anyone who had grown up with the stigma of being illegitimate would tell you that.

She opened her magazine to take her mind off it. There was a feature about the coffee bar craze, teenagers drinking cappuccinos in London's Soho. She tutted and murmured, 'And people wonder why girls go wrong these days.'

She read the advice for preventing a double chin – slap it briskly each day with a face flannel wrung out in icy water. She'd have to tell Win that one. *Femininity is the first and final asset of any woman*, it said.

16

Doris

When Stanley finally got up and let Doris and Laura in to his office, he showed Doris the typewriter and sat down opposite her to dictate some letters. Laura was bored, fidgeting around. Doris sent her outside to play. She came back half an hour later saying the other kids were throwing stones at her.

'What for?' Doris said.

'Bastard,' she said. 'They say me a bastard.'

Stanley looked at Doris and looked away quick, twiddling his hair.

'Just go and play in the back room,' Doris said, her face hot.

She worked for Stanley just mornings to start with. He seemed all right, he didn't lose his temper and he didn't lech over her. His office became part of her routine. She'd work until dinner time then go and sit on the sea wall to watch the pub in the afternoons. She missed her mornings, seeing

Vi come out to clean the step, but she was getting a bit of money together and they were eating better. Stanley set up a little desk for her in the corner of the office, said it looked good, having a secretary, decided against putting her in the back room. Laura made that her office and had a collection of treasures in there, her favourite sticks and her doll. She found an old Lyons' tin tea caddy that she called her treasure chest and played with that in the back when Doris was working.

She'd worked there a couple of weeks and Stanley seemed to be happy with her. One morning he was at his desk waiting for an appointment.

'I'm expecting someone in a minute,' he said to Doris. 'Sit tight and you might learn something – I might even have a little job for you, something that involves some field work. A bit of adventure, like I mentioned.'

Stanley licked his thumb and leafed through a pile of papers until he found what he was looking for. He squinted at it, his lips moving as he read. Doris waited, wondering whether the paper had her job on it.

'What sort of job?'

He gave a long sniff like he was thinking what to say and then there was a knock on the door, which Stanley kept locked. They both looked up sharply and Stanley got up to see. A proper gent came in, suited and booted with a little trimmed tash. He looked around the office and made a face. Stan shuffled back round his desk to his chair and waved his hand for the man to sit down, then leant forward to offer his hand.

'Stanley Blackshaw, Private Detective.'

'Philip Timpson, pleased to make your acquaintance.'

Posh voice. He went to unbutton his black wool coat then decided against. Instead he sat there clenching his jaw and looking around the room without moving his head, glancing at Doris then away again.

Stanley waited, quietly, just looking at the man, as if to unnerve him.

'I wonder whether you could help? It's something of a delicate nature.'

Stanley nodded wisely and lit a cigarette, not offering one to the man.

'Something of a matrimonial nature, in fact.'

'You've come to the right place, Mr Timpson.' Stanley squinted his eyes to look kindly and smiled a fake smile. 'You needn't worry, I am in the business of the delicate. These walls are your friends, Mr Timpson. And this young lady is a most trusted employee of mine.'

The man's bones seemed to soften a bit. He undid his coat buttons and took out a silver cigarette case, lighting one up.

'What exactly is the problem?' Stanley flipped open his tiny book and held his pencil ready.

'I wish to acquire a . . . divorce. I understand that you are the man to come to in these situations.'

'Of course. How long have you been married, may I ask?'

'Five years.'

Stanley looked the man in the eye and took a drag of his cigarette.

'A reasonable length of time.'

'Yes, I believe so,' said the man.

'Are you separated?'

'No, not really, not as such. I mean to say, I spend most

of my time in my London flat, my wife stays in our country home. We mainly stay in those respective places.'

'Are either of you cohabiting with another person?'

'I wouldn't say that exactly. I have a . . . friend who keeps me company on occasion.'

Stanley stared at him for what felt like ages but the man couldn't look him in the eye.

'I see. And your wife?'

'No, my wife, as far as I am aware, has not met anyone else.'

'And is your wife privy to your divorce plans?'

'She is, yes. She suggested it in fact.'

The man took a long drag of his cigarette and suddenly looked like he would cry, then shifted in his seat and fixed his face again.

'Mr Timpson, may I ask you a very delicate question in confidence?'

Mr Timpson took a deep breath through his nose and nodded.

'The friend who visits you, would they be of the female or the male persuasion?'

The man shot a look at Doris and back at Stanley and Doris's eyes opened wider. She looked over at Stanley's filing cabinet and mentally counted the drawers.

'Female, of course.'

'Now, now, that's fine, I need to know. I'm sure you understand?'

The man stared.

'So just to be doubly sure, neither of you has committed an indiscretion that you want to declare?'

'No.'

'Because, I'm bound to say, if you're telling me porky pies and you're *both* up to no good, you'll not get a divorce if you're found out.'

'I understand.'

'Now then, to brass tacks. I take it, Mr Timpson, that you are not the sort of fellow to offer your wife treatment of the rough variety?'

'What?'

'Rough treatment, I mean to say, persistent beatings, cruelty, things of that nature?'

'Good lord, certainly not.'

'And are we safe to say that neither of you has been deemed incurably insane?'

'No!'

'And clearly you have not deserted one another for a minimum three-year period?'

'No, we have not, clearly.'

'Then there is only one thing for it, Mr Timpson.'

Stanley made a church and steeple with his hands and pressed the steeple to his lips.

'Yes? Well, what is it?'

'We shall need to appease The Baron, Mr Timpson.'

'Who the devil is The Baron?'

'The devil indeed. Baron Blake Rutherford, President of the Probate, Divorce and Admiralty Division of the High Court of Justice. We shall need to appease him, Mr Timpson, and that is my line of business, you have come to the right place.'

The man looked like he suddenly realised he had no idea what he was getting himself into.

'And what does that involve exactly? A hotel, perhaps?'

'Ah, I can see you're privy to some of the realities of the matter, Mr Timpson. That's good. It's a difficult business, without a doubt. And it must hold up in a court of law. *Prima facie*, Mr Timpson, *prima facie*.'

Doris was impressed. Stanley certainly knew what he was talking about.

'The situation is this, Mr Timpson, and you'll pardon me if I put it in plain language because that is how I am?'

The fella gave a 'go ahead' motion with his head.

'You need to prove that one of you has committed adultery. The one who commits it is the respondent, the one who accuses it is the petitioner. The respondent is the one who has to get themselves in a situation that can be used as evidence. The petitioner is the one who has to appear in court before the old Baron. Now you and your wife have to decide who is which.'

Stanley leant back in his chair and threaded his fingers together on his chest, waiting for the answer. Without hesitating, the fella said, 'I'll be the respondent.'

'Right you are, save the lady's shame and all that, eh?'

'Indeed.'

'Now the question is, do you know a lady who you can be *caught* with, like? The friend who visits you, perhaps?'

'No, I'm afraid I do not. No, I wouldn't wish to involve the friend.'

Stanley puffed up like this was the answer he wanted.

'In that case, I shall arrange for a young lady who will agree to provide the evidence that you need.'

'Yes.' The man's shoulders sank a bit and Doris realised he'd been bunched up all that time, waiting to see if he'd come to the right place.

'Now then, Mr Timpson, I'm obliged to tell you that The Baron has tightened things up. He's no fool, he knows what goes on and he can smell a fishy divorce a mile off. I know how to get round it, as it were, but it don't come cheap.'

Stanley raised his eyebrows like he'd asked an invisible question.

'Yes, of course.'

As the man sagged back in his chair, Stanley's eyes twinkled and he puffed himself up even more, like he was taking the very air out of his client's body.

'Now then, this is how the land lies. You can go for your bog standard weekend-in-a-hotel bit – now don't go thinking a one-nighter will do the trick any more – but a weekender is the bog standard and what I mean to say is, that's what most of them try to get away with and that is what you're mostly up against, you get what I'm on about?'

'I think so.'

'With that, you'll need the *understanding* of the hotel manager and a chambermaid – this is all the costs what I'm talking about now, Mr Timpson, but don't worry, I've got all these contacts in place – you'll need a willing companion to be caught in bed with you – sorry for the impolite nature of it, Mr Timpson, but we're friends now – and you'll need a bit of extra evidence of being seen out and about, and that's where me and my camera and my eyewitness testimony come in, Mr Timpson.'

Stanley waited for all that to sink in.

'Now that's the basics, if you go for that you're hoping for the best, you're risking going through the shame of it all and not getting the result you're after. If you want some extra security, Mr Timpson, you'll live with the girl for a bit or have her working for you, plus all the out-and-about evidence and the hotel too.'

The gent jerked back his head.

'I know, I know, it's a shock to a gentleman like yourself, and it don't come cheap like I say. The thing is, Mr Timpson, it gets round the class problem if you like, makes it more likely. You can't help coming from your background and my girls can't help coming from theirs. Now, what's the most common place a man of your standing might spark up an association with a girl not in his social circle?'

'At work.'

'Quite right, at work, with his secretary. Now, that is a believable situation that is, Mr Timpson. If I was The Baron, I'd believe it, wouldn't you?'

'Yes, I suppose so. But living with me is out of the question.'

Stanley nodded. 'Where do you work, may I ask, Mr Timpson?'

'In the City.'

'Well, that's perfect.'

The fella looked at Stanley like it was anything but perfect.

'This is really beyond the pale, are these really the lengths to which people go? I was led to believe it would be relatively straightforward. What about the Royal Commission?'

Stanley screwed up his face like someone had told him the Queen was a cockney.

'*The Royal Commission?* They'll be just as likely to ban divorce altogether than make it more easier. Be my guest if you want to wait around for that lot to do anything useful.'

'Yes, all right, I take your point, Mr Blackshaw. I suppose I can find a temporary position for one of your young ladies as a secretary at my place of work.'

'Best advised, Mr Timpson, *prima facie*. Now then, a delicate question, Mr Timpson, will you be wanting to commit acts of intimacy or will you be wanting to give the impression that acts of intimacy have been committed?'

'What the devil?'

'Give the impression ... ' Stanley wrote it down in his book and the man gave a curt nod. 'That service requires a twenty-pound insurance fee.'

'What?'

'To protect the modesty of my employee, Mr Timpson.'

'But you just offered me ... otherwise.'

'In which case the fee would be twenty pound per act of intimacy committed. The insurance fee is the cost of me, personally, being nearby so as to ensure no such acts are committed.'

Doris was fascinated, Stanley seemed to be playing the man like a barrel organ.

'This is all highly irregular.'

Stanley gave a little snort of surprise. 'Did you expect otherwise, Mr Timpson?'

All he got back was a cold stare.

'I can assure you, I provide the highest quality service with the highest likelihood of success. I have sat in them courts of law, Mr Timpson, and I know what The Baron wants to hear and what he'll say yes to and what he'll say no to, and I've got a good understanding of the costs and employees involved in supplying such a service. This is a very niche business, Mr Timpson, very niche. You are most welcome to try your luck elsewhere, otherwise endure a three-year separation period, otherwise commit persistent physical cruelty against your wife, otherwise hope she is diagnosed an incurable lunatic, otherwise wait around for marriage to be up to the State and not the Church. Up to you. Entirely.'

The man pursed up his lips and looked at Stanley like he wanted to kill him. Doris looked to the door and wondered how fast Stanley could unlock it.

'Well, it seems I have little choice. What, in addition to my solicitor's fee and your "insurance fee", would your high quality service cost exactly?'

'Yes, sensible, Mr Timpson, most sensible. Let's say a one-month position at your place of work, you'd pay the going rate for the position to the girl of course, plus the same amount to me for supplying the girl. There'll be the hotel bill for two nights, plus the hotel manager and the chambermaid, both will have to testify in court, you understand. There'll be my fee for out-and-about evidence and you'll need to take the girl out for dinner and such for at least four evenings to make it look realistic. We're looking at, and this is approximate, I'll need to do a proper account of it all, but I reckon it'll be three hundred pound, plus the cost of meals and drinks and the fee for your own counsel of course.'

'Three hundred pounds?'

Doris had never seen the colour drain out of a face like that. And she couldn't believe the amount either; she was surprised Stanley even let her stay there to hear it all.

'I'll need all your information, name, address, where you

work and all that. Fill this in please and we'll get the ball rolling.'

In a daze, the man took the piece of paper from Stanley and got up to leave, his face still white.

'Come and see me again next week and leave the arrangements to me and I'll be in touch. No letters, no telegrams, no telephone calls. You don't know me, you've never met me, your wife has hired me. Don't you worry, we'll be reading about you in the *News of the World* before too long.' Stanley got up to let the man out and patted him on the back.

The man whipped his head around and dropped his jaw to speak.

'Ha ha, and the *Sunday Times*, don't you worry. The divorce announcements, Mr Timpson, that's all, ha ha.'

The man gave Stanley a weak bit of a smile and left.

Locking the door after him, Stanley turned to Doris and winked. 'Poofter,' he said.

'No! You sure?'

'It don't make no difference either way. If he said he's a poofter they'd lock him up. He has to pretend he's not a poofter. He'll have to make out he's had intimate ways with another woman to get his divorce, whether he's a poofter or not. You've got a lot to learn, young lady.'

It all sounded Irish to Doris, and not a bit immoral. She'd never met a poof before. It hit her then, the job Stanley was talking about.

'Is it me? Am I the young lady who's going to be the secretary?'

17

Doris

On a sunny May morning, Doris stood on the pavement of London's Leadenhall Street and looked up at the imposing stone facade of the General Insurance Company. She knew Stanley was standing a short distance away; he had shown her the way. He had stood on the Tilbury station platform fifty yards up from her, she had watched him get off at Liverpool Street, had followed him down Bishopsgate, watched for him to signal the right building by taking off his hat and putting it back on again. She hadn't taken her eyes off him, terrified of getting lost, of being in London for the first time in her life.

She had read the magazine feature about what you should wear if you are a girl who works in an office. She had cut her own pattern based on the shin-length, slim-skirted pinafore dress in the picture and had hand-stitched it in a pale green gabardine bought with her wages. She had paid for a haircut and set, had made a little cloth bag from the same gabardine and had borrowed some heeled shoes and Woolworth heart-red lipstick from Fred. She was fairly confident that she looked the part.

'I'm here to start a position in the New Business department,' she said to the girl on reception, careful not to mention Mr Timpson's name, the man who wanted Stanley to get him a divorce.

Going up in the lift to the third floor, she blotted the moisture on her upper lip with the side of her finger and wished she had made up the dress in a light cotton and not a heavy gabardine.

A woman called Minty welcomed her to New Business. Minty had stepped out of Doris's magazine, her make-up and hair and clothes looking exactly as the advice said she should look. Doris didn't miss Minty's sweeping glance over her own outfit and hoped it met with her approval.

'Where did you say you were from, Brook Street?'

'Yes, that's right,' said Doris, careful to establish her story just as Stanley had told her.

'And you've worked in a typing pool before?'

Doris nodded and smiled.

'Well I must say, you're awfully lucky to go straight in. There are girls here who have worn the clerical overall for two years before being allowed in the pool. You have shorthand too?'

Doris nodded.

'A word of advice, darling, the dress . . .' Minty scrunched up her nose and shook her head.

Doris looked down in horror, wondering what was wrong.

'You're not going to make your catch dressed like that,' she winked. 'The men here like the girls to be smart, neat and immaculately clean, nails short and shining. They want something nice to look at all day, don't they?'

Doris felt instantly uncomfortable and thought everyone would be thinking the same thing about her dress. She wanted to run out of there.

Minty led her through to a half-partitioned section with twelve desks, eleven of them occupied by typists, a desk at the front with a spectacled older lady. Minty leant down to speak into her ear. The older lady nodded and stood up.

'Doris, this is Mrs Pearson, who'll be your supervisor. I shall catch up with you later.'

'Where did you train?' said Mrs Pearson without any niceties.

'The Grays typing school,' said Doris.

'Grays?' said Mrs Pearson, frowning. 'That's a first. My girls have all trained at Mr Box's Academy in Brighton. I know where I stand with them. With you we'll see. Take these over to that desk and bring them back for checking when you're finished. Two carbon copies for each.'

Mrs Pearson handed her a folder of work. As Doris walked to her desk, she saw the eyes of the girls flicker away from their work to assess the new girl and flicker back to their typing. Doris could feel her armpits dampen and hoped it wouldn't show too much through the green fabric.

Luckily the typewriter was very close to the one she had used at typing school. As she worked she looked around, wondering where Mr Timpson's office was and when she'd have an opportunity to strike up the 'discreet friendship' that Stanley had talked about. The other girls were much faster than her, and it took until lunchtime to complete her work. And when lunchtime came, the other girls stopped, opened their top drawers and took out objects to freshen up their faces and hair. Doris had seen the exact same thing in her magazine and was thrilled to be part of such a scene in real life. She looked forward to spending some of her new wages on make-up and keeping it in her top drawer. Stanley said she'd get four pounds and ten shillings per week. She stood up, smiling at the other girls, wondering where they would go to lunch together. Perhaps one of the city coffee bars she'd read about, perhaps they would eat spaghetti and drink cappuccinos and chat about men and dresses.

'Hello, I'm Doris,' she said to the group of girls making their way to the lift. They made no answer. 'Hello, I'm Doris,' she said a little louder, as they were so busy chatting that they hadn't heard her. She moved closer to the group, bustled along with them. One of the girls turned to her.

'Yes, sweetheart, we get it. Doris.' She looked Doris up and down and turned to her friend and giggled, heading towards the lift together, squeezing Doris out of the group.

Doris stood still, watching them go. They looked over their shoulders and laughed as they waited for the lift.

'Hello there, new are you?'

Mr Timpson stood there with a delightful smile on his face. Doris nodded and the girls stopped giggling and paid attention.

'Mr Timpson, New Business Manager, pleased to make your acquaintance.'

'Doris Walsh,' she said, holding out her hand. The bell of the lift pinged and the girls got in, turned round to face out.

'Well, you'll make a lovely addition to the office,' said Mr Timpson loudly, patting her cheek and walking off.

Doris saw the outraged faces in the lift as the doors closed and she smiled at the stuck-up bitches. Mr Timpson turned and came back to her and, just as Minty was passing by, said, 'As it's your first day, I'd be glad to show you a nice place to lunch?'

'That'd be lovely, thank you,' said Doris, playing her part.

'Meet me here in twenty minutes?' he said, looking at his watch.

Minty raised her eyebrows at Doris and walked on by.

Mr Timpson took her out to a little Italian restaurant on Lime Street. He ordered cannelloni alle Parmigiana and a frothy coffee for them both. Doris thought the food tasted too rich and smelt of something strange and pungent, and she wondered what the purple-skinned things were but she did her best to eat some of it. After checking the restaurant several times, to make sure there was no one from work, he leant over the table and whispered. 'What on earth are you wearing?'

'What's wrong with it?' she said, looking down at herself.

'It looks like you made it yourself.'

Doris felt the prickle of tears in her eyes. 'I did,' she said. 'I did my best seeing as I didn't have a sewing machine.'

'I didn't realise I'd have to dress you as well,' he said, dabbing the corners of his mouth with a white cloth napkin. 'Give it a few days and I'll take you up town.'

Doris picked up her napkin and wanted to dab her mouth too but it was so clean and white, she couldn't bear to soil it. She could feel Mr Timpson's eyes on her and didn't want to disappoint him, so wiped the crisp cotton across her lips and looked at the smear of tomato sauce and remnants of Fred's heart-red lipstick and folded it away in her lap.

With a small jerk, Mr Timpson plastered a fake smile on his face and motioned with his eyes towards the front window. Stanley was out there on the pavement by a lamppost with his camera. Doris remembered why she was there and gave her dining partner a doting smile, reached across the table with her hand. He did the same, his smile dipping into a grimace and back again. They held hands, gave Stanley ample opportunity to take their photograph and then let go.

Back at the office the girls in the typing pool took a sudden interest in Doris. There was no talking allowed during work hours but at tea break, one of them, Letty, came over to her.

'That was fast work,' she said.

Doris looked at her with wide eyes, faking innocence.

'Where did you go for lunch?'

'What, with Mr Timpson?'

Letty nodded with a spiteful smile.

'Oh, a lovely Italian restaurant down the road. Really lovely it was,' said Doris, making a pretence of looking for something in her homemade green cloth bag.

'You'll not get anywhere there, he's married, you know.'

'I don't know what you mean, he was just being kind because I had no one to have lunch with.'

Letty sucked in her cheeks and then laughed. 'Well you'll

just have to come for lunch with us tomorrow, won't you? Where are you from anyway?'

She said it as though Doris had just landed from outer space.

'Tilbury.'

Letty shrugged as if to say she didn't know where that was and so it was of no importance to her.

True to her word, the following day Letty invited Doris to lunch with her and the other girls. They went to a coffee bar and sat on high chromium stools, they drank cappuccinos and ate little pastries and reapplied their Elizabeth Arden lipstick in their Max Factor compact mirrors. They talked about the Young Farmers' Club dances and the Tatler tea rooms, asked Doris which hunt meets she attended and how often she went to tennis club. Doris of course had nothing to contribute to the conversation and they soon grew bored with her. She listened in carefully though, when they talked about the men at the insurance company, learned how Letty had been working on a Mr Price for some time and expected some sort of return some time soon. How a Mr Smythe smacked Felicity's bottom at least twice a day and that this indicated a good chance of being taken out to dinner. They told Doris, again, that Mr Timpson was married and that she shouldn't waste her time with him.

She shrugged. 'I like him, as friends,' she said and they frowned and suggested she try her luck with one of the filing clerks from the basement.

Doris grew used to her commute to London over the first week, enjoyed walking along the busy streets with the other office workers. She left Laura with Lil at the boarding house.

When Doris got home, Laura would be cross with her for a little while and then would be clingy and annoying, telling Doris she didn't want her to go. But Doris had a job to do and she was enjoying herself.

On her third day, Mr Timpson asked Doris to lunch, loudly, so that the typing pool girls overheard. He took her to Harrods on the underground train and bought her a Terylene suit in pale peach, two blouses and a full-skirted dress. She put her bags in left luggage at Liverpool Street station so as not to arouse suspicion at the office and couldn't wait to get home to try them on.

The next day at tea break the girls crowded around Letty to read a magazine feature about men at the office.

'It says that you shouldn't get carried away when a nice man pays attention to you, it may make you feel grown up but he might only be thinking of you as a pretty thing to have around the office.'

The girls all pretended that this didn't apply to them and they looked at Doris with pity in their eyes.

'You see, Doris?' said Felicity. 'I wouldn't hold much stock in Mr Timpson taking a real interest in you.'

'I never said I did,' said Doris and Felicity kept quiet, looking with great interest at her hands in her lap.

'The married ones are the worst,' said another girl, Tiffany. She lowered her voice. 'Mr Brown is an office wolf, he's married but he flirts all the time and he told someone, I can't say who, when she threatened to leave, that her references would suffer if she gave notice.'

'You're talking about Serena, and she's still suffering. It's worse when you're the secretary to a wolf,' said Letty. 'Anyway, it says here that friendships with your female colleagues are very important and will make you more popular with men.'

Letty looked straight at Doris and raised her eyebrows. Doris wanted to laugh but didn't.

'That's an awfully nice suit, Doris. Where did you get it?'

'Harrods,' she said.

'Goodness me, it must have cost fifteen pounds.'

'Yes, about that much.'

The girls exchanged glances and went back to their work.

At the end of the first week, Mr Timpson suggested a picnic in the park after work. Stanley had told her two nights previously that he'd be coming up to town on the Friday and to let Mr Timpson know. Doris brought sandwiches and boiled eggs. Mr Timpson brought some gooey French cheese and a bottle of white wine. They sat in Finsbury Circus Gardens, on a lovely patch of grass near the immaculate bowling green. It was a perfect haven, the trees rustling in the May breeze, the late sunshine dappled through the maple trees. Doris spread the full skirt of her new dress out over her legs, curled up by her side.

'You do look lovely in that dress,' said Mr Timpson.

'Thank you.' Doris couldn't help but blush. Mr Timpson looked handsome in his tailored suit but she daren't say so. He had brought a smart picnic basket with glasses and plates. He opened the wine and held out a glass to her, poured one for himself and they clinked and sipped and Doris thought the whole thing was delightful. She was even starting to think the way the typing girls spoke. Delightful, super, extraordinary.

'The weather is really extraordinary lovely,' she said, sipping more wine and feeling it go to her head.

'Yes,' Mr Timpson laughed, 'it really is.'

Doris looked at his fine face, his sculpted cheekbones, the way his fringe fell forward when he took off his suit jacket.

'Delightful,' said Doris, 'really delightful.' She lay back on the grass and looked up at the sun sparkling through the trees, thought how much she was enjoying the act, even that it felt like more than just an act.

Mr Timpson leant over to her on one elbow, placed the back of his hand on her cheek, stroked it slowly and gently. Doris felt a jolt of electricity ping through her groin and gave a small gasp. She turned to him and smiled, looked around the park at other couples lounging there, in love, just enjoying one another's company.

He picked up her hand and kissed it. No one had ever kissed her hand before, it was such a gentlemanly thing to do. He moved in closer to her, leant down so that his face was an inch from hers and she could smell his cologne, a heavy musky scent. Doris froze in the moment, mesmerised, looked at his skin, his eyes. When he kissed Doris's mouth, she neither resisted nor kissed him back, but let his lips touch hers, softly, so gently. Pulling away slightly, he looked lovingly into her eyes, turned to glance at something and sat back up, smoothed down his trousers and broke off a piece of bread to eat. Doris sat up too, put her hand over his.

'It's all right,' he whispered, pulling his hand away. 'He's gone.'

Doris frowned and looked in the direction that Mr Timpson motioned. She just saw the back of Stanley's green tweed coat as he disappeared through the exit on the other side of the park.

'Jolly good, well done,' he said. 'You're very good at this. It's a strange business all right,' he said, laughing, 'a very strange business.'

Somehow Doris managed to stay composed. She turned away to look at the trunk of a nearby birch tree, focused on the white bark, how it had split, the deep gashes revealing the dark beneath. She kept her face in check, turned back to him and smiled.

'Extraordinary,' she said.

18

Doris

'You from Africa?' said Laura to Claude.

Doris was surprised to hear her say it – she must have picked up some new words in the boarding house when Doris was at work in London. It was Saturday, a day off. She was sitting on the kerb outside the boarding house eating a meat paste sandwich and Claude had wandered out to join them. Doris didn't want to have to make conversation with him but Laura, as usual, talked to anyone.

Claude regarded Laura for a moment while she waited for an answer.

'No, but my great-great-great-grandfather was born in Africa. I was born in Jamaica.'

Laura looked at him, chewing her sandwich.

'Look,' he said, picking up a chip of red brick from the gutter. He drew Africa and Jamaica on the pavement flagstones. 'It's all the way across the ocean. How come I was born in Jamaica and he born in Africa?' he said.

Laura shrugged and watched him intently.

'He was taken from Africa, he didn't want to go but they made him go, they bought he like an animal and took he to Jamaica. He was a slave then.'

Laura stopped chewing. 'What means slave?'

'It is when someone owns you, you are not free, you work for your owner your whole life for no money and they treat you bad, like you are not a real person, just a thing.'

Laura swallowed her bread and didn't take her eyes off Claude.

'You know who did it? Who took him from Africa?'

Laura shook her head.

'Your country.'

Laura's eyes widened, then she looked at Doris as if Laura herself was being blamed for the slave trade.

'Not me,' she said to Doris.

'No, not you,' said Claude, with a chuckle, crouching down. 'Your country a long, long time ago, and other countries too.' He drew Britain on his map and chalked the trade route. 'They did send boats to Africa to buy the people and took the people to Jamaica to work on the land and grow sugar, lots of sugar. They were paid in sugar, not money, for those slaves. They took the sugar all the way back to your country so the rich people could sweeten their tea – with slave sugar.'

Laura took another bite of her sandwich and looked at Claude's map, coming closer to him to see better.

'You know how many slaves there were in Jamaica all that time ago? A hundred and fifty years ago?'

'How many?' said Laura.

'Three hundred thousand slaves,' said Claude. Laura looked at Doris to see how much that was. 'That's a lot,' said Claude.

Laura scrunched up her face, trying to understand.

'Let's see,' said Claude, taking off his hat and putting it back on again. He took his chip of brick and drew ten tiny stick men on the pavement. 'You count, how many is that?'

Laura frowned, squatted down, pointed with her finger. 'One, two, three, seven, four.' She looked at Claude with bright eyes, happy with herself at being so clever.

'Together,' he said, counting to ten with her. 'So that is ten, let we do another ten, get that piece of brick.'

They drew another line of ten and another. 'We do them in rows so we know how many,' said Claude, hunching down with Laura.

Doris watched them, wanted to join in but didn't want to talk to this man, so strange and unfamiliar. She wondered how he knew so much. She had heard the punters in the pub say that the coloureds were stupid and slow, not as clever as the British.

Laura concentrated hard, crawling along the rough pavement on her knees, happy that someone was playing with her, giving her attention. After a while they had drawn many rows of stick men and she stopped and sat up.

'I'm tired, my arm hurts,' she said.

Claude sat up on his haunches. 'You know what the boss did do to the slaves when their arms did get tired?'

Laura shook her head. 'No, Caude.'

'They whip them. They weren't *allowed* to get tired.'

Laura's eyes opened really wide, and she looked like she'd cry. 'You gonna whip me, Caude?'

'Nah,' he laughed, 'I am not in the business of whipping slaves. Tell you what though, let us show those poor slaves how we feel about them, let us carry on with our tired arms so everyone knows how many souls whipped for England's sugar.'

Laura nodded and hunched down to start drawing stick men again. They both did, and as they drew, Doris heard Claude say, 'They are in heaven now and they are looking down with tears in they eyes, but you making them smile.'

Laura looked up to the sky and across at Claude and carried on drawing the stick men.

'We do it together,' said Claude.

Once they'd drawn the first ten rows of ten, Claude drew a line across and started on the next block. They worked their way down the pavement on their hands and knees. Children gathered at a distance to watch. Doris sat on the kerb and smoked, her new pastime, watching Laura and Claude, both concentrating hard, working side by side. For an hour they worked. Doris looked south – although she couldn't see The Empire pub from there – and thought about the slaves. She had been forced away from her family too.

Claude got up to go back down the pavement, counting his hundreds of stick figures. He helped Laura up and they looked at the long line of tiny stick people.

'We done it! We done it!' Laura did a little lop-sided jig and laughed. Claude stood there, wiped his hand across his face and gave Laura a weak smile.

'A lot, isn't it, Blaze?' The figures stretched out a long way down the pavement. 'But you know what? That is only ten thousand. The real number is three hundred times that much.' Laura looked at him and frowned. 'That is right to the end of this road, and all along down the other side, and up and down the next two streets,' Claude explained. Laura's jaw dropped in amazement.

'You know, when Christopher Columbus found Jamaica, he said it was *the fairest island that eyes have beheld; mountainous and the land seems to touch the sky.* We got to think about it – we got to remember them, right?'

Laura looked up at him, all serious now.

'Yes, Caude, I will, I've got a good remembery.'

Laura wandered off to play, leaving Doris there alone with Claude.

'She's a good girl,' he said.

Doris looked at him and shrugged. 'She's a pain in the arse.'

Claude's eyebrows raised. 'Must be hard looking after her by yourself.'

Doris squinted at him, wondered who he'd been talking to about her. 'My own dad went to war when I was her age, my mother coped.'

'You don't live with your family?'

Doris gave a cynical laugh. 'I lost that right when I had her.'

'They kicked you out?' Claude frowned.

Doris shrugged. 'Looks like it.'

'We don't worry about such things at home. Anyway, what about old Henry the Eighth? He had at least six children out of wedlock.' He chuckled, 'So you are the black sheep of the family?'

Doris swung her head to look at him teasing her.

'And she is your black lamb?'

She couldn't help but smile. 'You could say that.'

One of the street residents came walking along the pavement, looking down at the chalk drawings. She was taken by surprise to see Doris and Claude there on the kerb. The moment she saw them she crossed the street.

'Is that for you or for me?' said Claude.

'For me, probably. Respectable housewives don't mix with bad lots like me.'

'So that is why you live here?'

'I grew up in The Empire pub, just down there by the river.'

'The Empire? The pub with that sign in the window?'

'That's the one. They might as well add bastard children to that sign. She's the reason I'm not allowed back.'

'She did not ask to be born.'

'No, and I didn't ask for a baby.'

At that moment Laura came hobbling down the road, crying.

When Doris didn't say anything to her, Claude asked, 'What is wrong, Blaze?'

'They don't let me play.' She swung her arm behind her, indicating the group of children playing further down the road.

'Why not, you too clever for them?'

Laura wiped her nose on her arm. 'Cripple,' she said. 'Mongrel.'

Claude frowned and looked at Doris who just sighed and shook her head.

'You know they don't play with you so why do you bother going down there?'

Laura let out one sob and shrugged her shoulders.

'I think I better count your ribs,' said Claude, with a serious face. 'Just make sure you in one piece.'

He beckoned Laura to him and she went, frowning.

'What means ribs?'

'Come,' said Claude, and patted his lap. Laura looked across at Doris first and then climbed up on to Claude's lap. 'I just need to count your ribs,' he said, running his thumb along her side. She jerked wildly as he tickled her, squirming and shrieking with glee. 'One, two, three, four ... oh no, you only got four ribs that side, you a cripple mongrel!'

Laura screamed, then stayed still, waiting for more. Claude pressed his fingers along her other side, grinning at her deep belly laugh, which Doris had never heard before, until she cried out for him to stop.

'You got enough ribs, you not a cripple mongrel.'

'Caude, you funny,' she said, staying on his lap, leaning into his chest.

Claude laughed. 'You know what I do when I am sad, and sometimes when I am happy too?' Laura shook her head. 'I look at the sky.' Laura looked up and back at Claude's face. 'I look up at the sky and I think to myself, what do I want to be? That way, I don't see all the other people around me, I do not think I am not as good as them, or I am better than them, I just look up and it is only me and the sky and I can be what I want.'

Laura looked up at the sky and so did Doris. The clouds moved in wisps across the matt blue canvas.

'Why you called Laura?' said Claude, and Laura looked at him blankly.

'It's after Laura Knight, the artist,' said Doris.

'Oh? You like art? You draw?'

'Used to.' Doris looked away. It felt like a hundred years ago that she'd sat in the pub window and drawn the people in the street.

'Not any more?'

'Nope.'

'You should. I would like to see your work.'

Doris felt herself blush. She had forgotten how to draw, she had forgotten what it felt like to *want* to draw, that part of her was dead. The thought made her want to cry. She had become so good at burying everything down in the dark. Looking at the damn sky wouldn't do *her* any good.

'So what you doing here, then?' Doris didn't want to talk about herself.

Claude laughed. 'To live the high life, of course. To see Buckingham Palace and Trafalgar Square, and so I can write and make something of my writing,' he added. 'In Jamaica they say the streets of London are paved with gold.'

Doris scoffed. 'No they're not.' She knew, she had seen the streets of Leadenhall and they were paved with flagstones and the heavy tread of workers' feet.

Claude nudged her with his elbow and smiled. 'I know, I just teasing.' He picked up a twig and drew lines in the dirt road. 'It have no opportunity in Jamaica, and I was brought up British so it make sense that I come here to improve my life and my prospects, no?' Doris gave no answer. 'My father fought and died for the British Empire, my passport is British. But the British have not been kind to Jamaica. They tired of us now and my old Uncle Norton says if the hurricanes do not flatten the Jamaican economy, the British Empire will finish it off.'

'Yeah, but there's nothing here for you.'

'No?' Claude seemed taken aback at her abruptness. 'I have to find that out for myself. That is how it is.'

He drew the union flag in the dirt.

'It was Empire day on Tuesday. Don't you have a parade here?'

'Don't think so,' she said. 'My mum puts union flag bunting up on the pub on Empire day, that's all I know about it. Uncle Archie used to talk about the good old days when Britain was great.'

'I sometimes went to Kingston for the Empire day parade. In Jamaica it is a big deal. I got there early so I was close enough to see the platform draped in union flags at the statue of Queen Victoria. Later the crowds stand twenty deep back from the pavement. The roofs and balconies of the grand colonnaded buildings would be strung together with bunting. The policemen in their white helmets would stand guard rod-straight along the street and the school children would come marching along, saluting to the Governor on the platform as they went past. I would wave my union flags and wait for the band to start up the National Anthem and I would sing it with all my heart and soul.'

Doris tried to imagine him doing that in Jamaica. One of the women came out of her house a little way down the road. The group of children were telling her something. She came to see the pavement, covered in stick people, and she looked at Claude and Doris sitting there on the kerb. She went back into her house and came out with a large tin bucket, stood with her legs astride on the pavement and sloshed the water down to wash the drawings away. She went back in, came out with her broom and started to scrub at the path with all her might.

Claude stood up, made the sign of the cross with his forefinger and kissed it. Laura copied him, and watched him go back inside the boarding house.

19

Vi

Ever since Doris had come back to Tilbury, Vi went to church on Sundays. Going to church, and being seen to go to church, put a safe wedge between her and her daughter's behaviour. She was siding with decency and it was important to Vi that everyone knew it. She enjoyed being reminded about what was right and what was wrong by the vicar at St John the Baptist – it gave her a sense of righteousness, and confirmed to her she was doing the right thing.

On the way back she'd make sure to walk slowly down the roads of Tilbury, from the church on Dock Road, over the hairpin bridge and down St Andrew's Road, along Fort Road to The Empire pub on the river. She'd walk with her gloved hands clasped together, her eyes lowered respectfully to the ground, contemplating the sermon she had just heard. The residents of Tilbury would see her walk by, and she imagined that those who hadn't attended church would wonder why a respectable woman like Vi was down on her luck, would admire her for making steady her virtues and carrying on like a good woman should.

On that late May Sunday Vi shook hands with Reverend May as usual, said thank you and goodbye and made her way home. As she walked down Dock Road, she passed the junction with Ship Street, and naturally averted her gaze. It was the seedy part of town, where the merchant sailors and the gamblers went. Half of the street had given way to sin and debauchery and there was nowhere else like it in Tilbury. Vi felt for the decent residents at the far end of the street and wondered how they coped with the noise and the wickedness. It wasn't the hearty and wholesome recreation enjoyed at her pub, that much she knew.

She allowed herself a glance when the sound of a football caught her attention. In the few seconds it took to quicken her step and move on, she saw her own Doris sitting there on the kerb at the bad end of the street. There was a coloured man in shirt sleeves hopping around in the road playing football with a little girl. It was Doris's daughter, Vi could tell from the blonde curls and the limp. The coloured man was calling and laughing and Vi caught the glimpse of a smile on Doris's face as she watched them play.

Horrified, Vi trotted home. It was worse than she could have imagined. Doris was so desperate for a father for the child that she would even consort with black men. And what was she doing in that area, was she earning her keep in some unimaginable way? And out in the street like that on a Sunday too, without a care for decent behaviour.

'She's hanging around on Ship Street of all places,' she said to Archie upstairs in the pub flat. 'And letting that child play football in the street on a Sunday.'

'What do you expect from a tart and a mongrel like that?' said Archie, sitting at the kitchen table reading a paper.

His words cut Vi, inside where it didn't show. He wasn't Doris's father, he should show some respect for her as Doris's mother. But she knew he was right.

'I've got some beef dripping,' she said brightly, tying on her apron. 'I'll make you some on toast before we open up. That'll be a nice treat.'

She squeezed past him, letting her backside press against his arm. He glanced at the door for Win and put out a hand behind him to catch her leg. She let herself be caught, let him slide his hand up inside her dress, let his fingers work their way around her knickers and touch between her legs.

Win came into the kitchen reading a letter. Archie turned the page of his paper and let his arm fall and Vi bounced into a step as though she hadn't broken her stride. Win paused for a second, then sat down at the table with Archie. Sneaking a look behind her, Vi's stomach fluttered when she saw Archie suck his finger as though he'd been eating buttered toast.

'She's only hanging around Ship Street with that child playing football in the road on a Sunday,' Vi said to Win.

'So that's where she's got to, is it?' mumbled Win, sitting down next to Archie. 'A letter came from Jim in the last post yesterday,' she told Vi, her eyes lighting up.

'That's nice,' said Vi.

Archie leant in close to his wife, their heads together,

reading about their son. He had gone to sea to work as a porter on the P&O cruise liners. They would read the letter over and again with each other, they always did.

'He's in Brisbane.' Win smiled over at Vi. 'Touring around, imagine.'

'The City in the Sun,' Archie read. 'Sub-tropical, swimming pools, raceway, seafood. Sounds all right, doesn't it? Ask him when he's coming home when you write back.'

Vi forced a smile. She would have given anything to sit at the kitchen table with her Cyril.

Downstairs, Vi pulled the towels off the pumps as Archie unbolted the pub doors.

'Having a lie-in, were you?' said Jack, still with his muddy wellies on from the field.

'All right, it's only a minute past, keep your hair on,' said Archie.

There were six men waiting for the doors to open. Vi smiled. They couldn't wait to get away from their wives to their pint and bar stool.

'How's yourself, Vi, love?'

'Can't complain, Harry my darling, I honestly cannot complain.'

'That's a girl,' he said.

Vi didn't need to ask him what he wanted, she knew all her regulars' orders by heart. She pulled Harry's pint of mild and he gave her the right money.

'What's happening in the world, Harry?' Vi nodded towards his *News of the World*.

Harry tutted and shook his head. 'The blue cards are giving the white cards aggro in the dock strike, love. We came out on the green for a talk from the union boss – he stood on the bonnet of his car. A few of ours have come out but they're sending some of the London ships here so I don't know what we'll do.'

'Well I hope you get what you want. You men work hard enough, Harry,' said Vi.

'Hear, hear,' said Jack. 'But the rail workers might go out on strike next week as well,' he said, reading his own paper. 'That'll muck up the pigeon racing. And the miners striking already. What's the country coming to?' Jack took a long swig of the pint that Vi handed him and smacked his lips.

'Robots set to take over the world, love,' said Harry, turning his page.

'You won't see a combine harvester on my farm, I tell you that,' said Jack.

'Jack, the day you get a combine harvester is the day I get a robot to wash my step,' laughed Vi.

'The trial for that Ruth Ellis has been postponed.'

'Let's see,' said Vi, pulling Harry's paper round. She pushed it back again. 'Wonder when it'll be,' she said.

'She'll hang, I bet you.'

'Well, you make your bed, you lie in it,' said Vi.

She picked up her magazine, flicked through, looked at the new Gipsy Queen heeled shoe with a leather bow on the front. Archie didn't like her spending money on new shoes. She made hers last with Blakey's and polish. A condiment to please men. She might try and get some for Archie. Electric washing machine for thirty guineas. Archie didn't spend on the flat. He didn't mind keeping the pub nice though and to Vi that was the main thing, to stay true to Cyril's spirit and keep the place well. Vi turned the page. Someone moaning that her husband didn't give her enough money, that women couldn't sign HP agreements or get mortgages themselves. At least she had a husband. Nice pattern for a bed jacket that Archie might like to see her in. A seven-day beauty plan. Vi turned the corner of the page to go back and read that one in detail. How to keep that schoolgirl complexion, how to make Savoury Sailing Boats with luncheon meat and salad cream, how to keep him happy, how to stay lovely, how not to try to be the boss.

Vi read with interest the advice for women. They should behave correctly, standing back to let their husbands conduct the business. Women should be happy enough to be married and provided for, men didn't want a silly woman trying to control things. With a surge of satisfaction, Vi nodded as she read the articles that confirmed everything she stood for. She wasn't married to Archie, but he was the head of the household now and Vi shouldn't try to be the boss even if The Empire was her pub. She should defer to him, and that is exactly what she had been doing.

Reading the magazine was like lifting a weight from her mind. She was doing the right thing and she would carry on doing her bit to keep Archie happy. Vi and Win needed him there at the pub; they wouldn't get a licence without a man. Vi was sure Win knew the arrangement – that Vi was helping to keep him sweet.

Vi made up her mind to make a special meal for Archie. She had a nice bit of liver upstairs in the larder. Yes, it would be a sight easier if they had a fridge to store food in. She looked at the advertisement page for the 'English Rose' kitchen — a perfectly groomed woman in her best dress and apron, taking out her individual trifles in little glass dishes from the fridge and placing them on her hostess trolley. She and Win took it in turns to go shopping every day. Standing in the queues for up to an hour in the various shops on the high street. But if Archie didn't think it right for them to spend money on a fridge, then so be it. Having him there gave her a feeling of safety, security. That was worth more to her than a fridge any day of the week.

20

Doris

'Get a bag packed, you need to go up to town right now.'

Stanley had called Doris down from her room in the boarding house.

'What? Why?'

'Rail strike, all kicking off tonight, you need to get up to town and stay at Mr Timpson's until the trains are back on.'

'Does he know?'

'You'll have to tell him when you get there, I can't risk sending a telegram.'

Doris gawped at Stanley. Mr Timpson wouldn't be too happy with her turning up on his doorstep.

'He's not gonna be too happy about that.'

'Well, we can't have a break from this now, we've got to keep it going, and it'll only help his case if you're living with him.' Stanley snatched a drag of his cigarette. 'Come on then, get a move on,' he said, making a wheel motion with his hands.

Doris turned to climb back up the stairs.

'I haven't got a nice bag to pack my stuff in.'

Stanley turned to Lil, there at the front desk. 'Lil, you got a nice overnight bag?'

'And what about Laura?' said Doris.

'Lil, you'll look after the kid, won't you?'

'Suppose I'll have to, won't I?' said Lil, pushing past Doris on the stairs to go and find a bag.

'Hurry up, there's a train at five o'clock and that'll be the last one,' Stanley called out to her.

Doris stuffed her things into the leather tote bag that Lil found for her.

'You'll stay with Lil, I've got to go away for a bit,' she said to Laura, who sat on the bed throwing her doll up into the air.

'You going 'way?' said Laura, letting the doll drop to the floor.

'I've got to, it's my job.'

Laura's lip curled. 'I want you stay here.'

Doris tutted. 'Well I can't, so just shut up about it. You'll be all right with Lil.'

Grabbing her bag and coat, Doris rushed from the room, leaving Laura there on the bed. She had to run for the train; she didn't have time to pander to the kid's tears.

She made it on to the train and studied the note that Stanley had given her with the address and directions. At Liverpool Street, get on the underground, take the Circle or Metropolitan line to Great Portland Street, walk five minutes along the Marylebone Road to Park Crescent and it's number twenty-two Park Crescent, flat number eighty-nine.

Doris sat back in her seat, looked at the cigarette butts and old train tickets on the floor. She was going to stay in London. The thought both terrified and excited her. She wondered if she would be able to find his flat. Her main concern, though, was Mr Timpson and what he would say when she knocked on his door.

At Liverpool Street she managed to get on the right tube train, and she got off at Great Portland Street. A station attendant helped point her in the right direction down the Marylebone Road and when she came to Park Crescent, she checked the street sign against her note several times before she could believe her eyes. She realised now why it was called a crescent, bending in a graceful arc, enclosing a posh garden area. It looked like a concave wedding cake, smooth and pale with tall double columns right along and a sweeping balcony that sat on top of the columns. There were hundreds of windows. Among the several cars parked along the road, she could see four Rolls-Royces from where she was standing, recognising the flying metal woman on the front from a magazine. She hardly dared to walk along with her note and her bag. If anyone had challenged her at that point she would have gladly run a mile.

Taking tentative steps, she crept along to the door that said twenty-two. It was black and had smart-looking shrubs in pots on either side. She knocked and waited. If it was a flat, she supposed she'd need to go through this door first and then look for the right number. She pushed and it opened. There sat a man in a uniform behind a desk. He looked at her with raised eyebrows and she wished she hadn't knocked first.

'Hello, I need flat number eighty-nine, please?'

'Who are you here to see, miss?'

'Mr Timpson. He knows I'm coming,' she added quickly.

'He's out, miss.'

'Oh, all right, thank you.' Doris gave him an embarrassed smile and went back out the front door. She stood there on the pavement, not knowing what to do, and finally decided it would be best to wait on the other side of the road and watch for him to come.

Two hours later and her legs ached from standing against the railing of the private gardens. Mr Timpson came walking along the path on the other side, looking down at the floor, his hands in his pockets, a little smile on his lips. When Doris crossed the road to him and he saw her there he quickened his pace, looked around, grabbed her by her arm and pulled her up short.

'What on earth are you doing here?' he hissed.

'Where have you been? I've been waiting ages. I'm starving and I need the lav.'

He muttered something under his breath. He held the front door open for her, nodded at the reception man and led her to the lift. The lift porter didn't need to ask them which floor was his. Mr Timpson couldn't wait to rush her down the corridor and he dropped his keys in his haste to open his flat door.

'The facilities are through there.' He waved towards a door.

Doris was impressed with the indoor toilet and plumbed-in bath, it was really fancy.

'It's smaller than I thought,' she said when she came back out.

'It's just a studio. I'm awfully sorry, but would you tell me why you're here?'

Doris took out the letter that Stanley had given her, passed it to Mr Timpson. He opened and read it, his face creasing with disbelief.

'What? You can't *stay* here.'

Doris shrugged. 'I have to, Stanley said. There's a rail strike and we need to keep things going and if I live with you it'll look good.'

Mr Timpson went rigid, ran his hands over his head, looked at the ceiling.

'Aargh,' he said. 'Aargh, this is damned bloody inconvenient.'

He took it quite well, he didn't hit Doris or throw her out. She looked around the room. There was a settee, a chair and a bed on the opposite wall. She peeped into another door to see a tiny kitchen, a lovely kitchen with all kinds of things.

'I can cook,' she said. 'I'll cook us some tea if you like. What have you got in?'

Mr Timpson sat down heavily on the chair. 'I've already eaten, I've been out to dinner.'

Doris was starving.

'All right, is there a chippy or anything near here?'

'A what?'

'Chippy. Chip shop?'

'For food? No, I'm not sure. There's some bread and cheese in the kitchen.' He got up, and Doris followed him into the kitchen. 'I'm sorry,' he said. 'It's just that it's something of a shock. Would you like some tea?'

'Yes, please,' said Doris. 'But you go and sit down, I'll make it. I'll find my way around if that's all right?'

'Yes, yes of course, thank you.' He sighed and went to sit down. She heard him light a cigarette and blow out the smoke with great force as though he was trying to blow her out of his flat. She looked at the cooker for a minute, turned one of the dials and saw one of the hob rings light up orange, put her hand above it and felt the heat. She smiled and put the kettle on.

When she brought the tea through, and some bread and cheese for herself, Mr Timpson was on the settee with his feet up. He swung them down to the floor and sat up for his tea. Doris sat on the chair and started to eat, looking at him and at the room.

'What's in there?' she said, pointing to a wooden cabinet.

'Television set.'

'Blimey.'

'Look, I think this is a case of making the best out of a bad situation. We're both adults, we can work together on this thing in a courteous way, don't you think?'

Doris nodded, her mouth full. She chewed quicker and gulped, Vi's words in her ear. *Never speak with your mouth full, it's rude.*

'Yes, course we can. It's nice here, I like it.'

'I expect the train strike will be over soon. It's just damned selfishness. They get one wage increase only to demand another, holding the country to ransom. It affects inflation, increases the cost of living ultimately. Look at me, living in a studio flat.' Doris looked and he continued as if talking to himself. 'Yes, we have the country house but we can't afford much help these days. It's a struggle . . .'

Doris nodded, wide-eyed, chewed on her bread. 'I like

your kitchen, the fridge and cooker are lovely. And your indoor lav.'

Mr Timpson looked at her and blinked. 'Thank you.'

He considered the room. 'I'm not sure about sleeping arrangements. It's all rather awkward, isn't it?'

'No bedroom then?'

'No, it's a studio flat, everything in one room. I was using it just for work initially, until . . .' He paused. 'I suppose I will sleep on the settee and you'll take the bed. It's all rather awkward but we'll just have to make do.'

At bedtime, Doris changed in the bathroom and slipped into bed. She could tell Mr Timpson was pretending to be asleep on the sofa from the sound of his breathing. She smiled to herself, sleeping in a posh flat in London. What would Vi say if she could see her now? Vi would love the fridge and cooker, and Win would love the television set. Doris hugged herself. Things were on the up, she was a typist and she lived in London. She wished she could tell Claude about it and it surprised her to realise that she missed him, wanted to share her thoughts with him.

In the morning, Doris felt funny with Mr Timpson seeing her in her nightdress and he said good morning to the carpet. He said it was best if he left for work before her, and told her which train to take.

When she arrived at the office, she took her folder of work as usual and went to her desk, took the cover off her type-writer and began tapping away. Within half an hour there was a strange atmosphere in the place. People were whispering, the other girls were looking around to see what was going on. A woman cried out somewhere in the offices and everyone stopped working to see. Sally, Mr Timpson's secretary, ran past crying. Letty followed her to the toilet and came back with an ashen face saying that Sally had been fired.

'For tardiness,' she whispered. 'She was late back from lunch by ten minutes last week and they've fired her for it, said she's a poor timekeeper and they won't stand for it.'

The other girls gasped and one of them sobbed into her handkerchief. Minty came into the typing pool to speak to the supervisor, who called Doris.

'Doris, you're wanted.'

Minty walked her along the corridor, and spoke in a sharp whisper. 'I don't know how you've wangled this, Doris, but Mr Timpson wants you as his secretary.'

Doris's stomach turned over. She said nothing to Minty but let herself be walked to her new desk, outside Mr Timpson's office. She sat down in a daze.

'Go and get your things and bring them here.' Minty leant down to say quietly, 'Honestly, Doris. Poor Sally, that's all I can say.' She leant down closer. 'You do know he's married, don't you?'

21

Doris

Clutching a parcel of socks and garters wrapped in brown paper from the swanky Austin Reed shop on Fenchurch Street, Doris walked confidently through the office. She bought Mr Timpson's intimate items for him now and she liked everyone to know it. She made his tea, sometimes coffee, and would also place a biscuit on his saucer. The girls in the typing pool eyed her through spiteful slits as she walked by. They hated her but she didn't care. They didn't know the half of it.

Taking a seat at her desk, she rolled a sheet of paper into her typewriter ready to touch-type a letter that Mr Timpson had dictated to her earlier – when it was just her and him in his office, when she collected his dirty cup and saucer and enquired whether he'd be needing her for anything else. They were going out that night. To the theatre to see something called *Salad Days*. Doris would wear the new dress Mr

Timpson had bought for her. The fact that Stanley had got word to them that he'd be around that day taking photos didn't really come into it. Doris knew they would enjoy their evening out together regardless. She imagined her arm through his as they walked along, perhaps she would rest her cheek against his shoulder for a moment to show him how she felt. He would put his hand over hers, grip it for a second, in a silent and private gesture of affection.

Before typing the letter, Doris wanted to pop in to let him know she'd found the socks he'd asked for. Brown silk. She'd say it casually, as if nothing would be too much trouble, he could rely on her, his right-hand girl. His door was half open and she heard him talking quietly on the telephone. She waited for him to finish, overhearing his conversation without really meaning to. In any case, they were very close these days.

'So coarse,' he said, his deep voice audible even when quiet. 'I mean, we can talk more when we see each other, but suffice to say ... charwoman type ... un-housetrained ... you know, biscuit on the saucer with the tea cup type-thing, it's terribly awkward. Anyway, I'm looking forward ... yes ... like a fish woman in a Harrods' suit ... ha ha, I know ... anyway ... until then.'

Doris stiffened, put her hand on to the desk to steady herself. It took all her effort to walk to the ladies' lavatory without crying. When she got there and closed the cubicle door she couldn't get any tears out. They were so mixed up with anger and shame and a half understanding of what was happening that they stayed under the surface, making her face feel bloated and red. She spat out a breath of bitter laughter and sucked it back in. In a flash she realised how foolish she had been, how impossibly idiotic it was to think that Mr Timpson would consider someone like her worthy of his friendship or anything else equal to him.

She concentrated on breathing. In through the nose and out through the mouth. *Composure was a sign of class*, that's what Vi used to tell her. Don't show your feelings, that was very important. If you wore your heart on your sleeve, if you were wet, you were *weak and vulnerable*. In a few minutes Doris came to her senses. She splashed cold water over her face at the sink, took out her compact from her bag and powdered the red blotches around her eyes and nose. A touch of Yardley's Calypso Pink lipstick and she stood tall and walked back out there to her desk, picked up the parcel of socks, tapped on Mr Timpson's door. She was there to do a job. She placed the parcel down on his desk with a slight nod of her head, her eyes closed for a second to indicate that he needn't say anything, and she went back to type his letter.

The evening went along. They moseyed down the Strand and she threaded her arm through his and leant her cheek against his shoulder to give Stanley the opportunities he needed to take photographs. The stylish London set were out, the girls in their full skirts and jive shoes, Teddy boys, men in black high-neck jumpers and tight trousers talking intently to their friends and snatching cigarettes from their mouths. One of those types stopped to talk to Mr Timpson, who looked very shifty about being seen with her. The man in black grinned at Mr Timpson, furrowed his brow in question, touched Mr Timpson's arm. Mr Timpson said they were in a hurry and got them away quick. It brought back the memory of what Stanley had said about him being a poofter.

Perhaps he was right. Perhaps that explained why he didn't like Doris. She looked at him sideways as they walked along. No, that wasn't why, it wasn't the only reason anyway. What had he said? *Coarse, un-housetrained.* Doris smiled wryly to herself. All the trouble Vi had gone to over the years to train Doris up to be respectable and decent and it still didn't wash with the likes of Mr Timpson, she was still a fish woman in a Harrods' suit to him.

In the Vaudeville theatre she looked around at the red velvet furnishings and gilt mouldings – she liked to think it was a fancy version of The Empire pub, not this place filled with rich people who could afford to pay to watch a boy and girl with BBC voices prancing around the stage to a magic piano. Mr Timpson grinned like a goon and tapped his thigh with the palm of his hand when the actors sang the gushing songs. He'd told her on the way to the theatre that salad days meant when you're young and carefree, inexperienced but having adventures. Doris was young but none of the other things. Watching the actors dance around made her sick to her stomach. Real life wasn't like that. Whoever wrote that play was a fool.

She smiled when he looked at her, nodded her head to the music and blinked back the sting of tears. It was just a job, not real life. It wouldn't be her real life in a million years. It was like she was being shown what she couldn't have. Like a waiter at a nice restaurant was making a big show of presenting a silver platter to her, then whipping it away before she could get her hands on it.

She thought of Laura back in Tilbury, and her stomach turned over. It was so easy to forget about her, to pretend she didn't exist. But it was like pretending the sky didn't exist. And then she thought about Claude and she wished she was with him. He was kind and he liked her, even though he knew what kind of life she really lived. He didn't care about that. He told her to draw, encouraged her, even though she couldn't find it in herself any more. She stole a glance at Mr Timpson. What would he say if he knew she was an artist, or used to be, or used to want to be? He'd probably approve of that. They liked all that, the posh lot. Her head, nodding to the music, instead nodded with the weight of the tears she was holding in. She hadn't been able to draw for three years. It was a part of her that was lying dead. She wanted to see Claude. She didn't really even know why. There was just a feeling that made her want to be near him. She had a few days left in London and then she'd be back in Tilbury. She was suddenly glad about that.

'They've reached a settlement!'

At work the next morning, Mr Timpson rushed out of his office as Doris arrived at her desk. Before she could take off her coat he was showing her the front page of his paper, trying to keep his voice down.

'The rail strike is over – the greedy blighters will get what they want – by six o'clock tonight most services will be running normally – you can go home.'

Doris glanced at his paper. 'That's good, then.'

'I'll say,' he said, going back into his office.

It was hard to be happy when he clearly didn't want her around, even though she wanted to go back home by then. She only had three more days left in the office anyway, and that would be her month up. She wouldn't be missed. No one in the office liked her – she didn't fit in with the classy husband-hunting girls who knew how to dress and how to speak. Minty liked her maybe a little.

Mr Timpson opened his door. 'Doris, a moment.'

Doris grabbed her notepad and pen and went through.

'I've been thinking, Doris. There's no need to do Thursday and Friday as well. Now the trains are running, why don't you make this your last day? We could make some sort of scene, that way it would look more realistic, rather than doing a complete month.'

Doris looked at him sullenly and shrugged. 'If you like.'

'Yes, I think it's best. You'll still be paid for the whole week, you can tell Stanley that. Look here, let's make a scene later. What'll it be? Let's keep it in line with Sally's dismissal. Why don't you take an overly long lunch break, then I'll lose my temper and tell you to leave. How about it?'

Doris hadn't seen him look so excited before. She shrugged again. 'All right.'

'When we have the row, you go back to the flat, gather your things, and you can be on the train this evening back to Tilbury. What do you say? You're as eager to get back home as I am to have my flat back I'll be bound?'

'Yeah.'

At lunchtime, Doris wandered around the city streets, finding herself down by the Embankment, the Thames the same colour as it was in Tilbury, greeny-grey. She could jump in and float her way back home. She felt she'd always drift back there no matter where she went. Strolling around, killing time, she peered into shop windows, got up the courage to go into a swish coffee bar by herself, pretended she liked the strong cappuccino, pretended she felt she belonged there with the coffee bar set. The fish woman in a Harrods' suit. Making sure she'd stayed out for two hours, she went back to the office and Mr Timpson came straight out of his door as soon as she came to her desk. He was flushed, self-conscious, he'd been planning the moment but was unsure now it had arrived.

'What the devil are you up to? You've been gone two hours, this is outrageous.'

He made sure his voice was good and loud so everyone in the office would hear. Doris played her part, stammered that she was sorry, that she had lost track of time. Minty appeared at her side.

'What's wrong?' she asked.

'I'm sick of the tardiness in this establishment, it simply will not do,' said Mr Timpson, wiping the flecks of spit off his chin. Minty frowned, as though she thought he was over-reacting.

'Doris? What happened?'

'I lost track of time, Minty, I'm sorry.'

'Mr Timpson, look, I'm sure we can talk about this in your office,' said Minty, taking Doris's arm and steering her forward.

'We most certainly cannot,' he said. 'Gather your things. You'll have no reference either from me. Minty, you shall not challenge my authority on this. Find me another secretary. This time, one who knows how to keep time.'

Mr Timpson turned on his heel into his office and shut the door.

Minty frowned again, looked at Doris. 'Doris, I'm terribly sorry, Mr Timpson is clearly very particular about timekeeping. You'd better collect your things. I'll arrange your pay for the week.'

'It's all right,' sniffed Doris, dabbing her eyes with her handkerchief. 'I knew he'd had enough of me, he's an awful cad, you know.' She spoke Minty's language and slipped Minty a meaningful look.

'Oh my dear,' said Minty softly, placing her hand over Doris's. 'Bloody men.'

Doris made her way back to the Park Crescent flat, collected her things and waited to say goodbye to Mr Timpson. At six o'clock she realised he wasn't going to come home; he'd stay out to make sure she had gone.

It was a relief to be on the train home to Tilbury. London had been a strain. An adventure, but a strain pretending to be someone she wasn't. She'd had a glimpse of other people's lives but it was a way of life not open to her. She plodded to Ship Street from the station, wondering how she could slip back into her old life when she had been living so differently – a secretary staying in a posh London flat. If Vi could have seen her, well. As she came onto the street she saw the girls hanging around outside the boarding house as usual. They waved to her, asked how she was and she smiled at them, glad to be home to familiar faces. Lil on the front desk had no smile for her.

'You're back at last, then. You can take care of your kid now, can't you?'

'Where is she? Thanks for looking after her.'

'She's up in the room. She looks after herself most of the time.'

Doris put a foot on the stairs and happened to glance down the hall to the back room, the betting shop. Claude was there and he saw her at the same time she saw him. Doris's stomach turned over, and she put her hand up to her hair. Claude stopped listening to the man talking at his ear and took a step towards her. His face lit up, then his smile dropped as though he wasn't sure. He looked at her face and he picked his smile back up again and walked towards her.

'Hello,' he said. 'It has been a while, how are you doing?'

'All right, thanks. It's good to be back.' His shirt was open at the collar and she had a strange urge to touch his neck.

'Yes, it is good. Can I take that for you?' He took her bag and went to move past her to take it upstairs. There was an awkward moment when he couldn't get past without brushing her and they both grinned and looked at the floor. She followed him up.

'What have you been up to, then?'

'Me?' he said. 'Doing a work for Stanley.' His posture shifted, his head lowered and he seemed to walk more heavily up the stairs.

'Oh yeah? What kind?'

Claude laughed through his nose, not a happy laugh but one that showed embarrassment and bitterness. 'Well, Doris, it looks like I'm in your line of work now.'

'What?'

'Stanley is amused by it all. Says I am a sure case-winner for his lady clients, the divorce clients. You know, the courts would always grant a divorce to a man whose wife had been with a black man.'

Doris frowned. 'What, you've been on a job like mine, pretending to be someone's fella?'

'That is right.' He didn't look at her, just put her bag down and tapped at the door. 'She has missed you like mad,' he said.

Laura came to the door, opened it a crack and peered out with scared eyes. When she saw Doris she started to cry, started to really sob there behind the door.

'What's happened?' said Doris.

'She missed you,' said Claude.

Doris pushed the door open and Laura crept in behind it.

'Come out then,' said Doris. Laura stayed where she was, sobbing quietly. Doris shrugged her shoulders at Claude.

'Ah, Doris.' It was Stanley, coming up the stairs. 'You're back. The trains are back on, you going up there tomorrow then?'

'No, Mr Timpson said I should finish the London job today, that there's no need to do Thursday and Friday but he'd pay me anyway. He fixed to sack me today, so it's all over.'

Stanley nodded, twiddled his hair as he listened. 'Righteo, but it's not all over yet. You're doing the Brighton quickie this weekend, didn't he say?'

'What?'

'I told you before, it's the bit where you have to be caught in the hotel with him for the last piece of evidence, to hold it up in a court of law.'

'That's this weekend?'

Stanley turned to leave, called out to her as he went back down the stairs.

'Get ready for it, you'll be going down to Brighton on Friday night.' He grinned. 'Ask your pal Claude for some tips. He's a pro now, aren't you, Claude?' Stanley laughed.

'Doris, you doing the Brighton quickie?' Claude said it to her quietly, his eyes looking worried.

'Yeah, I suppose, if it's part of the job, I'll have to.'

'Look, Doris,' said Claude, holding her arm. 'I don't want you to do it.'

Laura came out from behind the door.

'Where you been, Mumma?' she said.

Doris tutted and frowned down at her. 'I've been doing a job, I told you that.'

'You not going away again?'

'For god's sake, I have to work, all right?'

Laura started crying again and disappeared into the darkness of the room.

'I have to do it, Claude. Stanley's been good to me. It's all right, Mr Timpson's not too bad.'

Claude looked at her, like he was waiting for her to say something more.

'Doris, what will happen when the job is finished?'

She shrugged. 'I don't know, maybe typing in Stanley's office or another job like this last one I suppose.'

'Are you sure, Doris?'

His face was close to hers, his eyes looking so deeply into hers. She shook her head. 'I don't know.'

He put his hand on to the side of her face and she blinked at him. 'I'm worried about you, Doris. I don't want you to do this work.'

'It's all right, I'll be all right,' she whispered.

He kissed her forehead. It was such a tender thing to do, she didn't know how to respond. She smiled at him and nodded, went into her room and shut the door.

22

Doris

In the throng of Victoria station, Doris stood beneath the clock clutching her small suitcase, the hard corners poking her legs whenever someone busy brushed past her. Her eyes searched the crowd and there, with his arm up in the air and a bright smile on his face, Mr Timpson came striding towards her. He looked so happy to see her and Doris knew that Stanley must be somewhere in the station taking photographs of them. She offered her cheek to his dry kiss and let him take her suitcase and they hurried through the barrier to have their tickets punched.

'Brighton Belle?' said Mr Timpson to the ticket inspector.

'Platform two, sir.'

Mr Timpson led the way and showed his ticket to a man dressed in a brown and cream uniform, who immediately snapped his fingers for a nearby attendant to take the luggage.

They followed him alongside a beautiful train painted in the same colours as the guard's clothes. Along the side of each carriage stretched the word Pullman, and a woman's name – Mona, Hazel, Lucille. The carriage they stopped at was called Doris. Doris looked at Mr Timpson, who allowed himself a smile. When they climbed aboard, the inside of the train looked like a plush hotel. They were seated opposite one another across a little table covered in a white cloth mitred neatly at the corners, upon which was a tall lamp with a snowdrop shade, wineglasses and cutlery, sculpted napkins and salt and pepper pots and a cut-glass ashtray. Doris could only look at it all with wide eyes, too excited to speak and too afraid to say the wrong thing.

'The waiter will be along in a moment, sir, madam,' said the guard, leaving them.

Doris leant across to Mr Timpson. 'Why's it called Doris?'

'A nice touch, don't you think?' he said, lighting a cigarette. 'Now, smile for the birdie,' he said, indicating outside the window with his eyes and taking Doris's hand.

Doris took Mr Timpson's hand in both of hers and leant across the table to gaze into his eyes, a delighted smile on her face. She didn't need to act. Not really. She might as well enjoy it.

The electric train pulled away smoothly and a waiter appeared asking what they would like to drink. He came back with an ice bucket and proceeded to open a bottle of pink-coloured wine. Mr Timpson gave Doris the menu and tapped the section titled *à la carte main meal service*.

'You might try the kippers,' he said. 'They are famous.'

Doris wondered what the cold collation was and decided

on the eggs, bacon, tomato and sausage. Mr Timpson had the kippers. When the meal arrived and Doris mopped her egg yolk with her bread and butter, he exchanged glances with the man across the aisle. Through the remaining journey he sipped his wine and read his newspaper. Doris gazed out at the countryside rushing by and felt lightheaded from the wine and the luxury she had found herself in. She studied the other passengers. A woman in a smart white jacket and matching hat, a man in a bow tie smoking a cigar. She imagined the woman standing up, pointing at her and saying loudly to the other passengers in a Queen's Christmas message voice, *Stop the train! She does not belong here!*

There was a fine drizzle of rain when they stepped out of Brighton station. The off-white seagulls eyed them from fence posts and road signs as they made their way to the hotel, Mr Timpson consulting a piece of paper in his hand. He looked up at the Regal hotel and sighed. It looked all right to Doris, it wasn't big or very fancy but it looked all right. Mr Timpson motioned for her to go ahead up the steps, and struggled to hold both suitcases and hold the door for her, his face clouding at the lack of service.

A bell rang as they entered and a man popped out of a doorway behind the reception desk. He was very pale, his skin was almost see-through like those transparent spiders where you can see what they've just eaten, the dark veins forking through his forehead. His grey hair was long around the ears, his white shirt grey about the collar and cuffs. He wore no jacket and no tie. To Doris, he seemed half-way dead, only his coal-black eyebrows showing any sign of life.

Mr Timpson was lost for words for a few seconds. The two men stared at one another, as if hoping the other would speak first.

'A room?' said the pale manager in a cigarette-seasoned voice.

Mr Timpson coughed behind his fist. 'Yes, please.'

'Sign here.' The manager slid a guest book across the wooden surface and gestured to the pen and inkwell in the stand.

Mr Timpson looked at the man and down at the book, glanced at Doris without fully seeing at her. He wrote slowly and carefully. *Mr and Mrs Timpson, Ivy House, Mill Lane, Cookham, Berks.* Doris studied his writing and frowned and as Mr Timpson placed the pen back in the stand she suddenly remembered her acting role. She clutched at Mr Timpson's arm and crushed herself into his side. The sudden movement made him stumble and he looked at her with tight lips. They both recovered and faced the manager who was scrutinising them carefully. There was a knowing look in his eye and it seemed that he was trying not to smile. An awkward moment followed when the couple adjusted their postures to seem more comfortable together, the manager watching them still.

'It's late, would you like to take your dinner in the room?'

'Yes please,' coughed Mr Timpson.

'And I'm sure you should like the *special* dinner and a bottle of something *nice* for the lady?'

The manager grinned at them, revealing his tobacco-stained teeth. He seemed to be enjoying their discomfort.

'Yes, yes of course, thank you,' said Mr Timpson, flicking

his head to get Doris's hand away from smoothing back his hair.

The manager handed them the key. 'The honeymoon suite,' he said, 'top floor. You'll be all right with the luggage? There's no lift I'm afraid.'

'Well, if you might give us a hand?'

The manager clapped his hands together with a broad smile. 'Delighted,' he said, coming round from the desk and taking the cases. They followed him up the stairs, in the wake of his stale sweat. He opened the door of the room and placed the cases just inside.

Mr Timpson took the key with not quite a snatch but near enough. The manager stood nodding his head slightly. Doris shifted uncomfortably and looked around the room, which even she could see wasn't anything special. Mr Timpson jangled some change in his pocket and produced half a crown to give the manager a tip. The manager looked at it in his hand like it was some sort of curious insect and didn't move to go. Mr Timpson ground his teeth and placed another half-crown with it, and another, until the manager looked up and smiled and left the room.

'Blast that man,' hissed Mr Timpson as he took off his jacket. 'He knows damned well why we're here but we'll have to play this ridiculous charade.'

Doris stood in the room not knowing what she should do. She looked at the double bed.

'And this place is a bloody shambles,' said Mr Timpson, lifting his suitcase to the bed and starting to unpack his things. He opened the dark wood wardrobe in the corner and peered in uncertainly, took out a clothes hanger and hung his shirt from the outside of the wardrobe door instead. Doris followed suit, opened her little case, pulled out her full-skirted dress and hung it next to Mr Timpson's shirt. They hadn't been in there twenty minutes when there was a knock at the door. Mr Timpson gestured to Doris to lounge on the bed. She sat on the edge and leant back a little without lying down, her stomach hurting with the strain of the position.

A young chambermaid was at the door with a trolley of food. She wheeled it in and started to place the covered plates on the little table by the window. Mr Timpson went to stand next to Doris, picked up her hand to hold it.

'This looks lovely, darling,' said Doris, looking up at him.

'It's only what you deserve, sweet little thing,' said Mr Timpson, patting Doris's cheek. The maid placed a bottle of something in an ice bucket on the table and stood back to smile at them. Her smile wasn't altogether sincere; in fact it was more of a smirk. Mr Timpson jangled his pocket change again and delivered some coins to her.

'We'll take breakfast in the room at eight.' He said it slowly and clearly.

When she had gone Mr Timpson lifted the cover on one of the plates and leant over to inspect the food. He wrinkled his nose.

'Well we had better eat it, I suppose.'

Doris smiled and sat down. She remembered Vi's etiquette advice and placed her napkin across her lap. Mr Timpson examined his cutlery closely, buffing his knife with his napkin. With his fork he prodded the steak on his plate, felt it with the back of his fingers.

'Overcooked and lukewarm. How did they manage that? It must have been sitting around for some time.'

'Did the maid look funny to you?' said Doris, sawing her steak with the knife.

'How so?'

'I dunno, like she was laughing at us.'

'She's probably planning her trip to London.'

'What?'

'If it's the same maid in the morning, she'll be the one testifying in court that she saw us in bed together.' Mr Timpson coughed behind his napkin.

'So you reckon she knows what we're doing? Stanley will be cross.'

Mr Timpson snorted. 'He's probably paid them to do it, and they're taking full advantage with this food that will be overpriced I'm sure, and this hideous room, the so-called honeymoon suite. Pah! The manager will want to recoup his expenses I suppose, losing his staff to the courts for a day or two.'

Doris chewed her steak and watched as Mr Timpson glared at the label on the wine bottle, unscrewed the wiring around the top and leant away as the cork popped out.

'Lovely,' she said, sipping the champagne.

'That's lukewarm too,' said Mr Timpson, 'it matches the meat, at least.' He downed his glassful and refilled it.

'Will you go to court, too?'

'No, this is my part of the unpleasantness. My wife will have to take her turn and appear in court. She's lucky I agreed to do it at all.' He glanced at Doris and down at his food.

The wine hit Doris's head and she smiled, feeling better

about it all. By now Mr Timpson wasn't a stranger and they were used to sharing a room. He clearly wanted to get it all over with as quickly as possible but she might as well enjoy it. Staying in a hotel, drinking champagne, they weren't things you did every day.

'So why you getting a divorce then?' She'd wanted to ask him all this time but hadn't had the courage.

His chewing slowed as he thought. 'We have grown apart. But you can't obtain a divorce if you've grown apart, that would be far too sensible. No, you have to have been caught *in flagrante delicto*.'

'What's that, then?'

'It means having marital relations outside of your marriage.'

Doris nodded wisely and wondered exactly what those marital relations were.

'So, what do we have to do then?' She blushed and nodded towards the bed.

'Oh my goodness, not the real thing, if that's what you mean. Hasn't Stanley told you anything?' He looked at her with pity for a moment. 'No, absolutely not, we'll just need to be seen in bed together, in each other's arms so to speak, to give the impression of other, that is to say, other relations.'

'Oh yes, I see.' Doris didn't really see but to be seen in each other's arms in bed was something she could do without too much trouble. At least, the champagne made it seem like that. She gulped down half a glass and burped with her mouth closed, her cheeks puffing out.

'Stanley thinks you're a poofter,' she said, laughing.

Mr Timpson put down his glass with a bump. 'What the devil?' His face clouded with indignation.

'Oh sorry,' she said, waving her hands at him as if to waft away the comment. 'I didn't mean anything by it, it's just Stanley joking around.'

Mr Timpson gathered himself and dabbed the corners of his mouth with his napkin.

Doris cast around for something to say. 'Why didn't you put your London address in the guest book?'

He seemed to appreciate that she was trying to change the subject to save his embarrassment.

'It's supposed to be an accident. I *accidentally* gave my country address so that the hotel bill will be seen by my wife. She'll be able to use it as evidence in court.'

He flung his napkin on the table with a sigh.

'Look here, this is all very difficult. I think I'll turn in. What'll you do?'

Her head light from the wine, Doris wanted to laugh at his anxious face, but she nodded. 'I'll just finish my drink then I'll turn in too.'

She made sure to look at the window as he changed in the corner, kept her eyes fixed on the curtains as he got into bed, and stifled a laugh when he let out a squeeze of wind and coughed to disguise it.

When his eyes were closed, Doris changed too and climbed into bed beside him. The warmth from his body radiated on to hers as she lay there. She knew he wasn't asleep. What if she put her hand across to touch him? The thought made her want to giggle and she fell into wine-softened dreams.

There was a knock at the door. Mr Timpson shook her arm. Doris blinked at the light pressing through the brown curtain fabric, giving the room a nicotine hue. She sat up with a jolt, remembered what was happening this morning. Mr Timpson looked at her anxiously; he looked tired. He put out his arm and Doris crept in close to him.

'Ready?' he whispered. His breath was foul and she looked down the bed to see one of his feet out of the sheets, his hairy toes making her shudder. She nodded.

'Yes,' he called and the door opened. It was the same chambermaid they'd had the previous night. Her eyes were wide with anticipation and she had bitten her lips together as if trying not to laugh. Doris snuggled in closer to Mr Timpson's chest. She moved her knee upwards so as to get closer and it brushed Mr Timpson's groin. It was as if they had both touched a live wire. In a flap, Mr Timpson pulled at the sheets and Doris sat up a little. The maid was openly grinning now, glancing at them as she laid out the breakfast on the little table.

'Did you sleep well?' she said.

'Perfectly well, thank you,' said Mr Timpson, rigid with discomfort.

Doris needed the toilet and wanted to get away from Mr Timpson's pungent body. She tried to maintain a dreamy smile and half-close her eyelids to give the impression of perfect bliss. But the maid caught her eye on her way out and sniggered, making Doris's face blush hot.

When she'd gone, Mr Timpson tore back the sheets and stumbled out of bed, knocking his knee on the bedside table. He strode around the room with both hands smoothing back his hair.

'Well that was a bloody farcical performance,' he said.

Doris bit her fingernail and looked at the breakfast table, wondering what was there.

She badly needed a wee.

'And we have to be here another night, it's just interminable.' He lifted the cover from one of the plates and let it clang down again.

'We could go and have a look at the seaside,' said Doris, holding her bladder and taking a seat for breakfast. The smell of the bacon and eggs was too much to resist.

'Yes I suppose you're right, they would expect us to do it and Stanley is most likely lurking somewhere for his photographs.' He poured himself a cup of tea and stood to drink it while Doris tucked in.

Outside it was still drizzling and the gloomy seagulls were perched sentinel on every high surface, heads cocked with one eye on the ground for dropped chips. But as the day wore on the clouds cleared and the day trippers put on their sunglasses and spread down to the beach. Doris was excited about the two piers and told Mr Timpson it would look good if they went on some rides. He agreed, reluctantly, to try out the car track on West Pier. Doris threw back her head with joy and tore up and down, Mr Timpson puttered behind with a pained smile fixed in place. On Palace Pier, Doris said Stanley would like a picture of them on the waltzer. Mr Timpson turned green and hung on for his life, but managed to keep the smile there and put his arm around Doris. They ate chips on the beach side by side and Doris clapped her hands with delight as Mr Timpson threw stones into the sea. She tried to teach him how to skim them but he didn't take to it.

At about five, Mr Timpson said he needed a lie down and they made their way back to the hotel. In the room he took off his shoes and fell on to the bed.

'This is absolutely exhausting, I've never been through such an ordeal in all my life.'

Doris wanted to tell him to pull himself together, this was nothing compared to what she'd been through. She had had a high time on the seafront, had thoroughly enjoyed herself. Mr Timpson turned off the light and closed the curtains, said he needed a nap. Doris sat for a while but with nothing to do she lay down too for a bit of shut-eye.

They took dinner in the hotel restaurant, which looked like two tables in someone's front room. The manager served them lamb cutlets and more champagne, refilling the glasses at every opportunity. They managed to finish a bottle between them and Doris was losing focus.

'I'm sure you'd enjoy another bottle with the lady wife on your special weekend away?' crooned the manager. Doris laughed and said yes.

'This divorce is costing me a bloody fortune,' hissed Mr Timpson when the manager was out of earshot.

'It's funny, isn't it?' said Doris.

'What is?'

'It's funny, how you're buying your divorce,' she spluttered a giggle and reached over to wipe a bubble of white spit that had flown from her mouth and landed on Mr Timpson's chin. He swiped her hand away and then laughed a grotesque fake laugh as the manager appeared at his side.

'The fish course,' he said, placing plates before them and lifting the lids with a flourish.

'We didn't order the fish,' said Mr Timpson, his words slurring.

'Oh, I'm sure you ordered the seven courses, sir, you

distinctly said that nothing is too much for your wonderful wife.'

The manager stood there with a silly innocent look on his see-through face.

'Oh, you ... yes, of course, why don't you bring us more food and champagne than we could possibly eat in a week, that would be just bloody perfect.' Mr Timpson giggled into his champagne glass.

'Of course, sir, whatever you say.'

'I'm so full,' groaned Doris, laughing, 'But it's sinful to waste food, I just have to carry on.'

'Yes, carry on, that's the spirit,' he said, banging the table and then banging it with a beat and starting to sing. 'What's happening, what's happening, what's happening to me, I'm dancing, I'm dancing ...'

Doris joined in. It was one of the songs from the *Salad Days* musical they went to. 'What's happening, what's happening, what's happening to me,' she sang, swaying in her seat. There was no one else in the tiny restaurant. Mr Timpson suddenly stood up, his napkin falling from his lap. He held out his hand to her, pulled her into the gap between the tables and started doing the quickstep. Doris didn't know the dance but she was drunk enough to be able to follow his lead uninhibited.

'What's happening, what's happening, what's happening to me, I'm dancing, I'm dancing ...' they sang and quick-stepped around the room and danced back to their table, sitting down and laughing.

The manager brought in a tray loaded with cheese and biscuits. Doris had to try some, forced down a lump of veiny Stilton.

'This looks like him,' she said, spluttering a laugh and holding the wedge of cheese up on her fork. 'The manager . . .'

'Oh, yes I see – the veins.' Mr Timpson clutched the edge of the table and drummed his feet on the ground as he laughed.

When they got back to the room, Doris lurched from side to side trying to land on the bed. The second she lay down, she had an overwhelming desire to be sick. She managed to get to the little sink in the corner in time and didn't remember anything after that.

In the morning Doris heard the knock at the door filtering through into her dreams for a while before she opened her eyes. She looked across at Mr Timpson, who was still asleep, a line of drool joining his cheek to the pillow. She patted his arm. He groaned and rolled towards her, opened one eye.

'She's at the door,' whispered Doris.

Mr Timpson groaned again and nodded, wiped his cheek and held out his arm and Doris laid her head on his chest.

'Yes,' he called.

'Oh, sorry,' said the maid, the same one as before. 'I thought you said eight o'clock.'

'It's all right,' said Doris, sitting up and wincing as her brain banged against her skull. 'We had a late night, that's all.'

'Oh my god . . .' The maid covered her mouth and nose with her hand, looking towards the sink in the corner.

'Oh no, I'm really sorry, it was the champagne . . .' said Doris.

'Well I wouldn't normally do a Sunday shift, but you know, in this case . . .' said the maid, placing the breakfast things on the little table.

'Give her a tip,' said Mr Timpson, as if uttering his last breath. He fumbled on the bedside table for his wallet, squinted into it still lying down and gave Doris a one pound note.

Doris frowned. 'All of it?' she whispered. He nodded, so Doris got out of bed, straightened her nightdress and walked gingerly over to the maid.

'Thank you, for all your hard work,' said Doris, not knowing what to say. She had never given anyone a tip before.

'Gosh, thanks,' said the maid, looking at the note. 'This is turning out all right. Don't worry about the sink, I'll sort it out.'

She left, wheeling her trolley out of the room.

'That should seal the deal,' mumbled Mr Timpson. 'Make me a cup of tea, would you please? The devil is knocking at my head.'

23

Vi

Model Smiles at Death Sentence.

Vi read the news headline and shook her head.

'It just goes to show. The woman's got no morals. Who would *smile* when they're sentenced to death?'

Vi and Win were cleaning the pub ready for morning opening at eleven. Win leant over Vi's shoulder to read the piece on Ruth Ellis and tutted.

'Terrible. A crime of passion. What a waste of a life.'

Vi frowned. 'I wouldn't say that. She made her bed. When you go around like a tart you're asking for it.'

Win took her polish over to the furthest table, turned her back on Vi and started rubbing at it with gusto.

'What's wrong with you?' said Vi. Win ignored her. 'What is it?' said Vi, going over.

'I'm worried, Vi,' said Win, rubbing her duster in circles and not looking at Vi. 'About Doris.'

'Oh for god's sake, Win, why don't you just let it go?'

'You know she's hanging around Ship Street, aren't you worried? She'll get herself in bad trouble, Vi.'

Vi ignored her sister. Of course she was worried. Ashamed would have been a better word. But she had washed her hands of the ungrateful girl, who was already in bad trouble after all. She walked back over to the bar, pushed the newspaper away and opened her magazine to a page with a picture of a woman sitting up in bed fully made-up wearing a frilly nightdress and a satin bow in her hair, an open beauty basket on her lap.

'Seven-day beauty plan,' mumbled Vi. 'Seven-day beauty plan here, Win. Do you fancy it?' Win didn't answer; she was sulking about Doris. 'Liquid diet, water, soup,' mumbled Vi, 'facial, we can do one on each other, eh?'

Win looked over and shrugged. 'If you want.'

'Here, it says, for slimmer legs, you should pinch your calves in the bath. Pinch your calves – that's a new one. You should do that, Win.'

'Thanks a lot.'

'You know what I mean, you daft bird.'

'Pedicure. You can do that one yourself, I'm not touching *your* feet.' Win allowed herself a little smile at that one. 'Hair, do your hair like Princess Margaret with reverse pin curls, we can try that.'

Vi concentrated as she read the make-up day in detail. She fancied trying the monochrome look. It wouldn't suit Win so she didn't bother telling her about it. She did need sprucing up though. 'I'll do your make-up for you, Win, how about it?'

'What, so I look like that Ruth Ellis in the paper?'

'Don't be stupid, not a tarty look, something more peaches and cream.'

Vi didn't have a lot of make-up so she had to use it sparingly, but she wanted to do something about Win. The woman made no effort for her husband.

Archie came up from the cellar. 'The barrels are on,' he said, pulling the beer through into a tin bucket at the pump. He set it aside and pulled a half pint to drink, picked up the newspaper. 'She's had it, then,' he said. 'That Ruth Ellis, she's gonna swing for shooting Blakely.'

'I know, serves her right, too. Going around like that, this man then that man, I don't know,' said Vi, standing at his side to read.

'She was jealous because Blakely was seeing other women,' said Archie, turning the page. 'Christ, if jealous women were given guns, there'd be no men left.' He stopped laughing when he saw Win looking at him.

'She's got a bastard son,' said Vi, looking at Win. 'She was that type.'

Win shook her head at Vi and looked like she might cry but kept herself in check before Archie saw.

'She had a bastard son when she was seventeen and got into nude modelling and prostitution to scrape a living,' said Win, 'when the father stopped giving her money.'

'How do you know so much about it?' said Archie, gulping his beer.

'I take an interest in these things,' said Win, looking at Vi meaningfully. It was a swipe at her about Doris.

221

Vi scowled. She didn't want Archie wound up, didn't want there to be a row about Doris.

'Blakely was a violent drunk,' said Win.

'Oh, so he deserved to get shot, did he?' laughed Archie.

'He punched her in the stomach when she was pregnant and she lost the baby,' said Win.

'She shot him once,' read Archie, 'then stood over him and shot him three more times, once just half an inch from his back. The woman's a nutcase. A tart and a nutcase. "It's obvious when I shot him I intended to kill him," she said that in court yesterday.'

'She's just owning up to what she's done,' said Win. 'Doesn't mean she's not a victim herself.'

'What you talking about, woman?'

'Hadn't you better get on with the tables, Win?' said Vi. 'We're opening in ten minutes.'

Archie went back down to the cellar and Win moved to the next table, spat on her cloth and started polishing.

'She's a victim of the life she got into after being left on her own with a child, that's what I'm talking about,' she said.

Vi pretended she hadn't heard.

24

Doris

'I'm pleased, Doris, you did a good job.'

Sitting across from Stanley at his office desk, Doris smiled. She was glad he thought she'd done well. The job for Mr Timpson hadn't been that bad really, she'd even enjoyed some of it. On the Sunday they'd had a lie-in to clear their hangovers and then went to the seafront for a nice restaurant lunch before getting the train back to London. Saying good-bye at Victoria station, Mr Timpson had smiled at her, said thank you for making it bearable. Doris was a little sad to see him go in the end, after they'd had a laugh together on Saturday night in the hotel restaurant. He'd nearly swallowed his tongue when he saw the hotel bill.

'So, what's next?' said Doris, feeling like one of the staff now.

'Next?' said Stanley. 'Yes, next. Well I can't use you again for a divorce job, not for a year or so anyway, or it would look suspicious. I've got something for you down the road though. Lil's going into hospital for her plumbing and she'll be off for a couple of weeks. I need you on the front desk – can you do that?'

Doris's heart sank. She'd hoped to go back to the office.

'Don't you need me in here, doing the typing?'

'No, it's gone a bit quiet, I need you on the front desk while Lil's away. All you have to do is greet the customers, see which girls are free, time them and take the money. Oh and any other things they might want, you know, the bits and bobs that Lil keeps behind the desk.'

He lit a cigarette and peered at her through his smoke.

Doris was very intrigued by what went on in those rooms at the boarding house. She had realised when she'd moved in that not only did the girls live there, but they saw men in their rooms, different men every day. The rooms could be quite noisy, the bed springs groaning. It must have been marital relations type things going on in there. What exactly marital relations were, Doris was trying to guess. The kind of thing she'd done with Kenny probably. But why would they pay for it?

She gathered her courage to ask Stanley. 'What do they do in there then? In the rooms?'

'Ha ha,' Stanley laughed. 'That's good, that is. So you'll do it then? The money will be a bit more than you've been on if you do a good job.'

'I wanted to ask you about that, Stanley. Will I get paid for the divorce job now?'

He seemed to remember something all of a sudden, started

rifling through his papers. 'Yes, yes, I'll let you have that, Doris, but most of the payments went on expenses and child-care, you know, Lil looking after your Laura, so there's not a lot left, to be honest.'

'Really?'

'Yes, let's talk about that later, I've got a lot to do.' He seemed to find what he was looking for and started reading a letter intently and twiddling his hair. 'Why don't you pop along to see Lil, she'll train you up. Make sure you do a good job, mind, or I'll have to take your room for someone else if you're not working for me.'

He said this last part while he was still reading the letter.

Doris stood up, paused and left. It was harsh of him to say that to her when she'd just done the divorce job for him. She'd done a good job as well, had never done anything like it before and she'd just got on with it. He hadn't told her she'd have to pay Lil for looking after Laura either. And he'd said before that the boarding house was his friend's place, but he must have lied about that. He seemed to be the one running things there.

Laura was sitting on the pavement outside the boarding house playing with a pile of stones. She jumped up when she saw Doris.

'Mumma!'

Doris patted her head as she clung to her leg. 'Come on, let go now, I have to talk to Lil.' Laura made to follow her in. 'No, you stay out here and play.'

Lil was behind the front desk, her neckline scooped low showing her generous cleavage. Doris never knew where to look.

'All right, Lil? Stanley said you're to show me the ropes.'

'Ah yes, Doris, you'll be covering for me. Good job you came back today, I'm about to leave for the hospital.' She unhooked a key ring from her belt and gave it to Doris.

'Keys for the front and back doors, the money drawer and all the rooms,' she said.

Doris took the bunch of keys and felt the weight of responsibility that hung there too. Her stomach twisted with nerves. 'What have I got to do, then?'

'Well, you'll be the "maid". That's what the girl on the front desk is called. The maid's job is to welcome the customers – with a smile, but not too friendly if you know what I mean. You don't want them to think that they're in charge, otherwise things can get out of hand. Don't forget, you'll always have at least one lad around, it'll be Terry or Claude, or both. They get involved if there's any trouble, if the girls get hurt or if the customer won't pay, stuff like that.'

'So the customer pays . . . ?'

'Course they do, what do you think this is, a charity?'

'Well, how much?'

'Depends what they want.' Lil saw the clueless look on Doris's face. 'Christ, Doris, you've got a kid, haven't you?'

'Yes, but . . . '

Lil looked up at the clock on the wall by the desk. 'Look, don't worry, I'll tell the girls to tell you how much, all right? You just sit here and look professional and don't take any shit from the punters.'

Lil gathered up her handbag and nodded up at the clock. 'Fred's just taken someone up, always give them twenty minutes, if it's any longer than that, give one of the lads a nudge and they'll be ready to go up and knock on the door. Right then, that's me off.'

With that she left, forgetting to tell the girls to tell Doris how much for each customer. Doris edged round to sit down at the desk. It was in the hallway, across from the foot of the stairs. She turned to see through into the back room, the betting shop where there were always men hanging around. The bunch of keys was still in her hand. Lil hadn't told her what to do with them. She tried the top drawer of the desk but it was locked, then tried several of the keys until she found the right one. There was a quantity of cash in the drawer. She shut and locked it quick. The next drawer down was unlocked. Inside there were some small tins. She opened one and frowned. Inside, lined up like sardines, there were four cream-coloured rubbery things each wrapped with paper around the middle. She looked up as one of the girls, Bette, came in with a man on her arm. Doris put the tin back and slammed the drawer shut without meaning to.

'What you doing, honey?' said Bette, smiling but not in a friendly way.

'I'm watching the desk while Lil's away.'

'Really? Well look, honey, I'll be taking Bob up, all right?'

The man touched his cap and guided Bette towards the stairs.

'Yes, all right,' squeaked Doris. She looked up at the clock, it was ten past seven.

Laura came in. 'Mumma, I'm hungry.'

'You can't be in here, Laura.'

'But Lil lets me. She tells Fred to get me bread and jam.'

'Well, Fred's busy,' said Doris. She'd forgotten what time

Fred was supposed to be coming down and didn't know whether to tell one of the men about it. 'I'll get it for you, come on.'

She led Laura through to the little kitchen out the back, next to the betting shop. There wasn't any bread, but there was a cold cooked pie in the larder so she gave that to Laura, taking a huge bite of it herself first.

'Now skedaddle, go on.' She shooed Laura out onto the pavement to eat her pie. There was a man waiting at the desk with his cloth cap in his hand. When he saw Doris he looked embarrassed.

'Hello love, Lil about?'

'No, no she's not, sorry, I'm here for now,' said Doris around her mouthful of pie. 'Do you, do you want to . . .'

'It's Bette I normally see, she free?'

Doris looked up at the clock. It was twenty-five past seven. 'No, she's upstairs, she's busy.'

'All right, love, I'll wait out the back then.'

'Oh, yes, that's a good idea, all right then.'

The man frowned and nodded and disappeared down the hallway.

Doris chewed her thumbnail, realised that if Bette only had five minutes left then Fred should have come down by now. But she didn't want to get it wrong and cause a fuss. She'd just leave it another five minutes.

There was a big cheer from the back room that made Doris jump. There were loud voices and someone shouted. She went part way down the hallway and she could see Terry the Teddy boy in there, standing between two men who looked angry with each other. She rushed back to the desk and sat down, scared what would happen, what the angry men might say to her because she was in charge. She wished Claude was there. She twisted her neck to look back to see Terry ushering one of the men out of the back door. Bette came down with Bob and stood talking with him by the desk, giving Doris meaningful glances when Bob wasn't looking.

'Doris will help you now, Bob, thanks darling.' Bette kissed him on the lips in front of Doris and turned to go up the stairs. Bob stood looking at Doris as he took out his wallet. She felt a flutter of panic, she needed to call Bette back down to ask her how much money she had to take. Bob handed her three greasy pound notes. She took them with a meek smile.

'My change?' he said.

Doris gulped and unlocked the drawer, fumbled with the coins.

'Er, sorry, how much change?'

'Ten bob, usually,' he said, his neck blushing red.

'Oh, yes, sorry, here.' She handed him two crowns and he turned on his heel and left.

Doris let out a sigh of relief and leant back in the chair. Her armpits were damp with sweat. With a jolt she looked up at the clock. It was twenty to eight. She jumped up and rushed down the hallway into the betting shop.

'Where's Terry?'

There were several men in there listening intently to a dog race on the radio. They turned to look at her as if she were a sheep just walked into a butcher's shop. From the kitchen next door she heard a man shout out.

'Where's my fucking pie?'

She ran round to the kitchen and saw Terry there with his head in the larder.

'Terry, sorry, is Claude around?'

'No, he's gone up town.'

'I need you to go up to Fred's room, she's been in there ages.'

'What?' he said, looking her up and down. 'What, Doris, is it?'

'I'm looking after the desk while Lil's away, Fred's been upstairs with a bloke for ages, you better go and check.'

He tutted and shook his head, mumbled that someone had taken his pie and went upstairs.

Doris waited at the stair foot biting her nails. She heard laughter and looked up. Fred was there with a man, smiling, arm in arm. They all came down and Fred glared at Doris when the man wasn't looking. Doris leant into Fred's shoulder, whispered *how much?* into her ear.

'Three quid,' whispered Fred, rubbing her neck.

'That'll be three pounds, please,' said Doris with a smile as she sat in the desk chair.

The man smirked at her and handed her the right money.

'See you then, darling,' said Fred, and kissed the man on the cheek. He smacked her backside and left without saying anything.

'Has Lil gone then? What the hell are you playing at?' said Fred, leaning over the desk at Doris. 'I've been up there with him for a lifetime. He told me his bloody life story and sucked on my neck like a hungry baby.' She drew her hand away and Doris saw a large red sore on Fred's neck. 'And I had to beat the living daylight out of him again. It's really quite tiring,' she said, sitting on the edge of the desk and lighting up a cigarette from the pack on the windowsill. 'Bloody ex-army, they like their beatings.'

Doris stared at Fred wondering what on earth she was talking about.

'I'm really sorry, Fred. I'm new at this. There was a row out the back and Bette had a customer and ...'

Doris felt herself starting to cry and wiped her nose upwards on the palm of her hand, something Vi always told her not to do because it wasn't ladylike. But she didn't have a clean hankie and now Fred was cross with her and she liked Fred.

'Hey, it's all right, you daft thing. I'm all right, aren't I? If I'd come down with a couple of shiners I'd have been pissed off, but I was just getting bored up there, that's all.'

With her cigarette between her lips, Fred came round to Doris's side of the desk and leant down to put her arm around Doris's shoulders. She hugged Doris towards her and sat on the edge of the desk there.

'Don't worry, chicken, all right?'

Doris sniffed and nodded.

'Sorry, Fred.'

'You'll get used to it. Lil reckons she'll be back in a couple of weeks or less. This is a good way to get you used to the set-up for when ... you know ...'

Fred looked at her with pity and reached out to stroke her hair.

'What?' said Doris.

'Hasn't Stanley said?' Fred looked like she wished she hadn't said anything. 'He's a bugger, he is. Well, you might get a better offer between now and then.'

Laura came in from outside, bits of pastry and gravy from the pie around her face.

'Hello, chicken,' said Fred. Laura went up to Fred and hugged her leg, and Fred leant down and kissed the top of Laura's head. 'Besides, you don't want this one living here much longer, do you?'

'Why not?' said Doris, wondering why Fred was kissing Laura. 'It's all right, it's better than where we were living before. I can't afford anything else. Stanley hasn't even paid me for the job I've just done.'

'Yeah, you've got to watch that one – slimy, he is. But this is no place for a little one to be living, as much as I love having her here. Had fun, didn't we? When your mum was in London?'

Laura nodded and smiled. Fred wiped the food from Laura's face with her hand, licked her thumb to rub at a stubborn patch of dirt.

'Stanley said Lil looked after her when I was away.'

'Lil? Ha, that's a good one. No, I kept an eye on her for you.'

'Thanks Fred, that's good of you.'

'Always a pleasure,' said Fred, stubbing out her cigarette on an ashtray on the desk and reaching down to pick Laura up. 'You'd better not hang around here, little one, it'll be getting busy soon. Why don't you go to your room and do some colouring before bed, all right?'

'Did you get her that colouring stuff?'

Fred nodded. 'Yep, just a little treat from Auntie Fred. Say night to Mum.'

'Night, Mumma,' said Laura. Fred carried her up the stairs, Laura's head resting on her shoulder.

25

Doris

On the kerb outside the boarding house, Doris sat smoking and playing cards with Fred. They were placing small bets and Laura was there, making little towers with the pennies. Fred had her hair up in rollers beneath a turban. Doris had pinned hers back from her face.

'Hello ladies.' Claude came out the front door, greeted them with a lift of his hat. His Jamaican accent didn't sound so strange any more.

'Doris, I'm going over to see the boys if you fancy coming?' he said, picking up Laura and turning her upside down as she squealed with glee.

Doris looked at Fred, who tutted. 'Go on then, don't mind me. I'll watch the little one for you.'

'Cheers, Fred.'

Doris felt a little rush of joy at Claude asking her to go

along with him. As they walked, he played at brushing her hand with his as though he was going to hold it. And then he caught it and threaded his fingers through hers.

Looking at the ground, Doris tried without success to stop a wide grin spreading across her face. She stole a glance at Claude, who angled his head just enough to smile deep into her soul.

'I been to London to see the Queen, Doris.'

'What?'

'I been up to the Big Smoke to look around.'

'Oh yeah?'

'Yeah, and I'm excited, Doris. I met some people up there, West Indians, but they're not like the boys – negative and homesick. The people I met, they're strong and looking forward to a bright new day.'

'All that, eh?'

'I went to Notting Hill, where the boys said all the islanders live. It have boys living eight to a room and paying six pound each a week, some of them doing a day shift of work and sharing a bed with someone doing a night shift of work. No bath, run down, like where I live here for free.'

'Six pound a week?' Doris was horrified it cost that much to rent a shared room.

'Because they're black, Doris, that's why,' said Claude, explaining to her. 'It have a big deal landlord there, a real crook, who knows they've got nowhere else to go. One of the boys there told me to go to Brixton, where all the Jamaicans live.'

Claude's hand was warm and big. Doris relished the feeling of hers in his.

'I got to Brixton, all these Jamaican boys were hanging around the Labour Exchange and I got talking to one of them and he said he knows a group of West Indian writers living in London.'

He was swinging her arm as he spoke and waving his other hand around for emphasis, the way the other boys did, like they didn't need words sometimes.

'He told me he'd introduce me to them and to some folks who are campaigning against the unofficial colour bar. Think of it, Doris.'

'I thought you wanted to write books.'

'Yes, that too of course,' he said, his voice toned down a notch. 'This fella, he told how bad things are, how blacks can't live where they want, landlords don't want them, landladies afraid of what the neighbours will say if they take black tenants, how blacks are sent for a work by the Labour Exchange but they get there and the work is gone, but at the Labour Exchange the next day, the work still vacant.'

He paused for breath.

'That doesn't sound very good,' said Doris, not really surprised by what he was saying.

'I know it, he says how the churches don't want the blacks, they afraid the whites won't come if they let the blacks in. He says how some of the pubs don't serve the blacks – some of the pubs, Doris, like your pub.'

'My mum's pub, you mean.'

'Yes, that is what I mean, it is the same in London. He says it have a group of them campaigning for anti-racist laws, Doris, because there are none. Those signs, I see them in

London: No blacks, no Irish, no dogs, I see them and they are legal. I see the KBW graffiti, six feet high on the walls.'

Doris frowned.

'Keep Britain White. Fascist groups, Doris, there are fights. It's like a pressure cooker, this fella says, the tensions, the government doing nothing about it.'

Doris didn't understand why he was so excited about it all. It sounded terrible and hard to believe anyone would be able to change something like that. They arrived at the tenement building, and walked round the back way into the inner court-yard where the other boys were cooking something over a fire.

'You're just in time for a cooked rabbit.' It was Homesick.

'What happening, Shakespeare? said Smallie, waving his hand from where he sat in his chair.

'I been up to London to see the Queen,' grinned Claude. 'Here, Homesick, I got you a present from the Big Smoke,'

'London? Nah, not interested, thank you,' said Homesick, waving away the offer.

'You haven't seen it yet. Here.' Claude handed him a brown paper bag.

Homesick opened it and smiled. 'Ah, Shakespeare, you know how to put a smile on Homesick's face. Jamaican hots.'

He took out a small squashed red thing on a stalk. Doris looked at Claude.

'Scotch Bonnet pepper, very hot,' he winked.

Homesick started dancing around like he'd just won the pools.

'Where'd you get them, Shakespeare?'

'A little place call Brixton Island,' laughed Claude.

'Ah, Brixton, I didn't like it there. You get any salt fish?'

'Nah, man, be grateful you got that.'

'Thanks, man.' Homesick put his arm around Claude's shoulders and jiggled him up and down.

'So, what did you think of it, then?' asked RAF, sitting in one of the chairs, prodding the sticks on the fire. 'A damned disgrace? A racist pit? Not your God Save the Queen on Empire day back home, eh?'

'So you wanna go back home now, eh Shakespeare?' called out Goodfor from his chair.

'What? Nah, I'm excited,' said Claude.

'Why is that?' said RAF.

'I met a Jamaican boy, hangs around with a group of Jamaican folks that campaign for black rights, civil rights.'

The boys fell silent.

'He told how bad it is in London for us, the colour bar, but said we got to think about the times, how Britain is hurting from the war, housing crisis and job shortage, and how things will get better, we just got to stay positive.'

The boys looked at each other and said nothing.

'They're campaigning for a change in the law, to bring an anti-racist law in. They're strong, they are *survivors*.'

'It's big talk,' said Homesick. 'I have been asked enough times *Where's your tail?* and *How come you can count?* to know that blacks will never be welcome here.'

'The white girls don't mind us so much,' grinned Goodfor, winking at Smallie.

'This fella said it's lucky the white women sympathise with us.' Claude gave Doris a sheepish smile. 'Says they know what it's like to be used in the war and then shoved aside, them back to the kitchen and us back to the plantation.'

Doris hadn't been used in the war, but Auntie Win always talked about how she'd loved helping with the war effort and how keeping house was boring compared to that.

'I can relate to that,' said RAF.

'I think we should do something instead of sitting around here cooking rabbits,' said Claude.

'Like what?' said Homesick, laughing. 'You gonna make rab, change the law, Shakespeare?'

'No, but we should make a stand, like with that racist pub, The Empire.' Claude shot a look at Doris. 'We should campaign against its colour bar. Is a damned cheek, not serving us in that pub, who they think they are?'

'They're your folks, aren't they, Doris?' said RAF.

Doris nodded. 'Yes, and they turned me out, didn't they?'

'They very choosy about who is allowed in their pub,' said Smallie. 'You're right, Shakespeare, I'd like to do something to show them up. Why should we just sit around and take it?'

'I don't know, we could get arrested or something,' said Goodfor, sitting forward in his chair.

'Peaceful protest, man,' said Claude. 'They do it in America. We just stand up and say this ain't right, we are human beings like you, we are British like you. We will shame them.'

Claude looked at them and nodded his head when he saw the look in their eyes.

Doris was excited. Claude had managed to get the boys riled up for a protest against the pub. He had taken Doris to one side.

'Doris, you all right about this?' he said.

'The pub protest? Why wouldn't I be?'

'The boys say you should join us, it will make us stronger if you are with us.'

'Because I'm English?'

'Yes, and you the owner's daughter. It makes them look bad, Doris, but you don't have to do it, we understand if you don't want to.'

'No, I will. I want to.'

Doris felt something bubbling up inside her. She thought it must be revenge. For the way she'd been treated. It was a strong feeling, and it wanted to push down her need to go back home – she didn't care if she was jeopardising being allowed back. Because that wasn't ever going to happen. And now she had Claude and he inspired her to be strong. He was saying no to injustice and she'd never felt it was her place to say anything at all. She wanted to do it to please Claude, but she also wanted to do it for herself.

Claude cupped her face in his hands and kissed her forehead. 'You are strong, Doris. You don't even know that yet.'

She gritted her teeth and pushed the tears away.

Smallie had come up with the idea of making signs. The boys pulled off door panels in the empty tenement flats and made placards with an old tin of white paint Claude had found in the boarding house cellar.

No Colour Bar said one placard. *Racist Pub* said another. *I fought for Britain*, said RAF's.

'We can take turns to stand up on a box and speak,' said Claude, 'like the union boss does with the dockers.'

Goodfor made a face. 'I'm not standing up on a box,' he said.

'RAF? You can tell about the war,' said Claude.

RAF nodded.

They gathered their placards and trailed over to The Empire pub. Passing the docks, they saw a large number of dockers hanging around on the green outside the entrance. They had been on strike for a couple of weeks. A line of ships stood in dock waiting to be discharged, the cranes idle and a smell of food rotting. The dockers watched the group file past.

They made their way down Fort Road and, placing his apple crate down on the ground outside the pub, Claude stepped up on to it. Doris could see he was nervous. She held her sign aloft, *Let the Coloureds Have a Pint*, hers said, it was her idea. She thought the punters in the pub would sympathise with that. On the other side she had painted *Let Us Live*. She winced as a splinter caught in the skin between her forefinger and thumb but held up her sign and started to walk in a wide circle around the apple box with the other boys.

When a couple of passersby stopped to see what was going on, Claude jumped up on to the crate and started to speak.

'See that?' He held out his hands. 'Stained red by the bauxite in Jamaica's earth. My feet are red too. You ask any Jamaican peasant farmer to show you his feet, they are red.' The bystanders looked at each other and shrugged. 'The bauxite is what makes bananas grow like magic. But even bauxite didn't magic away the 1944 hurricane. It shook up the island and nearly blew her away. I was ten and my father was fighting in the war for the British. My Uncle Norton cried when he saw his crop razed. But we ploughed the fields and re-planted and laid off some workers and then another hurricane came. Uncle Norton said to me, "Claude, we can't make it this time." He said the British Empire have flattened our economy, we didn't need a hurricane to do it. But I remember my father. He died fighting for the British. He used to say we are British citizens, and George is our King. In Jamaica, we all know plenty about the Royals, I can tell you Henry the Eighth's wives no problem. As a child I marched up and down on Empire day in my school uniform happily enough, and singing the National Anthem stirs in me a pride, a pride that my father fought for something he loved.'

It was hard to walk the circle with her placard and listen to Claude properly. His words touched her and she hoped other people would be touched by them too. But when she came round the bend of the circle, she saw the onlookers shake their heads and walk on.

When RAF stood up on the box he talked about fighting in the war for the British and how unwelcome he was after the war, how he couldn't rent a room or get a good job, how he couldn't have a drink in a pub. Goodfor and Homesick trudged around the circle, slouching and looking embarrassed. But Smallie and Claude marched around with their heads held high. When RAF finished speaking and a group of dockers walked by to go into the pub, Smallie suddenly jumped up on to the box.

'You want to rub my skin, see if the colour comes off?' he said. 'You want to touch my hair for good luck? You want to ask me where my tail is and tell me to go back to the jungle? I was brought up British under colonial rule, my country is still ruled by your country, my ancestors were brought there as slaves by your country, and now you tell me I can't have a work? I can't have a drink in the pub?'

The dockers had paused to listen to him, some of them looking angry when they read the placards. Smallie looked around wildly as he ran out of things to say and jumped off the box to join the circle again. The dockers laughed and said things like *Get out of it* and *Can't understand what you're saying* and went into the pub to have their drink.

Within minutes of them going inside, Archie stormed out to see what was going on. Doris's stomach turned over. She knew this would happen and had tried to prepare herself. She had joined the protest for Claude, yes. Because it was unfair how they were being treated, yes. But also for herself. It was a private protest between her and Vi. When Claude had said it was time to stand up and say something, Doris agreed with him for a different reason. Doris was angry. She didn't deserve any of this. She had Claude now, and he gave her the strength to say she'd been wronged.

'What in god's name are you playing at?' shouted Archie.

26

Vi

'Ruth Ellis has decided not to appeal,' said Win, reading from her newspaper as Vi sat with her at the kitchen table opening a tin of salmon for tea.

'Well good, the vulgar little tart knows she deserves it,' said Vi, struggling with the tin opener.

'Says here she changed from a quiet girl to a murderer. It's not surprising, is it, the way she was treated by those men and left on her own? I'm worried the same thing will happen to Doris.'

Vi tutted. 'What? That she'll shoot some fella in the back and get hanged for it? Don't be daft.' The rank smell of tinned salmon filled the air as Vi forked it into a bowl. 'It's bad blood, that's all. You and me have got bad blood but we're keeping our heads above water.'

'Should she hang for it though, Vi? Says here, capital

punishment is savage and it should be banned and the Home Secretary should save Ruth Ellis from the rope in three weeks' time.'

'You know what I read? That she's given orders to have her expensive evening clothes sold to put towards the keep of her ten-year-old boy. She knows what she's done and she's gonna swing for it, that's all. What's that racket?'

Vi went over to the window and looked out, saw a group of West Indians down there outside and heard Archie shouting.

'Something's up,' she said, running down to see.

Lifting up the bar flap, Vi rushed through the pub, where the punters were standing up to look out of the windows, and outside, where Archie and two Teddy boys from the pub were facing a group of coloureds holding up placards. Vi tried to read the signs and listen to what Archie was saying, tried to hear what the coloureds were saying when she saw Doris there. Vi frowned, not understanding. She read Doris's sign, *Let the Coloureds Have a Pint,* and wondered what on earth was going on.

'What's going on here?' she said loudly over the din.

Archie turned to her. 'They're having a protest,' he said with disgust, 'against the pub not letting them in.'

'What? Why would we want you in here?' Vi couldn't understand what the fuss was about, they could go and drink elsewhere. 'Now clear off, the lot of you, before I call the police.'

One of them stood up on an apple crate and started some sort of speech about being a farmer in Jamaica. Vi was so astonished she just stood there to listen. He talked about how the British destroyed the Jamaican economy with their one-crop agriculture, about how he was brought up under the British education system, how he had a British passport and had as much right to drink in the pub as anyone. He got off his crate and picked up a sign that said *Stop Racism* and walked around in a circle with the others, Doris included, with the kid hopping along with her.

Vi snapped. 'I don't know what the hell you think you're doing here but you can just bugger off,' she shouted. 'Archie.'

She beckoned to Archie to get rid of them. He grabbed the jacket of one and shoved him off. The two Teddy boys strode in looking like they expected a fight but the coloured who had spoken told the others to go and they went off. Doris looked back at Vi as they walked away peacefully. Vi had never seen her look like that before and her hackles rose.

'If you come around here again, Doris, I'll call the police on you, I'll make them take you away, you ungrateful piece of work. How dare you do this?' Vi was shouting and Doris just carried on walking with her disgraceful friends, the kid staring back at Vi with a look of confusion.

'How dare she?' Behind the bar, Vi poured herself a large brandy. 'How bloody dare she? Hanging around with that lot is bad enough, but making a big scene like that outside my pub. I'm fuming.'

'Stupid little cow, if she does it again, we call the police,' said Archie.

Vi nodded at him and downed her drink. She was shaken up. How could Doris do such a thing? Did she put those men up to it or the other way around? And in her special place, too. Her special place where, years before, Vi had met her Cyril when she had a job in the docks mending bed linen.

She would eat her lunch on the sea wall right there outside the pub. And they would sit there together when they were courting. The thought of Doris and that lot soiling it made her sick.

'It's all well and good them talking about being British. We should keep the colonials in order where they belong, that's our duty,' said Archie, rolling a cigarette.

'Roll me one, Arch,' said Vi.

'It's a damn bloody cheek,' said Archie.

'The dockers are on strike, maybe they thought they would copy them. But the dockers have got a right to protest, haven't they, Arch?' Vi felt herself starting to cry and held it back. Seeing Doris out there with them was a shock. 'My punters don't want to be bothered with the likes of them stirring up trouble. They work hard, they just want a drink and a smoke and a paper, that's all.' Vi's voice caught in her throat. As she held the roll-up for Archie to light, her hand shook. The shame of it. If Doris came round again Vi didn't know what she would do.

27

Doris

'It was a good start,' said Claude, back at the tenement court-
yard. The boys were sitting in the chairs or on the ground.
Doris squatted on the upturned apple crate that Claude had
spoken from and Laura was chasing a seagull that seemed to
be playing with her.

'It did not do any good,' said Homesick. 'That is not gonna
change anything.'

'That is not the point, is it?' said Smallie. 'The point is
that we have started something. It is about having a voice,
speaking up, saying what is wrong is wrong.'

'That is right,' said Claude. 'I think we did well. We should
go again soon and see what happens. As long as we keep it
peaceful they cannot do anything to us. If the police come,
they'll just move us on, won't they?'

'Who knows?' said Goodfor. 'I don't want to go to jail.'

'What about you, Doris?' said RAF. 'Your folks?'

'Yeah,' said Doris. 'I dunno, they didn't like it but we've given them something to think about. Come on, Laura,' she said, 'I've got to get to work.'

'I'll walk you over,' said Claude, standing up.

As they walked the ten minutes through the Tilbury streets to the boarding house, Doris slipped her hand into Claude's. He smiled at her.

'You had courage to do that today.'

Doris shrugged. 'I'm sick of the way they treat me. I'm glad we're doing it.'

Claude nodded. 'You're having your own battle, aren't you, Doris?'

She nodded and forced a smile.

'How is work?' he said, his brow creasing with concern.

'All right, I suppose. It's a bit odd.' She didn't like to say she was completely befuddled by it all. Those men paying money to go in, some of the things that Lil kept behind the desk. One of the girls asked for a horse whip the other day. Doris hadn't wanted to touch it.

'What has Stanley said?'

'What about?'

'I don't know, just are you staying on the desk or what?'

'Don't know, Claude.'

He pulled her hand to make her stop, put his hands on her shoulders and looked down into her eyes. 'I don't want you working there, Doris.' He stroked her cheek.

'Me, me!' said Laura, 'Tickle me, Caude.'

'Oh, you naughty little pig,' said Claude laughing, and

he lifted Laura up and swung her around, turned her upside down and held her arms while he tickled her. She writhed with joy and tried to scream out but couldn't.

Doris smiled. He was so good with the kid. She wondered what he meant about not wanting her to work at the boarding house. Perhaps he had plans for them. She didn't want to hope for anything, but he seemed very taken with London. Maybe he'd suggest they go up there to live together and he'd look after her and Laura.

'Isn't there anything you can do, any help you can get? I thought with the welfare state and all . . . ' said Claude.

Maybe Doris had guessed wrong. He just wanted to help her. Maybe he wanted to help her to help herself first of all and then other things would come later.

'The welfare don't help people like me,' she said. 'There are enough ex-servicemen on the housing list. If you're unmarried with a kid you're nothing, just a shameful disgrace. When I was at the Salvation Army home they were talking about something, I can't remember now, some kind of place that helped people like me, but it wasn't the welfare. I can't remember now, I didn't think I needed it then because I was planning to go home. Look how that turned out.'

'Maybe you should find out, Doris?'

Claude put Laura down and took Doris's hand again. A surge of pleasure ran through her body. She looked at him. She'd never imagined she would fall for someone like him. Although, apart from how he looked, he wasn't so different from Kenny – funny and kind – at least the Kenny she had known before he'd turned his back on her. Claude squeezed her hand. Yes, he must have plans for them. He wanted to see if they could get any help together.

'The Lettice Fisher Fund,' exclaimed Doris, surprised that she had remembered. 'That's it, the Lettice Fisher Fund, I remember thinking what a funny name it was.'

'Write to them, Doris, eh?'

She nodded. She felt uplifted, fresh, like there was a change for the good on the horizon. There was something about this man, like if you knocked him down he'd just get back up again. When Doris had been knocked down she'd stayed there not expecting anything else. A fallen woman. Why shouldn't she pick herself up again?

Up ahead in the road she could see a man pushing his barrow along. His back was stooped, going up a slight incline. She couldn't see his face but could feel the effort he was making, the tendons in his neck taut, each step hard won. She had a sudden urge to draw him. And then she knew for sure things were getting better.

As they passed a telephone box, Claude stopped.

'Here, let's try something,' he said.

They squeezed into the box, Claude and Doris pressed together in the small space. Claude picked up the telephone and dialled the operator.

'Hello, could you give me the address for Lettice Fisher Fund please? Lettice Fisher,' he repeated.

He waited and smiled at Doris, laughed when he saw Laura pressing her face against the glass from the outside, her nose and eyes squashed and deformed.

'Yes, yes that must be it, thank you,' he said, taking out a small pencil and notebook from his inside coat pocket and leaning on the little shelf to write something down.

He hung up. 'The National Council for the Unmarried Mother and her Child.'

'Yes, that's it,' said Doris, excited.

'Twenty-one Coram Street, Russell Square, London,' he said, reading his note.

He tore off the section of paper and handed it to her.

'Write to them, Doris, tell them about your situation and see what they say.'

Doris looked at the piece of paper. 'I will, Claude, thanks.' She turned the paper over, saw some writing there. *Pick a colour, any you please. The ruddy reds of burst vein cheeks. The milky cream run through with soft green lines.* 'What's this?' she said.

'Oh,' Claude laughed, embarrassed. 'Just a little poem I was working on. It is all right, I will remember it.'

28

Doris

'It's too big,' said Doris, laughing.

She was trying to carry a placard along the road towards the pub for another protest, but the new one Smallie had made for her was six feet high. She was dragging it along the ground.

'I'll help, Mumma,' said Laura, trying to lift up the tail end. The two of them struggled along, like Jesus carrying his cross.

RAF whistled a tune and swayed his hips as he walked along Fort Road carrying his sign. The boys were all up for it this time. Claude had talked to them, told them it was their duty to stand up and speak out that what was happening was wrong. And it did the trick.

'Hey, Homesick,' called out Smallie. 'Here's a new boat coming in now,' he said, pointing out to the river. They all looked out to the water. A large passenger ship was docking at the landing stage of the passenger terminal. They could see the men and women waving from the decks, the dark faces alight with expectation.

'Do you want to tell them or shall I?' said RAF to Claude with a wry smile.

'Well, let's hope they get straight on the boat train and don't come this way. It'll be some kind of greeting to see this,' said Claude. 'Let's rest here for a while,' he said, putting his placard down against the sea wall and leaning his elbows there to watch the boat.

'I feel like an old timer and I haven't been here long,' he said as Doris and Laura put their sign down next to his. 'It's been a baptism of fire, coming here.'

'I'm glad you did, though, Claude,' said Doris, leaning against him as they looked out to the water. He put his arm around her shoulder and pulled her to him, kissed the top of her head.

'You send that letter off?'

She nodded. 'Yep, I told them all about it, and said I need some help.'

'Well, let us see what they say. Come on,' he called to the others.

This time they set themselves up a little further away from the pub, about a hundred feet along the sea wall. Claude put his apple crate down and Smallie jumped on to it straight away, eager to say his piece. A few people stopped as they passed by to hear what was being said. Some of them expressed their disgust but for the first time one woman nodded and smiled and this gave them all the encouragement they needed.

Doris kept her eye on the pub. It gave her a thrill to think she was annoying Vi and Archie. The net curtain was pulled aside at the top window. Auntie Win looked down and gave her a little wave and then a gesture as if she was shooing Doris away, her mouth saying something Doris couldn't hear. The sound of an approaching police siren made it clear.

The police car pulled up along the road outside the pub, a constable got out and walked over to them. Claude jumped up on to his box and started to speak.

'I know I was luckier than some in Jamaica, but is that any way to justify a life? Is it godless to make do and not strive for more? I'd go to Kingston, spend whole days in the library. I read things my uncle had no interest in. He told me to go and work for United Fruits, said they have irrigation ditches and don't water each plant by hand, but he'd rather fall on his machete than do the same himself. I told him to try going into sugar now the market has started to pick up. He says in his dreams he's one of the old English landowners who own eighty-five per cent of Jamaica and he wakes up in a sweat . . . '

'Get down off there, mister.'

'Why, constable? I'm doing no harm.'

'You're disturbing the peace, now do as you're told and get down off there, and you all take your signs and go home. You're not wanted here.'

Claude refused to budge and just as the police constable reached up to take Claude's arm, Claude saw something that made him freeze.

'Yes, yes, constable, no problem,' he said, and Doris wondered why he'd changed his tune so suddenly. He jumped down from the crate, still looking intently at something. 'I am sorry, of course.'

The police constable backed away and leant against the bulbous bonnet of his grand black car to make sure they left. Doris followed Claude's gaze – he had such a look on his face. He put his placard down by the sea wall and started running along the river front in the direction of the docks' passenger terminal, which was just along the river from the pub. Doris looked beyond him to see what on earth he was up to.

There in the distance stood a woman, a coloured woman in a smart coat and hat, and by her leg a small child. Doris squinted her eyes – it was a boy, about Laura's age. The woman walked a few steps towards Claude, and broke into an awkward run herself, her suitcase hindering her. Her mouth moved as she said something to the boy. He looked at Claude and shouted out, ran ahead of the woman and when the boy and Claude met each other, Doris had the sickest feeling of dread as Claude lifted the boy up, swung him around, turned him upside down and held his arms while he tickled him.

Doris looked on, her brain trying to find other ways of explaining what she could see. But when the woman reached Claude, he put the boy down and caught her up in his arms, put his face close to hers and kissed her as they spun around. Doris felt lightheaded; she swallowed with her mouth open, her jaw slack with shock.

The woman pulled away from Claude's grip, smoothed her skirt and checked her hat was on straight. Doris could tell she was conscious of the group of people watching her. Claude looked along at Doris, seemed to take a deep breath as he glanced at the ground and back at her again. As he took a step towards her, so Doris took a step back. Claude put his arm around the woman and held the boy's hand, led them towards his friends.

Doris dropped her placard and backed up. The space between her and Claude had become solid, pushing her backwards until she bumped against the sea wall with a shock. Claude and the woman reached RAF.

'RAF, this is Albertina, and this is our son, Gem.'

Doris retched, looked around for Laura, grabbed her hand and strode away.

'Doris,' called Claude. He ran to catch up with her, held her arm to stop her. 'Doris, look . . .'

'Look?' She wanted to speak but her face crumpled into tears. 'I'm looking, Claude,' she said, her voice strained and whining, 'and I can see something that looks like a great big lie to me.'

'No, Doris . . .' Claude shook his head woefully. 'No, I wanted to tell you. I'm sorry, Doris. I don't know how to say this. Albertina, we've been together for years, we have a son. She's why I was waiting in Tilbury. But you, I didn't think I'd meet someone like you, Doris.'

Doris stifled a sob, pressed the back of her hand against her mouth. She felt like she'd been cast out all over again. Like a bit of rubbish, just thrown out when she wasn't any good for anything. Claude clutched her arms. 'Doris, I'm sorry. I want you to carry on, Doris. Carry on with the protest and the boys. I want you to get out of Stanley's place, Doris, are you listening? It's no good for you there. I want you to draw.' Claude was crying now, and Doris let her tears fall. 'I want you to draw and shine.' He wiped his eyes. 'I'm so sorry.'

He turned to gesture to Albertina that he was coming.

'And you,' he said to Laura, picking her up and giving her a kiss on the cheek, 'you look after your mumma, all right Blaze-A-Glory?'

'Where you going, Caude? Who that lady, Caude?'

Laura's little face looked so worried. She grabbed Claude's collar when he tried to put her down.

'I've got to go to London, now, little piggy, all right, but I'll come back to see you, I promise.'

Claude gave Doris a weak smile and walked back to his wife and child.

29

Vi

Vi saw the whole thing. The leader of the damned coloured group that was causing trouble for the pub, the one who appeared to be Doris's fella, going off with a woman and child just off the boat.

Vi felt a deep satisfaction that the group had their own troubles now, that him leaving might mean the rest of them giving the protest a rest. Who did they think they were anyway, with the dockers just down the way with something real to moan about? And Doris, who seemed like a stranger as Vi watched from her window. She wasn't the innocent young girl Vi had nurtured and educated to grow up to be a good wife and mother. Vi felt altogether distant from her. She didn't hide behind the curtain but stood in full view. She wished they would all, Doris included, just clear off for good. The time would come when Archie would stick to his word and send her away if she didn't go of her own accord.

She turned back from the window and jumped when she realised Win was standing at her shoulder.

'You made me jump,' she said, putting her hand to her chest.

'Poor Doris,' said Win. 'Why don't you just take her in, Vi?'

'Take her in? Are you off your rocker?'

Win sighed and went back to the kitchen table to finish her 'nigger minstrels' cakes.

'Can't you think of something else to make? You've been doing those for years.'

It was a post-war recipe, for when there was no fruit for cakes, when you had to be inventive with food ideas. The 'nigger minstrels' were made out of stale chocolate cake crumbs moulded together into a ball for the head, with an upside-down ice cream cone for the hat.

Win looked wounded. 'Archie likes them, he thinks they're funny,' she said, icing white eyes and mouths onto the heads.

Vi tutted. They just reminded her of that lot outside. She went to her bedroom, felt like taking a look at the pub books to take her mind off things. Archie didn't seem to want her to check the books any more but she'd done it herself for years and missed keeping an eye on the pub's affairs. The safe had always been kept in her room, Cyril had installed it there. She turned the dial to the usual combination, Cyril's birthday – twelve, ten, thirteen – and pushed down on the handle. It didn't open and she tried again. The combination had been changed and she felt a stab of anger in her gut.

'Where's Archie?' she said, striding back to Win in the kitchen.

'Gone out to watch the football, the dockers are playing Monday Leather Factory, why?'

'I need to talk to him.'

Archie's chaffinches hopped and twittered in their little cage. There were four of them in there, jerking their heads with tiny quick movements. One of them jumped to the side of the cage, its claws clinging to the wire bars and its wings flapping pointlessly. Vi had a strange urge to open the door and set them free.

30

Doris

'He left this for the little one.'

RAF sat on the kerb with Doris outside the boarding house, the morning sunshine blocked by cloud. He handed her a little wooden horse.

'He was carving it for her. It's nearly finished, he said to give it to her when he left for London.'

Doris didn't take the carving. Instead she lit a cigarette.

'He was very sorry, Doris, he didn't mean to have feelings for you, he said, but he couldn't help it.'

RAF sighed when Doris gave no reply.

'I don't know how much he told you about himself, but you heard his apple crate speeches. He told me that on the day King George died, Albertina told him she was with child. They're not married, those two. In Jamaica, we don't believe you have to be married to be together – that's why Claude wanted to ease you up, being treated like you are because you have a child on your own.'

Doris tilted her head back and blew out smoke.

'Claude told me he was so sad,' continued RAF, 'when Albertina told him she was having a baby, but he said he was quick to smile and hold her tight and she fell asleep with his hand on her belly. But you know, Doris, he said he had the sickest dread inside him. All he could think was *What prospects does any child of mine have? What sort of example am I?* He fell into a restless sleep and he dreamt of his child pushing the plough, his hands and feet red with bauxite, with Claude up ahead pulling the pale, bone-jutting oxen just like his Uncle Norton did all his life. And Claude, he said he needed something more in life. He needed to come to England.'

Doris made no answer. She could imagine Claude saying this to RAF in his poetic way, but RAF's words didn't console her. Nothing would. RAF said goodbye and left and Doris was glad to see him go, he just reminded her of Claude. She sat there on the kerb and smoked. Any lightness of feeling that she'd had lately with Claude had gone. Her body was heavy, her every breath weighed her down. She'd drag herself to work, slump at the front desk and couldn't muster a smile for the customers. She'd have to drag herself to work tonight too.

She heard the tap of a man's footsteps along the pavement, and saw Stanley's slim suited figure from the corner of her eye.

'Doris, Lil's back so she'll be on the desk tonight.'

'All right,' she said, not caring.

He came and sat down on the kerb with her. She jerked her head in surprise.

'So I'll want you to take your first punter tonight, all right?'

He said it as though he was giving her a list of groceries to get at the shops. She frowned and turned her head to look at him.

'What?'

He didn't miss a beat. 'Your first punter, all right? Talk to Fred if you need to know anything. We'll give you someone good for your first go; don't worry, you'll be marvellous.'

With that, he stood up and walked into the boarding house, whistling as he went.

What he'd said wouldn't go into her brain. Did he mean he wanted her to go to a room with one of the customers? To do what? Her heart fluttered with panic. She felt a sudden need to run away quick. But where would she go? Stanley had been good to her, given her a room and a job. There was no one else to look after her and the kid.

Fred came out to sit with her.

'Stanley sent me out,' she said. 'Want one?' She offered her pack of cigarettes. Doris held up hers to show she already had one.

'Look, Doris, we all remember our first time with a punter. It's not as bad as you think it's gonna be. And we're all here for you, all right?'

'I don't want to, Fred. Can't I just stay working on the desk instead?'

'You'll be all right,' smiled Fred, nudging Doris with her elbow. 'Look, you can only get these from the doctor if you're married, but Stanley got hold of a couple for me. I've rinsed one off, you can use it for the time being.' She smiled as though she was giving Doris her last crust of bread and handed her a little rubber cup thing with a rim of hard black leather.

'Squeeze it together and pop it up there. Don't rely on making yourself sneeze if he won't wear something. We don't want any more little Lauras, do we?'

Doris took it with the tips of her fingers and gave Fred a weak smile of thanks.

'We'll give you someone nice for your first one. They're all right really, when you get used to their funny ways. You'll get regulars who ask for you and they'll give you a bit extra on the sly upstairs. Don't tell Stanley if they do that or he'll want his cut.'

She might as well have been talking French.

'You know, it's much better here than in London. Tilbury's not half as bad as some of the places I've been. But all docklands are the same in a way, you get the waifs and strays, the spivs and tarts, that's why I came here.' She smiled bitterly and shook her head to clear it away. 'You get all sorts washing up at the docks. They're cracking down in London though, since the Festival of Britain, scared of shocking the tourists and all that. They arrest you, put you in front of the magistrate at Marlborough Street court, you get fined thirty shillings and then you're back on the street. You don't get all that nonsense here, probably because there's only one brothel in the whole of Tilbury.' She laughed.

'Brothel?'

'Yes, chicken, that's what a place like this is called, a knocking shop. God, you *were* born yesterday, weren't you?'

Doris looked back over her shoulder at the boarding house. It was a brothel. She'd heard the word before. The tarts on Ship Street, that's what Vi and Archie used to say. Was she a tart on Ship Street now? In the brothel. She thought of Claude and how he used to say he didn't want her to work there. The heaviness came upon her again. What did she care anyway? She was just the type, surely – unmarried mothers were considered immoral, not real women, that's what Vi had always told her.

'We'd better get you spruced up a bit. Got any dressy sort of clothes? Make-up?'

'I've got a bit of make-up.'

'Hm, well, come up to my room, I'll lend you something to wear for now.'

Doris dragged herself up to standing and followed Fred up the stairs. Fred's room was much like her own except there were scarves hanging here and there and a lot of cheap jewellery hanging from the dressing table mirror. She pulled a green dress from her wardrobe and handed it to Doris.

'Try that on,' she said.

Doris pulled off her cardigan and day dress, turning her back to Fred, embarrassed to be seen undressed. The green dress fitted her but was a bit short and her bra showed around the halter neck.

'Take it off, your bra, with that dress.'

Doris unhooked her bra and pulled it off.

'Here,' said Fred, handing Doris a long string of black beads. 'What size shoe are you?'

'Five.'

'That's lucky, here.' She passed Doris a pair of black stilettos.

'You know what? You look pretty good, Doris. You got any red lipstick?'

Doris shook her head and suddenly wanted to cry. She leant down to apply Fred's bright red lipstick with a shaky hand in the mirror.

'Good, very good. I think you're ready,' said Fred, applying some lipstick herself and adjusting her chest so that more of her cleavage showed. 'Let's go down.'

Fred might have said *Let's go to the cinema* or *Let's go to the butchers*, the way she said it. Numb and heavy, conscious of her bra-less chest, Doris followed her down the stairs and out onto the pavement. Bette was there already, leaning against the wall and smoking. She looked surprised when she saw Doris.

'All right, Doris? Don't you look a treat, the punters'll love *you*.' She gave Fred a look when Doris didn't answer. The two of them chatted for a while before the first customer came along. It was the ex-army man who had seen Fred before, that time Doris was on the desk for the first time and had lost track of the time.

'Hello, love,' said Fred, putting her arm around the man's waist. 'Come to see Fred, have you?'

The man chuckled and guided her inside. Doris looked after them with horror. Fred was supposed to be helping her, wasn't she?

'Don't worry,' said Bette. 'Someone'll be along for you soon, you can go next if it's someone nice.'

Bette stood there on one hip picking her nails and Doris didn't know what to say to her, or even how to speak any more. After twenty minutes a man came walking from the other direction. He was on the other side of the road and she hoped he wouldn't cross, but he did and he came straight over to them.

'Evening, girls, who's this then? Fresh meat?' The man was big, taller than Doris and half as wide again, he wore a suit but his belly bulged through his suit jacket beneath the button. He laughed, his lips pulling away from his teeth. He seemed to have a strange amount of teeth, or were they just very wide, Doris couldn't decide. There were small fleshy lumps on his face, around his mouth and his left eye.

'Hello, Percy, this is our Doris, a sight for sore eyes, isn't she?'

Doris looked at Bette. She was selling her like she was a hot chestnut. Women for sale, that's what they should put above the door. It brought to mind Claude's story about the Jamaican slaves.

Percy sidled up to Doris and put his hand on her backside and squeezed it. 'Oh yes, I think she'll do nicely,' he said, laughing again, this time into Doris's face. She did her best not to lean away but gave a small smile instead. 'Come on then, I can hardly wait. See you Bette, love, maybe your luck will be in next time.'

In a daze, Doris held Percy's hand and led him up the stairs. She could see Lil watching her but didn't turn her head. If she did that she wouldn't make it up the steps. On the landing she turned left and opened her bedroom door. Laura was in there, looking out of the window.

'Get,' said Doris, and Laura took one look at Doris's face and ran out of the room.

Percy closed the door and came straight to Doris, pawing

267

her body, his podgy hands squeezing her breasts hard, and reaching up inside her dress, worming into her knickers and touching her between her legs, his fingers going in. Doris turned her face away, feeling like she was going to throw up.

'Get undressed,' he said.

She took a deep breath and looked at the wall as she undid the halter bow at the back of her neck, let the dress fall down around her waist. Percy had his hands in his trousers, touching himself and grunting.

'Take it off,' he said.

She pulled the dress down, hesitated, left her knickers on and stepped out of the dress, leaving her stockings and shoes on.

'Undress me,' said Percy, in a breathless, frantic voice.

Doris paused, not wanting to touch him. Going to him half naked, she felt like a meat carcass hanging in the butcher's window. She unbuttoned his shirt and pulled his tie free, eased his sleeves off. There were more fleshy little lumps on his body, a lot more. His stomach was huge and round, his nipples hanging downwards. She pulled at his trousers, which he had already undone. He groped her with one hand while rubbing himself down there with the other. His trousers around his ankles, he pushed his pants down and Doris saw in his hand his thing, massive and stiff and grotesque, his balls hanging long beneath.

He pushed her with one hand towards the bed. She stumbled and fell against it. He turned her so her back was facing him and she nearly passed out from a wave of shock when she remembered she had been there before.

We don't want any more little Lauras, do we? Percy's body came up against her backside as he pressed her shoulders down and pulled her hips upwards towards him. *Just shut up and keep quiet. I've seen you with Kenny, you little tart.* We don't want any more little Lauras, do we? Percy prodded at her with his hard thing. *If you say anything about this I'll tell your mother and I'll have you put in the madhouse.* Percy reached down and grabbed her breasts in both his hands, rubbed them round and round like he wanted to grind them back into her body. We don't want any more little Lauras, do we? *Shut your fucking mouth, one peep out of you and you're in trouble.* Percy jabbed and poked her backside with his thing until he found his way in, and as soon as it went in, Doris retched and was sick on the satin eiderdown.

'What the . . . ?' Percy pulled out and knelt back on the bed. 'What the hell?'

Doris swung around to face him, climbed off the bed, pulled the green halter neck dress back on, left Percy kneeling there on the bed with his thing sticking out in front, ran down the stairs holding on to the banister to stop herself falling in the high heels. Lil looked up from the desk at the sight of her coming down in a state.

'Doris!' she said, half standing.

Doris didn't stop. She ran out the front door, stumbled across the road.

'Doris!' It was Fred, calling out to her from the pavement, but Doris kept going until she came to The Empire pub and ran past it, stopping at the sea wall, leaning against it to catch her breath.

The pub, where it had happened four years ago. Archie,

coming to her room that time. He had forced himself on her and she hadn't even known what was happening. To her it was violence, a sick violence with him jabbing his body into hers and it was so much of a shock that she did as she was told and shut her mouth. For days afterwards she had been unable to speak, afraid to look at anyone in case they guessed what had happened. If she'd been able to speak she wouldn't have known how to describe it or give any reason for what he'd done anyway.

And to think that Laura was Archie's baby, she must have been, Doris had only just realised it. Vi had always told her she didn't need to know where babies came from, that it wasn't for young ladies to know about these things. At school the girls would giggle about things but wouldn't include her; she was stuck up, that's what they said anyway, because she wasn't allowed out and couldn't join in. In class the teacher talked about plants reproducing and farm animals having babies but nothing was said about how it was done. She had loved Kenny and she had let him kiss her and that's why she thought the baby was his, because isn't that what a husband and wife do, love and kiss each other? She'd seen Win and Archie having a kiss and cuddle when they thought no one was watching and she had a vague memory of her parents doing the same thing when she was little. The realisation that it was what Archie had done to her, what Percy had done, and that's how babies were made – good god, no wonder Vi didn't tell her and the teacher didn't tell them. It was a brutal attack, a disgusting invasion. How could she have been so stupid?

A surge of sickness and anger overcame her. She realised

the group of boys were there, protesting with their placards. She stumbled over to them and they stopped dead to see her in the dress and heels and lipstick. Doris grabbed the placard out of Goodfor's hands and started stomping around the apple crate in a circle, thrusting the placard into the air with every step, and with every step she shouted out like an animal, *Let us live, let us live, let us live.* She screamed it and the boys stood still, staring at her with surprise.

'Doris,' said RAF gently, coming over to her. 'What is it?'

'Let us live!' she shouted. 'Let us live!'

She watched the door of the pub, willed it to open and it did. Vi came out, followed by Archie.

'Stop her,' shouted Vi. 'Look at the state of her, the awful tart. Stop her, Archie.'

'Yes, Archie,' said Doris, slowing down, throwing the placard down and stepping up on to the apple crate, wobbling on her heels, leaning forward to shout. 'Come on, Archie, what have you got to say for yourself?'

Archie hesitated, could see something was up. 'Come on, I'm calling the police if you don't clear off . . .' he said uncertainly.

'Ha ha ha,' laughed Doris. 'What a marvellous idea, *Uncle* Archie, why don't you call the police? I'm sure they would be very interested in what I've got to say.'

'What are you talking about, Doris, have you gone mad?' said Vi, stepping forward.

'Did you know, Mum?' she said, a sob catching in her throat.

'Know what?'

'Did you know what *Uncle* Archie did to me?'

The colour drained from Vi's cheeks, her rouge standing out like a rash.

'What are you talking about?'

'It's what the men at the brothel do to the girls there, that's what. He's the one who made me have a baby.'

'No.' It was a statement of fact. Vi said it quietly. Just *No*.

'You're off your silly head,' said Archie. 'Time to call the madhouse I think, Vi.' He let out a fake laugh. Doris saw the boys exchange glances, sizing up the situation.

Vi stood there, silent but visibly shaken. Archie turned on his heel and headed back into the pub. 'Come on, Vi, we've got a business to run.'

Vi shook her head at Doris and followed Archie.

'It's all your fault, Archie, all of it's your fault,' Doris called after them and Vi hesitated, slowed her step and then carried on inside.

31

Vi

Vi walked back into the pub. She looked at her punters enjoying themselves. She was proud of her business, her position in society. Archie was back behind the bar, talking to Sally the Whelk, who passed a little bowl of jellied eels over to him. He winked at her and smiled. Archie knew about business, knew how to keep the punters happy. Vi was exhausted. She could have fallen into a chair and nodded off, but she had a pub to run. The sight of Doris out there in that dress and that smudged red lipstick looking like a cheap tart. It was the last straw. And saying those things about Archie, who had done so much for them.

'Usual, love?'

Smiling, she took the empty glass from Ted, the war veteran with a dodgy leg who ran bets for the local bookie. She knew what time he'd be there until and how much he paid Archie his weekly cut.

Squeezing past her, Archie paused, leant down to whisper into her ear.

'All right, Vi?'

She knew he meant was she all right after Doris's outburst. It was good of him to say it, considering what he'd been accused of doing. She nodded and wished they were alone together upstairs. She needed some company tonight.

'Talk later?' she said and he nodded and held her waist as he went by.

Jack and Harry were sitting at their usual places at the bar.

'I don't know, Harry,' said Jack, shaking his head at his newspaper. 'It doesn't seem right.'

'What's that, Jack?' said Vi, cocking her head to see the newsprint.

'That Ruth Ellis girl, going to the gallows.'

'You going soft, Jack?' said Vi, laughing. 'Why should the rules be any different for someone like her?'

Jack and Harry looked at her.

'A good-time girl, shamelessly doing what she likes when the rest of us are trying to keep decent and moral.'

'Well, don't mince your words, love,' said Harry, chuckling. 'I'm on your side and so's the wife. That Ruth Ellis, she's feeble-minded, getting herself into situations. It's no excuse for going on the game and leaving your kids.' He faltered, realised what he'd just said. But Vi had distanced herself from that – she wasn't going to be tarred by that brush, whether the punters had seen Doris just now or not.

'Exactly,' said Vi, accepting a light from Harry.

'Sounds to me like she's had a hard life with those brutes she's ended up with, knocking her about. I don't think she should swing for it. Do a stint of time, yes, but not die,' said Jack. 'Blakely had tried to strangle her, says here. Thousands of signatures have gone to Lloyd George to try and get a reprieve.'

'She should pay for what she's done, Jack,' said Vi. 'Some people go bad no matter what chances they've been given.'

'Where did she get the gun from, anyway?' said Jack.

'Who cares? What difference does that make?' said Vi.

That night after locking up, Vi and Archie went upstairs. Win was already asleep, Vi could hear her snores. When Archie turned in the direction of their bedroom, Vi caught his arm, gestured with her head to go with her. In her room, she shut the door and sat on the bed.

'She's out of order, Vi.'

'What? Who is?'

Archie looked confused. 'Doris, who do you think?'

Vi hadn't wanted to bring it up, she was so tired with it all. 'I know. I'm sorry, Arch, it upset me seeing her like that today.'

Archie sat on the bed next to her, put his arm around her shoulders and pulled her head to rest on his chest.

'It's gone too far now, Vi. I can't have her hanging around out there any more. I mean, look at her, what a state, it's bad for business. It looks like she's on the game, Vi. And with that little kid. I think it's best if she goes somewhere for a while.'

Vi drew her head back to look up into his face.

'For her own safety as much as anything. She's mad, Vi, she needs locking up.'

'I know,' said Vi. 'You're right.' Vi just wanted to block it all out. Thinking about it was too much, it would drive Vi mad herself. All she wanted at that moment was to be held and to feel safe and not have to worry about anything. She put her hand on Archie's belly and looked into his eyes, moved her hand lower down past his belt and could feel that he was of a similar mind.

As she walked along the pavement the following week, Vi looked down at her shoes. With each step, they were taking her closer to something she had dreaded doing. It was almost as if they were walking of their own accord, that they knew what was best. It wasn't so much that she was afraid of doing it, but that going to the doctors now was the final confirmation that she had failed, that Doris had fallen despite all of her efforts. Vi had read the paper that morning, a headline about Ruth Ellis. *I'm content to hang*, it said. Vi had taken a week to think about it and now she was here. Tell them to lock her up and throw away the key – that's what Archie had said. Archie wasn't happy with Doris affecting business and Vi had her position to think about. She depended on Archie for a lot of things.

'Mrs Walsh, it's been a while,' said Dr Peters, showing her in and motioning for her to sit down in a chair across from his desk.

'Hello, doctor,' she said and all of a sudden she had no idea what she was going to say. The shame of it was terrible.

'What can I do for you?'

'It's my daughter, Doris. She's gone astray, doctor, and I'm terribly ashamed.'

She twisted her gloves in her hands and looked at her lap. 'Go on.'

'She . . . she had a child out of wedlock three years ago.' Vi glanced up to see him frowning.

'I see.'

'That's not the worst of it, doctor. We sent her away to the Salvation Army home to give the baby up for adoption but she came home with it, can you imagine? She came home with it and I threw her out, doctor. I'm not proud of that but her behaviour was disgraceful, and there was no way we were going to take her and her bastard child in.'

'And the father?'

'A local boy, his folks didn't want to know or do the right thing. Anyway, I thought she was mad, back then, but since then things have gone from bad to worse. She's living in Ship Street, at the . . . the brothel, and she's hanging around with prostitutes and coloured men and she may well be a prostitute herself now, and all this with her daughter in tow, it doesn't bear thinking about. She's not right in the head, doctor, not morally right, she needs sending somewhere for her own good.'

'I see. This is very unfortunate, Mrs Walsh.' The doctor tapped his fingers on his desk blotter and thought for a moment. 'Very unfortunate.'

'Last week she was screaming outside the pub that she'd been raped. She's just getting worse, it's a disgrace.'

'Why did she say she'd been raped?'

Vi tutted. 'It's just the latest in a string of ways she's making trouble for us. She's been protesting about coloureds not being let in the pub, too. Marching around outside the pub carrying placards. She's not right in the head. She needs putting away somewhere to keep her safe.'

'I see. That would mean her child being taken away, you do understand?'

'Yes. That's what should have happened anyway. She's an unfit mother, that much is clear.'

The doctor drew in a long breath through his nose and wrote something down. 'Leave it with me, Mrs Walsh,' he said, and stood up to show Vi out.

32

Doris

'Fancy a cuppa?'

Fred knocked on Doris's bedroom door the morning after the night with Percy and when Doris nodded, she slipped away to fetch the drink.

'What's wrong, Mumma?' said Laura, already awake and sitting up on the bed playing with her knitted doll.

'Everything. Everything's wrong,' said Doris, lying on the bed heavy with the weight of what had happened the night before.

She closed her eyes but all she could see was Archie coming into her room, telling her to shut up, his hand over her mouth like an iron mask. His rough hands on her skin when he pushed her onto the bed, pulled down her knickers with one hand, his urgent breath next to her ear. *I've seen you with Kenny, you little tart,* he said. *If you say anything about this I'll tell your mother and I'll have you put in the madhouse.* It was like a strange, terrible dream – the more he spoke, the faster he hurt her inside. *Shut your fucking mouth, one peep out of you and you're in trouble.* And then it was over and he was gone, like nothing had happened. Just the wet stuff she had to wipe off and his stink and the echo of his words that never left her. It had been such a shock that she hadn't known what to think about it. When she'd seen Archie in the kitchen the next day he had acted completely normally, didn't say a word about it, and she wondered whether she had gone mad. She felt changed after it in some way she couldn't put her finger on; she never felt quite the same after. But Kenny hadn't done anything like that to her. No wonder he was shocked that she had a baby, no wonder he didn't want to speak to her. He knew that another man must have made her pregnant.

She could hear muffled voices outside her door on the landing. Stanley and Fred. He sounded cross and she sounded like she was trying to calm him down.

'Here you are, then,' said Fred, sitting on the side of the bed and putting the cup and saucer on the bedside table with a clatter. 'What's all this about, then, eh?'

'What did Stanley want?' said Doris, sitting up and reaching for the tea.

'Oh, don't worry about him. He knows we don't all take to it straight away. It can take a bit of getting used to. What happened with Percy, then? He's usually all right.'

Fred peered at her with a mix of sympathy and curiosity. Doris sank into herself, her face creasing with sobs. She tried to speak, she wanted to tell Fred.

Fred took the saucer away from her.

'It's all right. Whatever happened, I bet it's already happened to Fred,' she said, talking about herself and smiling. 'I've been through enough stuff, you know.'

'It's just ...' Doris paused. 'Laura, go downstairs.' Laura grabbed her knitted doll, scrambled off the bed and went.

'It's just, when Percy ... did that, I didn't know what he was going to do, I've only ever done that once before and I didn't realise what it was at the time ... I was ... it wasn't ...'

'You were forced?' said Fred. 'Raped?'

The word was shocking. But yes, it was that. Doris nodded her head.

'Oh, Doris, poor thing, no wonder.' Fred stroked her hand.

'So I always thought Kenny was Laura's dad because he was my boyfriend, but we'd never done that together.'

Fred nodded. 'So, who was it? Who did that to you? Can I ask?'

'My uncle. Archie,' said Doris. And it was a relief to say it out loud.

'My god. That bastard. He's a customer here, did you know?'

'What? No.'

'Yes, and he's a rough one too, no one likes to have Archie.'

Doris cried, and tried to cover her face. It was all too much. What would Auntie Win say if she knew?

'You know what, Doris?' Fred peered down into Doris's face, 'I know how that feels.'

'Yeah?'

'Yes. Why do you think I'm here? Not out of the love of it. No, I was raped too, when I was younger. And I had a baby, too.'

Doris looked at her in surprise. 'You've got a baby?'

Fred shook her head and swallowed, it was hard for her to say it. 'Nope, she was adopted. Because of my situation, because of who her father was.'

'Who?'

'My own dad, can you believe it?' Fred gave a wry smile and looked at her hands. 'It wasn't the first time, either. He'd already got me in the family way once and taken me to a dodgy abortionist who half killed me. Didn't stop him, though. And when it happened the second time, they threw me out. My own mother disowned me.'

'Oh god, Fred.'

'Yep. And I don't even know where my daughter is or if she's all right.' Fred dissolved into tears, shaking her head.

They both jumped at a knock at the door.

'Go away, Stanley, it's not a good time,' called out Fred, as she wiped her nose with her hankie.

The door opened. Lil stood there looking unusually ruffled.

'Doris, you're wanted downstairs. It's the police.'

'What? What for?'

'I dunno, but you'd better get down there quick. It's very bad for business with them hanging around.'

Doris looked at Fred and Fred shrugged. 'You'd better go down,' she said. 'I'll come with you.'

Doris dressed quickly and walked down the stairs slowly. She noticed the pattern in the stair runner, purple and brown swirls, and the little brass runner clips keeping everything in place. When she looked up she saw two policemen standing in the hallway with Dr Peters. They were all staring at her with grim faces. The doctor was holding Laura's hand. She called out *Mumma* when she saw Doris and tried to come towards her, but the doctor held her back. She clutched her doll to her chest.

'Doris Walsh?' said one of the constables.

She nodded.

'You are being detained under the 1913 Mental Deficiency Act,' he said, reading from his notebook. 'You will be committed to Cleavalls mental hospital . . . '

Doris was confused, she couldn't understand what they were talking about. She looked around. Lil had gone, Stanley wasn't there, there was no one down the hall in the back room, it had all gone quiet. Only Fred was there and she was staring at the men and had gone very pale.

'No,' said Fred. 'You can't, she was raped, she hasn't done anything. Go and arrest Archie the landlord at The Empire for rape. He's the one you should be taking away, not Doris.'

'Doris, your mother has given permission, it's for the best,' said the doctor.

'Mumma?' Laura tried again to get to Doris but was pulled back, her face grimacing with the pain of the doctor's grip on her arm.

'Is this your child?' said one of the policemen.

'Yes,' said Doris.

The men looked at each other meaningfully. 'You must come with us,' they said and Doris didn't know which one said it – it was like they were all saying it together.

'I'll take the child first.' That was the doctor.

He held Laura's hand with both of his and led her to the front door. Doris took a step towards them.

'No, wait, where are you taking her?'

The two policemen were at each side of Doris; she felt their hands on her arms.

'Wait,' she said. 'She's still got her nightie on, wait.'

Laura looked back and cried out, 'Mumma!' She tried to pull away but the doctor ushered her forward roughly. She stumbled over the doorstep with her bad foot and he dragged her up to standing.

'Oi, you can't do this,' shouted Fred. 'Bring her back, I'll look after her, she knows me.'

They ignored Fred and Doris lost her voice, a cold panic coming over her. Laura craned her neck to see the last of Doris as she was taken out to the doctor's car, never letting go of her knitted dolly. Doris struggled against the policemen's hold. They pulled her arms around her back and she felt cold metal around her wrists and heard a click and when she tried to bring her arms forward she couldn't. They held her there like that for a few minutes, listened for the doctor's car to go. Fred was at the door watching, her hand on her chest. 'Please,' she said. 'Please, if you take her there she'll never come out, that child will never see her mother again. It's not right, please don't do it.'

'Madam, I suggest you step aside or you'll be coming with us to the station.'

Doris felt herself propelled forward against her will. Her feet shuffled out of the door. They led her to a black police car, opened up the back door and helped her inside. One of them sat there in the back with her and the other went to the front. The engine started and the car eased forward, with Fred's face at the window staring in. Doris watched as the car drew away from Fred, saw her friend disappear from view. And as the car turned at the end of the road, Doris saw Vi standing on the pavement opposite the boarding house with a strange look of grim satisfaction on her face. She had seen the whole thing.

33

Vi

'Vi!' Win came running, breathless. 'What's happened?'

'They've taken her,' said Vi, looking down the road after the police car. 'And good job too.'

'What? Where's she gone?'

'To the loony bin, where she belongs.'

Vi looked at her sister dispassionately. The woman could be so emotional, so inappropriate sometimes. Look at her now, crying and gibbering in the street. What a disgrace.

'Pull yourself together, people will see.'

'What have you done, Vi?'

Win had her hands over her mouth, her eyes horrified.

'I've done what's best, what should have been done a long time ago. She's better off in there, Win. She's in a right mess here, you can't deny that.'

'What about Laura?'

'They've taken her to a home. They said she can't be adopted because of her foot, so she'll be in a home.'

'Vi . . . how could you do it? After what we went through? To send her to one of those places? I don't understand, Vi, I don't . . .'

Win steadied herself with one hand against a garden wall and gasped for air.

'Oh, for god's sake.' Vi left her sister and walked away, back to the pub. It was done now, there was no worrying any more about Doris turning up, hanging around and shaming them all. Perhaps the whispers would die down, the elbow nudging in the shop queues when they thought she wasn't looking. Vi could get back to normal. She'd manage somehow to put it all behind her and carry on. It had been such a strain and now there was a sense of relief that it had all been dealt with. Archie would be pleased too.

'It's done,' she said to him when she got back to the pub. He had just opened up and was taking the towels off the pumps.

'Good job, too. And the kid?'

'Yes, they've taken her to a home.'

Archie nodded. 'We can get back to normal now, eh?'

Vi nodded and picked up a newspaper from the bar. She needed to do something ordinary like read the paper to take her mind off things.

'The brewery are coming today, to talk about how things are going. So I'll be out the back for a while around two,' said Archie.

'Oh? I didn't know that. I didn't see a letter.'

'I open the brewery letters, Vi, there's no need for you to worry about that.'

'I don't worry about it, Archie, I like to be involved. It is my pub after all.'

Archie gave a snide laugh. 'The brewery don't want to deal with a woman. It's men's business, so just leave it to me.'

'I'll come to the meeting, too, Archie, Win can watch the bar.'

'No, Vi, like I said, I'll deal with this.'

Vi was lost for words. He was telling her to back off, almost as if it was his pub. She had asked him for the new combination to the safe and he made an excuse, wouldn't tell her. The books and the deeds were in there.

'Suit yourself,' she said.

Win came in, panting. 'Archie, it's terrible, Doris and Laura have been taken away.'

'Keep your voice down, woman, we'll have punters in soon.'

'I don't care,' said Win, her voice shrill and loud, 'that's my niece we're talking about, they've just carted her off like she's a lost cause. And little Laura, they've taken her too. I can't bear it, Arch, it's too much . . .'

'It's all right,' said Archie, going to his wife and putting his arm around her shoulders, steering her round to the back of the bar and through the hallway to the back room.

Vi heard his voice low, talking to his wife, calming her down. Win was weak; she knew what was best but didn't have the stomach for it.

Vi turned the paper over and recoiled when she saw the front page. *Ruth Ellis hangs this morning.* Her stomach turned, she suddenly felt sick and lightheaded. *At nine o'clock Ruth Ellis will hang.* Vi looked at the pub clock behind the bar. It was ten past eleven. She clutched the paper with both hands, squinted to see the print through the film over her eyes. The bag of sand left overnight to stretch the rope. The white hood placed over her head. The medical officer will go to the pit beneath the trap door to check she is dead. The body will be left to hang for one hour.

Vi ran through the hallway, out the door and got to the lavatory in the back yard quick. She put one hand on the wall and vomited into the bowl.

34

Doris

'Doris? Doris? Wake up, Doris.'

Doris was so sleepy. She rolled her head from one side to another but couldn't open her eyes. So groggy, like she was still asleep but not. Someone was shouting and there was a terrible smell of rotten apples.

'Doris? Come on now, sit up.'

Someone was shaking her with rough hands, their fingers digging into her arms. She struggled to open her eyes, saw a nurse with a starched cap and a dark blue dress and white apron. The nurse looked impatient and was trying to pull Doris up to sitting in the bed. Doris did as she was told: she pushed herself up with her hands, opened her eyes to slits.

'Right, open up now.'

The nurse pushed a spoon of warm mush against Doris's lips until she widened her mouth. Porridge. Plain porridge.

She squashed it with her tongue against the roof of her mouth and wanted to go back to sleep. The nurse pushed another spoonful in, and another, and soon Doris was allowed to lie down and close her eyes.

It felt like a dream that kept happening over and again. The nurse and the fingers digging into her arm and the spoon pushed against her mouth. And then the mist started to clear and Doris was able to think again and remember where she was. Cleavalls. The mental hospital. The loony bin. A shock of fear ran over her in ripples, tightened her throat and made her want the toilet. She sat up in bed, rubbed her eyes. She was in a hospital ward, a long wide room with beds down each side and an open fire in the middle of one wall. The other beds were empty but she could hear the faint murmur of voices coming from nearby. There was a desk at one end where a nurse sat, writing something down. She looked up at Doris, looked down again and continued writing.

'Please . . .' said Doris. But the nurse didn't hear. 'Please, nurse.'

The woman looked up.

'I need the toilet.'

The nurse pursed her lips and put down her pen. 'There's a chamber pot underneath your bed. Now is as good a time as any to get out of bed yourself to use it.'

With that the nurse resumed her writing. Doris frowned, pulled back the sheet and grey blanket and looked at the rough calico nightdress she had on. Her legs were wobbly when her feet touched the floor. Holding on to the bed, she pulled out the pot, looked around and squatted down on it, covering herself with her nightie. The sound of it echoed around the room. The nurse looked up to watch her and Doris felt her face blush hot. There was nothing to wipe herself with so she tried to clench out the drops before she climbed back into bed.

'Your uniform is under your pillow. Put it on,' said the nurse. Her voice ran around the walls of the empty ward; she seemed a long way away.

Doris felt beneath the pillow and found a dress made in a floral pattern, thin from over-washing. She felt for some underwear but there was none – she was too embarrassed to ask the nurse. Cringing from the lack of privacy she pulled off her nightdress and let the dress fall on to her shoulders. It was big, shapeless, short-sleeved. There were several cigarette burns on the skirt. A pair of flat black shoes with one bar across sat on the floor. She put them on and stood up.

'Good. Come with me,' said the nurse, standing up. 'You've seen the Superintendent, haven't you?'

'Oh yes,' said Doris, with a jolt of recall. She had seen him, the man in the office who looked like he was a king, or a god. There was something about him; the way he spoke as though no one would ever question him.

The nurse led her into a large room with high windows. There were lots of women in there, all wearing the same kind of dress Doris had on, except in different floral patterns and some in stripes. Some were sitting in chairs, some were wandering around, there was a lot of noise, and Doris tried to identify where all the noises were coming from. One woman was letting out a shriek as she walked along, some were muttering to themselves. There were two women having an argument. Doris wanted to turn around and go back to bed.

'This is the day room,' said the nurse. 'Let her sit down,' she said to a woman in a wing-back armchair. The woman scuttled away, looking back at them over her shoulder. Doris sat down and the nurse left her there.

She tried to think about arriving in this place. She remembered looking out of the window as they drove through the countryside, saw the fields of cut wheat, a yellow-beige expanse of harsh bare stubble dotted with the black of rooks pecking at the ground. The police had driven her up to a grand building with an impressive entrance, then she was taken into an office, a doctor in a white coat examined and questioned her and took her to the Superintendent's office. He talked to her for a long time. She was upset, crying and numb in turns, but he just talked at her.

'You have a child,' he said, looking at his notes. 'Out of wedlock?'

Doris nodded.

'Having a child out of wedlock is an offence against God's and Man's laws.'

He just said it like a simple fact.

'You know,' he said, with a little laugh, 'in the old days, unmarried mothers were put in the stocks and whipped, or sent to a house of correction for a year of hard labour.'

He expected no answer, it seemed.

'Filius nullius,' he said, pronouncing the words with authority like they belonged to him. 'No one's child.'

Doris couldn't think of what to say or even where to look. He wasn't looking at her, but at the wall or the ceiling, like he was practising a speech.

'In the Victorian days, unmarried mothers and their

293

illegitimate children went to the workhouse. It is widely believed that illegitimate children do not go to heaven when they pass away.'

This went on for some time. He told her that bastards were idiots, that low morals were passed down through generations. It all made Doris feel sick and worthless. He finished by telling Doris that all certified patients were not to be trusted, they could be violent at any point, they did not act with reason or intelligence and they were always trying to escape. And he told her that she had been certified insane, a moral defective, by the doctor she had just seen.

She had been taken away to the ward then and injected with something that put her to sleep. She had vague memories of feeling trapped and no idea how long she had been in that bed.

The woman who had been sitting in the chair sidled back over, seemed to want her chair back but didn't ask for it. She paced up and down in front of Doris, muttering something. Doris strained to hear what she said.

'Twenty, she'd be twenty now, twenty-one she'd be, twenty-one now ...'

The woman looked old beyond her years, sort of folded up. She couldn't have been more than forty, Vi's age, younger even, but she was pale and there were dark circles under her eyes, and she fidgeted with her hands, picking at the cuticles, which made Doris look away.

'Peony.'

Doris jumped. A woman had popped out from behind the wing-back chair, just her head poking around the side, her greasy brown hair streaked with grey.

'What?' said Doris.

'She's Peony, that one.' The woman grinned, showing her discoloured teeth. 'Been in here for donkeys, she has. Came in as a teenager. Had a bastard.'

Doris started back in her chair. The woman grinned at her as though Doris was a funny sight, her eyes sparkling.

'Annie,' she said, presenting her hand at the side of her head.

'Doris.'

They shook hands very briefly and Annie made no pretence at hiding as she wiped her hand on the front of her dress, her short stocky body appearing by degrees as she stood up to perch her wide behind on the arm of Doris's chair. Doris didn't want her there – she remembered what the Superintendent had said about the patients being violent.

Annie let out a big sigh and looked around the room, appraising the view before her.

'Here, watch those two,' she said with a chuckle, leaning in to Doris. Doris looked to where she nodded. One woman was scrubbing the wall with a brush, really putting her back into it. She had a bucket of soapy water into which she dunked the brush, carefully waiting for the drips to minimise before going to the wall with it. The other woman Annie nodded at was coming around the room, wiping her hand along the wall. If someone got in her way, she'd leave her hand in place until the obstacle moved itself, or she stepped over it, never taking her hand away. When she came to where the woman was scrubbing the wall, she wiped her hand straight across the clean wet wall, whereupon the other woman shrieked loudly as though she'd been bashed over the head with something.

She continued to shriek until the other had gained some distance, only to work her way around again.

Annie slapped her thigh and laughed out loud, looked at Doris's horrified face and laughed again. 'Don't worry, duck, you'll get used to it.' She dug her elbow into Doris's shoulder to emphasise her point.

All this while, the scuttling woman continued to pace up and down in front of the chair, saying, 'Twenty she'd be, twenty-one now, grown up she'd be,' and picking at her cuticles.

'How long have I been here, do you know?' said Doris.

Annie sucked her teeth, made a show of thinking about it.

'It's usually four to five days they put the new ones out. Phenobarbitol they give you. To relax you, they say. Keep you under control more like.'

Doris felt like she was in a bad dream. She couldn't take it all in, still felt groggy from the medicine. 'How long have you been here?' she asked Annie.

Annie blew out her cheeks. 'Long time,' she said.

'Why are you here?'

'Why? You don't ask people that, duck. I didn't ask you, did I?'

Annie suddenly jumped up and stamped on something on the floor. Startled, Doris looked to see what it was. She couldn't see anything there.

'Beetles,' said Annie, sitting back down. 'Damn beetles, everywhere.'

At five thirty the nurses led the women to the dining room where they were given bread and margarine, a small piece of cake and an enamel mug of tea to drink. Doris nibbled her food, looking around at the other women and their performances. Most sat silently, one woman shouted that she didn't like the cake, another that she wouldn't eat margarine and where's the butter. At seven thirty they were led to the sleeping ward, given a dose of syrupy medicine and told to get into bed.

Doris didn't think she'd be able to sleep. It all went around inside her head. The Superintendent's words about unmarried mothers, how worthless she felt – she laughed at herself, thinking she'd be able to be a secretary in London when the only reason she'd been there was because of Stanley's divorce job and that was only because he was buttering her up for the brothel. She realised that now. She could hear sheets rustling and women groaning, and one woman slid out of bed and got into bed with someone else. They fidgeted around until the nurse came over to tell that one to get back to bed. Doris stifled a sob when she thought where she'd ended up, remembered Fred's words that if she came in here she'd never get out. She could see herself going mad like the other women and she thought of Laura, Doris's undoing, how everything had gone wrong since she'd had Laura. Kenny hating her, all the places she'd been in and out of, the Salvation Army home, the refuge in Southend, the derelict tenement, the brothel and Claude's betrayal. And when Archie came into her room that time, how she hadn't known what he was doing, and how much she hated him, how he had always threatened to send her here and now here she was, he had finally got his wish. Then, to her relief, her eyes closed and she felt sleep pull her down to nothingness.

35

Vi

Every day now, Vi would scour the paper for more about the Ruth Ellis case. There was a big debate about whether hanging should be abolished. One of the papers held a poll, thirty thousand people voted, two thirds of them said hanging should be stopped. The other day there was a piece about the morning of Ruth Ellis's execution, how she was the calmest woman who ever went to the gallows. And there was a bit about where she got the gun that she shot Blakely with. Turned out another man she'd been seeing gave it to her, he'd shown her how to use it too. Something about it made Vi think she'd been wrong, that maybe the woman did deserve some sympathy after all. Beholden to the men in her life, badly treated by them. It made Vi think about the men in *her* life, how she'd been so in love with Cyril and how she'd had to cope without him during the war. The bloody war.

Vi looked up from her paper, leant back in the wooden kitchen chair and lit a cigarette. It both comforted her and made her feel resentful to think how she had played her part in the People's War, did as she was told, kept cheerful on the outside and slapped on her face every single day. She wondered how many people cried behind closed doors like she did, how many women didn't have the heart to get out of bed in the morning and put on their rouge and lipstick. You had to, it was a wartime crime to be caught down in the dumps, and they wanted the women to cheer the men's morale – there was a reason they didn't ration make-up, and even then she had to melt down the last of the lipstick with cooking oil to make it go further and use beetroot when it ran out. Vi took it upon herself to do her bit. She kept things lively in the pub, fixed on her smile as she opened up each day. Gave the pub garden over to a veg patch too, dug out the spuds herself sometimes, got Doris to help. She had liked pulling the lettuces and checking the leaves for slugs.

During the war, the pub gave Vi a reason to keep going. Keep things ticking over for when Cyril got back. He'd written sometimes, but he didn't say much – it was what he hadn't said that worried her.

It wasn't all roses in Tilbury, though: the docks were a prime target and the sound of the planes going over got to her nerves. She'd find herself wringing her hands then realise what she was doing. You never knew whether the Luftwaffe were carrying on to London or not, so every plane was a worry. Her body would clutch up, she'd crouch over Doris if she heard the whistle of a bomb. She wouldn't be able to sleep for the worry of it and the noise, down in the damp cellar with the beer kegs and a candle in a flowerpot, waiting for the end to come. Then she'd have to get up the next day and carry on, scrimping and smiling and dreading the coming night. Seeing the fires and hearing screams and fire engines and people wandering around dazed and staring.

She took people in who'd lost their homes, so the garden veg came in handy and the dockers would bring her the odd thing or two on the quiet. Win did her bit too. Vi needed her in the pub but she volunteered for this and that, did fire watching duty and helped Vi with Doris. They came and put a big poster on the side of the pub: *Your Courage, Your Cheerfulness, Your Endurance. Will Bring Us Victory*. It was the people's call to the colours, those at home – and to think of Cyril out there doing god knows what, you damned well found your courage, you damned well stayed cheerful.

Even throughout the Blitz when they'd cower in the pub cellar and hear the windows upstairs blow out and bits of plaster would rain down on them. Even when they'd go out in the morning and houses and even The Anchor pub had fallen, squashed like the hand of God had come down and pressed on them hard and the wallpaper flapped in the breeze and people's pots and pans rolled around the street. Even then, The Empire stood. Nothing could bring it down, and Vi was sorry for the people who lost their lives and their homes, but she was proud of the pub, it was a survivor. If it had fallen, Vi would have fallen herself in more ways than one.

When D-Day came, Vi was in bits because she knew Cyril was in it. She found out later he landed at Arromanches – god help them, what did it take those men to make the journey across the water knowing what was coming? Five thousand perished the first day but not her Cyril. Her ear was next to the radio and her eye on the paper and the King gave a speech like a wet rag. Then Hitler sent the doodlebug to slaughter more of them. Months passed and Cyril hung on and they all kept saying, why doesn't Hitler give it up, for god's sake? Then the pictures of those poor souls in the German camps, and Hitler shot himself, damned coward – she wanted him strung up.

The day before VE day, when they were all waiting for news, Vi got in what extra stocks she could, ready for the celebrations. Finally, at nine at night, as the punters all sat with an ear by the wireless and Vi was wiping down the bar, the bloke on the news said it would be two days' holiday from tomorrow. And that was that, the Nazis had come undone. Everyone went quiet and a couple of people cheered. The rag fell from her hand and she dropped down onto a chair. All that killing, all those lives, our boys and theirs, the civilians blown up in their beds, countless screaming souls. And it was over. Vi couldn't take it in at first, didn't believe it. Cyril would be coming home and she had kept things going for five years.

She heard people out in the street, and more came crashing through the pub doors. They wanted a drink and quite right too. Vi wanted one herself. She went outside and all the house lights were coming on, everyone ripping down the blackouts. Someone lit a bonfire and there was music and they were dancing in the street and all the little ones were up and lighting firecrackers, Doris too. A couple of the old bints came around complaining, saying it was too soon to celebrate, what about the Japs. The Yanks'll get them, Vi shouted, kick up your heels, you're not queuing for mutton.

A month later, in July, a telegram arrived. Vi didn't want to take it off the boy but her hand reached forward anyway. She didn't remember reading it, she felt like she died herself that day. Her Cyril, gone, just when it was time to come home.

On VJ day that August at midnight the ships' horns rang around the docks and the church bells were bedlam. Little Doris ran into Vi's bedroom but Vi turned over and covered her ears. Doris shook her and when she turned back she could see in her eyes that Doris felt the same as she did, but Vi had nothing left to comfort her with and Doris lay down on the floor and cried by herself.

Outside they were singing God Save the King, over and over, and they started pounding on the pub doors. Unfeeling bastards, no respect. Vi went down in her nightdress, put a sign up in the window saying *NO BEER* and went back to bed. What did she care if the war was over, if the Yanks had blown up half of Japan? She couldn't care less, they could drop an A-bomb on Tilbury and put her out of her misery.

She'd been through all of that without Cyril and for what? To be left on her own, with Archie and Win, Archie assuming control over her pub. Because women weren't deemed strong or clever enough to do a man's job and because it was easier and safer to just let him take over. She wondered how Ruth Ellis felt on her final day, alone and cast aside by society. But everyone was alone in the end, weren't they? No. It wasn't true. We died on our own, but we didn't have to die lonely, we could die with love. Wasn't that the final test of our lives, how we died? Cyril died with love, and the thought of it made Vi glad enough to choke. But then he left her, didn't he? She thought of Doris as a child, how she loved to draw and colour and chalk on the pavements, thought how hard it was bringing Doris up on her own. Vi hadn't really considered before how Doris had coped on her own with Laura before she went into hospital, only how shameful it had been for her.

Vi knew the consequences of being raised illegitimate, how you feel like a mistake, a disgrace. She just wanted Laura to go to a good home and not have to live with that disgrace. Being born a bastard had affected Vi's own life so deeply – it tainted her in every way, and she couldn't abide the thought of her grandchild being that way. Vi had always struggled with her feelings for Doris. She did love her, but she found it so hard to express it. She had been so fiercely attached to Cyril, he was her identity and survival, whereas Doris was her project, re-creating herself in a decent image. But she had got it wrong.

She wondered how desperately unhappy and trapped Ruth Ellis must have felt to leave her two children behind, to shoot Blakely knowing what it would mean. Vi had read in the paper that Ruth Ellis said she took it all because she loved him so much. Vi tutted. Bloody men.

She opened her magazine, flicked through it, frowned at an advertisement for a bank for business women that she hadn't noticed before. A piece about married couples who shared housework, something telling women not to be a slave to their house, something else saying it was a woman's world. It was funny how you only saw the things you were looking for sometimes.

She sighed and put the magazine aside, stood up and paced the living room. Her feet took her to Doris's room. She hadn't been in there for a long while. Sitting down on Doris's bed, she noticed something poking out from underneath. There were a number of sheets of paper, drawings, in pencil and charcoal. She didn't realise Doris had been drawing at home. From the look of it, she'd been sketching from her bedroom window, looking down at people there, ordinary people going about their business. The drawings were accurate, with a likeness that Vi recognised, but also there was something else there, a touch of sadness or wonder or something that made you pause and think, *Who is that person and what do they want?*

36

Doris

It had been raining for days. A heavy rain, insistent and unending. Doris stood by the window of the day room watching the raindrops running down the glass outside. The drops left traces of themselves in their journey down the glass, until there was barely anything left of them in the end.

Someone was having an argument behind her, but she didn't bother turning around. She was already used to the noise in the place: it was frantic one minute and unbearably calm the next. Some of the women had retreated inside themselves, found somewhere to go. Annie told her that if they were given the chance to leave, most of them would stay. They had been there too long, had become cemented in the daily routine of meals, meds, exercise, sleep, always the same, a predictable safety. Annie had tapped her own head, said she had her own place in there, that it was the only way, that they couldn't take away your dreams and memories.

From the corner of her eye, Doris saw something fly past her. A chair hit the window and smashed the glass before she heard the sound and her brain could register what had happened. She jumped away to one side, looking to see who had thrown it. It was one of the troublesome women, who argued a lot. There were shouts as the nurses called to one another. In an instant there were five of them there, grabbing the woman's arms, pulling her to the floor, holding her down. The woman seemed to know the drill. She relaxed and let them take her away.

'She only does it for the paraldehyde.' It was Annie, at her side. 'She's addicted to it, acts up so they put her in a side room and sedate her.'

Doris watched as one of the domestics came to clear up the broken glass. The other patients were flapping and anxious about the incident.

'You have to watch out if you're bad in here, though. Dr Death will chop your brain up.'

Doris stared and Annie nodded with authority.

'I'm not joking. I've seen bodies carried out of here in bags. There's a surgeon here, he does experiments on patients' brains. Sometimes it works and sometimes it doesn't . . . ' She tapped the side of her nose and Doris didn't know whether to believe her or not.

'If you stay good, you might get a job in the laundry with me,' said Annie, smiling.

'Good?'

'Yes, you know, if you don't try to hurt anyone or try to

kill yourself. Then you can get a job and you're one of the lucky ones who gets out of this room for a few days a week.'

Doris couldn't imagine having a job there. It made it all seem so permanent.

'Otherwise you sit around here for hours every day and it sends you barmy. Look at Peony.' Doris looked at the woman sitting in the wing-back chair picking at her cuticles. 'She's been here so long she's gone inward, sitting around here or shuffling around the airing courts.'

'She's here because she had a baby?'

Annie nodded. 'Yep, disgraced the family and they sent her away. And once you're locked up here, there's only three ways of getting out.'

'What ways?'

Annie lowered her voice and counted out the options on her fingers. 'You escape, or Dr Death chops up your brain, or you ... ' She drew her finger across her throat and Doris felt a shiver down her back. That couldn't be right. She couldn't be in here forever, that just didn't make any sense.

'She's not the only one,' said Annie, watching her closely.

'What?'

'Her,' Annie pointed to another woman sitting quietly in a chair. 'And her.' She pointed to a woman standing at the window further along. 'All here for having babies and not being married.'

Doris felt sick. She didn't want to ask but had to know. 'How long?' she said.

Annie blew out her cheeks. 'Long time. Long, long time.'

One of the nurses called Doris.

'You have a visitor.'

Doris followed her through to the part of the hospital she'd only seen when she'd arrived. Past offices and into a room with some chairs screwed to the floor. Auntie Win sat there looking wretched and holding a small tin in her lap.

The nurse stood over in the corner of the room and Doris went to sit down.

'Hello, love. How you holding up?'

'I didn't know I'd have visitors.'

Auntie Win nodded and pressed a handkerchief to her nose. 'I'm so sorry, Doris, about all of this, I don't know what to say.'

Doris stared at her. This woman whose husband had raped her, had ruined her life.

'You can say you've come to get me out of here.'

'I can't,' she sobbed. 'I can't do anything about it, Doris, I'm so sorry.' Win ran her hand over the surface of the table, wiped it off for bits.

'Why not?' Doris raised her voice. 'Uncle Archie raped me. Laura is his baby. Why can't you do something about that?'

Win shook her head. 'Your mum doesn't believe it, Doris. It's up to her, it's her say whether you stay in here or not.' She hesitated, brushed off the table again, wiped her nose again. 'Doris, are you sure that's what happened?' She whispered it as though the words themselves would make it true.

'Yes, I'm sure.' Saying it brought back the memory of Archie in her room and she shook her head to clear it away. She looked at her Auntie Win's face. She remembered her dad saying when she was little that you can tell when someone is lying to you because they can't sit still. 'You knew, didn't you?

That's why you brought me stuff when I was in the tenement. You knew it was him.'

Win looked pained, her eyes darting this way and that. 'No, Doris, I don't know. Maybe I suspected, but I didn't know for certain.'

'And you're still living with him, sleeping in his bed?' Doris said it with disgust.

'This is Laura's, I thought you might like to have it,' said Win, changing the subject and handing the tin to Doris.

It was an old Lyons' tea caddy and, opening the lid, Doris realised it was Laura's treasure box. Doris had never bothered looking in it before, and Laura had always kept it stashed away safely. Inside were some pebbles that Laura had polished to a shine, a button, three sticks, and a piece of paper curled around the inside, which Doris drew out. It was a pencil drawing of two people, both with big heads and stick limbs, both in triangle skirts and both smiling. One tall, the other small. The small one had a large boot on one foot and a left arm that was freakishly long, winding up snake-like to meet the right hand of the tall one. Doris swallowed and bit her lips together.

'Where is she?'

'They took her away to a home, the doctor won't tell me where.' Win's face wobbled with emotion.

'Like the one you grew up in?'

'I don't know, Doris.'

Doris stood up, clutching the tin, and turned to leave. The nurse stepped forward and held out her hands. 'You can't have that, we'll keep it for you.'

Doris looked at the nurse as though she hadn't heard right. 'Why not?'

'It's the rules. Give it here.'

Doris looked down into the tin again, at the little things in there, so precious to Laura, then looked at the picture again.

'Can't I just keep this?' she said, holding out the picture.

'Yes, all right then.' The nurse took the tin and opened the door.

Doris didn't look back at Win or say goodbye to her. The useless woman wasn't going to help her. She trudged back to the day room.

'What's that?' Annie was at her shoulder.

'Nothing,' said Doris.

The charge nurse blew her whistle and the women shuffled over to line up. Doris did too, she was used to the routine by now. She stood in line and waited to be counted, then followed the woman in front out of the door into the airing court. The outside garden space for her ward, fenced in by high wooden panels. She trod the familiar path, walked around in a circle with the others, a slow walk, a slow, sad walk to nowhere. She clutched Laura's folded-up picture in her pocket and squeezed her lips together. She hadn't thought much about Laura since she'd arrived at the hospital. But now she realised with a frightening intensity that she missed her daughter. She missed her with all her heart and soul. She wanted to see her, needed to know she was all right. She had always blamed Laura in a way for what had happened – being cast out of home, ending up in those places, and finally at the brothel. It was all because of Laura, because Laura was there, shaming her, branding her a pariah. She heaved a sob. It wasn't Laura's fault, none of it was. She didn't ask to be born, just like Claude said. It was Archie's fault, all of it. Doris hated him, she hated him so much she wanted to kill him.

But even more than that unsettling thought, she missed Laura and needed to know she was safe. She wanted to be her mother. Doris buried her face in her shoulder for a second to wipe away her tears. She'd been a terrible mother, terrible. She'd shown Laura no love, she'd given her no sense of hope or happiness, she hadn't done her best for her daughter. And how had Laura paid her back? By being naughty? By hating her? No, she felt the picture in her pocket. Laura had stuck with her, Laura had known what was right all along, that they belonged together. And now look what had happened. The poor little mite was stuck in a home with god knew what kind of people looking after her. And Doris was stuck in the hospital with no way of getting out and finding her. What had the Superintendent said to her, what had he called Laura because Doris wasn't married? *Filius nullius*? No one's child. Well, Laura was Doris's child, and she was going to find a way of getting her back.

37

Doris

Annie was right. Doris had 'stayed good' and they had given her a job in the laundry. At nine o'clock on her first morning, she lined up in the ward to be counted with the other laundry workers and was taken to the wash-house by a laundry maid, one of the staff members who worked there, who had a big ring of keys secured to her belt. They were led through corridors that Doris hadn't seen before, a cold wind blowing through slit-like windows that had no glass in them.

'Bats fly through here at night,' Annie told her, walking behind.

'How do you know?' said Doris.

'Because I came down here when I escaped,' she said, as if Doris should have heard about that by now.

'You've escaped?' said Doris, disbelieving.

'Course I have, twice. But they've always caught me and brought me back. That was a long time ago now.'

Stopping at each door to be unlocked and relocked, they filed outside and through the main gardens, past the walls of the individual wards' airing courts and past the patients who were allowed open access to the grounds.

'Gave me a serious blast of electric shock each time too, like those poor sods.' She nodded at the patients in the gardens, some walking or sitting as if dazed. 'It makes you forget ... although some people like it, say it helps.'

Doris looked at them, wondering if it had helped them.

'They told me if I try escaping again it'll be a leucotomy – Dr Death will chop my brain up,' she added. 'You know, like that one in the corner of our ward?'

Doris nodded. She knew who Annie meant. There was a woman who always sat in the same corner of the day room, just sat there staring into space. Sometimes her head would fall forward and a line of drool would dangle from her mouth and no one would wipe it away.

'I need to talk to the Super,' said Doris. 'Tell him I shouldn't be in here, that I'm not mad.'

Annie chuckled. 'They all say that, duck. If you say it, they'll just give you electric shock and you'll be marked out as trouble.'

'But they can't just leave people in here.'

'Can't they? There's a woman been in here a long time, her husband was seeing someone on the side and wanted rid of her. She's not mad either, least she wasn't when she first came in. There are men in here for getting into fights, and that's all.'

'But it's not right, it's against people's rights.' An image of Claude talking about politics jumped into her mind. He would have said it was wrong to treat people like that.

Annie laughed. 'You haven't got any rights once you're in here, duck. That's just the way it is.'

'How do you know what men are in here for anyway?'

'My boyfriend told me, that's how, Miss Smarty Pants.'

'Your *boyfriend*?'

'That's right. Geoffrey. He works in the woodworking shop on the other side.'

Doris stared at the woman. For all she knew, Annie was a liar. She could have been making it all up.

They arrived at the wash-house. It was huge but suffocating, the air humid with moisture, the smell of soap and steam and sweat seeming to settle on Doris's skin and coat the inside of her nose and mouth. It reminded her of what Vi used to say if ever she copied the grown-ups and swore. *I'll wash your mouth out with soap and water.*

'I'm on the hydros,' said Annie, nodding over to what looked like a set of enormous spin dryers. 'They might start you off on the foul wash,' she said, stifling a laugh unsuccessfully, 'just to see if you've got the stomach for it.' She walked away, her shoulders shaking with laughter.

The laundry maid beckoned to her, led her to a sectioned-off corner, with a sign above it that said *Foul laundry*. The smell was overpowering as she approached the room, and she instinctively covered her nose and mouth with her hands. There was a large wooden trolley that Doris recognised from its being wheeled through her ward to collect the dirty sheets and sanitary towels that were made up from old sheets in the sewing room by the patients. The laundry maid showed her how to grab a bundle from the trolley, undo the knot holding it together, and tip the contents into a large tank of cold water to soak. Doris gagged when she did one herself. The sight of blood and the stench of shit made her retch into her shoulder but she managed to keep the sick down somehow.

'I said I'd come in here to help you.' It was Annie at her side. 'Smells rotten, doesn't it? It's all the bad patients in the chronic wards. They chuck their chamber pots around for sport.'

'I can't stand it, I'm gonna throw up.'

'Keep it down if you can, then they'll give you a job on the hydros or the colanders, otherwise they'll send you back to the ward and you'll have nothing to do.'

Doris thought she'd rather do nothing all day than wash someone's soiled sheets and sanitary towels.

'Here, I'll do that, you take them out and put them in there,' said Annie, handing Doris a set of large wooden tongs and indicating the steaming copper boilers. Doris tonged the sheets out of another cold tank and into the hot water, putting a few feet between her and the worst of it.

'Thanks, Annie.'

'Well, if you work in the laundry you've got a better chance of escaping,' she said quietly, checking for eavesdroppers.

Hot water splashed up on to Doris's wrist, making her wince. 'What?'

'You know, when they bring you over through the gardens, you can slip away from the line.'

'But what about the walls?'

'The boards? I know, high, aren't they? But they can be

climbed. The staff climb them when they come back late from dances. I've seen them out the window. You know which ones fell in the ditch on the other side before making it over – they're soaked through.' Annie chuckled.

'Have you done that, then?' said Doris, leaning over to Annie and making sure no one could hear.

'Nah, I got out at night. Pinched some keys from a nurse on paraldehyde, once I'd let her feel me up a bit.'

Doris recoiled. 'What do you mean?'

'Ah, nothing, they like the ladies, a lot of these nurses, you just get used to that in here.' Annie laughed at Doris's expression. 'Anyway, I reckon it's a good plan, slip away from the line, creep around the bushes and get over the boards, then make a run for it.'

Doris thought about Win. She wasn't going to help her get out. And Vi wasn't going to either. If what Annie said was true, maybe escaping was the best way. It might be the quickest way of getting to Laura. And if she was caught, what would happen? She'd get some electric shock treatment and end up back where she was – it was a risk she might have to take.

'I dunno, Annie.'

'Did I tell you that there's a law?' said Annie, wrinkling her nose as she emptied out a bundle of soiled linen into the cold tank. 'If you escape out of a mental hospital and you're not caught in fourteen days, then you're free and don't have to come back.'

'No, you didn't tell me that.'

'Yeah, I just haven't managed it yet, that's all. I end up making a nuisance of myself and they always find me and bring me back. Tell you what though, I'll do it with you, we can get out of here together if you like?'

Doris couldn't tell if anything Annie said was true. But if it was, then it sounded like there was a chance of escaping.

'We can help each other over the boards, see? We'd have a better chance that way. I can get Geoffrey to nick some little nails out the workshop and we can push them through the soles of our shoes, to help climb over, see?'

Doris nodded at her and smiled.

'There's a dance on Saturday. I'll get word to Geoffrey.'

'A dance? In here?'

Annie nodded. 'They let the men's side and the women's side mix once a week. They keep a strict eye on the goings-on though . . . ' She winked and clicked her tongue. 'They haven't told you yet because you're new but they'll let you go this time I bet.'

Doris made a decision. She'd go to the dance. If Annie's Geoffrey existed and came up with some nails, then she'd have a reason to trust that Annie was telling the truth.

For the next two days Doris was on the foul wash. She learned to breathe through her mouth, which helped with the stench, and she scrubbed her hands with carbolic afterwards, so she didn't feel contaminated when she was back in the ward. Annie had told her that the staff's clothes got washed on a day when none of the patients worked in the laundry, so that their clothes didn't get infected by the patients. Doris wondered whether madness was catching. She would watch Peony sitting in her chair, quiet and staring, and wonder what was going on inside her head and how long she, Doris, would be able to stand being in a place like that. She thought

317

about Laura to keep herself going. She fixed Laura's face in her mind, but sometimes she felt the image slipping away. In the day room she asked the nurse for something to draw with. She was given a piece of paper and a black crayon and she sat at a table to draw a picture of Laura. For a while she forgot where she was, she was so focused on what she was doing. It felt so good to draw, and drawing Laura, thinking about every detail of her face, made her feel close to her daughter, made it feel like she was touching her in some way.

'Who's that?' It was Annie, peering over her shoulder.

'My daughter,' said Doris, and felt a swell of pride in her chest. She looked around and Annie had gone. Peony heard and got up from her chair, drifted over to where Doris sat, and stared at the drawing, mumbling her usual mutterings.

'Twenty, she'd be, grown up, twenty-one she'd be now, twenty-two . . . '

'Is that your kid, Peony? How old she is now?'

Peony went silent, looked with round eyes at Doris and shuffled away. Doris finished the drawing and looked at it for a long time. Her throat ached with a longing to see Laura. She needed to know she was all right, she wanted her back and she wanted to make up for everything she hadn't done during Laura's short life.

Two of the patients were waltzing around the room together, excited about tonight's dance. Once they'd had their tea at five, they were told to wash their hands and faces and brush their hair. Doris wondered who would be allowed to go, then realised it was obvious who would be staying. Those women who sat in their chairs all day, not speaking or mixing with anyone, they wouldn't be going to the dance.

Peony wouldn't be going. Doris washed her hands and face and ran a brush through her hair. They had no other clothes to change into, just the one work dress at any one time that was replaced by a clean one once a week. They were told to line up and were led through the corridors and into a large room, told to sit in the chairs along one side. So the dance was real, that was one point for Annie. She was excited, sitting next to Doris.

'They'll bring the men in now,' she whispered.

Once the women were all seated, the door opened and a male nurse led a line of male patients into the room. They were dressed in shirts and trousers of varying drab colours, and black shoes. Doris watched them as they filed in. Some of them looked normal, some looked excited or anxious. They were other-worldly, with pallid faces and drooping, hopeless shoulders. Some openly stared at the women, some stole glances and looked at the floor. They took their seats opposite the women. Annie waved to someone and fidgeted in her seat. She elbowed Doris.

'There's Geoffrey,' she whispered and pointed to a man diagonally right from them. He had patches of bright white amongst his brown hair but looked too young to be grey. There were brown puddles of skin below his eyes, but apart from that he looked all right. He was grinning at Annie. Several of the other patients were waving too.

'They're waving at their fancies,' said Annie. 'There might be someone there for you, too.'

Doris couldn't help wrinkling her nose at the thought of it. Two nurses wheeled in a gramophone on a little table, and put a record on. The sound of a waltz started up and the patients knew the drill. As soon as the music started, it was like horses out of the traps: they all ran onto the dance floor, looking for their 'fancies'. Doris jumped when a man strode over to her, stood there holding out his hand and grinning as though that was his normal expression. She felt she couldn't really refuse, as she had come to the dance after all, so she took his hand and let him lead her to the floor. He continued to grin, his large teeth even larger up close, but his eyes seemed dead and didn't match his mouth at all. He pulled her close to him and she strained her body backwards as they stepped into the dance, tried to keep him at the proper distance. Annie and Geoffrey waltzed by, but they were pushed up against one another, kissing and grinding. Other couples were doing the same and Doris looked at the nurse attendants standing around the edges of the room, wondered why they weren't imposing rules, pulling people apart.

One of the attendants stepped forward towards a couple who had stopped dancing and were squashing their faces together, and her hand was down the front of his trousers. The attendant told them to go and sit in their respective chairs, which they did, panting and wiping their mouths. Doris saw Annie rubbing the front of Geoffrey's trousers and he had his hand up the front of her dress. But they were still managing to keep dancing and they weren't told to stop and go and sit down. Another couple stopped dancing and the man yanked his trousers down to his knees. He wore no pants and his thing stood out on end through his shirt tails and he was pulling the front of her dress up when two attendants rushed over, pulling them apart. The man patient resisted, pushing them away, and two more attendants came

and took him away with force out of the room. His partner wailed and screamed, but the other couples carried on,
taking the opportunity to rub and kiss while the attendants
were distracted.

Doris shivered. It reminded her of Archie and of Percy in
the brothel. Her partner tried to get closer to her, and with
every step of his, she would step backwards, until they were
on the outskirts of the dance floor and she couldn't go back
any more. His right hand travelled up her arm and across
to the front of her dress. He managed to grab her breast
before she tore herself away and went to sit down, close to
where one of the nurses was standing. Luckily there were
only two more records played, and Doris managed to fend
off the other men who tried asking her to dance. When
the last song had finished, the patients were told to resume
their seats. The nurses and attendants had to physically pull
people apart and shove them back to the walls. The women
were led out first.

'That's Geoffrey,' said Annie, out of breath, her eyes shining. 'Ooh, I love the dances,' she said. 'That's one reason to
stay good in here. They don't let you come if you're bad.'

'What did he say about the nails?' said Doris.

'He'll get some. I told him they're just for you because he
wouldn't want me to go, I didn't want to upset him.'

That was two points for Annie. Geoffrey did exist. If he got
the nails, Doris thought she would do it, she'd try to escape
with Annie. She trusted her now.

38

Vi

Three o'clock and Archie bolted the doors closed on the afternoon opening. Coming back round the bar, he popped his
head into the back hallway to check for Win and slipped over
to Vi, grabbing her from behind as she checked the optics.
He ran his hands over her body, pressing himself against her,
untucked the front of her blouse from her skirt waist and
slipped his hands in over her breasts. Vi's heart quickened.
She hated it when Win could walk in at any moment, but she
loved the thrill of it at the same time.

They jumped apart when they heard the clang of a tin
bucket in the tap room. Vi tucked her blouse back in and
checked the gin. They needed a new bottle brought up.

'Grab a gin while you're down there, Arch,' she called to
him as he descended into the cellar.

'You all right, Vi? You look a bit flushed.' It was Win with her bucket of cleaning things.

'What? Oh yeah, just coming down with something, I expect.' Vi wondered whether Win had seen them and had clanged her bucket to give them a chance of separating before she came in.

There was a knock at the pub doors. It wasn't the usual bang from the punters who were waiting for their pints, but a softer tap.

'Who's this now? Can't they see we're closed?' said Vi, going to see and unbolting the door.

There stood a woman Vi hadn't seen before. She looked like a tart, at least there was something about her that suggested as much. Vi couldn't put her finger on it. The woman's hair was neat enough. Her dress was a tad on the short side though, and her heels were a touch too high, perhaps her eyebrows were slightly over-plucked.

'Yes, love?'

'Is it Vi, Doris's mum?'

Vi felt herself harden at the mention of Doris's name.

'That's right.'

'I couldn't come in for a minute, could I?' The woman ducked her chin and smiled, lifting her shoulders apologetically.

'I suppose so, but we're closed.'

'I know. I waited till you were closed. This is a bit delicate and I thought it best to wait. Is Archie around?'

'What do you want with Archie?' said Win, coming round from the bar.

'Nothing, actually. I want to talk to Vi. Who are you, please?'

'This is my sister, now what's all this about?' said Vi, impatiently.

'Win, is it?' said the woman.

'Yes,' said Win. 'Who the devil are you?'

'My name's Freda, but everyone calls me Fred. I know Doris. I worked with her for a bit, before she was taken away.'

Vi and Win exchanged glances. The woman looked nervous, like she had something important to say.

'Go on,' said Vi.

'Well, I was very sorry to see Doris – and her daughter Laura – taken away. I was very upset about it. And the thing is, Doris had told me about what happened to her, why she'd been thrown out of home.'

'Yes, we know about that, thank you very much,' said Vi. She looked at Win, who had gone very quiet and pale. 'What's that got to do with you?'

'Well, nothing, not with me exactly, but I like Doris, and Laura, and I don't like to see them in trouble like this when it's not their fault.' She paused, took a deep breath. 'When it's someone else's fault, someone who should be held to account.'

Vi laughed. 'What on earth are you talking about?'

'Archie. That's who I'm talking about.'

'What do you mean?' Vi's voice sounded smaller to her.

'I mean, I work on Ship Street and Archie is a customer there. That's how I know him.'

'No! Get out of here, you little tart. She's one of them tarts, Vi, you can't trust a word she's saying.' Win stepped forward as if to push Fred away, but Vi stopped her instinctively.

'So?' said Vi, trying to stay composed and not wanting to believe that Archie had visited the brothel.

'So, Doris told me that Archie raped her, that he's Laura's father.'

'Vi! Stop her!'

'Win, for god's sake, just shut up,' said Vi.

Fred took another breath, looking at them both warily, judging whether she was in danger. 'And, the other night, Archie came in and I took him upstairs for his usual, but this time I took a bottle of whisky and got him drunk and asked him about Doris and he told me . . . he told me that he'd done it.' Fred paused to take a breath. '"*So what?*" That's what he said, "*So what?*" I didn't tell him this, but I wanted to say you can do time for that, that's so what.' Fred's eyes misted with tears, her voice wobbled. 'And I wanted to tell him that I'll stand up in court and testify that he said it, that's so what.'

Vi said nothing and neither did Win; they both stared at Fred. Very slowly the pub door opened behind Fred, and of all people, Kenny, the potboy who'd been sacked, poked his head through the front door. Fred nodded to him and in turn he nodded at someone behind him and then came into the pub, with a coloured man following him in.

Vi couldn't think straight. Was this girl telling the truth? She could feel herself starting to go, and she fought to keep her composure. She was confused. What the girl was saying didn't seem possible. Archie was a scoundrel, yes, but a rapist? Would he have done that to her Doris when she was sixteen?

Kenny and the coloured man stood next to Fred and Vi could only stare at them. All she had wanted was a home, somewhere safe. She had tried to protect it, that's all. She had lost her daughter and her granddaughter. Her thoughts were jumbled. She needed something to prove it, but couldn't think what. Her first impulse was to throw them all out of her pub, put a stop to it but she resisted saying anything when she remembered how Doris came back to the pub that day, when all that coloured lot were outside with their banners. Doris said that Archie had raped her. Now this girl saying it too. If it was true, that meant she had thrown Doris out for nothing, that she had put Doris in the asylum for nothing. That it wasn't Doris's fault, none of it – it was Archie's fault. That Laura was a scapechild. How could she know whether it was true?

The cellar door slammed and then Vi knew. She'd look into Archie's face and that would be proof enough. Everyone in the pub had fallen silent. There were just the sound of Archie's footsteps approaching and the sound of the bottles he held clinking together. He stopped when he saw the people in the pub.

'What the hell's going on?' he said. He saw Fred first. 'What's she doing here? And what the fuck are they doing in here?' he said, nodding to Kenny and the coloured man.

'Arch,' said Vi, walking over to the bar, facing him across it. 'You know this girl, Fred?'

'Dunno, seen her around, I suppose,' he mumbled, putting the bottles down on the bar.

'Arch. I've got something important to ask you.'

He smirked and looked around at everyone, but his confidence slipped when he sensed that they were all there waiting for him.

'Arch? Did you touch my Doris?'

'What? No, course I never . . . ' he spluttered.

'Arch. Fred here says you told her you did. And Doris said it too.'

At that moment, Vi turned her head slightly to look at Win, and what she saw there was the worst of it.

'Oh my god, Win, you knew?'

Win covered her mouth with her hands and choked back a sob.

'Arch?' Vi looked at him again. His expression changed from defence to attack.

'So what if I did? What are you gonna do about it? You're as much of a tart as your daughter and this one standing here. Don't try and say you're not.'

Vi put back her head and closed her eyes, crying for her own stupidity, for putting her trust in this loathsome man. She lunged towards him, struck the side of his face with her fist.

'You know what, Vi,' said Archie, pushing her away and rubbing his cheek, 'this is a good time to tell you I've taken over the deeds for this place. Me and Win are gonna run it and you can just piss off.'

Vi opened her mouth but didn't know what to say. The shock of their incomprehensible betrayal was too much.

'So what, did you say?'

Vi swung around at the sound of the voice, a deep voice with a heavy accent. It was the coloured man. Vi was sure it was one of those who had been protesting outside the pub. He strode over to Archie, went round the bar and got hold of him by his shirt front. 'So what? You've ruined that young girl's life, that's so what.'

'Get off me, you black bastard,' said Archie, red in the face with outrage and struggling against the man's hold on him. He grabbed hold of one of the bottles of gin on the bar but the coloured man took it away from him.

'Bastard? I wouldn't care if I was one, and being called black is no insult to me, man. My name is Claude, and you can call me that or nothing at all.' Claude held Archie's stare and called back over his shoulder. 'Kenny? Call the boys in here.'

Kenny opened the pub doors and shouted. Four other coloured men came into the pub and Vi could only watch.

'See this piece of dirt here, this man who raped his niece?' said Claude to his friends. 'He reckons he's taking this pub when it doesn't belong to him. But I know different. I've spoken to Stanley Blackshaw who knows a fair bit about English law, and he says this rapist dirt can be arrested and thrown into jail.'

'I'm calling the police,' said Kenny. 'You let everyone think it was me who did it. You deserve to go down for what you've done, you son of a bitch.'

'No, don't!' cried Win. 'Don't do it, please Kenny. We'll go. We'll just go, won't we, Arch?'

Archie stopped trying to free himself from Claude's grip and relaxed. The other men had crowded around him and he had nowhere to go.

'Looks like you got no other option, man,' said Claude, into Archie's face. 'You and she got ten minutes to get your things and get out of here.'

'I can't understand a damn word you're saying,' hissed Archie.

'Starting now,' said Claude, pushing Archie towards the back hallway. 'Understand that?' Archie went and Win scuttled after him, the four West Indians following them up the stairs.

39

Vi

In the flat above the pub, the West Indians were standing guard while Archie and Win packed their things. Archie looked fit to blow – he wasn't a man to be told what to do but he knew he had no choice. Win whimpered and ran about, picking up this and that and bundling things up into sheets tied at the top.

'What's the new combination for the safe?' Vi asked Archie as he headed towards the bedrooms.

'Mind your own fucking business,' he said.

Rage bubbled up in Vi's chest. She hated him, she wanted to kill him for what he'd done to Doris.

Claude and one of his friends caught hold of Archie and bent his arm up behind his back. 'Tell her,' they said.

Archie took the pain until he couldn't stand it.

'We'll break your arm,' they said.

'Twenty-four, oh five, fifty-five,' he said, as though the very words burnt his mouth to say them.

Vi ran to the safe, dialled the numbers. They were the date for this year's Empire day. The deeds were in the safe and still in her name. Archie had been bluffing, or maybe he just hadn't got around to changing them yet. That might have been his plan all along, to take the pub over in his name. Perhaps he thought he was keeping Vi sweet, just as she had been doing to him. She had no idea what she'd do though, now she had no male figurehead to obtain a licence.

Win wouldn't look at her. That's what hurt the most. Vi thought they were in it together, like they had been all their lives, since they were children in the home all those years ago. She thought they'd had an unspoken bargain, that they would do what was necessary to keep things going, to make sure they were seen to lead decent lives and to keep a roof over their heads and a good living. Just like maggots that are born in filth. They grow wings and they fly away.

'Were you really going to take the pub off me, Win?' She asked her the question as Win bustled around, but her sister only gave her a dirty look and said nothing.

'After everything we've been through together? How could you, Win?'

Win paused in front of Vi. 'How could I? Are you joking? You've been going with Archie behind my back all this time. How much longer did you think I'd put up with it, Vi? You lost your husband so you thought you'd steal mine, eh? And you're blaming me for trying to protect what's mine? Come off it, Vi.'

Win had never spoken to her like that before.

'Archie raped Doris, Win,' she said, screwing up her face with revulsion. 'And you knew about it, didn't you? You disgust me.'

'Ha, the feeling's mutual, Vi. Get off my knitting, I'm taking that.' She grabbed the half-knitted jumper that Vi was sitting on and put it on the pile of things on the sheet on the floor, then went into her bedroom to get her clothes.

The West Indians hurried them along, got them downstairs with their bundles. Archie went to the till and opened it. Claude went and put his hand over the money but Vi called out.

'It's all right, let him have it. He won't be coming back for any more.'

Archie cleaned out the till and stuffed his pockets with the cash. The boys herded them out the front door and Vi watched as Archie brought his motorcycle round from the side alley. Win got into the sidecar and Archie passed the bundles of things to her. She stuffed them down between her feet, by her sides, and on her lap. Sitting astride the seat, Archie started the motor and as they pulled away, neither of them looked at Vi. They kept their gazes fixed forward but Vi knew that Win's heart was pumping ten to the dozen, just like her own.

As the sound of the motorcycle gradually faded, so Vi wanted to crumble with relief. But the shock of what had happened gripped her body and kept her upright. Turning to go back in, she paused to look up at the sign of the pub. The Empire. A painting of a cargo ship in Tilbury docks. To her the British Empire conjured images of power, wealth, loss and men. Archie had tried to take her empire over, but it was hers and she'd find a way of keeping it going.

But a more pressing issue was upon her first. She understood her priorities now. Her daughter Doris was sitting in a mental asylum. Doris had had her daughter taken away from her, had been to hell and back over the past few years and Vi had some atoning to do.

When she went back into the pub, Claude and his friends were waiting for her, with Fred and Kenny too.

'Thank you,' she said to them, and her voice broke as she spoke. 'Thank you for doing this, I can't thank you enough. I need to find Doris, I need to go and get her.'

The group looked at one another with nods and smiles. It was what they had been hoping to hear.

'Kenny,' she said, walking over to him. 'Kenny, I'm so sorry, I honestly didn't know, how could I have known?'

He nodded.

'Could you . . . could you stay here and watch the pub for me while I go to the asylum? I'm worried they'll come back while I'm gone.'

'I'll come with you,' said Claude, 'and the boys will stay with Kenny to watch the pub, won't you, boys?'

'Really? You'd really do that? I can't thank you enough,' said Vi, wondering why they would be so kind to her. 'I've got to get Doris.'

She ran up for her bag and walked to the train station with Claude.

'I can't believe what just happened,' she said. 'How did you do it, why did you all come?'

'We came for Doris,' said Claude. 'I live in London now. Fred came to find me. She came up to London on the train, Stanley had an address for me, and when she told me Doris was in trouble, I came straight away.'

Vi nodded, wondered at the strength of the friendships Doris has made. This man, Claude, and that girl, Fred, who had been so brave to come to the pub to tell Vi about Archie. Vi hadn't a chance to thank her — she must have left when they'd all gone upstairs to watch Archie and Win pack up.

Vi and Claude had to take a train and a bus and then walk down a long country lane to get to the mental hospital. Vi hadn't been there before and she felt a pang of guilt that she hadn't visited Doris. The building was large and grand and quite sinister as they passed through the high stone archway and into the reception rooms.

'I need to talk to someone about getting my daughter released from here,' she told one official-looking man in a suit. They were told to wait to see the Superintendent.

In the Super's office Vi took a seat while Claude sat in the waiting room. The man considered her gravely for a moment, pushing his top lip upwards to feel his thin moustache.

'I understand you're here to discuss your daughter, Doris, Mrs Walsh?'

'Yes, that's right,' Vi started uncertainly. 'I'm afraid she's been put in here by mistake, by me by mistake,' she added.

'In what way?' said the Super.

'I thought she . . . needed to be here for her own safety because of the people she was going around with, but it turns out I was wrong about that, so I want to use my power as her only parent to have her released.'

The Super nodded and looked at his hands. 'May I ask, when was the last time you saw your daughter, Mrs Walsh?'

Vi blushed. 'Around two months ago, when she was taken away, when I asked the doctor to have her certified.'

The Super nodded at his hands for longer this time.

'I'm afraid I have some distressing news for you, Mrs Walsh, and please be assured that this only came to my attention this morning and we were about to contact you to inform you.'

Vi's heart squeezed with fear. 'What is it?' she said, leaning forward.

'Your daughter has managed somehow to escape from here, Mrs Walsh, and I cannot apologise strongly enough.'

Vi let out a breath of air and sank back into her chair.

'What? Where's she gone then?'

'We don't know. We have contacted the police a short while ago and there will be a local search party being put in place as we speak. I wouldn't wish to alarm you, Mrs Walsh. This is Doris's first stay in a psychiatric hospital, is it not?'

Vi nodded.

'Well, in these cases – I mean, they are very few you do understand, we have a comprehensive security system in place here – but in a high percentage of these very rare cases, the patient is found, usually confused and lost, and is brought back in by the police with no harm done.'

Vi didn't know what to say. She almost felt a sense of pride that Doris had managed to escape, but was also frightened that she would be hurt and lost with nowhere to go.

'Well, we have to find her, don't we?' she said. 'She'll be frightened.'

'Yes, that's imperative. I'll call the police to let them know that you are here.'

40

Doris

'He put them in my pocket at the dance.'

Annie opened her hand when the nurses weren't looking, to show Doris several very short flat-headed nails. It was the final proof that Doris needed. Her heart gave a little leap as she made the decision that she would try to escape with Annie. She hadn't believed that Annie had a boyfriend who could get some nails, she'd had to wait another week for the next dance to know for sure. And if that was true, then Doris had to trust that the rest of what Annie said was true – that she'd be able to slip away from the laundry line, she'd be able to climb over the boards and that if she hid for fourteen days, she wouldn't have to go back to the asylum and that meant she'd be able to find Laura and get her back.

'Well done, Annie,' she said. 'So when shall we do it, then?'

The shine of achievement from getting the nails faded from

Annie's face. 'I don't know yet, we'll need to plan it properly,' she said, wrapping the nails in a twist of paper and putting them in her pocket.

Doris nodded and looked at her expectantly. Annie checked for nurses and started walking slowly round the day room, talking in a low voice, with Doris matching her stride. 'We should do it on a day when that Teresa comes to get us,' she said, thinking. 'She's new and scatty and finds it hard keeping us lot in the line when she takes us over. She'll be worrying about the keys too much to count us up.'

'Yes, all right. Do we do it on the way over to the laundry or on the way back, and in the morning or afternoon?'

Annie put her hands behind her back and leant forward as she walked and Doris tried not to laugh.

'It's tricky. If it were winter, we'd be better off in the dark but it doesn't get dark till around six at this time of year. Unless we do it on the way back for tea at five, then we could hide in the bushes until the light fades and then jump the boards?'

'They'd realise by then and be searching the grounds, though, wouldn't they?'

'Yes but if there was some sort of diversion . . . I know, we can make itching powder out of the rose hips in the garden and put it down the backs of the women's dresses.' Annie laughed and rubbed her hands together. 'Then they wouldn't be bothered counting us, they'd just be trying to work out why everyone's itching.'

Doris nodded. 'It might work, Annie, it's a good idea.' Annie smiled to herself, saying things under her breath. 'Then what?' Doris asked.

'Then what?' said Annie, distracted with her own thoughts. 'Then we slip away into the bushes and wait for dusk, and help each other over the boards.'

'We can put the nails in our shoes while we're waiting.'

'Yes,' hissed Annie. 'Who'll go over first? You're taller than me so you should give me a bunk up and then I'll hang on the top and try and hoist you up. Then we'll just have to drop down into the ditch. We'll just have to get wet.'

'Can't we . . . no.'

'What?'

'Can't we throw a dry dress over to change into?' said Doris.

'But how? They only give us one dress.'

'But we work in the laundry, Annie, we could get two more dresses and wrap them up, and you could throw them clear of the ditch when you're on top of the fence?'

'Yeah, good thinking, duck. We can throw our coats over too. Make sure we put our coats on when they take us for work.'

Doris nodded and bit her thumbnail. Her stomach twisted in knots when she thought about escaping. If they were caught, they'd give Doris some sort of punishment, some electric shock or something and then she'd be branded bad and they'd take her job away and any other chance of escaping; she'd be there years before she'd get another chance. But Annie would get worse, she'd get an operation on her brain and then she wouldn't be Annie any more.

She exchanged worried glances with Annie, who she could tell was thinking the same thing.

'It's a good plan,' said Doris. 'Is there anything else you can think of that could go wrong?'

'I don't know,' said Annie. 'Argh, beetles!' She leaped ahead to stamp on the floor, jumping up and down on the spot.

Doris watched her, knowing nothing was there.

When Doris woke up on Monday morning, she wondered whether this would be the day. She ate her breakfast porridge and some bread and butter, trying to fill up in case she didn't know where her next meal would be coming from. When they were called for work, she looked at Annie who shook her head. One of the experienced laundry maids had come to collect them, and she kept a tight ship. She marched them through the gardens in an orderly line, turning back to shout at Annie who was faffing around with something. She counted them through the door of the laundry and Doris could see that it wouldn't be any use trying to escape under her charge.

'Here, look,' said Annie, sidling up to Doris in the foul laundry room. She held her dress pocket open for Doris to see – there were around ten shining red rose hips in there. Doris looked at Annie's triumphant face and smiled.

'Well done,' she whispered. 'You're good at this, Annie.'

'I know,' said Annie, and bounced away back to the hydros.

The same laundry maid took them back to the ward for their midday dinner. But when they were lining up to be taken back for their afternoon shift, it was Teresa who came to get them, the young maid, the scatty one.

Doris and Annie looked at each other with wide eyes. They had both remembered to put on their coats too. When they got to work, Annie put a few rose hips into Doris's dress pocket.

'Pick them apart,' she said. 'Get the hard red bits off, and just have the fluffy itchy bits from inside. Then stand close to the boiler – the steam will make them itchier.'

'All right,' said Doris. 'What about the spare dresses?'

'I'm gonna try and get them in a minute.'

Annie went back to her work and while Doris stirred the dirty linen in the cold tank, she had one hand in her pocket. She dug her nails into the rose hip skin, picked it away enough to be able to pull out the itchy bits, which she transferred into her other pocket. It hurt her nails but she was fired up and carried on. When she'd done them all, she tonged the linen out of one of the cold tanks into the hot water, standing with her pocket close to the boiler.

Somehow Annie found a way of ducking back into the foul laundry room. 'Don't ask me how I did this, I had a bit of luck when my hydro broke down.' She winked at Doris so much it looked like she had a tic in her eye. She must have done something to block up the machine. 'I grabbed a couple of clean dresses and stuffed them into our coat pockets while the maids were all trying to pull out a sheet that had got stuck in there.' She grinned. 'Can't believe I did it.'

'You're a real star, Annie,' said Doris with admiration. She felt more and more confident that they might actually do it.

Doris watched the clock on the wall. Five o'clock came around very slowly. It would all depend on who would be taking them back over to the ward. The head maid called them all into line and Doris got her coat on and shuffled into place in front of Annie. Her heart sank when the head maid stood at the front of the line and indicated that they should follow her. Doris looked back at Annie, who gave a frantic shake of her head.

The tension was unbearable and Doris felt sick. She didn't want to have to go through this all again tomorrow. She felt a tug on her dress and heard Annie's panicked voice low in her ear.

'You go on, I'll do something to distract them. You go on as planned and I'll come and find you.'

She slipped away. Doris tried to watch where she was going without causing suspicion. Annie weaved through the machines and disappeared. The head maid started counting from the front of the line. Doris felt a sense of agitation running through the women ahead of her. They were looking up and pointing, murmuring and mumbling. Doris followed their gaze and started back. Annie had climbed on top of the high water vat somehow. She was holding a sheet, she was reaching up towards the ceiling, to the copper piping that ran along there, she was feeding the sheet over one of the pipes. The head maid hadn't noticed. Annie got hold of the other end of the sheet, now looped over the pipe. She let out a great whooping shriek, and jumped from the vat, swinging from the pipe on the ends of the sheet.

Doris imagined it was what monkeys sounded like in the jungle. The patients started jumping, hopping, calling out. The head maid cried out in horror when she looked up and saw Annie up there, swinging from the pipe.

'Get down!' she screamed. 'Get down, this instant! Call the nurses!' she shouted at the staff, running closer to Annie, looking up at her. 'Get down, now!' she shouted.

'Yeeeeeeee-hah!' called Annie, somehow managing to keep hold of the sheet.

Doris realised where Annie was. Below her, next to the

water vat, were the huge copper boilers for washing the sheets. The lids were off, steam billowing upwards. She grabbed the arm of the woman next to her, an elderly woman, who winced at the touch.

'The boilers,' said Doris with alarm. 'The boilers!' she screamed at Annie. 'Annie, get down, you're above the boilers.'

The smile on Annie's face shifted as she tightened her grip on the sheet. Annie was small but not a slim person, it must have taken a lot to hold her own weight like that. Doris gasped when Annie started to bounce – it seemed as though she was trying to test the strength of the pipe. She tugged on the sheet, pulled on it, and everyone went quiet when they heard the groan of metal and one of the brackets holding the pipe in place came away. Annie dropped a few inches and nearly lost her grip on the sheet. The women screamed out. Annie looked down at the boiler, at the boiling water below her. She looked at Doris, who shot her arms out towards her friend. And Annie let go.

Doris saw her fall, saw the water slosh over before she heard the sickening metallic thud and splash. Annie thrashed about and Doris saw one of her legs, the shoe still on, heard Annie bang against the side of the copper. The laundry staff ran to the release valve, to let out the water from the tank. Their faces told what they saw. Doris knew Annie couldn't have survived.

'Get them out,' shouted the head maid, indicating the patients, who were groaning, pulling at their faces. One of them was laughing, an eerie hysterical laugh. 'Teresa, get them out.'

The young maid skidded around to the head of the line, her face as white as the linen she washed every day. She fumbled in her pocket for the ring of keys hanging from her belt, her hand shaking as she unlocked the laundry door. She held it open and waved the women through. Doris was pushed from behind by the old lady when her feet wouldn't move. She wanted to scream and cry, she felt sick and numb at what Annie had done. There was one word going round and round inside her head. *Why?* Why did Annie do it? She was going to escape, she was going to get out. *Why, why, why?* She shuffled forward, keeping in line, without any will, just by rote. They waited while Teresa locked the door behind them and then ran to the front to lead them through the corridor that led to the gardens. The gardens.

With a bolt of terror, Doris understood. Annie had created a diversion. For her, for Doris to get away. But she had given her life. Why had she done that? Doris felt her face crumble into tears. They were going to escape together, they had their plan. The shock of what had happened was almost too much to see through. But something made Doris watch Teresa as she unlocked the door to the gardens, watch as Teresa waited by the door to see them through. *They get the sack if they leave even one door unlocked even once.* Annie had told her that. The women waited in line until Teresa was at the head again, and they then started their walk through the gardens. A voice in Doris's head told her to wait for a moment, to bend down to fiddle with her shoe until the other women behind her had gone by. It was the voice of survival, it told her to stand back up and reach into her pocket.

It was a piece of luck that the woman at the back of the line was Vera. Vera wore a bunny suit, it was like an all-in-one boiler suit but it had feet in it and it did up at the back, because Vera was one of the women who liked to take her clothes off and when you had a bunny suit on, you couldn't take it off by yourself. Doris reached in her pocket and put the whole lot of rose hip fluff down Vera's back. And with a huge jolt of fear and strength, she made a run for it. She dashed across the lawn and crashed into the large rhododendron bush, batted her way through the leaves into the cavern of branches, went deeper into the growth and sank down on the cool earth, shivering with fright.

There was a scream from the gardens. Doris couldn't see but she guessed that Vera was clawing at her back, trying to get the fluff out, that Teresa would have been even further distracted than she already was, that she'd have trouble herding the women back into the main hospital building. Teresa wouldn't be counting the line, she'd just be desperate to unlock the door, get them in and lock the door again. Doris couldn't think straight. She urged herself to stay strong, to not give up now. She didn't know how long it would be before they noticed she was gone. And she didn't know how on earth she was going to climb over the boards without Annie.

41

Doris

In the huge rhododendron cave the leaves were all on the outside, green and shining, creating a protective barrier, but inside it was dark, the branches twisted and bare, turning this way and that, winding around each other in a confused state. Doris sat on the bare earth and the shock of what she had just seen started to filter through her brain. She hugged her legs to her chest, pressed her face into her knees and tried to stifle the sound of her sobs. Poor Annie. She must have really been mad after all. She'd done a good job of seeming quite normal, whatever normal was. Doris wasn't sure she knew.

In her mind, Annie must have thought she was helping the escape plan, but she must have wanted to end her life too. But why – did she think they didn't really have a chance of escaping, that she'd be found and brought back and have her brain operated on? Maybe she took her chance of ending it before they could do that to her. Doris would never know for sure. But it made her doubt whether she should try to escape, if Annie had been so unsure they could do it.

Doris tried to breathe, wiped her face on the skirt of her dress. As she sat there in the semi-darkness she didn't know if she had the courage to try it on her own. She was scared. What if she couldn't climb over the boards . . . what if she fell and broke her leg on the other side . . . what if she couldn't find her way home . . . what if she couldn't find Laura when she got there . . . She pulled the papers from her dress pocket. The picture she had drawn of Laura and Laura's picture of them both. The sketches made her cry again. All those times she had threatened to send Laura away when she was naughty. She wished she'd never said those things. She wished she'd shown her more affection, made her feel safe and loved. Everything Vi hadn't given to her, she should have given to Laura.

In her coat pocket she felt the spare dress that Annie had stuffed in there and in the other pocket her half of the little nails from Geoffrey's workshop. She listened hard and thought she could hear voices. Creeping quietly to the edge of the bush, she peered through the leaves and stiffened. One of the nurses was holding the laundry door open. Two male orderlies carried out a long black bag. Doris covered her mouth with her hands when she realised that Annie was inside that bag. The two orderlies and three nurses made their way over to the main building and disappeared through the door. Poor Annie. She gathered the nails in her hand inside her pocket, squeezed them until the sharp ends dug into her skin. She remembered how Annie would appear at her shoulder in the day room, tell her a secret or a piece of information, tell her something funny that wasn't really funny, and how she'd suddenly leap across the room to stamp on beetles that were never there. She'd try it. She'd try to escape, for Laura but also for Annie.

As she looked out, she could see that the sun was going down. Annie had said wait until the sun fades and then jump the wall. Doris tried to think where she was, how close she was to the boards. She made her way through the centre of the bush, ducking under and stepping over branches, and through to the other side. She could see a patch of garden in the lawn and beyond that the boards. She was less than a hundred feet away from the perimeter. She waited another twenty minutes until the light had faded. There were no voices. The women would have had their tea by now and would be washing for bed. If they hadn't already noticed she'd gone, they would definitely notice when they checked the beds. She had to go now. She unbuckled her shoes, took out the nails from her pocket and pressed one of them into the inside. It went through the first layer but she had to press it very hard with her thumb to get it to pierce the leather sole. Just the very tip of the nail came through and wouldn't go any further. She hoped that when she put the shoe on, the nails were so short and the heads so big that her weight would push the sharp tip through enough to give her the spikes she needed.

Sucking her sore thumb, she managed to press three nails into each shoe sole and buckled them back on. *One, two, buckle my shoe, three, four, a knock at the door.* The childhood rhyme played through her head. She took off her coat and tied it with the sleeves into a ball with the spare dress inside, then fed her arm through it so it hung on her shoulder like a bag. Muttering the rhyme under her breath to give her strength, she pushed her way through the leaves. One quick look around to confirm there was nobody there and she ran for it. She streaked across the lawn, round the flower bed and to the fence. She leapt up against the boards, gripping the joists with her fingertips and grinding her shoes against the wood to find purchase. She clung there for a moment but couldn't get any further and dropped back down onto the grass. She looked around. No one was running towards her or calling for help. The boards were around eight feet high. She was five feet five. If she could just get high enough to grab the top, she might be able to pull herself up.

Taking a deep breath she jammed her foot against the wood, feeling the nails dig in. The fence posts were wide apart. She could only reach one and clutch it as she leaped upwards, jamming her other foot into the wood, clutching the post higher up and lunging for the top. Her fingertips reached and then folded over the top and she had it. She pulled herself up, kicking her feet against the boards and grimacing as she flung her upper body over and stopped, her stomach cut in half by the top edge of the fence. Trying to breathe, she pulled the coat bundle off her shoulder and looked over the other side of the fence. It was almost dark, she couldn't see the ground clearly, but Annie had told her there was a deep ditch of water at the base of the fence on the other side. She lobbed her coat as far as she could, heard no splash and hoped she'd thrown it clear.

With a sob at the pain of sliding herself over, she managed to do it so she was facing the fence on the other side, hanging there by her fingers. She kicked her feet against the wood and they held. She didn't know how to get down – she didn't want to just drop down in case she broke her leg. At that second she remembered something her dad had told her when she was little. In the army they had shown him how to fall properly. *You tuck your head down,* he had said, *elbows in together, you bring your knees up and together, and when you fall you land sideways so the side of your leg hits the ground first, then you roll so your hip hits the ground next and then last the side of your shoulder. That way you protect your feet, your back and your head.* They had practised it together and it came back to her now. Gingerly she clutched the fence post and lowered one of her feet, finding purchase in the wood. Once again with the other foot and then she lost her grip, let out a shriek and fell.

It was almost as if her dad was there with her, helping her do it. She tucked herself up and in and landed on her side with a splash in the cold dark ditch. She swallowed a mouthful of foul-tasting water as her head dipped under. Lunging upright, she struggled to her feet, felt her way to the bank and clawed her way up it, slipping and trying again, and pulled herself out of the ditch onto the dry ground, heaving for breath. She had done it, with no broken bones.

Feeling around on the ground for her coat bundle, she found it, grabbed it and ran for cover under some nearby trees. She didn't know where she was. A pale moon afforded a weak light as darkness fell. She carefully circled the perimeter looking for the front of the estate until she came to the country lane that led away, lit by the lights at the hospital entrance.

Careful to stay on the verge in case she left footprints, she followed the road, staying under the shelter of trees where she could, running along arched over, scared out of her wits and dripping wet. Once she had been running for fifteen minutes she had to stop, she had a painful stitch in her side. Drawing away near a patch of large bushes, she stripped off her wet dress and put on the dry one, which was much too big for her, and her coat, and she felt better for being dry. She pulled off her shoes and shook out the water, left them upside down on the ground while she rested for a few minutes. An owl hooted nearby and made her jump. Her breathing was the only sound and when that calmed she looked around, up at the sky, now dark, wondered at the myriad stars that made her feel small and afraid, wondered how the world was all still out there and going on when she was so alone and wretched. She thought about what Claude used to say about the sky and pushed the memory of him away.

Hungry and tired, she got up and trotted onwards, following the road until she came to a row of cottages. She shrank back from the light in the windows, edged into the darkness and along further. Some houses loomed and a proper street, and she stopped, not knowing what to do. She remembered Annie saying that the hospital was in Pitsea and they would find the train station and walk the track. She skirted the houses until she came to a little bridge and when she looked over, her heart leapt. She thought she could see a railway track.

The bank of the railway was steep and clogged with gorse and broom. Doris stumbled down, scratching her legs on the gorse, until she was by the iron track. She looked each way and realised she had no way of knowing which way to go. She couldn't make out the station anywhere nearby and anyway, she couldn't risk being seen, so she turned right and started off down the track, trudging along in her wet shoes.

Up ahead, a fox saw her, held its ground and stared. The sound of an approaching train made them both dart away off the tracks. Doris crept up the bank to hide behind a gorse bush and the train thundered by, leaving a trail of soot and smoke in the air. Three more trains passed her as she carried on. She must have walked for over an hour when she saw lights ahead and what looked like a station. She slowed down and craned her neck to see the station sign as she drew near. Benfleet. It was Benfleet station. Her heart sank. She knew from her time in Southend that she had been walking in the wrong direction. She dropped to the ground and burst into tears. She'd have to turn around to walk back the way she had come. It'd be over an hour to get back to Pitsea, then she'd have to walk to Stanford and East Tilbury before she'd get to Tilbury station. That would take her all night, and then she didn't know what to do or where to go. The strength drained away from her. She felt completely alone in the world. She didn't have the energy to stand up, let alone walk for miles, cold and hungry. She thought about Annie and how she had chosen to end her life. What if Doris just lay down on the track and waited for a train to come? It'd be so easy.

42

Vi

The hospital Superintendent had been keen to get rid of Vi. He told her to go home and await news from the police.

'She's gone,' she said to Claude, sitting in the waiting area. 'She's escaped out of here.'

'What?' There was concern on Claude's face but also a hint of admiration. 'Where is she? Is she all right?'

'They don't know,' said Vi. 'They've called the police, said to go home and wait.'

Claude ran his hands over his head, took his hat from his lap and put it on. 'Let's go and look for her.'

'Yes.' It was Vi's instinctive reaction, she didn't need to think about it. They left the hospital, waiting to be let out of the front entrance by the gatekeeper.

'You think she went over the top?' said Claude, looking up at the high wooden fence.

'Dunno, it's too high, isn't it? That water looks deep too,' she said as they came out and saw the ditch.

'Let's walk around it.'

They walked around the perimeter and Vi looked at the ground as Claude was doing, looking for any sign of Doris. They could find nothing. As they did the full circle and came back round to the entrance, a police car had pulled up and was waiting to be let through. Vi ran over to it and waved through the window. The constable rolled it down.

'Are you here because of my daughter? Doris Walsh? She escaped.'

The constable frowned and got out of the car. 'Your name please, madam?'

'Violet Walsh, Doris's mother. We're worried sick.'

The constable looked Claude up and down, a tic in his left eye betraying his dislike.

'And who are you, sir?'

'Claude Vernon. A friend of the family.'

The tic twitched and Vi wished Claude wasn't there.

'Madam,' he said, ignoring Claude and turning to Vi. 'We will contact you should any information become available. Now if you'll please excuse me, I need to go in.'

He left them and drove into the hospital grounds, the gatekeeper holding the gate wide. They continued to look around, then walked back down the country lane, scouring the ground for any signs and finding none.

'When did she escape?' said Claude.

'They didn't say. I don't think they reported it straight away though.'

'So she might have made her way to Tilbury by now?'

Vi shrugged. 'I suppose she might, if that's where she's going.'

'I know somewhere to look in Tilbury,' said Claude. 'It is worth a try.'

They walked to Pitsea station in the fading light and took the train to Tilbury. Vi had a strange sensation in her chest, a desperation to find her daughter that made her breathing fast and her heart pump to keep up. If they found Doris, what would she say to her? Sorry? Sorry for throwing you out of your home? Sorry I didn't know what Archie did to you? Sorry for the past three years of misery you've endured on your own. It made Vi choke to think about it. Perhaps too much had happened to be able to go back and make things right. How could they just get back to normal after something like this had happened? It wouldn't be normal. That was the answer. It would never be as it had been before. But maybe they could make a fresh start and move on and look after each other.

Claude sat opposite her on the train. He didn't try to talk, he seemed to know she had no words for this moment, that she was grappling with her own thoughts. It was a private affair, something to be sorted out within the family. But this man, he was here to help, to help Doris. He cared about her and that ought to mean something.

'Thank you,' she said, the tears springing to her eyes as she spoke.

He looked away from the window, smiled at her. 'It is all right.'

It was dark when the train pulled into Tilbury station. As they walked out on to Dock Road, Vi was aware of people looking, looking at her walking along with a coloured man. It rankled, yes, but she had something to learn, she knew that. She held her head up high and went with him to Ship Street.

'Doris was living here, with Laura,' he said, indicating the brothel and raising a hand to wave to one of the girls standing on the pavement.

Vi just wanted to cry. How could she have let this happen, her daughter living in a place like this? With the tarts on the street outside and the wicked goings-on inside. How could she have ignored it so easily?

She hesitated on the threshold, peered inside. Archie had been a customer there, that's what that Fred had said. The thought made her shudder, disgusted her – she realised she didn't know him at all. Following Claude inside, she saw sitting at a desk in the hallway a stout woman with a large bosom and a low-cut blouse showing her cleavage.

'Lil,' said Claude, nodding at her.

'Hello, love, long time. How's the Big Smoke treating you?'

Claude smiled. 'Good, thanks, it is pretty good. Look, Lil,' he said, 'this is Doris's mudda.'

'I know who she is,' said Lil with a curt nod.

Vi was taken aback. She'd never seen this woman before. Did they all go around in shadows or something?

'We're here about Doris,' said Vi, summoning her courage. 'She's gone missing. Has she been here?'

Lil frowned and shook her head. 'No, she hasn't.'

'All right, thanks Lil,' said Claude. 'If you do see her can you get word to The Empire pub?'

'Course,' said Lil, taking a drag of her cigarette and eyeing Vi. 'Wait a minute, this came for her.' Lil handed Vi a letter addressed to Doris. Vi slipped it into her handbag.

Outside on the pavement, Claude put his hands on his hips. 'We will try the tenement,' he said.

'What tenement?'

'Where she was living before here,' said Claude.

Vi didn't know anything about a tenement. Had that been where Win went to see her, taking her those things? Thinking about Win gave her a bad taste in her mouth. Her sister's reasons for looking after Doris ... because she'd known about Archie all that time maybe. The thought made Vi feel sick.

'Did she live on her own there?' said Vi.

Claude nodded. 'Yes, with Laura. I lived over the other side, with the West Indian boys. Doris introduced me to them when I was in trouble and had nowhere to stay.'

Her little Doris, doing all these things. It didn't seem real. Vi swallowed the lump in her throat. She felt a sense of pride that Doris had managed at all. She'd gone down a wrong path that led to a brothel, of course, but she had stayed with her child. She could have put her in a home and come back to the pub but she didn't do that. She'd shown remarkable strength.

They came to the site of the derelict tenements, the gas lamps on the street casting a dim light over the abandoned building.

'Here?' said Vi, shocked. 'But no one lives here, it's bombed out.'

'Yes,' laughed Claude. 'You would only stay here if you were desperate and had nowhere else to go.'

Vi gave him a sideways glance. He wasn't judging her. He hadn't said a thing about her treatment of Doris, he just seemed to want to help find her. Vi felt an affection for him. He was a decent man, kind, she could tell that about him. She could understand why Doris had hung around with him.

They picked their way with difficulty across the rubble and along to where the flats were still intact.

'I was staying over the other side, but this is where Doris and Laura were.'

They walked up a flight of stairs, feeling their way, and Claude pointed to a door. Vi's heart quickened. She wanted more than anything for Doris to be in there. But she was scared stiff that Doris hated her, wouldn't want anything to do with her. Vi herself had grown up without parents, had longed for a mother, dreamt about her coming one day to scoop her up and take her home. Yet, look how she'd been with Doris. She wasn't fit to be a mother, she didn't know how. She'd had no love herself as a child and she didn't know how to show love as an adult, not even to her own child. She was broken.

Claude stood aside and Vi stepped forward to knock at the door. Time felt warped, and she was lightheaded. As her knuckles struck the door, so they rang the times Vi had turned her back on Doris. The sound was like a hammer to Vi's heart. If something had happened to Doris . . . if it was too late to make amends . . .

The door didn't open. There was no sound from inside. Vi and Claude looked at one another. Vi leant to one side to look through the window but sacking had been lodged up against the glass on the inside. Vi put her hand on the door handle and pushed down. The door opened a crack. She took a breath and pushed it open.

The flat was in darkness, the sacking blocking the windows. Vi wrinkled her nose. There was a strong smell of damp and of stale chamber pots. Claude struck a match, cast about for a candle and found one pushed into the neck of a glass bottle. Once lit, Vi saw there were only some upturned wooden crates in the front room, one having been used for a table.

'Vi,' Claude hissed in a loud whisper.

She turned to see. He was pointing to the table – there was a milk bottle there, half full. She picked it up and sniffed at it. It was fresh. Her heart lurched in her chest. She looked at Claude meaningfully and they both stepped towards the back room.

'Doris?'

Vi jumped when Claude called her daughter's name. She pushed open the bedroom door. It was even darker in there and she squinted to see. A large bed with a tarpaulin on it. She walked round to the far side and looked down with a gasp. Doris was there, sitting on the floor, holding her knees to her chest. Through the gloom she was watching Vi with round eyes.

'Doris, love,' said Vi and held out her hands towards her daughter. 'Doris, love.' Vi started to cry. 'Doris, I'm so sorry, I'm so, so sorry.' She stood there, not trying to cover her face, everything came to the surface and she was sorry, she just wished none of it had ever happened. Claude left the candle on the floor and backed away to leave them alone.

Doris broke into tears too. It looked like she didn't want

to cry, that it was important to her to stay strong but seeing Vi had taken away her need to be strong on her own. Vi crouched down in front of her daughter, put her hands on Doris's shoulders.

'Can you forgive me, Doris?' Vi whispered. Doris looked through her tears with hatred and relief. Vi reached for Doris's hand, pulled it gently, helped her to stand up. She held her at arm's length and didn't know what to do or say. Silently, Doris took one step forward and put her face into Vi's shoulder and the two of them clutched one another and cried.

43

Doris

Until recently, Doris had only ever wanted this. For Vi to take her back. As her mother held her, Doris felt the sting of resentment and neglect but she clung to her mother, needing her despite everything. The strain of the past few years wouldn't dissolve magically, Doris would never forget what Vi had done to her. Doris had learned the hard way how important it was to feel wanted and loved, but she was strong now, in herself. They clung to each other, neither wanting to let go nor knowing how to say the difficult words that needed saying. Finally, Doris thought all of that could wait. There was one thing she wanted more than she wanted to be taken back by Vi.

'Laura.'

'What, love?' said Vi, pulling back.

'I need to find Laura.'

'I know, love, we will,' she said, taking out her hankie and wiping Doris's face with it and then wiping her own. 'We will.'

'But I'm hiding, I have to hide for fourteen days.'

'Why?'

'I ran away from the hospital.'

'Yes, I know but that's all right now, I went there to ... I went there to have you let out. You don't need to worry about that any more.'

'Really?' said Doris. She sat down on the bed as though her legs couldn't take the shock. She'd been so worried about it, about being found and taken back there and given electric shock treatment or worse. She couldn't believe she didn't have to worry about it any more. 'Are you sure?'

'Yes, I'm sure. I just need to tell them you've been found. The police are looking for you.'

'Laura,' she said. It was all her brain wanted to think about.

'Yes, come on, we'll go and see Dr Peters.'

There was no sign of Claude as they came out into the dim light of the street.

'Are you hungry?' said Vi.

Doris shook her head. 'Yes, but I don't care.'

She'd existed on milk stolen from people's doorsteps and raw vegetables pulled from the allotments at night for the past two days. The long walk down the rail track had seemed to take forever. But once she'd made her mind up to do it, she just carried on and didn't stop until she got to Tilbury. And when she got there, she hadn't known what to do. She had to hide, so she couldn't even look for Laura. She crept into her old tenement flat, careful not to be seen, and she planned to stay there until the fourteen days were up.

They made their way to Calcutta Road, where Dr Peters lived in the flat above his surgery.

'It's late,' said Vi with a grimace as she rang the bell.

'Mrs Walsh, Doris,' said Dr Peters in surprise when he answered the door in his shirtsleeves, slacks and slippers. 'What on earth are you doing here? The police have contacted me.'

'It's all right, doctor, can you help us? I want Doris decertified, she's to be let out. Can you telephone the police and tell them?'

He mumbled something about it not being as straightforward as that and that Doris would need to be assessed, but he told them to wait while he opened up the surgery and let them inside. He sat Doris down and asked her some questions about her state of mind, seemed somewhat satisfied with their story about Archie. Doris waited patiently for him to report her appearance to the police on his telephone and when it was done she asked him, 'Where's my daughter?'

'Your daughter? She went to a foster home, I believe,' he said, standing up to look through the papers in his cabinet.

'I want to get her back,' said Doris, and Vi nodded when the doctor looked at her for confirmation.

'I see. Well, I can telephone them, let me see.'

He found the papers and made the telephone call and gave them an address. Doris looked at it. It was in Ockendon, several miles away. She looked at Vi helplessly.

'Doctor, would you . . . your car . . . would you . . . ' said Vi.

The doctor frowned, ran his hand over his Brylcremed hair.

'Please, doctor,' said Vi. 'This never should have happened. Doris is innocent ... I didn't know her uncle Archie took advantage of her ...'

The doctor surveyed the pitiful sight of them before him. 'Yes, yes of course.'

He grabbed his coat and hat and held the surgery door for them.

Doris slipped into the back seat of his car and Vi got in the front next to the doctor. For a second, Doris panicked. What if they were tricking her, and really taking her back to the asylum? She chewed on her nails and watched from the window, trying to tell which way they were going, but it was dark and she lost track of the roads and became breathless with anxiety.

They finally pulled up outside a house, and Doris peered anxiously out of the window. It looked just like a normal terraced house and nothing like the hospital. The doctor opened the door for her and she got out on shaky legs. She and Vi followed the doctor up the path and waited while he knocked at the door. It was opened by a woman who looked like she needed a good wash. She had one cigarette behind her ear and one in her mouth. A small child peered around the doorway at the visitors and Doris gasped when she thought it was Laura, then realised it wasn't.

Doris felt lightheaded, the air was thick. The doctor was talking in a formal way to the woman and her face turned nasty. She spat out some words.

'But what about my payments? For looking after her? I've got my own family to feed, you know.'

The woman stood barring the doorway, one hand on her hip.

'Look, this is the child's mother, and I'm her grandmother,' said Vi, her voice getting high and fast.

'I don't give a damn who you are, where were you when the child needed you, then? What's she doing here if she's got such a nice family?'

The doctor and Vi argued with the woman, their voices raised, and in the midst of it, Doris knew what to say.

'How much?'

They all went quiet. 'How much what?' said the woman.

'How much do you want for your payments so we can take her home today?'

The woman puffed out her chest with indignation as though she'd been accused of something she wasn't guilty of.

'Well, there's at least six weeks, that's what I was told anyway, until a place was found for her in a home. That's six pounds' payment, that is.'

'This is most irregular,' said the doctor.

'Right,' said Vi, opening her handbag. Doris was shocked to see her count out six pound notes. 'Here you are then. Can we see her now?'

The woman took the money and held the door open to let them in. Doris's stomach twisted with nerves. She was desperate to see Laura but she didn't know if Laura would want to see her after what had happened.

The woman led them through into a dingy sitting room where two babies stood up in a cot and three other children sat on the floor playing. Doris's eyes flitted from one child to the next. She checked them all and couldn't see Laura. There must have been some mistake. She must have been taken to a home already. She checked the children again.

'Mumma?'

Doris looked up. Over by the window, half hidden by the net curtain, stood Laura. On her face was a picture of disbelieving joy as though she thought nothing good would ever happen again. Doris held out her arms and, with a stumble, but without a second thought for why Doris was there, why Doris had allowed her to be put in the foster home and why Doris had shown her very little love in her short life, Laura ran towards her. Doris fell to her knees and clutched her daughter against her, put her face into her hair and sobbed with relief.

44

Vi

It turned out it might be possible for Vi to get a publican's licence. A woman in England had already done it in 1952, paving the way for women like Vi, who owned her pub and wanted to run it on her own without a man at the helm. Once Vi had found Doris, and Doris had found Laura, Vi wrote to the brewery stating her case. They said the pub was financially stable and she could stay in post while they looked into it. It was a relief that Archie hadn't let the pub fall to ruin, that he'd been keeping it viable for his own purposes. And Vi knew she would fight tooth and nail for the right to run her own pub. She'd do it for Cyril, yes, to keep his memory alive, but she'd do it for herself too, for her own pride.

She had done a lot of thinking lately. It was funny how you could let life's rules dictate your behaviour without really noticing it. But as soon as she did start thinking, it was a whole new way of life for her. She was going to try hard not to let outsiders rule her life. So much in life was done for the sake of other people who didn't even matter to you. Lives were ruined because of what the neighbours might say. It was hard to go against that but Vi had learned that the alternative wasn't something she could live with. She had sent her daughter away to avoid the shame of her staying. It wasn't right, it couldn't be.

It was only now that Vi could see herself clearly in the mirror. The way she'd been brought up, bearing the stigma of illegitimacy for all those years, so afraid of being found out, doing whatever it took to cling to a normal life, a decent life. Which, as it turned out, wasn't decent at all.

To have Doris back was so important to her. Doris was living in the pub again, with Laura too, and it was a delight to have them around. Doris had thought about moving into a bedsitter with Laura but Vi had begged her to stay. They had talked about things a little bit.

'You should have told me about men,' Doris had said to her.

'Men?' said Vi.

'Yes, about . . . relations. I didn't know.'

It broke Vi's heart when Doris sobbed.

'I didn't know what Archie had done, because you never told me anything about that. It was all such a terrible shock, when the baby came. I thought it was Kenny's because he was my boyfriend but me and Kenny didn't do anything like that.'

'I'm sorry, Doris.' What else could Vi say? 'People don't talk about those things. No one told me when I was growing up, you just have to learn it for yourself.'

'But look what happens, girls getting into trouble, not knowing how to look after themselves.'

Vi nodded and looked at her daughter. 'You're right. You are.'

Vi wondered what had happened to her own mother, to have put her two daughters into a home. Had she been led astray or been caught out by not knowing how to protect herself? For the first time, Vi started to forgive her mother. She lay curled up on her bed and cried for her. And then she made a decision. She wouldn't let the fear of shame taint her life any more. She hadn't been 'bred wrong', hadn't caused Doris to be the way she was because of her own mother's behaviour, because of 'bad blood'. Her past had made her strong, she could see that now. She'd use that strength to carry on without shame.

Archie hadn't made an appearance since they'd seen him off and it made Vi nervous to think he might turn up and make trouble. But she knew they could report him for what he'd done to Doris, and as much as the public humiliation of a court case made her shiver with dread, she would do it if necessary. She would.

Sitting at the kitchen table upstairs at the pub, she listened to the twittering and scuffling of the chaffinches in their cage. She was so used to having birds in the kitchen, she only just registered that they were Archie's and Archie wasn't there any more. She took the cage to the window, opened the casement wide and watched as each of the four birds jumped tentatively to the ledge of the open cage door, took flight and flew away to freedom. Vi looked out after them and hoped that they'd be all right.

45

Doris

'Mumma, look.'

Laura held up a picture she had drawn of a tree. They were sitting on the sea wall by the pub with the group of West Indians.

'Good, Laura. Look how each branch splits into smaller ones,' said Doris, pointing to an ash tree up the street. 'I think that skeleton trees in the winter are the most beautiful, don't you?'

'Yes, Mumma, the most beautiful,' said Laura, holding her pencil in her fist and colouring in the tree trunk, her little tongue sticking out with concentration.

Doris watched her drawing and felt a warmth in her chest, an intense pride. She had finally bonded with her daughter, found the bottomless pit of love that somehow had had a thick plank of wood over it, like the cover over a well. She looked at the tree and it reminded her of the rhododendron bush she had hidden in when she was escaping from the hospital. How, without their leaves, trees show their true selves, what holds them together, without fancy foliage to cover up what's really inside. The image of Annie hanging from the laundry pipe flashed across her mind again. Annie's leg sticking up out of the copper boiler. Doris didn't want to remember her like that. She pushed the image aside and thought about Annie's clever escape ideas, her funny way of poking her head around the side of the armchair, and how she'd stamp on invisible beetles.

Doris was drawing again and that alone gave her such immense satisfaction. She hadn't felt fully alive when she wasn't drawing. Laura loved watching and copying her, and Doris was teaching her daughter. It was something they could just sit and do together.

They were living with Vi above the pub. Doris had mixed feelings about being back there. It was something she had craved all that time, when she had sat where she was sitting now, watching for Vi to come out the front door to clean her step, hoping for a smile or a wave. But being back reminded her of what Archie had done and it was hard to forget that, hard to forget giving birth on her bedroom floor and hard to forget being told to leave. Her own mother having her committed to a mental asylum was something she wouldn't forget, or forgive, easily. A part of her wanted Vi to suffer for what she had done. Another part knew that Vi was already suffering from the knowledge that she had allowed Archie to hoodwink her.

Vi had passed a letter to her that had been delivered to the brothel. It was from the National Council for the Unmarried Mother and her Child, who she had written to when Claude had persuaded her to look for help. They had responded saying they would help her find a place in one of their hostels with childcare provided so she could get a job and start supporting herself, or they'd help her find a bedsitter with a sympathetic landlady. It was good to know that there was something else out there for her if she needed it. It was a shame it was so hard to come by any help though; she could have done with that much earlier on.

It was Claude who had told her to be positive, to look for ways to carry on. She was a fallen woman and it was Claude who had taught her how to stand up for herself. In a sense, she didn't need Vi in the way she thought she had needed her. She could probably go it alone. It would be a struggle, terribly hard, but for now she would stay at the pub. This time she was there on her own terms – she could come and go as she pleased, neither beholden to Vi's rules nor outcast. When she was trapped in the pub, she couldn't imagine being an adult, having a different life. She had the benefit of experience now. She had told Vi she was going to look for a college course, she wanted to study art, and Vi said they would find a way for her to do that. She'd look after Laura for her. That would do for now.

She had Fred to thank in all of this too. Fred, who understood from her own life what Doris had gone through, and had gone to London to find Claude, Fred who had confronted Vi. Doris and Vi had agreed to invite her to lodge and work at the pub. She had accepted and Laura was delighted that her 'Auntie Fred' was living with them. It turned out Fred could sing like an angel and Doris knew the punters would accept having her around eventually.

They would be all right. They would all look after each other. Vi, Doris, Laura and Fred. They were The Empire girls.

'So? What's happening with Kenny?'

It was Claude asking her. He sat beside her, had come to say goodbye before going back to his family in London. Doris had thanked him for coming back to help her. She knew they had strong feelings for one another without it being anything more. It was nice to think there was someone out there in life who she knew would always be there for her, and she hoped Claude knew that she would be there for him too.

'Kenny?' she said, trying to cover a smile.

Poor Kenny, he'd been blamed for something he hadn't done. He'd lost his job and borne the brunt of his family's rage. Vi had offered him his job back, and he had decided to take it, much to Doris's relief. Vi had made him second in command and he relished having some responsibility at work. And he and Doris had tentatively said they would go to the pictures soon, and to that milk bar they used to joke about.

'Nothing . . . yet,' she said to Claude and he laughed and dug her with his elbow. 'And what about you? You're looking forward to getting back to London?'

'Oh yes,' he said, smiling. 'My job at the station, sweeping the floors, oh yes I cannot wait to get back to it.'

'And your other things,' said Doris, nudging him with her shoulder. Claude had met some other West Indian writers in London and was writing a book. The cleaning job was paying for his rent and food.

'Yes, it is an exciting time, Doris. I want to publish my work and be known as a serious writer. That is something I could not have done in Jamaica. You know ...' he said, 'it is not easy here for me, Doris, the colour problem and everything, the way we are treated by some, but I think to myself, Claude, hold up your head and look at the sky, this will teach you to be strong and things can change. I have to find my own way here, Doris.'

'Well, you better write and tell me all about it, all right?'

'Yes, of course I will. Right then, boys,' he said clapping his hands together, 'I am off to the Big Smoke.' He stood up to shake his friends' hands. They slapped each other on the back and hugged and said goodbye. Laura jumped up, letting her tree drawing slip to the ground, and ran into Claude's legs, clutching him against her. He picked her up, lifted her high until she squealed with delight.

'Bye-bye Blaze-A-Glory,' he said. 'See you soon, all right?'

She nodded and looked sad.

'Remember to look at the sky, all right? Look at the sky and think *What do I want to be?*'

'Yes, Caude,' said Laura. 'Caude?'

'Yes, little piggy?'

'What if the sky white and the clouds is blue?'

Claude leant back to look at her, frowned and smiled.

'Then the world would be a different place, Blaze. You look after your mudda, all right? She needs you.'

Laura nodded and Claude set her down.

Doris stood up and frowned back her tears. 'Bye Claude, thanks again for everything.'

He opened his arms and folded her into them. She pulled

back to let him go, a movement at the downstairs window of the pub catching her eye.

'Claude, there's Mum,' she said. Doris knew Claude hadn't fully forgiven Vi for her treatment of Doris, but he was too busy with his own life to bear a grudge.

Claude turned to see Vi standing at the window, holding the net curtain aside and watching them. She reached out to take down the sign that he had seen when he first arrived – *No Coloureds, No Dogs* – and she gave Claude a smile and a wave that said *I'm sorry and thank you*, and let the curtain fall.

Acknowledgments

Thank you to: my editor Maddie West and the team at Sphere, my agent Laura Longrigg at MBA, The Arts Council England for a 'Grants for the Arts' award, Lele Gemma for her midwifery expertise, beta readers Louise Ryder, Shapla Hodges, Mark Wilsher and Nicola Moulden, my writing group Allie Burns and Tanya Gupta, friends and family for supporting my writing efforts and Kevin, who always tells it to me straight even though I sulk. Thanks to Mia and Molly for helping with field research – timing how long it takes to draw ten thousand stick figures on the pavement and helping to visualise the number of people in slavery in Jamaica two hundred years ago. Invaluable research resources included Thurrock libraries and the British Library periodicals archives, the Tilbury Riverside Project and many brilliant books about life in the fifties, the history of psychiatric hospitals and those written by and about the arrivants from the West Indies to fifties Britain. I took a daunting leap out of my own realm of experience to write this book and I hope I have done due justice to the experiences of others, with my apologies if I haven't. Lastly, to the residents of 1950s Tilbury, I trust I have captured the fascinating local history and I hope you don't mind my artistic licence too much!

Supported using public funding by
ARTS COUNCIL ENGLAND

LOTTERY FUNDED